To Fred, with love

# PART ONE

# Chapter One

The piercing wind rose to an anguished howl around the fancy pylons and pavilion tops of Hammersmith Bridge. Huddled against its icy blasts, pinched-faced pedestrians hurried across the Thames, grimly clutching their hats. Equally exposed to the elements, coachmen and motorists shivered and turned numb in their driving seats.

Apparently oblivious to the weather, a well-dressed man leaned on the varnished guard-rail of the bridge staring vacantly ahead. When his bowler hat blew into the river, he didn't seem to notice.

Daylight was already fading. A soft glow crept along the riverside mall as the lamplighter lit the gaslamps with a long pole. Through the swaying branches of the leafless trees, a row of fine houses looked out over the water, their elegant façades and columns suggestive of the Georgian era.

Surrounding this residential hamlet, the contrasting sweep of industry dominated the skyline. The black discharge from factory chimneys gusted across the sky, merging with banks of rolling grey clouds.

The river was at high tide. In the wharves an assembly of barges, red sails furled to the mast, waited for low tide when they would settle on the foreshore for unloading. In the incipient dusk, the lights of the town began to stud the landscape beneath an urban silhouette of chimney pots and church spires.

Above the roar of the wind a rough male voice could just be heard. 'Can yer spare a few coppers for a poor old man, guvnor? I ain't 'ad nothin' to eat for days.'

Receiving no response from the gentleman, the beggar

nudged his arm and repeated his plea, whilst erupting into a fit of coughing which made his chest wheeze and rattle.

Eventually, the gentleman turned and faced the unkempt individual who was toothless and hirsute with a straggly beard and long matted tresses. Even in the wind the noxious stench of gin and body odour was overpowering but, deeply preoccupied with his own affairs, the gentleman appeared unaffected. He seemed bewildered, looking uncertainly around him as though baffled by his surroundings. Suddenly understanding, however, he reached into the pocket of his tailored overcoat and drew out some coins. 'There you are, old man,' he said, offering copper and silver in the palm of his leather glove. 'Take this. You're welcome to it.'

A pair of blood-shot eyes glinted greedily on this unexpected bounty. Grasping the money in his filthy paw, the tramp moved back quickly. 'Gawd bless yer, mister,' he said, and shuffled furtively on his way before his benefactor could have a change of heart.

As it happened, his fears were groundless because that handful of cash was as a grain of flour in a bakery to Cyril Potter whose financial affairs were beyond repair. Little does the poor wretch know he's better off than me, he thought despondently, turning back to the rail.

Pursuing this unhealthy line of thought, Cyril Potter began to envy the tramp. It was true that the man had no worldly goods or position in society, but neither was he burdened with crippling obligations. Unlike Cyril, he had no fashionable Kensington address to maintain. No prestigious store to stock and wages to pay every week. He didn't have a pampered wife and daughters accustomed only to comfort, unaware that their provider was about to go bankrupt and they were to be evicted from their home.

The pressure of the last few months, added to the final blow Cyril had received in the post the other day, had culminated in a feeling of confused unreality which rendered him incapable of coherent thought or concentration. Alternating between unbearable tension and numbing fatigue, he was muddled and forgetful. For a moment just now when the beggar had interrupted his reverie, he'd even forgotten what day or time of year it was, and why he was here on this suspension bridge in the depths of winter. But all too soon the worry and remorse had flooded back and he'd known that it was February 1910 and he had come here because there was no other way out of his self-inflicted troubles.

Vaguely he recalled writing a letter to his wife, which he had left on his desk in his office at the store. Then he had walked here from Kensington, deeming it proper, somehow, to do what must be done outside the boundaries of his own neighbourhood.

Now that the decision was made, the fear and misery had changed to a sense of relief that it would soon be over. His body felt heavy with fatigue, his mind addled. He was suddenly so crushingly tired, he could hardly stand.

Wishing only to sleep, he took a cautious glance around, noting that everyone was far too busy battling with the weather to pay any attention to him.

'I'm sorry, Gertie,' he murmured wearily into the wind. 'I never was the man you thought I was. The truth is all in the letter.'

Without further delay, he heaved himself up on to the rail, wavered for only a moment then let himself fall . . .

The high winds that had swept across the capital earlier in the month had calmed into a crisp chilliness, and Sycamore Square lay quiet in the clear morning light, the picture of good taste. Pale winter sunlight enriched the grass in the central gardens, brightened the buds on the eponymous trees, bleached the stucco terraces to a dazzling white and made the black railings shine as though wet.

A thin, dark-eyed girl sat on the drawing-room window seat of Number Twenty, gazing gloomily through the window. Dressed in outdoor clothes, her black hat just a shade or two darker than her hair, Kate Potter wondered fleetingly if leaving the family home might have been easier to bear on a grey, dismal day. Being realistic, however, she knew that it would take more than a change in the weather to ease the trauma of this watershed for her mother, her sister and herself. As the eldest daughter, she considered it her duty to find the courage to accept their new impoverished circumstances and help her traumatised mother to do the same.

Two weeks had passed since her father's body had been dragged from the Thames. In that short time she had matured beyond her years, receiving an abrupt introduction to the harsh reality of life without money.

Having grown up under the aegis of a resident nanny, Kate had never been close to either of her parents. They had been distant, awesome figures, synonymous with respect and authority. It had been a shock, therefore, to discover that her stern, infallible father had been a compulsive gambler who had been steadily losing everything he owned for years, whilst cunningly misleading his family into believing that his evenings out were innocently spent at his gentlemen's club. It was no small disappointment either to find that her beautiful, vivacious mother appeared to have no capacity whatsoever to cope with her loss in a dignified manner or to comfort her young daughters at this harrowing time.

Kate had also had to come to terms with the fact that the privileged lifestyle she had always taken for granted was not a God-given right. Fortunately, although she was still feeling shaken at the sudden loss of her security, she had discovered a surprising fortitude in her own make-up which had helped to carry her through.

Anyway, there had been no time to brood for someone had to take charge. Her younger sister Esme was too highly strung to be of any real help, and Mother was apparently unable to make any sort of effort. Their few distant relatives wanted nothing to do with the penniless descendants of a man who had not only disgraced the family by gambling away the business he had inherited from his father, but brought shame on them all by taking the coward's way out of his troubles.

So, at fifteen years of age, Kate found herself carrying the responsibility for the three of them. A daunting burden indeed, considering the predicament her father had left them in. Not only had he mortgaged the house to pay his gambling debts, he had also run up a huge overdraft which had got out of control over a number of years. Finally, his debts outweighed his assets. His suicide had been precipitated by a letter from his bank notifying him of their intention to take possession of everything he owned to recoup their money. All the Potters' worldly goods now belonged to them: the house Kate and her sister had grown up in, the furniture, the motor car, even most of their clothes.

When the trio made their final departure from this house in a few minutes' time, they would take just one small travelling bag containing a spare set of clothes each. A trunk containing household linen, crockery, and a few personal effects had been sent on ahead.

Mother had been too upset to deal with even the most minor practicality, so it had fallen to Kate to find them somewhere to live. Fortunately the bank manager, confident that his company would get their money back from the sale of the Potters' effects, and not wishing the bank to be seen as inhumane, had allowed them to stay on in the house until after the funeral. The bank had also made them a small goodwill payment – enough for mourning clothes, something to live on for a short time, and the month's advance rent they had needed to secure their new home, such as it was. Already the luxurious furniture Kate had been used to was swathed in dust covers.

She stood up as her mother, Gertie, entered the room, a thin, haggard woman barely recognisable from the frivolous type she had been just over two weeks ago. Her blue eyes were red-rimmed, her pallor emphasised by the severity of her black coat which she wore with a matching hat, her fair hair drawn tightly back beneath its wide brim. The shock of her husband's death and its consequences had aged her well beyond her thirty-three years.

'Well, are you ready to go?' asked Kate, already becoming accustomed to the authoritative role she had been forced to adopt.

Gertie drew in a shuddering breath. 'As ready as I'll ever be, I suppose,' she said shakily, her eyes awash with tears.

Thirteen-year-old Esme appeared, dressed in dark outdoor

clothes, and stood nervously beside her mother.

She was a pale, delicate girl with Gertie's fair complexion and blue eyes.

'Ah, there you are, love.' Kate crossed the room to where they both stood by the drawing-room door and put a comforting arm around each of them, ignoring the fact that her own legs were trembling and tears threatening. 'Since we're all ready, then let's be on our way.'

'Have you called a cab?' asked her mother.

'Well, of course not . . .' began Kate.

'Why not?'

'You know why, Mother,' she said, striving to be gentle for she was aware of the fact that her mother had lost her partner in life as well as her position. It wasn't easy to stay patient with her feebleness and refusal to face facts, though. Couldn't she see how painful this move was for her daughters? Didn't she realise how desperately they needed her? 'How can I call for one when the telephone has been cut off?'

'Send someone to get one, then.'

'Who shall I send? The servants have all gone. Surely you haven't forgotten?'

Tears meandered down Gertie's cheeks. 'Perhaps I'd rather not remember.' She sniffed forlornly. 'Can you go and find one for us then, Kate dear?'

'I could do, yes, but there's no point since we can't afford to pay for it,' she explained.

'Then how . . .?'

'We shall walk to Hammersmith,' Kate informed her firmly.

'Oh, *no*, Kate.' It was almost a cry of physical pain. 'Having to *live* in Hammersmith is bad enough, but to arrive there on foot!'

'All right, we'll walk to Kensington High Street and take a bus from there to Hammersmith.'

The older woman's hand flew to her throat dramatically for she had never in her life travelled on public transport. 'But buses always look so crowded, and they're probably filthy. Lord knows what we might pick up.'

'A train then?'

8

'I'm sure that's just as bad.'

'A tram?'

'Never!'

'Public transport is something we shall all have to get used to,' Kate told her gravely.

'Couldn't we take a cab just this once, dear?' begged Gertie, sobbing into her handkerchief. 'Just so that we can leave the square with dignity.'

'We don't need a cab to do that,' Kate pointed out determinedly. 'We must leave this house with our heads held high for all the neighbours to see. After all, we've done nothing wrong.'

'Your father's disgraced us.'

'So we must show the world that we refuse to be ashamed of something we knew nothing about, and was not our fault.'

'How can we hold our heads up without money?' Gertie moaned. 'Without that we have nothing.'

Two weeks ago Kate would not have argued. But middle-class opinions were no use to any of them now. 'Nonsense! We have each other,' she said. 'There's no shame in being poor.'

'There is to people in our circle.'

'The people we have mixed with here in Kensington are not our circle any more, Mother. We're on the other side of the fence now.' Kate walked from the room into the wide hall where the portmanteau was standing by the front door. The sunlight shining through the stained glass window above the door spilled coloured patterns on to the marble-tiled floor. She gripped the handle of the bag. 'Come along then, you two.'

Esme started to cry. 'I don't want to go, Kate. I want Daddy.'

Kate stifled her exasperation, reminding herself that her sister had probably been more deeply affected by their father's death than herself, for all his paternal love had flowed towards his youngest daughter, maybe because Esme had always been delicate and prone to sickness. 'Now come on, love, you must try to be brave.'

Her sobs grew louder.

Gertie put her arms around her youngest daughter, copious

9

tears rushing down her own cheeks. 'There, there, darling,' she crooned uselessly.

'We *must* go,' Kate reminded her anxiously. 'I promised the man from the bank we would be out of here by ten o'clock.'

'I can't go,' wailed Gertie, still clinging to Esme. 'It's all too humiliating. I just can't bear it!'

'We have to go, Mother.'

Affected by her mother's lack of confidence, Esme became almost hysterical, clenching her fists and emitting a high-pitched wail for her father: '*Daddy! Daddy! Daddy!*'

Remembering how their nanny had once dealt with a similar incident, Kate dragged her sister away from the protective arms of her mother and gave her a sharp slap across the face.

'Kate!' reproached her mother as Esme stared wide-eyed at her sister in shocked silence. 'Was that really necessary?'

'Something had to be done to bring her out of it.' Kate herself was feeling emotional about leaving, and the burden of having to act as parent to her own mother weighed heavily on someone of such tender years.

'The poor girl is bewildered,' said Gertie.

'At least she's calmed down.' Kate gave her mother a sharp look. 'It would help matters if you could be a little more positive.'

'Is that any way to speak to someone whose nerves are in shreds?'

'I'm sorry, Mother, but someone has to stop the pair of you from going to pieces altogether.' Hot tears threatened. 'Look, I don't want to leave here any more than you. But we *have* to go. So please try to pull yourself together, for Esme's sake. You know how emotional she is.'

'I bet the neighbours will enjoy themselves,' Gertie whined as though Kate hadn't spoken, 'peering at us from behind their curtains, and gloating.'

'Then let's not give them the satisfaction of seeing we're upset.' She opened the door. 'Come on, take my arm.'

Nervously Gertie emerged into the sunshine and made her way down the small flight of steps to the pavement, followed by Esme.

Kate turned and gave the door a final slam, having left their keys on the hall table inside.

'Right,' she said, her constricted throat almost choking her as she joined her mother and sister in the street. 'Heads up and best foot forward.'

The sad little threesome took the path across the central gardens, past the neat lawns and flower beds splashed with orange and mauve clusters of crocuses. They didn't look back but continued on towards the main road. When they were safely out of sight of the square, all three succumbed to tears.

Beaver Terrace was a far cry from Sycamore Square, being a row of dilapidated tenement houses in a poor part of Hammersmith between the Broadway and the Thames. The cobbled street was crowded with ragged children laughing and shouting at their play. Gertie was horrified when Kate stopped outside Number Three, a sorry-looking abode with peeling brown paint and grimy windows.

'Please tell me this isn't it?'

'I'm afraid it is,' said Kate, recalling the hours she had spent walking the streets in the freezing weather to find a place to rent at a price they could afford. Not wishing to upset her already distraught mother with the miserable facts, she hadn't said much about the place, hoping that Gertie would be more able to accept it when faced with a fait accompli.

'But we can't live in a rundown area like this,' said Gertie. 'It's completely unsuitable.'

'It suits our pocket.'

'It's out of the question.'

'We don't have any choice, Mother.'

'It looks as though it's full of fleas and rats.'

'Our room is on the top floor. Perhaps the rats will stay downstairs,' Kate suggested lightly.

'Our *room*?' said Gertie aghast. 'You mean there are other people living in the house?'

'You don't get a whole house for the rent we can pay, even in an area like this,' explained Kate.

'We must pay more then.'

'We can't afford to,' she said, her patience almost snapping. Having been equally as spoiled as the others, this dramatic lowering of standards was just as difficult for her to take, and she could do without opposition every step of the way. 'Maybe we'll be able to get something better later on.'

A gang of children had gathered nearby and were watching the newcomers with unveiled curiosity. 'You come to live 'ere, have yer, missus?' said a dirty little girl of about seven years old, with ginger hair poking through the holes in her grimy woollen hat.

The question was directed at Gertie who ignored it and turned her face away as though the sight of these ragamuffins made her feel physically ill.

'Yes, we have,' said Kate, smiling bravely. She was surprised to find herself intimidated by these children whose confidence certainly wasn't diminished by their underprivileged status.

'Coo, 'ark at her,' said the girl. 'Proper la-de-da, ain't she?'

Raucous laughter erupted among the children who continued to stare at the strangers with unnerving candour. Kate admonished herself for being made to feel uneasy by a bunch of filthy infants. She, Kate Potter, whose education at one of London's most expensive private schools had included rigorous training in self-confidence. With a part of her she envied these impecunious youngsters who accepted poverty as normal and were not worried by it. Having been born to austerity, they were wise and fearless on the mean streets of this neighbourhood over which they held such a proprietary air. Whereas she, the newly poor, felt as helpless as a seedling in a sudden frost.

'What's that gel cryin' for?' asked their interlocutor referring to Esme, who was snivelling noisily. 'She's a bit big to be blubbering, ain't she?'

'She's upset about leaving her friends where we used to live,' fibbed Kate, sensing that any mention of the fact that they had known better things would be taken as lies or arrogance by the locals. And, anyway, it was irrelevant now that this district was to be their home.

'Aah, ne'mind,' said the girl sympathetically to Esme.

12

'You'll soon find new mates. There's lots o' gels your age round 'ere.'

Esme turned away sobbing, the prospect of having to mix with these smelly creatures only increasing her despair.

'Why aren't you at school today?' asked Kate of the girl, partly from curiosity and partly in an effort to seem friendly for she guessed this encounter would reach the ears of neighbourhood parents. Life was going to be tough and lonely enough. She didn't think it wise to isolate themselves from their neighbours, however much Mother and Esme might wish to.

The girl, who was clutching the hand of a small boy of about two, said, 'I ain't bin this week. Me mum needs me at 'ome. She's got a bad chest, yer see.' She looked down at the toddler. 'I've gotta look after me brother.'

'School,' said one of the bigger boys scornfully, 'sod that for a lark!'

'What about your parents?'

'They're too old to go to school,' said the boy waggishly, producing a roar of laughter from his friends.

'You know what I mean,' said Kate. 'Don't they try to make you go?'

'Nah, they ain't bothered if I go or not, long as I do me milk round and earn some dough in the day runnin' errands and that.'

'Yeah, school's a mug's game,' said another boy, to loud agreement from his pals.

'Oh dear, what appalling children,' mumbled Gertie under her breath. 'Let's go inside, for goodness' sake.' She spoke with urgency in her voice, almost as though these unfortunates were dangerous criminals.

'Yes, come on,' urged Esme tearfully, clutching her mother's hand.

'We'll see you again, I expect,' said Kate to the little girl.

'Yeah, I expect yer will, an' all,' said the girl breezily. 'I live at number three too. You've prob'ly got the room next door to ours. The other people 'ave moved out.'

'Goodbye,' said Kate, her refined accent seeming to ring with incongruity in these surroundings.

13

'Tata, mate,' said the girl.

There was no lock on the front door of number three which opened just by pushing it. It led into a hallway with dingy brown walls, bare floorboards and a stench that had them all stuffing handkerchiefs to their noses. Stale cooking, mildew, mouse droppings and the acidic smell of urine accumulated into a powerful miasma which seemed far worse to Kate than when she had first come to see the room.

The landlady, who lived in another street, had given Kate the key when she'd paid the advance rent. So she was able to lead her mother and sister straight upstairs to the room she had taken for them on the top floor of this three-storey house. With dread in her heart, she turned the key in the lock.

'At least there's a good view,' said Kate standing hopefully at the window as her mother stared in horror at the squalor around her. 'You can even see the river over the rooftops.'

'It's no better than a slum!'

'Oh, come on, it isn't so bad,' insisted Kate. 'At least there's some furniture. Some of the places I looked at didn't even have anything to sit on.' She glanced around the room in which there was a large bed with a stained mattress and a folded pile of rough grey blankets, a chipped wooden table and four chairs, a scratched sideboard and a wardrobe. Beside the fireplace was a single gas ring for cooking. Under the window sat a washstand with a cracked marble top on which stood a rose-patterned jug and bowl suffused with little cracks and brown stains.

'But how can we eat and sleep in one room, sharing the same bed?' begged Gertie. 'We'll suffocate.'

'We'll get used to it,' said Kate, managing to maintain a positive front, despite the despair in her heart. 'Once we've lit the fire and cleaned the place up a bit, it will seem more like home.'

'Home?' shrieked Gertie. 'It's more like a dog kennel than a home. Why, even our servants at the square lived in more comfort than this.'

Anyone would think I was to blame for our dire situation to

14

hear Mother speak, Kate thought, but said, 'What else can we do but live somewhere like this? I did my best but I couldn't get anything better without the money to pay for it.' She wrung her hands. 'I'm sorry you hate it so much, Mother, but I just don't know what I can do to improve matters for us at the moment.'

'There's nothing you *can* do!' screamed Gertie hysterically. 'It's all your father's fault. How could he have done it to us, how could he, leaving us with no home and no one to look after us?'

Imbued with a surge of pity, Kate went to her mother and put a comforting arm around her trembling shoulders. 'Please don't take on so. We'll all feel better once we have some money coming in. In the meantime, let's try to make the best of it.'

Gertie drew back from Kate's embrace and glared at her. 'How can anyone make the best of a place like this?'

Looking solemnly into her mother's face, Kate said, 'Lots of people do. Hundreds of thousands of them all over London are living in worse conditions than this.'

'And that's supposed to make me feel better, is it?'

'I hoped it might.' Kate felt so hopelessly inadequate to the situation, and so powerless. 'It certainly makes me feel less hard done by to know that other people are worse off. I mean, one hears about the poor, reads in the papers about children getting bitten to death by rats, but it wasn't until I actually went out looking for a place for us to live that I realised just how bad things are for some people. Many poor souls don't have a home at all, but sleep on the streets in doorways or barns. And all this ten years into the progressive twentieth century and just a bus-ride from Sycamore Square.'

'It's no use preaching at me about other people's problems, Kate,' bleated Gertie. 'I've enough troubles of my own.'

'I didn't realise I was preaching, I'm just trying to get things into perspective for us all. Just think how much worse it is for elderly people who are poor, and those who are sick.'

'People over seventy get five shillings a week now,' Gertie snorted.

15

'Yes, and that's all right for those with savings behind them, but it's not enough to live on.'

'There are the workhouses.'

'Would you like to go to one?'

'Well, no, of course not.'

'Count yourself lucky you have your health and strength and me to look after you then!'

'I can't help it if I've always had the best of everything,' moaned her mother. 'I've never had to struggle. It's hard, Kate, hard. My nerves are in a shocking state.'

Kate was confused by her own emotions. Annoyance at her mother's singlemindedness was immediately followed by guilt and compassion for this pathetic little woman to whom she was almost a stranger. Maybe she hadn't shown courage in the face of adversity, but it must be hard to lose your husband, your place in society and your home comforts all in one fell swoop. She must have suffered a blow to her pride too to discover that her husband had been deceiving her throughout their marriage. Kate herself felt betrayed by him, and she had never really known him.

'It's hard for us all.' She put a supportive arm around Esme who was standing tearfully beside her. 'We've all led such sheltered lives we don't have any stamina. But we'll soon toughen up. We'll have to, since poverty is no longer something we read about but a part of our lives.'

The sound of children shouting on the stairs and adults quarrelling somewhere in the house filled the room, as did a blend of unwholesome smells.

'I'll never be like these people, Kate,' said Gertie, shaking her head. 'Breeding is something that stays with you forever.'

'You could be right,' she said. 'But that doesn't mean you can't learn to be tolerant of those who don't have it.'

Gertie looked doubtful. 'Only time will tell about that.'

The utter helplessness of her mother and sister imbued Kate with new strength. 'I can promise you one thing, though.'

'What's that?'

'I shall move heaven and earth to make it possible for us to

16

move back into Sycamore Square, or somewhere like it, one day.'

This show of optimism brightened Gertie's expression momentarily. But reality wasn't far behind. 'But you're only fifteen. Too young to marry. And it will be impossible to find a rich husband when the time does come, unless our circumstances change dramatically.'

'So, I'll do it another way.'

'What other way is there?'

'I don't know. And I'm not saying it will be easy, or soon. Only that somehow, one day, I'll do it. In the meantime, let's make ourselves as comfortable as we can. The first thing is to make a pot of tea. I'll go downstairs to see if there's any sign of our trunk with the crockery in it. One of us will have to go out to get some provisions. There's a market quite near, I noticed it when I came to view the room.'

Every second that passed in their new home seemed to produce another drama. Even a minor task like purchasing groceries created a problem for people who had always had servants to do such things for them. Esme was too nervous to leave the house, Gertie too proud, so Kate went to the shop on the corner and bought a ha'penny twist of tea. Sugar, milk, bread and margarine were obtained in similar small measures, just to keep them going until later.

If the fact that they had to go the ground floor to collect water from a sink in a scullery used by all the other tenants filled Gertie with despair, sharing a lavatory in the backyard with five other families had her almost suicidal. Then there was the noise and the smells and having to prepare their own food, and in such primitive conditions too . . . and not having privacy to undress, or space to move without falling over each other.

Having soothed her mother through all these trials and tribulations as well as trying to comfort Esme, who collapsed into fresh tears at every opportunity, Kate also tramped back and forth to King Street and Bradmore Lane market for various much-needed commodities. There was coal, which she dragged home in a cart she borrowed from a boy playing in the street for the sum of a ha'penny; potatoes to be baked in their jackets in the fire for supper; and various other essentials including a newspaper to look through the Situations Vacant, firewood and matches to light the fire, carbolic soap for general use, and soda to wash the dishes.

By eight o'clock that evening, having spent ages on her knees trying to coax some life into a recalcitrant fire, cooked potatoes in it, collected umpteen buckets and jugs of water from downstairs, made the bed, washed the dishes and scrubbed the floor while her mother and sister sat about complaining, she felt the time had come for some plain speaking.

'As from tomorrow morning we must work as a team and establish some sort of routine,' she explained in a firm tone.

'Huh!' snorted mother, shrugging her shoulders dismissively.

'Obviously, I can't be expected to do everything while you two sit about feeling sorry for yourselves.'

'I really wouldn't know where to start,' said Gertie haughtily.

'You'll just have to jolly well learn then, won't you, Mother?' said Kate, who considered it vital that her mother have some sort of occupation to keep her from brooding. 'Because once Esme and I have found work we shall be out all day, so it will be up to you to keep house for us. I'm quite prepared to take some responsibility but you two must make your contribution too.'

'Me, go out to work?' said Esme, aghast.

'That's right,' Kate informed her briskly. 'We can't expect Mother to get a job, so it's up to us to support her.'

Fresh tears flowed at this news. 'But I can't!' Esme wailed. 'Girls like me don't go to work.'

'They do if they don't have anyone to support them,' Kate pointed out firmly. 'We'll both have to earn a living somehow.'

'You mean domestic work, don't you? Cleaning up after other people,' Esme sobbed, looking towards Gertie for support. 'Oh, Mother, tell her I don't have to do it, *please*?'

But her mother was too intent on self-preservation. Someone had to keep her now that Cyril had gone. 'It doesn't have to be that sort of work, dear,' she said sheepishly. 'Perhaps you could get a position as a shopgirl in one of the West End stores?'

Esme wept dramatically at this betrayal. 'I'm not going to do it, and you two can't make me,' she wailed.

Kate's patience snapped. As the elder sister, she had always been protective towards Esme, but there was no place for passengers in their harsh new regime.

'That's enough of that silly behaviour, Esme,' she said sharply. 'You're not a baby, so don't behave like one.'

'*I hate you!*' Esme hissed vehemently.

'And at this particular moment I'm not too fond of you either!'

'I'm just a child, you can't make me work,' Esme persisted. 'I'd still have been at school if Daddy hadn't died.'

'So would I,' Kate reminded her. 'But he did die and there's no money for us to continue with our education. We are both past the official school-leaving age so we must go out to work.'

'Shan't!' Esme said childishly.

'Don't expect me to keep you then,' said Kate briskly. 'I'm not going out slaving to put bread in your mouth while you sit at home moaning.'

Her sister turned pale as she finally faced the fact that life's necessities had to be paid for. 'You don't mean that?'

'Esme, love,' Kate said in a conciliatory manner, for she was fond of her sister for all her faults. 'Having to go out to work is just as humiliating for me as it is for you. But it's something we'll both have to put up with. I can't keep you and Mother without help. There simply won't be enough money to go round.'

The younger girl stopped crying and looked at her fearfully. 'It's just that I'll probably be hopeless at any sort of work.'

'Not if you put your mind to it.'

'But I'll feel so out of it among working-class girls. They're

19

so frightfully common, and they always seem so sure of themselves from what I've seen of them.'

'I'm not looking forward to it either,' Kate admitted. 'But we'll get used to it since we don't have any choice.'

'All right.' Esme sighed miserably. 'I'll try to find a job in one of the West End stores. At least I won't get dirty there.'

Kate hugged her. 'That's my girl. If we all pull together we'll come through this, you'll see.' She turned to Gertie. 'How about you, Mother? Are you going to look after things here for us – shopping, cooking, mending and so on?'

'I suppose I'll damned well have to,' Gertie agreed reluctantly.

Lying on the lumpy mattress that night with her daughters either side of her, listening to the persistent rattle of someone coughing in the room next door, Gertie wallowed in self-pity. Life had become a complete nightmare, with no hope of any improvement. How could she, a respected Kensington lady, have been reduced to sleeping three in a bed in the same overcrowded room where they did everything else?

As the daughter of an architect, she had been brought up in reasonable comfort in a nice home, looked after by servants. In fact, Gertie had never cooked a meal, or shopped for food in her life. More worrying than having to knuckle down to domestic chores was the daunting prospect of having to rub shoulders with the lower classes. What if she was thought to be one of them? How mortifying! She didn't even know how to pass the time of day with hoi polloi, let alone feel comfortable with them. And what was more, she had no intention of learning.

Her thoughts turned to Cyril and her mood became even more despairing. If only she'd made use of the Married Women's Property Act that allowed women to own and control their own income after marriage, and hung on to her inheritance from her parents. She and the girls would still have had to lower their sights, but at least then they could have bought a modest house instead of renting this flea-pit. But in common with most husbands of their class, Cyril had always looked after their finances and taken responsibilty for everything except the actual running of the house.

Trusting him as she had, she'd handed her legacy over to him without a second thought. Angry tears burned as she thought of how he had betrayed her. If he had cheated on her with another woman it would have been less heinous than gambling away her security, she thought wryly.

All those years and she had never suspected that he was leading a double life. And to think he had been contemplating suicide and she'd not realised anything was wrong! He'd seemed a little tense those last few weeks, but she'd just assumed it was pressure of business. And since her interest in that direction had never been encouraged, she hadn't questioned him about it. Which just went to show that she had not really known him at all.

The person coughing on the other side of the wall sounded as if they were about to choke. The high rasping sounds were undoubtedly female. Damned woman should get her health seen to, keeping decent people awake at night, Gertie thought harshly, refusing to allow practical considerations like doctors' fees to linger.

Turning her mind to her daughters, she realised that they had been little more than strangers to her until two weeks ago. Well, it wasn't done to have one's offspring around too much in a well-to-do home. Gertie and Cyril had had a busy social life. An hour or so with the girls after tea had been quite sufficient. After all, what did one pay a nanny for? Even when the girls had grown bigger and Nanny had been assigned to other duties while they were out at school, the system hadn't changed much.

Now, ironically, they were thrown together morning, noon and night. Despite all the disadvantages, though, Gertie drew comfort from having the girls close at hand, especially Kate who had proved to be such a tower of strength, even if she did have a hard edge.

Beside her in the bed, Esme twitched and fidgeted. She'll be worrying about the horrors of tomorrow, I expect, Gertie guessed gloomily. Esme always had been the more sensitive of the two girls. On Gertie's other side Kate was lying still, breathing evenly. Sleeping peacefully, her mother assumed, though how anyone could manage to sleep on this dreadful mattress which felt as though it was stuffed with bricks, and smelled as though it was riddled with bedbugs, was quite beyond her. Sighing, she closed her eyes and tried not to think of tomorrow. But the dread of it wasn't easily banished.

Kate's mother had been wrong to assume that her eldest daughter was asleep. She was actually wide awake and worried sick. But she deemed it wise not to mention this to Esme and Mother who needed to feel that she was in control of the situation. In truth, she hadn't the slightest idea what kind of work she should look for or how to set about finding it. This wasn't really surprising since she had been raised with the idea that she would stay at home and enjoy a social life through which she would eventually find a husband to keep her in comfort for the rest of her life. She knew all about deportment and how to make the most of her femininity, but any sort of useful skills were non-existent.

Yet, oddly enough, rising above the worry of where next week's meals were coming from, she could feel an unmistakable bubble of excitement.

The coughing from next door was now interspersed with the sound of retching. The poor soul sounds awfully sick, she thought. A germ of unease nagged at the back of Kate's mind. It had been there for most of the day but hadn't yet crystallised into a definite concept.

Oh, well, it's been quite a day, and heaven knows what tomorrow will bring, she was thinking as she drifted into a sleep of sheer exhaustion.

# Chapter Two

Kate was feeling somewhat dejected as she walked home in the late afternoon of the following day, having unsuccessfully tramped the streets for hours looking for work. Noticeboards on factory gates had been scanned for vacancies; shop owners had been approached. She'd tried the laundry, the dairy, the bakery, the brewery; she'd even enquired at the waterworks if they could use a strong, hard-working girl.

Trying not to panic, she'd decided to look further afield tomorrow. Maybe she would try one of these new government places they called Labour Exchanges. According to the newspaper, eighty of these offices had just opened across the country to help people find work.

But now dusk was falling and the streets were shrouded with a smoky mist which stung her eyes and throat. She passed a shop bearing the sign Women's Social and Political Union, the windows of which were plastered with VOTES FOR WOMEN posters. Standing in the doorway were two women, wearing the purple, white and green suffragette sashes, handing out leaflets and talking to a small group of females.

She was tempted to stop and listen to what was being said, despite having been warned against those 'dreadful suffragettes' many times by her mother who deemed their behaviour unfeminine. Personally, Kate thought they sounded rather courageous, though she had had the sense not to mention this to Mother. More pressing matters prevailing over a mild curiosity she passed on, anxious to get home and find out how Gertie and Esme had fared.

Being footsore, chilled to the bone and ravenously hungry, even the room at Beaver Terrace was a welcome thought. As she climbed the stairs, she was longing to warm herself by the fire and sink her teeth into some food. She was disappointed on both counts, for entering the room she found herself in a smoke-filled ice-box. Her mother was sitting by the unlit fire sobbing quietly. Esme was standing beside her, scowling. They both looked up when Kate entered, Gertie barely recognisable under a thick layer of coal-dust.

'The fire's gone out,' explained Esme crossly. 'And Mummy can't light it again.'

Curbing her irritation at what seemed to be such unnecessary incompetence, Kate spoke calmly to her mother. 'How did that happen?'

'Don't ask me.'

'But I lit the fire before I went out this morning and made sure there was enough coal and wood to last until tonight.'

'It just sort of died away,' Gertie sobbed.

'You mean you forgot to make it up?'

'I didn't realise it needed so much attention.'

'Surely you didn't think it would last all day, until I got home?'

'I didn't give the dratted thing a thought, to be perfectly honest,' confessed Gertie. 'I've tried to re-light it but it simply won't catch and we've run out of matches.'

'Why didn't you go out and get some more then?'

Gertie stared shamefully at her feet, her shoulders shaking. 'I couldn't.'

'Why not?'

'I just couldn't, that's all.'

'But we made an agreement yesterday,' Kate reminded her. 'Your job is to keep house, and that means keeping the fire in as well as making sure there's something to eat in the place.'

'Sorry.'

'Have you been to the shops at all?'

Her bowed head moved from side to side.

'So you've had nothing to eat?'

'No.'

'But the market is only a few minutes' walk and the housekeeping money is in a tin on the mantelpiece.'

'I know that.'

'Yet you didn't go . . .'

'I feel so out of place around here.' She looked up, her eyes filled with tears. 'I just can't bring myself to go out of this room, let alone out of the house. I've not had a cup of tea since this morning because there was no water left in here.'

'What about the . . .?'

'I waited until I was sure there was no one about before rushing down to the WC.' She brushed a nervous hand across her brow. 'And even then it was an absolute nightmare. I was terrified I might meet someone on the stairs. I just don't know what to say to these people.'

Gertie looked so utterly forlorn, Kate couldn't help but feel sorry for her. Misguided she undoubtedly was, but she really *was* suffering. 'But you can't hide away in this room indefinitely.'

'I shall have to because I simply cannot bear to go out.'

Uncertain how to deal with this new problem, Kate said, 'I'm sure things will all seem different when we've lit the fire and had something to eat.' She turned to Esme, hardly daring to ask the question. 'How did you get on up West?'

To her amazement, Esme said with casual indifference, 'Oh, all right, I suppose. I start tomorrow at Bailey and Peck in Oxford Street. Haberdashery department. Eight shillings and sixpence a week, and I can live at home as we are not far from the West End.'

'Oh, Esme, that's wonderful,' enthused Kate. 'Well done!'

'What's wonderful about standing behind a counter all day with a lot of dimwitted girls?' asked her sister, who had secretly hoped that no one would employ her and she would be spared the ghastly ritual of having to work for a living. 'I shall hate every minute of it.'

'I think you're very clever to have got a job at all,' said Kate.

'Nothing particularly clever about it,' she said dismissively, for she had deliberately set out to seem fat-headed with the idea of failing the interview. 'The woman who interviewed me liked the way I speak, that's all. An upper-class accent goes down well with their customers, apparently.'

25

'Well, I think it's good news anyway,' said Kate, switching her attention back to the immediate problem. 'Will you go downstairs and get some water, Esme, to make some tea while I go to the shop for matches? I'll get some food while I'm out.'

With a horrible suspicion that getting her mother back into the outside world was not going to be easy, Kate left the room and made her way downstairs with Esme en route for the scullery.

Parting company at the bottom of the stairs, Kate opened the front door and almost collided with a tall woman of about thirty with bright red hair swept up into her black straw hat and falling untidily in spiky wisps around her face. She wasn't fat, but noticeably big-boned and with wide shoulders. Noticing the large brown eyes that protruded slightly, Kate saw the likeness to the redheaded girl and her brother from yesterday's reception committee, both of whom were present now. The girl and the woman were carrying a loaded shopping bag between them.

'Whoops! Sorry, ducks,' said the woman breathlessly, dragging her heavy load away from her daughter as she staggered towards the stairs and flopped down on to the bottom one, gasping for breath and erupting into a fit of coughing. The bag bumped on to the floor, some muddy potatoes spilling out and rolling across the hall.

'It was my fault.' Kate began, collecting the potatoes and returning them to the bag. 'You don't seem very well.'

Answering for her mother, who was coughing fit to choke, the girl said, 'She isn't.'

Kate's own problems were immediately forgotten. 'Here, let me carry your shopping upstairs for you.' She picked up the bag which was weighty with vegetables. 'I think your room is next to ours from what your little girl said yesterday.'

The coughing abated but the woman's chest wheezed as she breathed. 'Kind of yer to offer, love, but there ain't no need. I'll be all right in a minute.' Her glance lingered on Kate, observing the tastefulness of her clothes, so completely at odds with her surroundings. 'So you've just moved in next door to us, 'ave yer?'

26

'That's right.'

'We ain't used to your sort round 'ere, and that's a fact.' She thrust forward a large, square hand which had the texture of sack-cloth. 'Still, you're welcome just the same. I'm Bertha Brent and these are me kids, Ruby and Georgie.'

Kate introduced herself.

'Sorry I ain't popped in to say 'ello,' said Bertha, 'but I've bin that bad. I felt so rotten yesterday, I couldn't get out o' bed all day. It started with flu and went down on to me chest. Always does, yer know. It's livin' in damp conditions, I expect.'

'Ruby said her mother wasn't well,' Kate said sheepishly. The uncomfortable feeling that had been bothering her now identified itself as full-blown compunction. She'd been told her neighbour was sick, but she'd been too immersed in her own affairs to pay any attention. Accustomed as she was to Sycamore Square where everyone had servants to tend to their needs, it hadn't occurred to her actually to make any sort of effort. And it should have since things were so obviously different around here. The least she could have done was to have made her sick neighbour a hot drink.

'I 'ope me cough didn't keep yer awake last night?' said Bertha. 'The bugger just wouldn't stop.'

'We were all too tired to notice,' fibbed Kate. 'But, anyway, you can't help having a cough so don't you worry about us.'

The woman stood up and went to relieve Kate of the bag. ''ere, I'll take that.'

'I'll carry it up for you, like I said.'

'Don't trouble yerself, ducks,' said Bertha cheerfully. 'You don't wanna troop all the way back up. I can see you're on yer way out.'

'Another few minutes won't make any difference,' said Kate, feeling completely at ease in this woman's company. 'We're in such chaos anyway.'

'Oh? Why's that?'

'My mother couldn't get the fire to light,' she explained, omitting details that might embarrass Gertie. 'I'm off for fresh supplies of matches. It's a case of smoke, smoke everywhere and not a flame in sight.'

Bertha gave a hoarse laugh and they began climbing the stairs together, chatting as they went, Bertha stopping every few minutes to catch her breath.

'I've got some matches you can borrow if yer wanna get the fire going straight away, to get the place warmed up.'

'That's kind of you, thank you,' said Kate. 'I'll replace them when I go out to get something for tea.'

When they reached their landing, Kate carried Bertha's shopping into her room and waited while she found the matches. The room overlooked the backyard and, although slightly larger than the Potters', was much more cluttered, mostly due to piles of ladies' hats in various stages of manufacture which covered the table and stood in piles on the floor. There were felt ones, straw ones, some with ribbons, some with bows or wax fruit. Cardboard shoe-boxes were open to reveal braid, ribbon, feathers, artificial flowers . . .

Glancing towards them, Bertha tutted. 'I'm all be'ind with me work, with bein' poorly. I'll 'ave to get crackin' or I won't make enough money this week to pay the rent.'

'Do you have a weekly quota to do?'

'It's piece-work, love,' she explained. 'You only get paid for what you do.' She tutted again. 'It's a blimmin' nuisance getting sick in the middle of the trade's busy season. I like to make the most of it, 'cos it'll slow down at the end of May.'

'Are you a qualified milliner?'

'Not in the true sense of the word. I don't make the 'ats from start to finish. I just does the trimmin' and finishin'.'

Kate's interest was immediately aroused. 'I think millinery is something I'd like to try,' she said thoughtfully. 'I'd enjoy working with all the different shapes and materials.'

'It's 'ard work,' warned Bertha. 'And it can be boring doin' trimming all day.'

'It must be interesting to design and make an exclusive hat, though?'

'Oh, yeah, I expect it is but that's a different branch of the trade altogether. That's the West End model millinery trade. The firm I work for produces lots of identical 'ats for stores all over the country.'

'Sounds fascinating,' said Kate, finding herself unexpectedly intrigued.

'I dunno so much about that,' said Bertha. 'I ain't got any choice but to sew 'ats. I've gotta feed the kids somehow. Me old man, Gawd rest 'im, kicked the bucket soon after Georgie was born. The poor sod was took bad with consumption.'

'I'm sorry about that.'

'So am I, but there ain't no point in moanin' about it.'

'I suppose not,' said Kate, hoping that in time her mother would find the strength for such a positive attitude.

'I've been out looking for work all day as a matter of fact,' said Kate chattily.

'No luck?'

'No.' She paused thoughtfully. 'Perhaps I could sew hats at home to make some money?'

'You'd 'ave to work at a factory to get trained,' explained Bertha. 'I used to work in one before I got married. I 'ave to sew at 'ome now 'cos of the kids. I'd sooner go out to work though, I enjoy the company.'

'Does the firm you work for have any vacancies?'

'I dunno.' She rummaged among the muddle of dusty ornaments and nick-nacks on the mantelpiece until she found a scrap of paper, then drew out a pencil stub from behind the clock and wrote something down. ''ere's the address. It's a place over at Wandsworth. No 'arm in askin', is there?'

Filled with new hope and enthusiasm, Kate smiled warmly. 'Thanks, Bertha, I'll go over there tomorrow morning.'

She frowned. 'You'll 'ave to watch the guvnor, Reggie Dexter, though.'

'Oh, in what way?' Having been a schoolgirl until recently, and led the sort of life where a young woman socialised with the opposite sex only with a chaperon present, Kate had no practical experience of men.

Bertha looked into that pointed little face dominated by striking dark eyes with thick curling lashes and rounded brows. For all her well-bred self-assurance, there was an innocence about Kate that was virtually non-existent in the streetwise young girls from round here. But Bertha sensed a pluckiness too, despite her elfin appearance. And the early signs of a beautiful woman were clearly visible in this skinny adolescent. Cissy Dexter is gonna have to watch that husband of hers like a hawk if they take this girl on, she thought wryly, but then Cissy was used to that. 'In the usual way, ducks,' she chirped. 'Let me know how yer get on tomorrer.'

'I will, and I'll drop a box of matches in to you later.'

'Any time, love. You know where I am if yer need anything.'

'Thanks, Bertha.'

Kate left feeling greatly warmed by her neighbour's friendliness, and happier than she'd been in ages.

After Kate had gone, Bertha thought, now that is one classy young lady, and not a bit of side with her either.


'Mr Dexter will see you now, Miss Potter,' said a bespectacled secretary the next morning as Kate sat outside the office of the owner of Dexter's hat factory, 'Knock and enter, please.'

'Thank you.' Kate walked boldly into the office where a dark-haired man with a neat moustache was sitting at a leather-topped desk. Heavily built with broad shoulders and a solid jawline, he looked about thirty and was smartly dressed in a grey suit with a waistcoat, a high starched collar and dark tie.

'My secretary tells me you're looking for work,' he said, observing her with interest.

'Yes, that's right.' Although her confidence was somewhat diminished by her reduced circumstances there was still an inherent self-assurance in the way Kate carried herself. 'And I'd like to work with hats.'

'Do you have any experience?'

'None at all, I'm afraid,' she admitted brightly, 'but I'm sure I would be quick to learn.'

He was completely taken aback by her. The girls who came to him for work were humble, badly dressed, ill-spoken. This one had swept in with such aplomb, a casual observer might have been forgiven for thinking that *she* was about to interview *him*.

'Indeed!' The fact that his rates were the lowest in the area and this was his busy season meant he was urgently in need of labour which was why he had agreed to see her. But he wasn't going to tell her that. 'I don't usually see people without an appointment.'

'Oh, really? Well, I'm very glad you decided to waive the rule on this occasion because I do need a job quite urgently,' she said assertively, unaware that her attitude might seem unusual. 'And I'm not afraid of hard work.'

She intrigued him more with each passing moment. 'You don't seem the sort of girl to be job hunting.'

Giving him a half smile, she said, 'Needs must when the devil drives.'

'Have you run away from your family or something?' he asked, eyeing her suspiciously.

'No, nothing like that,' she assured him. 'My needing a job is due to my family falling on hard times. My father died in very tragic circumstances, you see.'

So there was no father . . . that was even better. He deliberately let his glance linger on her slender young form. Not yet old enough to wear her clothes at full adult length, her coat reached to mid-calf and was worn with thick black stockings and sturdy lace-up shoes. For all her confidence, she was just a slip of a kid. Her curious mixture of innocence and arrogance excited him. He had every intention of giving her a job, after he'd teased her a little, but she was going to have to learn the qualities he demanded from his staff. Obedience, industriousness and deference towards their betters was compulsory for workers in this establishment. This girl obviously had breeding. Perhaps once she might even have been considered socially superior to him. But as one of his staff she would be inferior and never allowed to forget it.

'I'm sorry to hear that, my dear,' he said smoothly. 'And I'd like to help but I don't have anything at the moment.'

Her face dropped. 'Oh, but when you agreed to see me I thought . . .'

'Mmm. I felt there might have been a place for you in our workroom,' he said cunningly, 'but after thinking about it, no, I'm sorry.'

31

Disappointment flooded through her but she managed to retain her composure. 'Well, I'll not waste any more of your time then,' she said, rising.

His small dark eyes were completely devoid of warmth as they met hers, his smile seeming to mock her. It was then she realised exactly what it was that Bertha had been warning her about. Inexperienced Kate was, but her instincts were in perfect working order.

'I hope you find something soon,' he said, in a tone that indicated the opposite.

'Yes. So do I.'

Feeling his eyes on her back as she walked to the door, she was relieved to be leaving, as desperate as she was for the job. But as she crossed the factory yard, someone called her.

'Can you come back, Miss Potter?' shouted the secretary. 'Mr Dexter wants to see you again.'

'I can find a place for you, after all.'

'But I thought . . . I mean, you said . . .'

'So I've changed my mind,' he said. 'It's an employer's prerogative.'

'Well, I'm not sure . . .'

'Seven shillings a week while you're training, and you can start tomorrow.'

She knew he was playing some sort of a power game with her, and had sent her away with every intention of calling her back to offer her a job. She wanted to slap the complacent smile off his face and tell him what to do with his job. But she thought of the price of coal, and food, and the dwindling household fund. She remembered that there was a hole in the sole of her shoe from all the walking yesterday and that her mother needed new stockings. And at least this was a chance to learn a trade rather than being a shop girl forever. And since he didn't seem the sort of employer who would mix with his workers, she probably wouldn't see much of him during the course of a working day.

'Well, do you want the job or not?'

'Yes, I want the job.'

' "Sir", if you don't mind,' he demanded. 'I insist on my workers calling me sir.'

Having always been on the other side of the class divide, she couldn't help seeing the irony in the situation. 'Certainly, sir,' she said calmly.

'That's better,' he said with a triumphant smile.

Hatred wasn't an emotion Kate was accustomed to, but she loathed him with ferocity.

At that moment a well-dressed woman entered the room, and his manner altered completely.

'Ah, Cissy, my dear,' he said, rising and kissing her cheek, 'I've just taken this girl on for the workroom.'

The woman was swathed from head to foot in ermine, her mousy brown hair swept up beneath a fur hat. Her grey eyes scrutinised Kate thoroughly before moving to Mr Dexter. 'Have you indeed?' she said sourly.

'Yes, dear. I thought we needed a junior hand, what with it being our busy time,' he said obsequiously.

Caught in a crossfire of tacit conflict, and being acutely aware of the woman's power over him, Kate said, 'Well, I'll be on my way then.'

'I'm Mrs Dexter,' said the woman, as though issuing a threat. 'You'll be answerable to me as well as my husband while you are working here.'

'I understand, and I'm very pleased to meet you, Mrs Dexter,' said Kate amicably.

Up went Cissy Dexter's brows. 'My, my! That doesn't sound like the accent of someone who's used to hard work.'

'It isn't, and I'm not. But I've explained my situation to your husband.'

Mrs Dexter threw him a dark look. 'Yes, I expect you have.' Her gaze darted back to Kate. 'I hope he has made our position clear? We shall expect a good day's work from you, and we don't tolerate chattering on the job because it could affect our high work standards. Is that clear?'

'Quite clear.'

'Good. Be here sharp at eight o'clock in the morning.'

'Yes.'

'Yes, madam, if you please.'

'Yes, madam.'

'Off you go then.'

Kate left the room, knowing she had made an enemy in Cissy Dexter though she wasn't sure why. She also knew that working for the Dexters was going to be no easy ride.

Things at home had improved slightly when Kate got back to Beaver Terrace. Gertie still hadn't been out shopping, but at least she'd kept the fire in and tidied up. The news about Kate's job produced a mixed reaction. Whilst relieved that the Potters were not destined for the workhouse, she was dismayed at the prospect of being alone all day on a regular basis.

'Yes, I can see that you might feel lonely, but the shopping and the chores will help pass the time. You could always pop in and see Bertha next door,' suggested Kate, having already told her mother about her meeting with their neighbour. 'She'll probably be glad of some company, being confined to the home all day sewing.'

'I wouldn't have a thing to say to her,' said Gertie haughtily. 'We're from different worlds.'

'*From* different worlds, yes,' agreed Kate. 'But not *of* different worlds now that you're neighbours. It will do you good to make some friends.'

'I'll not mix with these people, Kate,' she said crossly. 'So you can stop suggesting it.'

'But you'll be so miserable if you cut yourself off from everyone.'

'I'll be even more miserable spending time with people with whom I don't feel comfortable.'

'Once you get used to them . . .'

'I am *not* going to get pally with some vulgar woman who probably doesn't even speak the King's English and will think I'm being stuck up because I do.'

'How do you know she'll think that? You've never even spoken to her.'

'I don't have to speak to her to know what she's like. Working-class women are all the same.'

34

'But *we* are working-class now.'

'We are not the same as them, Kate,' she interrupted crossly. 'And we never will be. Even if we were to sleep in the gutter or go to the workhouse, we would still be middle-class inside.'

'Even so, I think you should make an effort to be friendly.'

Gertie shrugged.

'How about coming to the market with me to get some groceries?'

'I've a headache.'

'The fresh air will help to clear it.'

'I said no, Kate, and in case you've forgotten, I *am* your mother. I'm the one who's supposed to tell you what to do, not the other way around.'

And that was something her mother only remembered when it suited her, Kate thought wryly, but said, 'I'm only trying to help.'

'Well, you're not, so stop trying to force me into things.'

'All right,' she agreed, but was very worried by her mother's attitude.

Dexter's hat factory was a square, two-storey building. On the ground floor were the offices, the packing room and the sale-room with counters on which finished hats were displayed in long rows for inspection by the representatives of firms of potential buyers. The upper floor comprised a workroom crammed with tables at which women in pinafores worked. Although rather austere with its dull grey walls, it was a well-lit room with lots of windows and lights hanging low from the ceiling, Kate noticed when she started work there the next morning.

Everywhere in the workroom were hats at various stages of production. They perched on papier mâché millinery heads; in piles on the tables; in boxes on the floor. The work-tables were littered with such necessities as ribbon, cotton, scissors, pins, petersham. At a workbench in the corner were a couple of gas rings to heat the flat irons, and steam kettles for shaping.

Having been raised to believe that good elocution and

deportment were vital to success in life, it was a shock to Kate to realise that such refinements were going to be a hindrance to her at Dexter's.

'Gor blimey, where did yer find ripe plums this time o' year?' said a young woman called Ivy when Kate, gathering pins from the floor and trying to be friendly, made a casual comment about the weather.

'What plums?' asked Kate innocently.

'In yer mouth, love,' Ivy said, grinning all over her round, freckled face. ''alf a pound o' best Victorias by the sound of it.'

Kate's tormentor had plenty of support apparently, for after a ripple of laughter another one of her workmates said, 'You'd better start talkin' proper if yer intend stayin' in the job. We don't want none o' that la-de-da talk round 'ere.'

'I can't help the way I speak,' said Kate.

'Yer can stop puttin' it on.'

'I'm not, honestly.'

'Yer don't mean that's your natural way o' talkin'?'

'Yes, it is.'

'Oh, do give over! If your so bleedin' 'igh and mighty, 'ow come you're workin' in a dump like this?'

Kate bit back her reply. She was feeling very lonely and confused. Her head was spinning with words and expressions she had never heard before. As well as unfamiliar cockney slang, she also had to contend with millinery terms. People talked about hoods and capelines, which were basic hat shapes before final shaping, and blocking, which was the shaping process, and sparterie, which was a material used for stiffening and moulding . . .

As a workroom junior she was required to run errands, make tea, gather pins from the floor and keep the place tidy. The sewing hands sent her to the stores for thread and trimmings, and the formidable female supervisor sent her all over the factory collecting and delivering various items. And all the time her workmates mocked her middle-class manner in low tones so as not to attract the attention of the supervisor who sat at a table apart from the workers. Kate longed for a kindly word, but she had enough common sense to realise that she wouldn't receive one from these people by being humble.

'That's my business,' she replied at last, meeting the woman's cool glare. 'I've as much right to work here as you.'

Ivy's brows rose at this unexpected show of defiance. 'Cor, dearie me! Did yer 'ear that, gels?' She looked along the tables at her workmates and launched into a parody. 'That's her business. Oh, my dee-ah.'

The crackle of mirth was halted by the supervisor, who heard the disturbance and left her place to remind them that this was a place of work not a fun fair, and that Dexter's didn't pay for shoddy work. But Kate was not left to go about her work in peace for long. That afternoon when the supervisor was with the Dexters in the office, Ivy decided on a little more sport at the new girl's expense . . .

Calling Kate over, she deliberately emptied a box of pins on to the floor and told her to pick them up. Immediately the pins were returned to the box, she smiled wickedly and spilled them again.

'Oh dee-ah,' she said in an exaggerated imitation of Kate's voice. 'Look what I've been and gorn and done. Pick them up, girl, and quick about it!'

Calmly, Kate met Ivy's hostile stare then got down on her hands and knees and collected the pins, pricking her fingers and making them bleed with the speed at which she worked. Within seconds of finishing the task, the pins cascaded to the floor again.

Some of the other women were enjoying the entertainment which livened up their dreary day, and watched with amusement.

Deciding it was time to make her position clear, Kate addressed the trouble-makers. 'You'll tire of this nonsense before I will, I promise you.'

'We'll see about that,' said Ivy.

'Why are you doing it?'

'We don't want your sort around 'ere.'

'Why? I'm no threat to you!'

''Cos yer ain't one of us, that's why, and yer makes us feel edgy,' Ivy explained. ''ow do we know you ain't part of the management, 'ere to spy on us?'

If she hadn't been feeling so wretched, that might have struck her as funny considering the way the Dexters had treated her at the interview. 'You only have my word for that. But I can promise you that whatever you do to me, I won't leave. I *can't*. I've a mother to support, and I'll put up with anything to get my wages.'

The others fell into a surprised silence as they tried to assess this outsider. 'I'll ask yer again,' said Ivy, 'if you're such a lady, why are yer working for the miserable rates the Dexters pay?'

'Anyone can fall on hard times,' she said candidly.

'Leave her be, Ivy,' said a woman working nearby.

'Yeah, leave the kid alone,' said another. 'She ain't 'urting you.'

Realising the show was over, Ivy turned her attention to the hat lining she was working on.

Kate doubted if that would be the last time Ivy would try to make trouble for her, but at least there was some gratification in having stood up to her.

Gertie stood just inside the door of the room with an empty bucket, straining her ears for the sound of movement on the stairs. Satisfied that there was no one about, she stole softly from the room and began the trek to the water tap. Creeping down the stairs, she held her breath with every creaking footstep for fear she might attract attention and be forced into conversation.

Since the girls had started work a week ago, Gertie had managed to keep the household running without having any contact with the world outside their room. Quite an achievement considering the location of the water tap and toilet facilities. But by ignoring any knocks on her door, leaving her hideaway only when it was absolutely necessary, and leaving the shopping to Kate when she got home from work, she had avoided speaking to anyone.

Her aversion to her new neighbours had progressed beyond snobbery to fear. Although she considered herself to be superior to them, the fact that she was the odd one out gave them the upper hand. Sometimes, although she hated to admit it, she even felt envious of their natural heartiness which she could hear from inside her self-imposed prison as they noisily chatted on the stairs and landings. God forbid that she should ever become that common, she thought, though already her smooth manicured hands were getting to be as rough as those of the housemaids she had once employed.

She was nearing the bottom of the stairs when someone came through the front door. Damn and blast! It was that awful woman from the room next door and that grubby boy of hers. Kate had pointed them out to her from the window when they'd been in the street the other day. Gertie stopped in her tracks, aghast, wondering how she could escape back upstairs to her room without being seen. But when the woman staggered towards the stairs in a state of semi-collapse and clung to the banister rail, Gertie knew she was trapped.

'Here, let me help,' she heard herself utter in a timid voice as she eased the woman into a sitting position on the bottom step.

The boy started to cry, thick yellow rivers sliding from his nose. 'Don't, Georgie,' said Bertha, wiping his nose with a well-used piece of rag. 'Yer ma'll get yer a bottle of medicine to make yer feel better soon.'

'You ought to be in bed,' said Gertie.

'I know,' said Bertha. 'I don't 'alf feel rotten. I just can't shake orf this bloomin' bronchitis or whatever it is. I reckon I'll be lumbered with it till the spring.'

'You shouldn't be out in this cold weather.'

'You're right,' agreed Bertha. 'But Georgie's got the colic and I was on my way to the chemist to get 'im somethin' to settle it. I got halfway up the road and felt that faint I 'ad to come back.'

'Oh dear,' said Gertie.

'There's a shop in King Street I go to where they make up a bottle o' stuff that always puts 'im right,' she explained, wiping a weary hand across her moist brow. 'If the poor little beggar wasn't feeling so bad, I'd leave it till Ruby gets 'ome from school and send 'er for it.'

'Perhaps that would be best.'

'No, he can't wait that long,' she said. 'I'll be all right in a minute. It's only a spot o' weakness from this bad chest o' mine.'

'Let me help you upstairs.'

'It's kind of yer to offer, love, but I'm going out again soon as it passes.'

'But you're not well enough.'

'Being well enough don't come into it when you've kids to look after. You've gotta keep goin' even if yer crawl about on yer knees.' She gave Gertie a companionable smile. 'But you must be young Kate's mum, so you'd know all about that.'

Since Gertie didn't think it wise to admit that she had always employed other people to bear the inconvenience of her children for her, she just said, 'Have you no one who can help you out?'

'Me sister from Shepherd's Bush 'elps out when she can,' Bertha explained. 'But she's got four nippers of 'er own and 'er work to do. She does trouser finishin' at 'ome so she's got quite enough on 'er plate.'

'Does the doctor say you should rest?'

'Doctor? What doctor?' she exclaimed. 'I can't afford to spend money on doctors.'

'I see.' Gertie felt a sudden stab of fear as she was reminded that medical treatment was another of life's luxuries no longer readily available to her.

Bertha rose and clung shakily to the banisters. 'Gor blimey, that funny turn's shaken me up good and proper,' she said, her face ashen and damp with perspiration.

'Come on,' said Gertie, astonished at her own forcefulness. 'Let's get you upstairs. Then we'll worry about Georgie's medicine.'

This time Bertha didn't argue. When Gertie had settled her in a chair by her fireside with a pot of tea, and Georgie snuggled on her lap, she asked, 'Are you feeling a bit better now?'

'Still feel a bit dickie,' Bertha admitted. 'But I can't sit about for long, not with the medicine to get and a pile of 'ats to finish.'

The child began to cry again, drawing his legs up to his stomach with the pain, his skin grey with pallor. 'There, there, pet,' soothed Bertha. 'Your mum will get you something to make you better in a minute.'

The obvious solution to the boy's problem hung unspoken in the air. Gertie broke out in a nervous sweat at the thought of it and tried to ease her conscience with some plain facts. These people were not her problem. She had helped the woman to get upstairs and made her some tea. What else was she supposed to do? It wasn't her fault if the damned female was in no fit state to attend to the needs of her sick child. Gertie had problems enough of her own.

Georgie continued to whimper helplessly.

'If you tell me which chemist to go to,' Gertie heard herself saying, 'I'll go and get the medicine for you.'

Bertha's expression lightened. 'Oh, would yer, love? I'd be ever so grateful,' she said, smiling. 'Is it any trouble?'

'Of course not,' lied Gertie, smiling bravely. 'I've got to go out to get shopping for me and the girls. Give me a list and I'll get whatever you need.'

A few minutes later, a terrified Gertie took the first shaky steps out into an alien world.

By the time Kate had been at Dexter's for a month, she was beginning to feel like part of the workforce. Ivy and her cronies continued to treat her with suspicion and never missed an opportunity to snipe at her, but the majority of Kate's workmates now accepted her as being on their side of the 'them and us' divide between workers and management.

And their judgement was not misplaced because Kate found both Mr and Mrs Dexter more odious with every day that passed. From time to time they would tour the workroom together, examining the work, reminding their employees of the high standards expected of them and threatening to penalise those whose sewing was found to be below par.

Mr Dexter was completely dominated by his wife, and fawned to her every whim. The reason for this, according to factory gossip, was that Cissy Dexter held the purse strings and

41

he had only married her for her money and to get his hands on the business. His very presence made Kate's skin crawl, especially the way he looked at her when his wife wasn't around.

But now that she was getting used to the work, she quite enjoyed it. The hours were long and the majority of her tasks tedious, but in between fetching and carrying she was given tuition by the supervisor in basic millinery, such tasks as how to make hat-linings.

Although she was slow and clumsy to begin with, she enjoyed working with needle and thread and seeing the results of her efforts. The thing she found so interesting about the trade was the speed with which basic hoods became finished hats after moving through all the different processes.

Dexters specialised in ladies' hats for the cheaper end of the market, hundreds all the same. Kate still thought it would be more satisfying to work in model millinery where one was more personally involved in the creation of a hat from start to finish. But she was happy enough working here and went out of her way to learn as much as she could.

Things at home were better too now that her mother had overcome her fear of the outside world and was accepting the domestic chores as her responsibility. Even though she still complained about her lot, at least she was making an effort. With Bertha's help she was even learning to make cheap, nourishing meals like mutton stew and tripe and onions.

To Kate's surprise, Esme had settled down very well at Bailey and Peck and seemed to enjoy the job. Being rather easily led, the working-class girls she had so cruelly derided soon became her heroines. Much to her mother's chagrin, she came home full of tales of having a 'terrific lark' in her dinner break with her friend from the lingerie department who was a 'real scream' and could do a smashing impersonation of the 'fish-faced old fart' who was the head of her department.

The Potters were still considered to be oddities in the local community and were the subject of much speculation. But life was tolerable now, and with regular money coming in they could at least pay the rent and eat, albeit simply.

★ ★ ★

One day in April, Kate was somewhat perplexed to be summoned to Mr Dexter's office. She was so worried about the possibility of being dismissed for some unknown reason, she didn't notice the strange looks that passed between some of her fellow workers.

'I understand you want to see me, sir,' she said, standing hesitantly just inside his office door, having been told to go in by the secretary.

'Yes, that's right.' His little piggy eyes rested on her unwaveringly, sending shivers of fear up her spine.

She waited to know the reason for this summons, glancing around the room to avoid his unnerving gaze and wishing that his wife was present. It was a dreary office that smelled of stale tobacco and sweat. His desk stood on a brown patterned carpet, along with a dark green filing cabinet and two brown leather chairs.

He stood up and walked slowly around his desk towards her, his stare never leaving her face so that she was forced to meet his eyes. Instinctively, she moved back.

Giving her a lazy smile, he said, 'Don't be afraid, my dear. I'm not going to hurt you.'

His menacing tone indicated otherwise and Kate was rooted to the spot as he walked purposefully to the door and turned the key in the lock.

# Chapter Three

Petrified, she watched her employer cross the room and sit back down at his desk.

'Come here, girl,' he commanded.

Her throat was so constricted it ached, and her heartbeat was alarmingly erratic. In desperation, she scanned the room for something with which to defend herself, seeing nothing more lethal than an umbrella in the coatstand.

'What do you want of me?' she asked in a dry, high-pitched voice.

He didn't reply, but leaned back in his chair and put his feet on the desk. 'You must have been with the firm for a couple of months now,' he said, looking at his shoes.

'About that, yes.'

'Long enough to have learned that it isn't your place to question the orders of those who pay your wages,' he snapped, raising his eyes to her sharply. 'Now come here, and quick about it.'

In the absence of any alternative, she did as he said, frantically scouring her mind for an escape plan.

'That's better,' he said as she stood obediently before him.

She waited in agonised silence for his next move, which proved to be astonishing. Taking a freshly laundered handkerchief from his pocket, he handed it to her and said, 'I'm very fussy about the shine on my shoes. The toil of the day has made them dusty and dull. Polish them for me.'

The relief was sweet, but she thought she must have misheard such an odd request. 'Did you say . . .?' she began.

'Just do it,' he interrupted, 'if you wish to continue working here.'

Demeaning the task was, but compared to her expectations it was the simplest job she had ever had to perform in her life. She was uneasy being in the room alone with him, though, and was glad when he seemed satisfied with her efforts and dismissed her.

After Kate had gone, Reggie Dexter smoked a cigar in a mood of quiet satisfaction. Watching that little madam squirm had been almost a physical pleasure to him. By the time he'd finished with her, all pretensions to breeding would be eradicated forever.

Having bettered himself through having an eye to the main chance, Reggie had turned his back on his humble East End roots. He was thirty years old, five years younger than his wife, Cissy, who provided him with a very comfortable life. His wife was a late-born only child who had completely dominated her elderly parents. Reggie had been eighteen when he had first met her. He'd come to work at this factory as a general labourer when it had been owned and run by her father. Cissy had fallen for Reggie in a big way and had made all the running in their relationship. Naturally, her parents had disapproved of the daughter of the firm walking out with a mere minion, but they hadn't been able to stop the headstrong Cissy.

When they had married, Reggie had been given a managerial position for the sake of appearances. And when Cissy had inherited the business after her parents' death, she had stepped into her father's shoes with her husband as a sort of sidekick. Her flair for commerce had soon become apparent. Changing the name of the company to Dexter's had been her idea not Reggie's, and she'd only done so to leave the workforce in no doubt that the firm would be run to Mrs Dexter's rules, not those of her more lenient predecessor.

Everyone at the factory had to toe the line set by the redoubtable Cissy, most of all her husband who was powerless against her assertive personality and the fact that she held the key to his creature comforts.

Being so dominated at home, Reggie found escape by intimidating young girls like Kate whose employment was at

46

his discretion. They were beholden to him, as he was to Cissy. Finding an unusual one like the Potter girl was even more interesting. He'd given her a couple of months to settle in and feel secure. Now it was time to shake her confidence, to remind her of his power and make her grateful for her job. The fact that he had to ensure that Cissy didn't find out what he was up to only added spice to the proceedings.

The newspapers were full of Dr Crippen's capture at sea, and the workroom at Dexter's was buzzing with it one warm summer afternoon at the end of July.

'I read in the paper that 'im and 'is mistress were posing as father and son on a boat to Canada,' said one of the hands. 'The captain of the ship got suspicious when he saw 'em 'olding 'ands. He sent a message to Britain by radio. A Scotland Yard detective caught a faster boat and overtook the one Crippen was on. They arrested 'im on board ship.'

'Gor blimey!' said someone. 'Innit amazin' what they can do these days?'

'They found 'is poor wife's body buried under the cellar floor of 'is house in Camden Town, by all accounts,' said another.

''anging's too good for the likes of 'im.'

'Not 'alf.'

The conversation ended abruptly as the supervisor appeared on the scene with instructions for Kate to leave what she was doing and go to Mr Dexter's office.

With no more than a flicker of irritation showing in her eyes, Kate left the hat-lining she was working on and made her way downstairs to the office, wondering what odd little task lay in store for her today. Over the last few months, she had grown accustomed to her employer's eccentric games which were obviously intended to remind her of her humble station in life. And since she always returned to the workroom intact, she was no longer afraid.

In fact, when Mrs Dexter was not present at the factory, Kate now expected to be summoned to his office, where she would be ordered to attend to some personal chore for him such as tidying his desk, brushing his suit with the clothes brush, or cleaning his shoes. He always behaved in a menacing manner, and made a performance of locking the door, indicating that some drama was about to take place.

Because there was something so odious about these games, she never breathed a word to anyone about them. When her workmates asked her about her regular visits to his office, she just mumbled something about being sent on an errand for him. And since the supervisor valued her employment, she never confronted him about giving staff orders above her head.

This afternoon, however, the pattern was altered. He didn't lock the door and was very businesslike in his manner, telling Kate briskly that he required her to stay late this evening to give the storeroom a good tidying. Since this might mean a little extra money which she badly needed, she wasn't altogether displeased.

Gertie had fallen into the habit of having tea with Bertha of an afternoon. Not that it was 'having tea' in the style to which she had been accustomed at Sycamore Square. It was more a matter of having a cuppa and a chinwag while Bertha worked at her hats and Georgie played on the floor. But Gertie enjoyed it, for Bertha seemed genuinely interested in her anecdotes of middle-class life. To be able to talk to someone about her prestigious past had become vital to Gertie to ensure it remained alive for her. The only way she could tolerate her present squalor was constantly to remind herself that it was only temporary. If she dwelled on the unlikelihood of the Potters ever regaining their former glory, she became deeply depressed so refused to allow such negative thoughts to linger.

Today, though, Gertie's other life was forgotten in favour of Dr Crippen's capture.

'It's more excitin' than somethin' yer see at the cinematograph, ain't it?' said Bertha.

'Everybody was full of it at the market this morning,' said Gertie, having already furnished Bertha with the gory details.

'I wish I'd done me own shopping now,' confessed Bertha. 'I've missed all the gossip.'

And that was another thing that was becoming a habit. If

Bertha was behind schedule with her hats, Gertie did her shopping for her. Although Gertie hated to admit it, she was growing fond of her neighbour and felt a sense of security in having her close at hand. 'Still, at least you're up to date with your work,' she said.

'Yeah, that's true, so I'll come shoppin' with yer in the morning.'

'Good,' said Gertie. 'We can have a wander round the Broadway too.'

Bertha nodded. She liked this fussy little woman, for all her airs and graces. She'd certainly been a help to Bertha since that meeting on the stairs, even if she was a bit snooty at times. It couldn't be easy for someone like her to adjust to poverty after the way she'd lived. And in all fairness, she is beginning to come down off her high horse, Bertha thought, casting a shrewd eye over her new friend as she played a game with shirt-buttons with Georgie on the floor. A few weeks ago, she could hardly bear to talk to him let alone play with him. Beneath that weak and feeble exterior there's a strength that's going to rise to the surface one of these days, if I'm any judge of character, Bertha decided.

Looking up to see her friend observing her, Gertie gave a hesitant grin and patted her fair hair into place as though she had been caught out in some misdeed instead of just letting herself go and enjoying herself in a rather undignified manner. She's a funny one and no mistake, thought Bertha.

When Kate went to Mr Dexter's office that evening to find out exactly what he wanted her to do in the storeroom, she realised immediately that it had been a pretext. And since she wasn't prepared to play his ridiculous games after hours, she decided to make a stand.

'I'm not going to stay late after all, sir,' she said, backing towards the door in the hope of reaching it before he could lock it.

'Oh, really? Well, I'll be the judge of that,' he said, leaping up and lunging towards her, pinning her to the wall by gripping her arms.

'You don't want me to work overtime at all,' she rasped furiously. 'You just want me to inflate your ego by cleaning your shoes or brushing your coat or something. Well, I've got better things to do, so you can find someone else.'

'So you don't value your job here then?'

'Of course I do,' she said, revolted by the stale smell of nicotine on his breath.

'Then don't defy me. It will do you no good anyway. I'll have my way whether you like it or not.'

Until that moment she had been mildly irritated rather than afraid. Now a shiver ran up her spine as two things registered with alarming clarity. The first was a noticeable difference in him. He was trembling slightly and his eyes were glazed. The second was the fact that they were here at the factory alone.

'All right,' she bluffed. 'Just let go of my arms and I'll do what you want. What is it this time, Mr Dexter? Shoe cleaning, desk tidying . . .?'

'No, something a little more interesting.'

Although weak with terror now, she managed to retain a reasonably calm exterior. 'Let's get on with it then, shall we, sir?' she said, playing for time and waiting for the moment when she could make her escape through the unlocked door.

'That's better. I'm glad you've decided to co-operate.'

As he released his grip, she made a dash for the door, managing to open it and dart out into the corridor, making a bee-line for the main doors, her heart pounding, an icy sweat beading her skin. Gasping with relief, she reached the main door and grabbed the handle. It wouldn't turn! Rattling it, she realised that it was secured by iron bolts at the top and bottom.

His laughter echoed through the empty building. 'Every door in the building is locked.'

Struck with panic, she pelted into the sale-room, the rows of hats on heads and stands looking like people in the dim light from the corridor. Feeling him close behind her, she dashed through a door at the end and across the passage into the packing room, struggling to lock the door behind her.

But as her trembling fingers fumbled with the key in the unlit room, the door burst open and he stood in the doorway, blocking her way, his triumphant smile visible in the light from outside. He turned a switch inside the room to reveal a murky interior with dismal green walls. On long tables stood a collection of cardboard boxes, balls of string, scissors, brown paper, tissue paper. On the floor there were piles of wooden crates. He stepped inside and locked the door behind him, trapping her completely.

'Please leave me alone, sir,' she begged, breathless with fear. 'I'll not say a word to anyone about this, I promise.'

'Who would take the word of a factory hand against that of her employer?' he said. 'When I've finished, you'll be too ashamed to say a word to anyone, I can promise you that.'

In a frenzied attempt at self-defence, she grabbed a wooden crate and aimed it at him. It clattered against the table and dropped uselessly to the floor. She followed this with a ball of string which was equally ineffective.

'You can fight all you like, it will make no difference,' he said as he walked towards her, discarding his jacket.


On warm summer evenings, Gertie and the girls often took a stroll along the riverside as a respite from the airless atmosphere of their room. The horrors of winter at Beaver Terrace, the temperamental fire, the iced windows and damp running down the walls, had been replaced by swarms of flies, even fouler smells, and food that turned rotten because there was nowhere cool or ventilated to keep it.

'You're very quiet, Kate,' remarked Gertie, later that same evening as the three of them ambled along the Mall.

'Am I?' she replied. 'I don't mean to be.'

'Didn't eat more than a bite of your tea either.'

'Sorry.'

'Aren't you feeling well?' Gertie had become aware of a new kind of tension in her life. A closer relationship with her daughters meant a keener sensitivity to their moods and feelings. Having perceived that her eldest daughter seemed troubled on her return from work, Gertie's concern was not entirely altruistic but tinged with the fear that some problem had arisen with which she herself would be unable to cope. A problem with the job, for instance, upon which she was dependent for her keep.

'I'm fine, really.'

'Anything wrong at work, dear?' Gertie probed.

Kate turned sharply to her mother. 'No, there's nothing wrong at work, or at home, or anywhere at all,' she snapped with uncharacteristic impatience. 'Now can you please let the subject drop?'

'Sorry I spoke, I'm sure,' Gertie said, noticeably peeved.

The waterfront had a gentle bustle about it as Londoners flocked here to escape from the hot, dusty streets. People strolled under the trees, chattering, looking at the water, feeding the swans and filling the riverside pubs. The late sunlight was deep gold, tinting the brown waters an olive-green shade in places. The river was crowded with a mixture of commercial and pleasure craft. Mingling with grimy tug-boats towing lighters behind them, and sailing barges carrying goods from the docks further downriver, was an assortment of rowing boats, little sailing boats and skiffs. Occasional houseboats sat on permanent moorings in quiet stretches under the trees, decks awash with pink geraniums and multi-coloured pansies in pots and troughs.

In one such shady spot where dog roses straggled over the grassy banks, and the splash of oars mingled with the rustle of leaves, Kate found herself with thoughts of her father who had sought peace within these muddy waters. For the first time, she felt a glimmer of understanding as to just how low he must have sunk to have taken such action.

Kate was feeling so wretched she almost felt driven to do the same thing herself. What had happened in the packing room this evening had changed her irrevocably. She didn't feel like the same clean-living girl who had walked along this riverside last evening. She felt filthy and degraded, the whole disgusting incident having stripped her of all self-respect.

She wanted to destroy all her clothes and immerse herself in water, try to wash away the hateful memory of Reggie Dexter against her, *inside her*. Oh, God, she felt so guilty, as though she was somehow to blame for what had happened. The thought of it made her skin burn with shame. She felt exposed, as though the whole revolting episode was blazoned upon her person for all to see. And to add to her misery was the dread of having to face that monster at the factory tomorrow.

There was no way she could avoid it because she needed the wages. She couldn't afford to lose one day's work which meant going into Dexter's every morning until she found another job. At all costs she *must* avoid letting Mother know there was anything wrong. Gertie wasn't built for problems. She would probably have a complete mental breakdown if she ever found out what had happened to her daughter today.

'I'm sorry I was a bit snappy just now, Mother,' Kate said, managing a smile as she took her arm. 'It's just the time of the month.' She linked her other arm through her sister's in a companionable gesture and forced herself to make this outing into the pleasant interlude it usually was. 'Look at the ducks preening their feathers on that driftwood. Aren't they just the sweetest things?'

Bertha was a great advocate of a 'bloomin' good night out' as a cure for all ills and problems. She recommended it to Gertie one day in September as the latter confessed to being worried about her daughter who had 'not been herself for weeks'.

'She probably just a bit rundown,' opined Bertha. 'A night at the music 'all is better than any tonic yer can get at the chemist shop.'

'Do you really think so?'

'I swear by it meself,' said Bertha, peering at Gertie over the brim she was sewing to a hat. 'They get some really good turns at the Shepherd's Bush Empire. Big names an' all, like George Robey, Vesta Tilley and Marie Lloyd. It won't cost too much if yer go in the cheap seats.'

'Hardly the sort of entertainment for a young lady like Kate,' objected Gertie.

Unoffended, Bertha stopped work with her needle and thread and thought about this for a moment. 'Oh, I dunno so much. A bit o' sauciness won't do 'er any 'arm. Anyway, the workroom at Dexter's ain't exactly a finishing school for young ladies. She'll 'ave learned a thing or two since she's bin there.'

'Even so . . .'

'Some of the comedians do get a bit naughty, I admit.' Bertha chuckled hoarsely. 'But you can always put yer 'ands over yer ears when they come on, can't yer, ducks?'

'Me!' exclaimed Gertie, as the practicalities of this scheme became evident. 'I can't possibly go with her. I wouldn't be seen dead in a music hall!'

'Yer don't know what yer missing, love,' sighed Bertha wistfully. 'I used to really enjoy a good show. Me and my Albert used to go every week when we were courtin'.' She stared mistily into space. 'Cor, the times we 'ad. A glass o' stout in the interval, jellied eels after the show. I never go anywhere like that now I've got the nippers to look after.'

Gertie chewed her lip anxiously. She didn't know if there was any truth in Bertha's theory, but she was willing to give it a try. Something was the matter with Kate, despite her pretence to the contrary. Gertie had felt the bed shake with her stifled sobs when she thought her mother and sister were asleep. Thank goodness it couldn't be the sort of trouble every mother dreaded. And it certainly couldn't be that because the girl didn't even know any young men, let alone keep company with them.

'Would you go with Kate if I pay for your ticket and look after the children while you're out?'

'Cor, not 'alf!' grinned Bertha.

Realising that she was being packed off to the Empire as some sort of cure for the blues, Kate went along with the idea to please her mother.

In fact, she did feel a certain sense of relaxation as she sank into the plush seat and waited for the curtain to go up, the warm anticipatory buzz in the auditorium lapping around her in a soothing tide. It was good to get out of that stuffy room for a while, away from her mother's constant observation as she wondered what was the matter.

Kate had tried to hide her turmoil, but it was almost impossible to keep anything secret from her room-mates, especially as Mother seemed to have developed some sort of extra-sensory perception regarding her daughters just lately. Lord knows what would happen when she found out what the trouble really was! Kate had thought things couldn't get worse after that revolting incident with Reggie Dexter. But she had been wrong because now they were a million times worse.

Bertha nudged her excitedly as the curtain rose and the show opened with a row of grinning chorus girls in ballet skirts who high kicked their way across the stage. They were followed by a juggler, a team of acrobats, a female singer and a comedian. Kate's arm was bruised by the excited pinching of her companion who kept up a steady stream of enthusiastic comments. 'Good, ain't she?' she'd chirp. 'Ooh, ain't that a pretty costume?' Or: 'You'll love this next act. I saw it once with my Albert . . .'

In the interval they joined the crowds at the bar where Bertha guzzled a glass of stout and Kate sipped ginger beer. The second half of the show began and Kate was carried along by the lively entertainment and the enthusiastic response from the audience. There was a contortionist, a woman delivering monologues, a handsome male singer who filled the auditorium with a moving rendition of 'Ah, Sweet Mystery of Life'. Beribboned, tricycle-riding poodles pranced and paraded to a great deal of oohing and aahing. And the show was brought to a magnificent close by a cockney singer called Mabel Miller who had Bertha sniffing into her handkerchief with her sentimental version of 'If Those Lips Could Only Speak'.

Outside, the evening was crisp and dry with a hint of autumnal mist. Street lights beamed brightly over the crowds who were piling on to trams and queueing at the bus-stop.

'Good show, wannit?' said Bertha.

'Lovely.'

The older woman linked a friendly arm through Kate's. 'Now, what do yer say we sit on the bench on the green and 'ave a chat until the crowds thin out a bit? We won't stay long enough to get cold.'

'Yes, all right,' said Kate dully, her worries returning after the brief diversion.

'And you can tell me what's the matter, if yer like,' Bertha continued as they wove their way across the road to the green, through a congestion of horse-drawn and motor traffic. 'A problem shared is a problem 'alved, so they say, and it might be easier to talk to me than it is to yer mum.'

The lamplight shining through the trees on Shepherd's Bush Green illuminated a blaze of autumnal colours, dazzling shades of yellow and red, gentle russet brown. It was curiously peaceful sitting on the bench under an oak tree in this haven at the heart of the busy town. All around them trams clanked and rattled, motor vehicles revved and roared, almost drowning the clip-clop of the horse-drawn hackney cabs that trotted by. A multitude of vehicle headlights flashed and winked with the movement.

Having intended to decline Bertha's invitation to confide, Kate found the whole story spilling out to this sympathetic woman. The relief of sharing the problem was enormous but it didn't make the situation any less grim.

'Are yer sure you're pregnant, love?' asked Bertha worriedly.

'Yes, quite sure. I've missed two periods and I've been feeling very queasy,' she explained. 'I didn't think it could be that at first. I didn't know it could happen the first time.'

'Oh, yeah, once is all it takes,' said Bertha, lapsing into a stream of invective that would have had Kate's mother reaching for the smelling salts. 'He's a bleedin' menace, that Reggie Dexter!' she continued, having let off the worst of her steam in stronger language. 'You ain't the first young girl 'e's tormented. He needs a good seein' to, the bastard!'

'He certainly does!'

'Is 'e still pesterin' yer?'

'No, that's all stopped – for the moment anyway. His wife has been at the factory more often lately so he hasn't really had the chance, thank goodness. He still gives me those looks of his though, when she's not with him, just to remind me of his power. I'm scared, Bertha, I dread going to work.'

'Course yer do, love. Who wouldn't under those circumstances?'

56

'I've been looking out for another job, but now I've got this other problem there doesn't seem to be any point . . .'

'No, there ain't.'

'I just don't know what to do, Bertha,' Kate said, wringing her hands. 'God knows what'll happen to Mother if I can't work to pay my share of the rent and food. Esme's money alone won't keep us. Once my condition becomes obvious to the Dexters, I'll be sacked with no chance of getting another job.'

'Yeah, yer will an' all,' agreed Bertha. 'And there ain't no point in askin' that bugger to pay for 'is pleasure, 'cos 'e'll deny all liability, the rotten swine!'

'We'll end up in the workhouse!'

'Don't panic,' said Bertha, 'we'll think of something.' They fell into a thoughtful silence, both searching for a solution to an insoluble problem.

'Why not go and see Cissy Dexter?' suggested Bertha at last. 'She's the actual boss of the firm, he's just 'er lap-dog. Tell 'er you're pregnant and ask if yer can work at home for them when yer starts to show and can't go into the factory. Appeal to 'er as another female. But for Gawd's sake don't tell 'er who made yer pregnant or you'll be in worse trouble.'

'You think it might work?'

'I think it's worth a try,' she said thoughtfully. 'A woman is bound to be more sympathetic to this sort o' problem than a man, it stands to reason. She's 'ard though, and won't do yer no favours. You'll earn every penny they pay yer, but they usually need people who are willin' to work for a pittance at 'ome. And if yer do the decent thing by confiding in 'er at an early stage, it might just do the trick.'

'And if it doesn't . . .'

'You'll be sacked on the spot.'

'And lose the money I could have earned while I was still able to hide the truth?'

'Mmm, that is a risk,' agreed Bertha. 'But I think it's a chance worth takin'. You'll feel better if yer know yer can at least earn something later on. It'll help when yer eventually break the news to yer mum.'

Kate clutched her head in anguish. 'Mother will probably go into a complete decline.'

'Don't yer be so sure about that,' said Bertha. 'I think there's more to that lady than meets the eye.'

'She's led such a sheltered life.'

'She's toughening up nicely though,' Bertha pointed out. 'There's nothing like 'ardship for puttin' starch in yer backbone.'

'I'm dreading telling her.'

'I'd do it for yer, love,' said Bertha, 'but there are some things in life we 'ave to do ourselves and that's one of 'em.'

'I know.'

'Anyway, what's 'appened ain't no fault of yers, love,' she pointed out. 'You just remember that.'

'It isn't easy.'

'You come and see me when yer need remindin',' said Bertha. 'But go and see Cissy tomorrow and get it over with.'

'Yes, I will.'

Bertha shivered. 'Time we was on our way. The bus queue ain't so long now.'

They walked over the green and crossed the road, Bertha chattering happily about getting some chips on the way home from the shop near Beaver Terrace.

But Kate was too full of dread of tomorrow to want anything to eat.

# Chapter Four

Cissy Dexter listened to Kate's confession dispassionately. The girl could never have guessed the turmoil those impassive eyes concealed as they observed her from the other side of the desk. Cissy was only too well aware of her husband's lecherous tendencies, and had known the minute she'd clapped eyes on the Potter girl that she would become a target for him. She was also certain that he was to blame for her plight, which was why she was so upset.

The fact that Cissy turned a blind eye to Reggie's transgressions didn't mean that she condoned his behaviour. In the early days of their marriage it had hurt her deeply. She'd begged, threatened and cajoled; he'd made promises that had been honoured only until another pretty young girl had appeared on the scene.

As Cissy had no intention of ending their marriage, she had trained herself to ignore his constant need to prove his masculinity. She simply waited for him to tire of his current fancy which he always did quite soon. Once he had made his point, he lost interest.

She was well aware of the fact that she was the dominant partner in their relationship, and that Reggie's diversions were simply his way of redressing the balance. God knows why she loved him. He was weak and self-seeking and had only married her for her money. But love him she did, with ferocious passion, and for that reason she intended to stay with him for all his faults. Theirs may not be a marriage made in heaven but it worked well enough, maybe because they were two of a kind, united in the view that altruism was mere stupidity.

Reggie didn't share her acute longing for a child, though, so didn't suffer as she did over the fact that she had not conceived after nearly twelve years of marriage. Now, confronted by this wretched girl who had the one thing that Cissy *really* wanted, she could have screamed with the unfairness of it. Especially as this pregnancy would do nothing for the girl but shame her and ruin her life.

'Anyway, madam,' Kate was saying in conclusion, 'my mother and sister are reliant on my wages, so I was wondering if you might let me stay on here until I start to show, then allow me to work for you at home? I've enough experience to do linings and basic trimming.'

Vicious jealousy scorched through Cissy. How she *hated* this creamy-skinned fifteen year old for her youth and pregnancy – a pregnancy that should have been hers!

Leaning back in her chair, the older woman's eyes brightened at the beginnings of an idea which she considered for a few moments before replying. 'That's out of the question, I'm afraid. It's against our policy to employ girls who find themselves in trouble,' she said smoothly. 'It's bad for the reputation of the company.'

Kate's ashen face flushed rebelliously. 'But it wasn't even my fault . . .'

'It never is, my dear,' Cissy interrupted sarcastically. 'But trying to shift the blame won't change anything. There's no place in society for an unmarried mother or an illegitimate child.'

'I know that, madam,' Kate said, regretting having taken Bertha's advice.

'However, if you are prepared to answer one question truthfully, I may be able to help you,' said Cissy surprisingly.

'Oh, well . . . fire away,' said Kate with renewed hope.

'Was it my husband who made you pregnant?'

Dumbstruck, Kate stared at her in silence, a scarlet flush creeping up her throat and suffusing her face.

'Answer me, for goodness' sake!'

Assuming that any offer of assistance would be lost if she answered in the affirmative, Kate said evasively, 'Whatever makes you think that?'

'I know my husband,' Cissy said sharply. 'I've seen the way he looks at you.'

'Oh . . .'

'I know it was him,' she snapped, 'but I want to hear you say it.'

Since there was no longer any point in denying it, Kate braced herself for the ensuing explosion as she said, 'Yes, it was him.'

Her nerves were jangling as she waited to be banished from Dexter's forever. But it didn't happen that way. Instead her employer said in an even tone, 'There is a way Mr Dexter and I can get you out of trouble.'

'Is there?'

'Yes. We will support you financially throughout your pregnancy and look after you during the confinement and lying-in period,' Cissy explained. 'We will also guarantee you a job in another millinery firm afterwards. We have plenty of contacts in the trade.'

'And what would I have to do in return?'

'Hand the child over to us immediately after the birth, for us to bring up as our own.'

This was the last thing Kate had expected and she was shocked and confused. She couldn't bring herself to think of the seed inside her as the beginnings of a child, merely the frightening result of an act of brutality. But this suggestion did seem drastic for all that. 'I'm not sure I would want to do that . . .'

'You're hardly in a position to choose, are you?' snapped Cissy. 'After all, you've nothing to offer a child. As you have just been telling me, you are struggling to help support your mother, and you probably live in some ghastly tenement. If you keep the baby it will grow up in poverty as a bastard, shunned by society, and you'll carry the stigma for the rest of your life. If you accept my offer, the child will have a good home with no expense spared to give him or her the best possible start in life. It will have the best of everything money can buy, and you can make a fresh start, with your reputation intact.'

'I'm still not sure . . .'

'With immediate effect,' Cissy continued stridently, as though Kate hadn't spoken, 'you can stay at home and take things easy, secure in the knowledge that we will pay your wages. I'll make arrangements for you to go away somewhere before you start to show until after the birth, so no one except your immediate family need ever know that you had a child. You will return home afterwards and pick up your life as though nothing has happened.'

'Yes, but . . .'

'Obviously, we wouldn't want you working for us,' she went on, ignoring Kate's attempts to interrupt. 'In fact, all contact with us must cease, in everyone's best interests, especially the child's. We would insist that you agree never to try to contact the child at any time in the future. We will arrange to have a midwife attend at the birth who will be given an incentive to co-operate when we register the child as our own.'

Kate's head was spinning. Everything the woman said made sense, but still something held her back. She knew from factory gossip that the Dexters were childless after several years of marriage. Mrs Dexter must want a baby desperately to come up with a scheme like this, which meant she would be a good mother, even if she did seem heartless to those who worked for her. But what about that husband of hers? 'Will Mr Dexter want the child?'

'Mr Dexter will do what I say! And since raising a child is a woman's business, it won't make any difference to him.'

'I see.'

'Well, what do you think?'

'What happens if I don't agree?'

'You will be immediately dismissed and I shall make it my business to mention your condition to all my contacts, so you won't find work anywhere in the London millinery trade.'

Whilst appalled at the idea of blackmail, Kate knew she was powerless to resist. She imagined her mother's anguish at being forced into the workhouse with a daughter who had disgraced her; she thought of her child being raised in misery and deprivation. With the Dexters it would have fine clothes, creature comforts, respect, a promising future to look forward to in the family business. She really had no choice.

'All right,' she said. 'I'll go along with what you have to offer.'

'Good girl.' Cissy was all smiles now that victory was hers. Maybe the child wasn't her own, but as her husband's it would be the next best thing. 'Now you can collect your things and go home.'

'But I don't want to give up work yet.'

'Maybe not, but you've someone else to consider now,' Cissy said excitedly. 'We don't want anything to go wrong with the baby, now do we? You must take extra care of yourself to make sure you give birth to a healthy child.'

'Surely I can carry on working for a while yet,' Kate insisted. 'I shall get very bored sitting around doing nothing.'

'You will *not* be working here again,' said Cissy forcefully, 'So please do as I say and collect your things and go home. Call at the office on your way out and I'll have some money ready for you. Regular payments will be sent to you throughout your pregnancy, so you have nothing to worry about. And you will be informed of arrangements for later on in due course.'

Breaking the news to her mother proved to be every bit as awful as Kate had feared. Bertha's theory about Gertie having hidden depths seemed totally inaccurate. She simply collapsed into tears and took to her bed, refusing to listen to the details of how her daughter's condition had come to be.

'And so now the final humiliation,' she sobbed. 'Is it not enough that my husband disgraced me and brought me to shame and poverty? Now my daughter has to make things even worse.'

'But Mother . . .'

'I thought I'd sunk as low as any woman of my calibre could,' she ranted. 'But now my daughter has made it impossible for me to hold my head up in the street, even a place like Beaver Terrace!'

No amount of persuasion had any effect. She refused to leave her bed except to go downstairs to the WC. Even regular deliveries of such nourishing treats as calves' foot jelly and top quality meat and vegetables, intended for the mother-to-be but enough for three and paid for by the Dexters, failed to appease her.

On hearing about this childish behaviour, Bertha decided to pay her friend a visit when the girls were not at home.

'Well, you're a bloomin' sight and no mistake!' she said, running a disapproving eye over Gertie's unwashed face and tousled hair. 'Yer ought to be ashamed of yerself.'

'Oh, and why is that?' asked Gertie, feigning innocence and peering guardedly at her friend over the bedcovers.

'As if you didn't know,' reproached Bertha. 'I thought you had the guts to come up trumps in all this, and said as much to Kate.' She paused at Gertie's aggrieved look. 'There's no call to look at me like that. I know all about Kate's trouble.'

'How dare she tell anyone outside the family?'

'Thank Gawd I'm there for her, the poor gel,' said Bertha. 'She needs someone to turn to, and you ain't no use to anyone!'

'Thanks very much,' snapped Gertie haughtily. 'And what gives you the right to interfere in our family business?'

'Someone's gotta intervene on behalf of those gels of yours, poor dears,' Bertha said. 'Call yourself a mother? Why, my little Ruby's more grown-up than you. Layin' about in bed when yer should be makin' this place into an 'ome for yer gels. Thinkin' only about yerself and 'ow yer daughter 'as shamed yer. Always jabberin' on about the posh 'ouse yer used to live in, and trying to carry on 'ere in Beaver Terrace like yer did there. Well, I'll tell you this much, Missus High and Mighty Potter, yer can't! And the sooner yer face up to real life, the better.'

'Well, really, I've never been so insulted . . .'

'When yer don't have money, yer ain't protected from the outside world like you used to be in that posh square o' yours,' Bertha continued, determined to activate the better side of Gertie's nature. 'Bad things sometimes 'appen to people like us through no fault of our own. Kate's trouble ain't 'er fault. She was raped.'

She paused as Gertie winced. 'There's no need for you to make faces, mate. It didn't 'appen to you. That gel o' yours is going through 'ell. She needs her mum right now, so pull yerself together and give her some moral support through this next few months.'

'It's the shame I can't take,' said Gertie, her affront turning to feebleness.

'Shame? What shame?' exploded Bertha. 'No one outside these four walls will ever know about Kate's baby, the Dexters are seein' to that.'

'People might suspect.'

'So let 'em, they can't prove nothin'. What sort of an example are you to the young 'uns, givin' up at the first bit o' trouble?'

'My life has been nothing but trouble since my Cyril died,' wailed Gertie.

'Well, yer lucky then, ain't yer, to 'ave 'ad it easy for so long?' raged Bertha. 'Some of us 'ave never known anything but 'ard times.'

'Can I help it if the shock of hearing about Kate's condition has made me feel ill?' Gertie said defensively.

'*You* feel ill?' Bertha roared. 'How do yer think young Kate feels after what she's bin through – suffering abuse from that monster, then finding herself pregnant and 'aving to carry the child, knowing she's got to give it away? Think about it, woman, do.'

'I don't have to listen to this,' objected Gertie hotly, struggling against a surge of compunction. 'Get out! Go on, you nosy parker, get out.'

Bertha turned and left without another word. But outside the door, she grinned. Gertie would be out of that bed within five minutes, or her name wasn't Bertha Brent.

Later that day when Kate returned with the shopping, a fire glowed in the hearth, taking the sting out of the autumn chill. The room was tidy and her mother was up and dressed and sitting by the fire, toasting some bread.

'Here, let me take those bags,' she offered, rising and

smiling rather sheepishly at her daughter. 'You shouldn't be carrying anything heavy.'

Kate put the shopping bags down and hugged her mother without saying a word. The least said about the last few days, the better, she thought.


Propped up in bed with her baby son in her arms, Kate gazed through the window at the sea, tinted a greenish-blue in the uncertain April sunshine. The Bognor seafront was almost deserted on this out-of-season afternoon, for the weather was cold and showery, the pavements still wet and puddled from a recent downpour.

Still only a little over twenty-four hours old, the baby stirred against her, making little snuffling noises. She held him close, gazing into the tiny sleeping face, pink and mottled against the white shawl, a fine layer of black down covering his head. Kate thought she had never seen anything so beautiful or felt such love. It hurt in its intensity.

This boarding house in which she had been staying for the last few months was owned by a discreet friend of the Dexters called Mrs Ludlow. Acting upon Cissy Dexter's instructions, she had spared no effort to make Kate comfortable. To give Cissy Dexter her due, she had gone out of her way to make sure the girl had wanted for nothing during her pregnancy. Admittedly it was all being done for the sake of the baby, but it was still pleasant to have had a spell of good living.

Kate's heart lurched with the realisation that her baby would soon be taken from her. She'd seen Cissy Dexter arrive in a cab a few minutes ago with a nursemaid in a grey uniform, having presumably been notified of the birth by telegram. Right up until the baby had actually entered the world, Kate had not realised just how hard it would be to let him go. Now she just didn't know how to bear it. But the Dexters wouldn't allow her to change her mind. And even if they did, what sort of a life would he have in that cramped room in Beaver Terrace where the damp and cold would give him a bad chest, if not pneumonia?

The nursemaid entered the room and marched to Kate's bed, followed by Cissy.

'Take the baby please, nurse,' she commanded briskly.

'No, no! Not yet, please,' cried Kate, desperate to keep him, and clutching him to her protectively.

'Allow the nurse to take the child,' ordered Cissy sharply, the concern she had shown for Kate during the pregnancy now non-existent.

Kate held him tighter, frantically searching for a way to escape from these people. But, weak from the birth and outnumbered, she was no match for them. In a swift, efficient movement the child was prised from her by the nurse and taken from the room.

'Please bring him back! Bring him back, he's mine . . .' cried Kate, getting out of bed and swaying with faintness as her feet touched the floor.

'Stop that stupid nonsense at once and get back into bed,' rasped Cissy.

'I've changed my mind! I just can't let him go,' came an anguished cry.

'For goodness' sake, pull yourself together,' demanded Cissy. 'You made an arrangement with us, so please honour it without a fuss. You will stay here for your lying-in period and be looked after by Mrs Ludlow. Two weeks from today our obligation to you will be at an end and you must leave here.' She put a piece of paper on the bedside table. 'When you get back to London, go to this address where there will be a job for you. We will then have fulfilled our part of the deal in total. And neither Reggie nor I want to see you ever again. And you are not to try to see the child. Is that clear?'

'Yes, quite clear.' The pain was excruciating. Nothing had hurt her like this before. And she knew nothing would again.

Without another word Cissy marched to the door, closing it quietly behind her.

Alone, Kate stared out of the window at the seashore. As though in tune with her mood, clouds had gathered, darkening the landscape and threatening another shower. The sea looked black against the angry sky.

'I didn't even have the chance to kiss him goodbye,' she wept, covering her face with the sheet as the tears fell in a torrent.

On her return to London, Kate picked up her life as before, applying herself diligently to her new job. The events of the previous few months were never mentioned. She behaved as though she had not had a child. Her mother and sister could never have guessed that she carried him everywhere with her in her heart, and not a day passed when she didn't miss him and agonise over having let him go.

Bertha knew that she was fretting, though. Oh, yes, very little escaped the shrewd eye of that lady who had become mentor and friend to each member of the Potter family.

'The boy is better off where 'e is,' she said one evening when Kate called in to return a cup of sugar they had borrowed. 'It ain't no good tormentin' yerself about 'im.'

'I can't stop thinking about him,' Kate said. 'I didn't realise that I would have such strong feelings for him when I agreed to let the Dexters have him. I think what I did was terrible. I'm his mother. I should be looking after him. I want to so much.'

'I can understand 'ow yer must be feelin', ducks,' Bertha said gently. 'But it's 'ow things are gonna be for 'im later on that matters. Just think 'ow much misery you've saved 'im by letting 'im go. People can be very cruel, and he'd 'ave been hurt every day of his life, growing up as a bastard. This way he'll 'ave a position in life, a good future.'

'Yes, I know all that, but still . . .'

'You'll 'ave the chance of marriage now too,' Bertha continued. 'And you'll have nippers later on – more than yer bargain for probably, like so many of the women round 'ere.'

'I don't think I could ever feel so strongly for another child.'

'You will when they come along,' Bertha assured her. 'There's always enough love to go round in the heart of a mother for her young, nature sees to that.'

'It isn't easy for me to believe that right now.'

'Course it ain't,' said Bertha. 'You're only sixteen. There's plenty of time to worry about 'aving kids, though. Life's 'ard enough. Don't make it worse for yourself by worryin' about something that can't be altered. Loving someone is all about doing what's best for 'em. You've done that, so stop punishin' yerself.'

'I'll try to,' promised Kate, but knew in her heart that she never would.

Situated in Fulham, Maple's Hats was a smaller firm than Dexter's, with a friendlier atmosphere altogether. Having already gained some experience in the simpler aspects of hatmaking, and relieved of the constant threat of Reggie's evil ways, Kate settled down quicker than she had at Dexter's. The boss, Mr Maple, was as hard a taskmaster as any other employer, but he had a much pleasanter manner than either of the Dexters. He was white-haired and avuncular, respected and liked by his workers.

The only real drawback to the job was the pay, which was even lower than at Dexter's and left a shortfall in the Potters' budget even though Kate worked overtime whenever she could. After weeks of robbing the milkman's money to pay the baker, and using the rent to subsidise food bills, thus falling short and having to borrow the difference from Bertha, it was obvious that something must be done.

Since there was no payrise in the offing for either of the girls, there seemed to be only one solution to the problem. But in this remedy Kate saw the answer to something else that had been worrying her, for she had thought for some time that an additional occupation for her mother would increase her self-reliance.

'I hope you won't be upset by what I have to say, Mother,' she said, 'but if we are to keep a roof over our heads, you're going to have to do some sort of paid work.'

'Me, work?' said Gertie, appalled.

'I'm afraid so. Just something part-time to see us through until I gain experience and can earn more.'

Gertie was not so much lazy as lacking in confidence. No sooner had she begun to get the hang of her new impoverished lifestyle than further effort was being demanded of her.

Unfortunately, she knew Kate was right. In fact, her conscience had been troubling her for ages about the amount of time she had on her hands, given the limitations of domestic work when you lived in one room. But she had kept her feelings to herself because it was simply too degrading for her to have to go out to work. Why, Cyril would turn in his grave!

'But what work is there available for a widow woman of my age?' she asked in her most pathetic voice.

'You're only in your thirties, dear,' Kate pointed out optimistically.

'Still quite young,' agreed Esme, glimpsing the possibility of retaining more from her own pay-packet with another wage-earner in the family.

'Yes, but finding something suitable won't be easy,' said Gertie miserably. 'I'm not a strong woman.'

'Perhaps one of the local shops might need someone?' said Kate undeterred. 'You sometimes see older women working behind the counter in grocery stores.'

'I doubt if they take part-timers,' said poor Gertie, appalled at the idea of being 'on show' on the servile side of a shop counter.

Kate didn't mention charring, which was the most likely possibility, because she thought that would be *too* much of a blow to her mother's pride. Realising that it was the thought of being *seen* going out to work rather than the actual work itself that was upsetting her mother, she said, 'Would you find it easier to do a job at home?'

Gertie brightened considerably at this. 'Yes, I think I would.'

Personally, Kate thought it would be more beneficial for her mother to be out among people, once she got used to it, but she didn't have the heart to press the point. Later on perhaps her mother might feel more able to mix.

'Maple's use a lot of outworkers,' said Kate. 'I could ask Mr Maple if he needs any extra hands. The fact that you have no experience will go against you, but if I tell him I'm prepared to show you the ropes and keep an eye on you until you get used to the work, he might be able to use you.'

'It would be good if you could persuade him.'

'The work will be tedious for someone without any training,' Kate pointed out. 'You'll probably just be sewing labels into hats for a very low rate of pay.'

'I'd rather do that than stand behind a counter cutting up cheese and weighing out biscuits all day!'

Because the pay for homeworkers was poor, factory owners could often find work for willing hands, especially if there was someone to guide them. And so it was that Gertie went into the millinery trade, albeit in a minor way. The little extra money this produced was just enough to put the Potters back on course, and gave Gertie a more fulfilling day. So much so that when Esme was given a payrise, Gertie had got so used to having her own work there was no question of her giving it up.

The more Kate learned about millinery, the keener she became. By the time she had been at Maple's a year she had progressed from making and sewing in linings to a variety of other jobs, including cutting out silk scarves, hemming them, pressing them with a flat iron, and using them to trim hats. Among other things, she also sewed badges on to school hats and worked on children's summer sun bonnets. A great deal of the work was boring and repetitive, but became less so as she progressed. She kept a sharp eye on the more experienced hands, never missing a chance to learn something new.

Using her practical skills and growing fashion sense, she practised at home, re-modelling her own hats and those of her mother and Esme. A twist here, a snip there, and some new trimmings could make the shabbiest old hat elegant enough for another spell of Sunday best.

Esme continued to enjoy her work in the West End. The delicate, highly strung girl from Sycamore Square had become a fun-loving young woman attracted to the bright lights. She kept her mother and sister entertained with amusing accounts of her encounters with the rich and famous who shopped at the store. One day she gave her mother severe palpitations with a lurid tale of an attack on the store windows by the suffragettes during a window-smashing rampage through the West End of London.

71

'It was ever so exciting,' she told them exuberantly. 'They had hammers and stones hidden in their muffs. And I'm lucky working on the ground floor because there was such a commotion, me and one of the other girls had a chance to dash outside into the street to have a look!'

'Oh, Esme, you didn't?' reproached her mother. 'That sort of behaviour could end in dismissal.'

'Don't worry, nobody noticed,' Esme assured her brightly. 'They were all too busy taking a peek themselves.'

'Really, Esme, you are the limit,' said her mother.

'There were lots of policemen around,' she continued, 'and some of the women were arrested. Someone said Emmeline Pankhurst was taken in at some point during proceedings. Imagine that! And I was right there in the thick of it.'

'Disgraceful goings on, on the part of those awful women,' said Gertie.

'I must admit to admiring their guts,' said Kate. 'It's us they're fighting for, after all.'

'They ought to be ashamed. Damaging other people's property.'

'That isn't right, I admit,' said Kate. 'But they've been driven to it. The government not only refuses their demands but claims they don't express themselves forcibly enough!'

'Personally, I'd rather leave politics to the men,' said Gertie.

'Not all women are content to do that these days,' Kate pointed out. 'That's obvious from the thousands who support the movement.'

'To me it was just a bit of a lark,' said Esme, who had not the slightest interest in the serious side of life.

'I bet your employers didn't think so,' said Gertie. 'You just keep well away from anything like that in future, my girl.'

'Yes, Mother,' she replied, without any intention of heeding her warning.

Now that Gertie was contributing to the domestic budget, life became easier for the Potters and they were able to have an occasional treat: a visit to the cinematograph or even a day at the seaside on an excursion train. They learned to love such plebeian delights as fish suppers, jellied eels and plates of cockles, as sold on the seafront at Southend.

Despite Gertie's very best endeavours to keep their life in Kensington alive and at the forefront of their minds, inevitably it slipped into the past against the all-consuming reality of everyday living in Beaver Terrace.

Because the workforce in the hat-making trade tended to be dominated by the female of the species, eligible young men were something of a novelty in millinery workrooms. So, when the elderly odd-job man at Maple's was replaced by a well set up twenty year old called Claude Brooks in the summer of 1913, hearts were set fluttering.

Claude was broad-shouldered and fair-haired, with clean-cut features and smiling blue eyes. Warm-hearted and cheerful, he made it clear to the workroom staff that he was their man against the management and was only too happy to collect items from the baker's or grocer's for them whenever he was sent out to collect materials or deliver hats.

Since the supervisor also benefited from this arrangement, she ignored the fact that it was contrary to usual practice and put her order in with the rest. Everyone knew when Claude was around because of his singing and whistling of popular songs, a particular favourite being 'Waiting for the Robert E Lee'. To the older women he represented a son they could be proud of; to the younger ones he was the sort of boyfriend a girl could show off to her friends.

'Watcha, gels,' he'd say as he breezed into the workroom to fix a machine or change a light bulb. 'I reckon my luck was in when I got this job, 'cos I get to 'ave a chat with you bunch o' beauties every day. Better than workin' in an engineerin' factory any day o' the week!'

At eighteen Kate wasn't immune to his charms, especially as they seemed to be aimed in her direction most of the time.

'What lovely dark eyes you've got,' he'd say laughingly as he passed her place at the table.

'All the better to see you with,' she would retort sportingly.

Her workmates would tease her and say he was sweet on her, and she would blush and say it wasn't like that at all.

73

But it *was* like that for him apparently, and one hot August evening he was waiting for her at the factory gates after work.

''ello, princess,' he said cheekily. 'Can I walk yer 'ome?'

'I don't see why not.'

As they strolled through the dusty cobbled streets in the humid air, he told her that he was the son of a railway worker but both his parents were dead and he lived with his grandmother in rooms in Fulham. Kate didn't supply her personal details and when they got to Beaver Terrace and she stopped outside Number Three, he said, 'Blimey!' I didn't think a gel like you would live round 'ere, what with yer posh accent and everything.'

'And everything?'she said quizzically.

He gave a casual shrug. 'Ain't it obvious? You're different to the rest o' the gels at Maple's. You've got class, ain't yer? It stands out a mile.'

'Oh dear!'

'What's the matter?'

'Being different isn't the most comfortable feeling,' she explained, 'but it isn't easy to shake off fifteen years of easy living in just three.'

'Don't worry about it, you're nice just the way yer are.'

'Thank you.'

'Only sayin' what's true,' he said earnestly. 'What brought you to these parts, anyway?'

'It's a long story.'

'You can tell me all about it when we know each other better.'

'You're sure of yourself!'

'Mm, I know,' he agreed cheerfully. 'I always was, even as a nipper. No point in being otherwise, me gran says.'

'You've made quite a hit with the girls at the factory.'

'I ain't got much competition, have I, since I'm the only bloke around under fifty?'

'The attention hasn't turned your head, then?'

'Nah, course not. I ain't the type.'

'I believe you,' she said lightly.

'Anyway, do yer fancy coming out with me tonight?'

Having grown up in an environment where you only went out with men to whom you had been formally introduced, she was doubtful. 'Where to exactly?'

'Wherever yer fancy.'

'I don't know what sort of thing you have in mind,' she admitted. 'I usually only go out with my mother and sister.'

'High time you spread yer wings then, innit?'

'I suppose it is . . .'

'We could go to a show, if you like, or the pictures, or just for a walk by the river.' He smiled into her eyes. 'Well, what do yer say?'

'All right, I'll come.'

'I'll call for you at half-past seven.'

'Fine,' she said. But she knew it would be anything but fine when she told her mother she was going out with a young man she didn't even know, and an unskilled labourer at that!

# Chapter Five

'Just because we happen to find ourselves in reduced circumstances, doesn't mean we should do away with standards altogether,' pronounced Gertie on being told of Kate's plans for the evening. 'It just isn't the done thing for a young lady to walk out with someone who has not been approved by the family.'

'It is among the girls I work with, Mother,' Kate informed her. 'They go out with boys they meet on the street . . . in the park . . . anywhere.'

'Well, of course, that sort of behaviour is only to be expected from that class of person,' said Gertie pompously. 'But there's no reason for you to do the same.'

'I *am* that class of person now,' her daughter sensibly pointed out.

'Don't be ridiculous,' exclaimed Gertie. 'You went to one of the best schools in London. You've mixed with top drawer people.'

'But I don't any more,' Kate reminded her forcefully. 'Nowadays my friends are ordinary girls from poor homes.'

'And you've allowed them to drag you down to their level,' accused Gertie.

Kate sighed in exasperation. Working at home, as Mother did, she could still pretend that lower-class customs did not apply to the Potters. Her contact with the outside world was limited to shopping at the market and trips to the factory to collect and deliver work. Stubbornly clinging to an outmoded attitude, she had studiously remained aloof from their local community, apart from Bertha. Naturally, being older and more set in her ways, it was harder for her to adjust than her young daughters, Kate realised that. But after more than three years, it really was time she faced up to the situation. 'How can they drag me down to their level when I'm already there?' she challenged.

'What a wicked thing to say,' objected Gertie, aghast.

'It isn't wicked, it's simply the truth.' Kate cast her eyes around the room that could pretend to nothing but poverty for all its cleanliness. Shabby furniture; worn lino; a chipped washstand; clothes hanging over the backs of chairs; piles of unfinished hats. All this and much more crammed into one room hardly conjured up images of affluence. 'Look around and what do you see? A clean but poor home. You must do the same as Esme and me, and accept the fact that middle-class ways no longer apply to us. I'm sure you'll be happier if you do.'

'Never!'

'You would be if only you'd give yourself a chance,' insisted Kate. 'I don't mind living in Beaver Terrace now that I'm used to it. I like the people round here. They're not lesser human beings just because they don't have money or breeding, you know.'

'They're not our peers, though, are they?' said her mother. 'I mean, we won't live here forever.'

'Maybe not,' agreed Kate. 'As I gain experience, my pay will go up. And Esme will earn more as she gets older. Quite soon we might even be able to afford a two-roomed flat or something. But it will still be a far cry from our home in Sycamore Square.'

'What about all that talk of yours about getting us back to the square? Just fine words, I suppose?' said Gertie mournfully.

'No, I still intend to do it, somehow,' said Kate, 'but it could be a very long time into the future.' She waved her hand. 'In the meantime, this is where we live and there's no point in thinking ourselves different from our neighbours, because we're not.'

'I'll always think of myself as different,' Gertie stated with infuriating recalcitrance.

* * *

Claude arrived on time looking spruce, his grubby working overalls replaced by a navy blue suit, white starched collar, and a checked cap worn at a jaunty angle. His manners couldn't be faulted, even if his demeanour was a little less formal than Kate's mother was used to. Fortunately, he said exactly the right thing to Gertie.

'I knew your Kate was a girl with class, the minute I clapped eyes on 'er,' he said breezily. 'And now I've met her mother, I know why.'

'Oh, really?' said Gertie, smiling and patting her hair, her disapproval tempered by this unexpected acknowledgement of the Potters' superior class. 'It still shows then?'

'Not 'alf,' he assured her airily, moving a pile of clothes and a copy of *Woman's Weekly* from a chair and sitting down. 'It stands out a mile.'

'Does it?' said Gertie, flushing with pleasure.

'Course it does. A cut above the other gels, yet not a bit of swank with 'er, that's Kate.' He winked across at Esme who was sitting on the edge of the bed. 'Just like 'er little sister, eh, ducks?'

'I'm very glad to hear it,' said Gertie before Esme could reply. 'One mustn't let standards slip. I was only saying so to Kate earlier, wasn't I, dear?'

Kate gave a dutiful nod. The sisters exchanged sympathetic glances. As much as they loved their mother, she could singe the roots of their hair with embarrassment at times.

'I couldn't agree more, Duchess,' said Claude in the companionable manner of an old friend. 'Me gran's a stickler for standards. She still clips me round the ear 'ole if she spots a tide mark on me neck. And me turned twenty an' all!'

'Really?' said Gertie, somewhat deflated by his lesser idea of standards.

'Oh, yeah,' he said chattily. 'She brought me up, yer know. Mum died of TB when I was a baby and me dad buggered off.'

'I see.'

Esme stifled a giggle at her mother's poker face as she

79

struggled not to show her disapproval at his coarse language and unimpressive pedigree.

'I could murder a cuppa tea, if yer makin' one, Duchess,' he said cheerfully. 'Me mouth feels like Southend sands on an 'ot day.'

'Isn't it time we were off?' interjected Kate, unnerved by his casual approach to the redoubtable Gertie, and deeming it to be only a matter of time before she exploded.

'Not yet, sweet'eart,' he said, winking at Kate. 'We can spare a few minutes while I get acquainted with yer ma, so she'll know 'er daughter will be in good 'ands. I thought you toffs liked all that sort of thing.'

There was an awkward silence during which Kate waited for her mother to take umbrage. But, astonishingly enough, she smiled and said, 'Very thoughtful of you, young man. I'll put the kettle on.'

Deciding to adopt Claude's outspoken attitude, Kate said, 'Just to set the record straight, we're not toffs, as you put it, not now.'

'You are to me,' he told her, with a heart-stopping smile. 'You may not live in style but your polish is still there. Ain't that right, Duchess?'

'Quite right, Claude,' Gertie said with a beaming smile. He might be at the bottom of the pile, socially, but at least he had the intelligence to recognise breeding when he saw it.

By the time Kate and Claude actually left Beaver Terrace, they had missed the second house at the Empire and it was too late to go to the pictures, so they just walked by the river, talking and getting to know each other.

'You're looking very smart this evenin',' he said, glancing at the white cotton blouse she wore with an ankle-length navy blue skirt, her dark hair swept back beneath a straw hat trimmed with blue ribbon.

'Thank you,' she said graciously. 'I can't afford many clothes but at least it's a change from my working pinafore.'

Although it was only late August, the scent of incipient autumn spiced the air as dusk fell. In places, the sweetness was tinged with the sour smell of hops from the breweries and the pungent whiff from the mud banks, exposed when the river was at low tide. Unloading was in progress at some of the wharves, and the riverside mall was bustling with people out for an evening stroll.

The Creek was crowded with sailing barges as they crossed by the wooden footbridge and looked for somewhere to pause awhile. Pub landlords were doing a roaring trade but Claude managed to find an empty table on the vine-covered terrace of The Doves where Kate sipped a lemonade shandy while he enjoyed a glass of beer. Waterside gas-lamps gleamed through the trees, swarming with midges like clouds of dust and moths which fluttered helplessly against the glass.

Kate felt relaxed in Claude's company, though the atmosphere between them was oddly charged. She gave him a brief account of the events that had brought the Potters to Beaver Terrace.

'Must be 'ard coming down in the world like that,' he remarked chattily. 'When you've been used to the best of everythin'.'

'Yes, it was very daunting because we'd been so pampered,' she explained. 'We've toughened up a lot, though I think Mother still feels bad about it.'

'That's understandable. It can't be easy for a mature lady like her to 'ave to rough it,' he said companionably. 'Different for the likes of me and me gran. What you've never 'ad, yer don't miss.'

'Mother will survive.'

'I'm sure she will.'

'And we should be able to afford better accommodation before too long,' she told him. 'I can earn more as I gain experience.'

'You planning on staying at Maple's?'

'For the moment, yes,' she said. 'They're a good firm, they've trained me well.'

'They've 'ad more than their moneysworth out of you, though, I bet,' he said. 'Like most employers in the clothin' trade.'

'Maple's isn't so bad,' she said. 'Some millinery workrooms are real sweatshops from what I've heard, despite the Trades Board Act.'

'I know, I've done odd jobbin' in some of 'em.'

'For all the efforts of campaigners like Clementina Black, there still seems to be a lot of sweated labour in the clothing trade,' Kate went on. 'You hear stories of shocking conditions from new girls who come to work at Maple's. Makes you realise how well off you are.'

'If you do decide to make a move, why not try one of the big stores?' he suggested. 'Most of 'em have millinery workrooms. Liberty's are good to their workers, so I've heard.'

'I'll bear that in mind if I do decide to look for another job.'

'I shouldn't be encouragin' yer, should I?' he said lightly. ''Cos I'd miss yer if yer left.'

'Would you really?'

Grinning, he reached over and took her hand in a firm cool grip. 'I would an' all.'

'That's nice.'

'Well, don't look so surprised,' he said, smiling into her eyes. 'I ain't exactly made a secret of the fact that I'm sweet on yer, have I?'

'No,' she said, blushing, 'I don't know why I was surprised.'

That wasn't true though. The scars of the rape, three years ago, still had not healed and the natural development of her feelings towards the opposite sex had been impaired by a deep-rooted sense of guilt. Sometimes she woke up in the middle of the night, sweating, the whole repulsive incident returning with terrible vividness. Her shame was still a physical pain which deterred her from regaining her self-confidence, even though her earlier training in good deportment had made a positive outward manner second nature to her. The cruel violation of everything she had had drummed into her about chastity had left her so full of self-hatred, she tended to forget that other people were not aware of her past.

Thoughts of the child she had given away still filled her with remorse too. So Claude's interest in her boosted her ego and filled a need, for she was at an age when she was ready to fall in love. He made her feel chosen and special, and she liked him very much.

'Anyway, if yer did leave, I 'ope I'd still be able to see yer?'

'I hope so too.'

'I want yer to be my girl, Kate. What do yer say to that?'

'I'd like that very much,' she said happily, though not altogether sure what the commitment entailed.

'Good,' he said, face wreathed in smiles.

She was aware of a new feeling of intimacy between them as they finished their drinks, surrounded by hollyhocks and roses growing on trelliswork.

'I think we'd better be going,' Claude suggested, after a while. 'If I get you 'ome too late, yer ma won't let me see yer again.'

'She can't very well stop me.' As she said the words, it occurred to Kate that the one good thing to come out of the Potters' social descent was a greater degree of freedom for herself and Esme. If things had remained as they were, family influences would have prohibited her from having anything to do with someone of Claude's station, except as a hired hand.

'I realise that but it makes things pleasanter for us all if she approves,' he said, taking her hand as they made their way back along the towpath.

That enjoyable evening with Claude was the first of many, and Kate couldn't remember ever being so happy before. As the nights drew in, they sat close together in the cosy ambience of the Cinematograph or a variety theatre, or walked hand in hand by the river as the glorious copper-coloured autumn darkened into the cold, foggy winter. And if Kate couldn't forget the past entirely, at least she could blot it out for some of the time when she was with Claude. His good looks and warm personality made him an easy man to love.

Much to her joy and astonishment, the initial rapport between Claude and her mother continued to the extent that he became almost like one of the family over the next few months. At first Kate had been on edge when he called for her, expecting her mother to erupt at his bluntness, and especially to being referred to as 'Duchess'. Yet his generally working-class demeanour seemed to be counteracted for Kate's mother by his friendly manner. Claude had a way of making people feel they mattered, and seemed to recognise Gertie's loneliness.

'Marie Lloyd's on at the Empire next week, Duchess,' he announced one evening in November when he came to call for Kate.

'Is she?' said Gertie without interest.

'How about comin' to see 'er with us?' he suggested. 'I'll treat yer. We'll go in the dear seats an' all.'

'Me?' She was taken aback.

'Yeah, why not? We'll all go, Esme an' all if she likes.'

'Ooh, yes please!' said the hedonistic Esme, who thought her sister's boyfriend was a real 'heart-throb'.

'Surely you don't want us to go with you and Kate?' said Gertie, touched by his offer which was nevertheless the last thing in the world she wanted. She hadn't yet sunk to such depths as to consider a music hall entertainment!

'I wouldn't have asked yer if I didn't,' he assured her breezily.

'It's very kind of you to offer,' said Gertie, deftly sewing a label into a hat, 'but it isn't my sort of thing.'

'Too common, eh?' he said, unoffended by her snobbery.

'Well . . .' she began dubiously, because she didn't want to hurt his feelings '. . . to each his own.'

'Wouldn't do yer any 'arm to see how your neighbours spend their leisure time,' he said. 'I realise it ain't really to the taste of a lady like yourself, but at least it would get yer away from that bloomin' sewin' for a few hours.'

'Music halls just aren't my cup of tea,' she said, concentrating on her work to avoid his eyes.

'It's a variety theatre,' he pointed out.

'Same sort of thing.'

'Our Marie ain't just any old entertainer, yer know,' he persisted. 'She's really special.'

'I'm sure.'

'Me gran wouldn't miss 'er for all the tea in China,' he went on determinedly. 'She's gonna see the show with 'er friend Ada.'

'Thank you for asking me, Claude dear,' said Gertie, sewing furiously, 'but I really wouldn't enjoy it, so you'd be wasting your money.'

He was sitting on the edge of the bed which was used as a kind of sofa during the day. He tapped his chin with his thumbnail meditatively. 'I tell yer what, Duchess, how about you and me havin' a bet?' he suggested eagerly.

'I never gamble,' she said, looking up quickly.

'Just a bit of fun,' he explained. 'You say you won't enjoy the show. I say yer will. So I'll buy us all tickets, and if yer don't enjoy yourself just a bit, I'll never ask yer to go again – *and* I'll wash all yer dishes for a month. But you've gotta be really honest and not pretend to hate it if yer really like it.'

Kate and Esme laughed heartily at this scheme.

Gertie flushed and tutted, then gave Claude an uncertain smile. 'You're teasing me.'

'No, I ain't.' He grinned. 'I mean it.'

'I think he does too,' said Kate.

'Go on, Mother, do say you'll go,' chipped in Esme. 'It'll be ever such a lark.'

The older woman looked from one to the other of them, then focused her attention on Claude. For the first time in her life, Kate saw her mother's eyes light up with spontaneous fun. 'I just hope you're a thorough dishwasher, young man,' she said, her face set in a deadpan expression, 'because I'm very particular about our crockery. Any spots or grease left on plates or pots, and you'll have to do them again.'

The foyer of the Empire was buzzing with excitement as crowds of people gathered in their best hats, laughing and chattering. Claude made a real occasion of it and splashed out on a box of chocolates which he handed to Gertie to look after before they pushed their way through to the auditorium.

'I hope you're not trying to sweeten me up with chocolates just to win your bet,' she said as they settled into their velvet seats in the fourpenny rows.

'You're a cynic, Duchess!'

Kate glanced at her mother, who was sitting between herself and Esme, with Claude seated on Kate's other side. Gertie was wearing a long brown coat and matching hat with two feathers in it, a relic from Sycamore Square. Her small, delicate features were arranged in a determined expression of hauteur, blue eyes darting disapprovingly around. Kate was somewhat doubtful about this plan of Claude's, for she had heard that Marie Lloyd could be quite saucy.

But he had been so genuinely keen to brighten Mother's dull existence, she hadn't had the heart to dissuade him. She hoped Gertie wasn't going to be too much of a wet blanket. After all, it was very generous of Claude to pay for them all out of his modest wages, especially as he'd treated them to fourpenny seats. It could get quite rowdy in the threepenny gallery, posh cushioned upholstery notwithstanding.

The show began with a moonfaced magician in a top hat and tails who made all sorts of artefacts disappear beneath coloured scarves, with the aid of an elephantine female assistant in a most unsuitable ballet skirt.

'Well, what did you think of it?' asked Kate, as they left the stage to loud applause.

'I could do better myself,' snorted Gertie. 'And as for that pudding of an assisant of his . . well really! Doesn't she know that decent women don't show their ankles, let alone their knees?'

'It's different for show people,' Kate whispered.

'Humph.'

All the acts in the first half received similar judgement from Gertie. There was a twitchy juggler who missed one of the coloured balls he was working with and sent the others bouncing crazily over the stage to loud jeers from the audience; a team of male acrobats, in red sequinned costumes, who threw themselves about in a programme of astonishing handsprings and cartwheels; a comedian with a waxed moustache whose trademark was melancholia strolled on to the stage in a loud-checked suit and did his entire comic routine without smiling, despite the fact that the whole auditorium, excluding

86

Gertie, erupted into fits. Then there was Percy and his performing poodles.

'Fancy dressing those poor little dogs up in blue jackets and ribbons and making them jump over hurdles like racehorses,' complained Gertie. 'Heaven knows what they do to the animals to get them to perform.'

A dashing fellow in a tuxedo, with shining black hair and dazzling white teeth, opened the second half in fine form with a good selection of songs, ending his act with a rousing version of 'You Made Me Love You', in which he was joined by the audience.

Gertie's reaction to this was, 'All right, I admit it, he knows how to put a song over.'

She quite enjoyed the monologues of a woman dressed as a man, was disgusted at the smut of a male comedian, and admitted that a female singer's rendering of 'Shine On Harvest Moon' was rather good.

And then it was time for the top of the bill. Electricity crackled through every row as they waited in hushed silence for the idol of the English music hall to appear. The whole place erupted as she walked on to the stage: a short, dumpy figure, resplendent in blue organdie with a large hat abundant with frills and flounces, and carrying a decorative parasol.

Stillness prevailed as she launched into her act, serenading them with her particular trademarks, including 'Oh, Mr Porter'. It was the first time Kate had seen Marie Lloyd, and she was instantly captivated by the magnetism of her unique personality. She was humorously improper, with a wicked wink which added innuendo, but never lewd.

Carried along by the entertainment, Kate forgot all about the wager between her mother and Claude. The warmth radiated by this amazing performer reached out to embrace her. It was as though she was singing for Kate alone. She sat entranced.

When the band struck up with the introduction to her final number, the song that had made her name and delighted her fans for many years, the audience roared and shouted, giving her a standing ovation. There wasn't a whisper to be heard anywhere in the theatre, just the tuneful notes of 'The Boy I Love is Up in the Gallery'.

The entire house united in a surge of emotion. Kate saw most of this final number through a blur of tears. When the final note died away, the whole place went wild. They were clapping and cheering and stamping their feet in the aisles. Throughout the theatre, handkerchiefs were in use – including the one belonging to the lady sitting next to Kate.

'Well, Mother?' she asked when the curtain finally came down.

'I don't know what it is about her,' Gertie said, blowing her nose. 'I've certainly heard better singers. But she's got something really special, and that's a fact.'

'So . . .?'

'So it looks like I'll be washing the dishes myself, after all,' she said, grinning.

In the New Year both Kate and Esme received a payrise which meant the Potters could now afford slightly better accommodation. They didn't go far, just round the corner to Dane Street, to a two-roomed unfurnished flat which they filled with second-hand pieces they found on junk stalls, and polished and painted to look like new. Although they still had to share a bedroom, at least now they didn't have to sleep in the same room in which they did everything else. And, joy of joys, there was a kitchenette in the corner of the living room, with a water tap of their very own.

'Proper toffs you'll be 'ere,' said Bertha, as she did a tour of inspection.

'Hardly that,' said Gertie, a touch scornfully.

'Well, maybe I am exaggeratin',' agreed Bertha, 'but it's better than you 'ad before.'

'Oh, yes,' agreed Gertie, who was pleased even if it still wasn't what she was used to.

'I'm glad yer didn't move far away though,' confessed Bertha. 'At least you and me'll still be able to 'ave a cuppa tea together of an afternoon, eh, Gert?'

'Oh, yes, I wouldn't want to miss that.'

That particular daily ritual was of immense value to her, since Bertha was still her only friend. The girls were grown up and preferred company of their own age. It wouldn't be long before they left home to get married. What would she do then, stuck in a flat all day, with no one coming home to her in the evening? How different things would have been if Cyril had lived. She would hardly have noticed her daughters leaving her if she'd still been involved with her Kensington friends.

Still harbouring delusions of grandeur, Gertie longed for company of her own type and an active social life. She missed the lighthearted gossip about clothes and parties and the theatre. To the people around here, socialising was a chat in the street or a visit for the purpose of borrowing sugar or tea. Gertie's neighbours always seemed to be jabbering on about such depressing topics, things she preferred not to think about, like unemployment or the latest victim of TB or scarlet fever.

It was surprising that Bertha wasn't like that, being of the same breed, Gertie thought. But she was different. In fact, they never seemed to run out of conversation. Bertha spoke her mind. If she thought Gertie was being selfish or pretentious, she was quick to point it out. But she was also generous with praise and, oddly enough, seemed to understand that Gertie couldn't bring herself to be a part of the local community. Though she was quite wrong to suggest it was only a matter of time.

'And we can still walk to the shops together of a morning,' Gertie pointed out, realising yet again just how much she had come to rely on Bertha's company.

There were few conversations with Claude which didn't feature 'me gran', a lively septuagenarian to whom Kate had been introduced early on in their friendship, and to whom he was devoted.

'Me gran's very partial to a night out at the pictures,' he'd inform the Potters proudly. 'She goes with 'er pal Ada from next door. Proper pair of film fans, they are.'

Or: 'I'm sorry I'm late, Kate, I 'ad to go to the Jug and Bottle for some stout for me gran. She enjoys a drink of a night.'

One evening soon after the Potters had moved house, he didn't appear at the appointed hour to call for Kate, but arrived at bedtime looking pale and distraught.

'It's me gran,' he announced, his voice shaking with emotion.

'What's the matter with her?' asked Kate.

'She dead,' he announced in a stunned voice.

'Oh, no!' said Kate.

'Yeah. Slipped away in 'er chair while she was waitin' for me to get 'ome from work,' he explained sadly. 'It must 'ave been then because the tea was ready and the table laid.'

'Oh, Claude,' sympathised Kate, hugging him. 'I'm so very sorry.'

Her feelings were echoed by her sister and mother who immediately put the kettle on.

'How old was she?' asked Gertie.

'Seventy-five.'

'Not a bad innings.'

'No, that's true,' he agreed. 'I suppose I thought she'd go on forever. She is . . . I mean she was, such a lively old gel.'

The silence was almost palpable as they all struggled for words of comfort.

'Anyway, I can't stay,' he said, his mouth trembling. 'I just popped round to let you know why I didn't show up earlier. I didn't want yer to think I'd stood yer up.'

'I wouldn't have thought that,' said Kate truthfully.

'You'll stay for a cup of tea?' said Gertie.

'No, I'd better not, thanks, Duchess. I don't want to leave Gran on 'er own,' he said sadly. 'Ada's with 'er, but she'll be wanting to go 'ome soon.'

None of them had the heart to point out to him that it really didn't matter any more. He had brought his gran so vividly into their lives, it was almost as though this was their bereavement too.

Claude was a kind-hearted and affectionate man who had made it plain from an early stage that he expected his relationship with Kate to end in marriage. But he was not blessed with a romantic turn of phrase, and this was very obvious one crisp February Sunday afternoon, as he and Kate took a stroll along the riverside Mall in the winter sunshine.

Noticing that he seemed preoccupied, Kate said, 'You're very quiet today. Is anything wrong?'

'Not wrong, exactly.'

'Still missing your gran?'

'I do miss 'er, o' course, but it ain't that what's on my mind.'

'What is the matter then?'

'Well, I suppose it is about me gran not being around in a way,' he explained cryptically.

'Can I help, or is it a secret?'

'Not secret from you.'

'Tell me then.'

'I was wondering 'ow the duchess would feel about you moving out?'

'Move out?' Kate said quizzically. 'Why on earth would I do that when we've just taken on a bigger place?'

'If you and me was to get married, I mean,' he said, grinning at her.

Marriage was, of course, the only acceptable state in society for a decent female, Kate was only too well aware of that. But since Claude tended to make flippant remarks about their eventual matrimony, *eventual* being the operative word, she wasn't sure if this was just a speculative remark or a proposal. 'Well, obviously, I won't be living with Mother forever so I suppose she's prepared for me to move out sooner or later,' she said. 'Though she'll miss my share of the rent.'

'Mmm, that is a problem,' he said. 'Maybe I could 'elp her out?'

'Since there are no plans that I know of for us to marry,' she said, annoyed at his presumptuousness, 'there'll be time enough to worry about that sort of thing when and *if* we do decide to take the plunge.'

'Um . . . well . . . that's what I'm trying to say, yer see. Now that I don't have Gran to look after, I can afford to support a wife.'

Shocked at what seemed a callous way of putting it, Kate

said sarcastically, 'How thoughtful of her to pop off so conveniently for you!'

He stopped in his tracks and turned to her, drawing her into his arms. 'It ain't like that at all,' he explained earnestly. 'Me gran meant the world to me, you know that. I would never have had 'er go short because I wanted to get married. But my wages will only stretch so far. I couldn't have kept two women. It was me duty to provide for 'er and I was 'appy to do that for as long as she lived. But she ain't here now, is she? And you are.'

'You might at least wait till she's cold in her grave,' snapped Kate. 'You only buried her last month. You're still in mourning.'

'So what?' he said, looking down at his long dark coat. 'I'm wearing black, ain't I? Gran didn't agree with people goin' about miserable for ages after someone had died. She told me straight. She said, "You get on with your life after I'm gone, boy. Don't yer sit about mourning for me. If I was to go tomorrow, I've 'ad a good life." '

Kate calmed down and warmed towards him. In her heart she knew he was genuine, even if he didn't have the eloquence to explain his feelings properly. 'Are you suggesting that we get engaged then?'

'Not really.'

'Oh, I thought that was what you meant,' she said, flushing with embarrassment.

'I was thinking of skipping the engagement lark and getting straight married.'

She couldn't help laughing. 'But if I agree to marry you, that means we're engaged.'

'Yeah, o' course,' he said. 'I meant, let's not make a big thing of that part, but get married as soon as it can be arranged. It ain't as though we don't 'ave somewhere to live.'

Suddenly, without warning, ugly thoughts of the past darkened her mood. Should she tell him the truth about herself and her child? But what purpose would it serve apart from causing him pain? The future was what mattered now. 'But, Claude,' she said recapturing her light mood, 'isn't there something a man is supposed to say when he proposes marriage?'

At least he had the grace to look sheepish. 'Well, that goes without saying.'

'Maybe it does, but I'd like to hear it just the same!'

Raising a few eyebrows among the riverside strollers, he kissed her, there on the towpath. 'I love you,' he said, loud enough to be heard by passers-by. 'And I'd like you to be my wife.'

'Shush! Everyone's looking.'

'So let 'em.' He turned to a dark-suited man in a homburg hat. 'I love her, yer know.'

The man's fur-clad wife looked shocked. 'Really,' she tutted. 'What are things coming to with young people canoodling in public, and on a Sunday too!'

Claude turned back to Kate, his expression becoming serious. 'I'll never be able to give you the sort of life you were used to in Kensington,' he said. 'But I'll see to it that you don't go 'ungry.'

'I know that.'

'The little flat I grew up in with me gran ain't a palace, but it's an 'ome – your 'ome, if you'll take it.'

At that moment her plans for getting back to Sycamore Square ceased to exist. 'Oh, Claude,' she said. 'Of course I will.'

He gave her a mischievous grin. 'Since we're doin' this whole thing properly, it's your turn now, I think.'

Her dark brown eyes glowed. 'I love you, and I'll be honoured to be your wife.'

As they turned towards home, they didn't notice the muddy waters of the river in the pale sunshine, or the murky ripples as the boats passed by, or the scavenger seagulls swooping in search of food. They were far too engrossed in each other.

'So as Kate doesn't have a dad, she needs your consent to get married, Duchess,' said Claude. 'And we'd love to 'ave your blessing an' all.'

Gertie had listened to the excited couple's plans with a heavy heart. It upset her terribly to think of the sort of marriage her eldest daughter would have made had things been different. The ceremony would have been a splendid affair with bridesmaids and pageboys. Claude was a sweet boy, but he *was* only a labourer.

'But why the hurry?' she asked. 'You have no savings behind you.'

'We're in love,' he explained.

'Yes, but . . .'

'Seems pointless to wait when we've got somewhere to live,' he said eagerly. 'We'll not be much better off if we leave it for a while. Courtin' is an expensive business.'

'But weddings cost money,' Gertie reminded him, brushing her brow with her hand anxiously. 'And it's my place as the bride's mother to pay . . .'

'Don't yer worry about that, Duchess,' he said cheerfully. 'I'll take care of it, as long as we keep it small.' He turned to Kate. 'Would you be happy about a small do?'

Since her ordeal of the past had left her feeling unequal to a big church wedding, she was relieved. 'The smaller the better as far as I'm concerned.' She looked at her mother, guessing she would be reflecting on what might have been. 'Sorry to do you out of a big wedding, but it is what we want.'

'I may not be rich but I ain't a pauper neither, yer know,' Claude pointed out as Gertie continued to look crestfallen. 'Me gran was a great one for makin' me put somethin' by for a rainy day. I ain't got much but I reckon there'll be enough to buy some food and drink for a party, and a new outfit for you, Duchess, as well as yer daughters.'

Gertie felt too emotional to answer. He really was the kindest young man!

'I know I ain't the sort of bloke you would 'ave chosen for your daughter,' he said, displaying his enormous tolerance. 'Naturally you wanted 'er to marry a gentleman, someone with a place in society. But I do love 'er, and I'll be good to 'er.'

'Yes, I know that, Claude.'

'And I should be able to help out with your rent if yer find it hard to manage without Kate's share . . .'

'That's very kind, but I couldn't possibly. . . .'

'I won't take no for an answer,' he told her firmly. 'As one of the family I'll consider it my responsibility to see yer don't go short.'

'There's no need for you to feel that.'

'Course there is,' he told her firmly. 'You won't be losing a daughter so much as gaining a son, yer know, Duchess.'

Gertie was too busy choking back the tears to reply.

'So what do yer say?' he asked, slipping his arm around his future wife. 'Do we get yer blessing?'

Gertie's thoughts were confused. She knew she was in a position of power, for as Claude had said, Kate was still underage and needed her consent. There was no doubt in her mind that Claude would always provide for Kate, but he would never take her out of the lower classes and return her to the sort of life to which she had been raised. They would probably grow old living in the same rented rooms in which he had grown up. As the wife of a man like Claude, Kate would have far too many children and spend her life watching every penny. By the time she was thirty she would look twenty years older, with rough hands and a permanent frown.

She observed her daughter looking at her hopefully, her pleasure in Claude's proposal clearly discernible. Gertie cast her mind back to a time not so long ago when that same young woman had looked strained and sad. She thought about the nightmares that still recurred to Kate and caused her to wake, screaming.

Dismally, she faced facts. The only sort of man Kate was likely to meet was someone from the labouring classes like Claude. The realisation filled her with an urge to scream with frustration at the injustice that had come upon her and her family. How dare fate do this to her? *How dare it?*

By Gertie's very nature, she tended to view things from her own personal angle, lamenting the fact that *she* had been robbed of a fine wedding and a connection with a prestigious family; that *her* dreams of regaining their former glory through Kate's marriage had been thwarted; that Claude didn't match up to what *she* wanted in a son-in-law.

Now, suddenly, as she looked at their anxious young faces,

95

flushed from the cold winter air and shining with love for each other, she found herself standing back from the problem and considering what would be best for Kate. It was true that Claude didn't have much in the way of prospects, but he was honest and faithful, which was more than could be said for a lot of men.

'It seems we moved into a bigger place just in time,' she said, smiling. 'We'll have enough space here for the reception.'

They all seemed to be hugging each other and talking at once, kisses being misplaced in the excited confusion. Gertie was completely baffled as to what was happening to her, for she had actually enjoyed putting their interests before her own. More than that, she was looking forward to making the wedding as splendid an occasion as possible within their limited means. I must be getting soft in my old age, she thought, and was surprised to find that she really didn't care.

Kate became Mrs Claude Brooks at the Register Office one cold blustery day in March. It was a small gathering; just a few friends from Maple's stood beside Gertie and Esme to watch the couple go through the formalities.

True to his word, Claude had supplied the money for the wedding outfits, and Gertie and her daughters had spent a pleasant few hours in Barker's of Kensington High Street.

Whilst Gertie was dignified in a rather matronly blue suit, and Esme looked pretty in red, Kate was stunning in a pink suit with a fashionably narrow, wrapover skirt, and a white blouse trimmed with broderie anglaise. She wore her hair in a soft loose style which complemented her pink hat trimmed with white ribbons and imitation roses. Carrying a spray of fresh spring flowers, she stood beside Claude who was looking very dashing himself in a checked suit and new hat.

Back at the Potters' flat, Bertha was waiting with her children to greet the wedding party with a glass of sherry, having put the finishing touches to the table while they had been out at the ceremony. She and Gertie had been up at the crack of dawn making dainty little sandwiches, cheese straws, and sausage

96

rolls. Assisted by her friend, Gertie had excelled herself by producing an iced wedding cake.

The party was noisy and cheerful. Toasts were made, speeches given, and the cake cut to loud cheers. Claude, in fine form and a little bit tipsy from the sherry, made a special toast to his gran whom he said was with him in spirit on the happiest day of his life.

It was early evening when the couple left the celebrations to start their new life, just fifteen minutes' walk away. Now for the difficult part, thought Kate, as she kissed her mother, hugged her sister and walked down the street on the arm of her new husband.

# Chapter Six

A commotion on one of the landings in a tenement house in Jarman Street, Fulham, brought the tenants to their doors, curious as to what all the squealing and giggling was about. Discovering that the disturbance was only the high spirits of Claude Brooks carrying his bride over the threshold, the residents smiled knowingly and went back inside. Claude was popular in these parts. His neighbours were glad he'd found such a 'nice respectable gel', even if he had been a bit sharp in marrying her so soon after his grandmother's funeral.

In the privacy of the young couple's rooms, the bride perceived a sudden change of mood in her groom. His exuberance seemed to drain away the minute they closed the door behind them. Had she not known him better, she might have thought he was nervous . . .

''ow about a cuppa tea?' he suggested, with unusual politeness.

'That would be lovely,' she said formally, infected by his seriousness.

'I'll put the kettle on then.'

'Shall I do it, since I'm the lady of the house now?'

'Plenty o' time for all that lark,' he said, his voice lacking its usual verve. 'I ain't lettin' yer do the chores on your wedding day.'

'It's your wedding day too, remember?' she pointed out, cringing at the dreadful banality of this conversation.

'Mmm, but everyone knows that the wedding day belongs to the bride.'

And the wedding night belongs to the groom according to rumour, she thought wryly, watching him fill the tin kettle in

99

the small kitchen area in the corner of the room, and put it on the gas stove to boil. Having set the tea-things out on a tray, he wandered into the living area, removing his jacket, unbuttoning his starched collar and putting them over the back of an armchair.

'Ah, that's better. I never feel really comfortable when I'm wearin' a suit.' He shivered. 'I think I'll put a match to the fire. I laid it ready this morning in case we needed it – yer never know what the weather's gonna be like in March. It could be warm as spring or colder than January.'

'Let me do it,' she offered in an effort to dispel the awkwardness between them.

'In yer smart weddin' clothes? I should ko-ko!' he said briskly.

'I don't mind.'

'Don't be daft.'

'I wasn't being . . .'

'You'll 'ave enough of the chores every day while I'm out at work,' he interrupted in a strained, staccato tone. 'So yer might as well make the most of a bit of spoilin'.'

Oh dear, he was behaving more like an indulgent aunt than a bridegroom. 'It's good of you,' she heard herself say as though he was some stranger who had given her his seat on the bus.

'You just sit yourself down or 'ave a wander round to get the feel of the place,' he continued stiffly. 'It's your 'ome as well as mine now, remember.'

Who was this strange man? she asked herself as panic rose. Where was the fun-loving heartthrob she had fallen in love with, the boy she had walked with by the river, laughing at nothing and kissing in the bushes and back alleys of West London?

Tensely, she sat down in a lumpy brown armchair near the hearth while he coaxed the fire into life by means of a newspaper held over the aperture. She studied him, hoping to revive the magic that had inspired her to become his wife. But he remained oddly different, and when the flames began to roar returned to the gas cooker to attend to the tea, studiously avoiding her eyes.

100

The warmth of the fire was welcome in this chilly atmosphere. She removed her jacket and laid it across the arm of her chair, feeling too ill-at-ease in her new home to go into the bedroom to hang it up in the wardrobe. The prevailing atmosphere made that particular region seem embarrassingly relevant.

She had brought her things round over the previous few days. Naturally her mother had been present at the time, since it simply wasn't done for a decent girl to be alone in a flat with her betrothed before the wedding. Together she and Gertie had stored all Kate's clothes away in the hideous mahogany wardrobe, and put clean linen on the bed Claude's grandmother had once shared with his grandfather. Mercifully this great iron monstrosity now benefited from a new mattress, purchased with Claude's savings.

Glancing around the fusty living room Kate saw dark, old-fashioned furniture, shabby lino, dismal walls spread with cheap pictures, and market-stall ornaments covering every available surface. In all due credit to Claude, he had made an effort to make it as nice as possible for her. The floor was freshly polished and the grate gleaming with black lead.

But that didn't alter the fact that every single item was his grandmother's, from the sad-eyed stuffed bird on the sideboard to the yellowing lace curtains at the windows. The only new things apart from the mattress were the bed-linen and some glassware and crockery they had received as wedding presents.

Naturally, Kate was grateful to have a home of their own, but she wanted to refurnish it in a more modern style and make it personal to Claude and herself. However, her ambition could not be realised as things stood at the moment because they couldn't save anything from Claude's wages. She had accepted the fact that as a married woman she would be expected to leave her job and devote her life to domesticity, because that was the way things were, but she could see no reason to waste her millinery training by not earning a few shillings at home.

On this subject Claude was adamant. 'What sort of a man do

101

you think I am?' he'd said crossly when she'd suggested that she do some sewing at home. 'Oh no, Kate. It's my job to bring in the money, yours to look after the 'ome.'

'But it doesn't make sense for me not to use my skills when it's work I enjoy, and we need the money so badly.'

'We are not so hard-up that I have to put my wife to work,' he'd insisted. 'You leave it to me to provide for us. It's an 'usband's responsibility.'

So she had been forced to concede defeat, for the moment anyway. But now, faced with the dreary room with its ugly sideboard and torn brown sofa from which straw stuffing poked through in places, she could see the sense to it even less. This, though, was not the moment to raise the subject.

''ere yer are,' he was saying, handing her a cup of tea and sitting down in the armchair on the other side of the fireside.

'Thanks, Claude.'

'Well, well,' he said, in an attempt at conversation, 'ain't this cosy?'

Cosy was the last thing it was, despite the lovely crackling fire. To someone who had been bracing herself for some sort of physical onslaught, this was an anti-climax indeed. For Kate, the excitement of the wedding preparations had been somewhat diminished by fear of the inevitable as the horrors of the past flooded back to her mind, making her feel tarnished and unworthy of Claude's love.

Naturally, their courtship had not been entirely platonic, but neither had they flaunted convention by succumbing to the full-blown 'unmentionable'. As far as Kate could gather, marriage gave Claude carte blanche in that department. Not that 'that sort of thing' was ever discussed. Mother had coyly muttered something about it being a woman's lot to endure, men's to enjoy, and that Kate was to look at 'that side of it' as a small price to pay in return for having a husband to support her and give her a respectable place in society.

Kate glanced across at Claude who was staring into the hearth, the firelight flickering over his handsome profile with its strong jawline and straight masculine nose, a stray lock of fair hair falling boyishly across his brow. He must have sensed her observation because he looked up, his mouth forming an uncertain half smile.

She knew for certain then that the poor love was just as terrified as she was, thus disproving the theory about all men being experienced as a matter of course. Dear, extrovert Claude, whom she had never known to be shy or lost for words, was not so confident after all!

All personal anxiety melted away in her concern for him. 'I love you, Claude,' she said softly.

He looked up, his furrowed brow softening in the warmth of her smile. 'Likewise,' he said, his voice trembling slightly.

She put her tea-cup down on a small table and stood up, reaching out to him. As she led him towards the bedroom, she couldn't help seeing the irony in the situation in a society that believed it simply wasn't acceptable for a woman to take the initiative.

The first time was a complete failure, mostly due to ignorance, nervousness, and the bitter March winds that rattled through the ill-fitting windows and turned the room into an ice-box. Subsequent attempts were little better. But nature eventually took its course and they soon became bold enough to be deliciously degenerate, having supper in bed as soon as Claude got home from work, and remaining happily ensconced there until morning.

During this honeymoon period, as the strong March winds turned to light spring breezes, Kate was thoroughly content in her role as Mrs Claude Brooks. She swept and scrubbed, beat rugs, dusted and polished the decrepit old furniture until their little home shone and smelled as fresh as a summer meadow. She cooked such nourishing and economical meals as mutton broth with suet dumplings, jam roly-poly and tapioca pudding. Every morning she religiously attended to her domestic regime before going to the market for the day's provisions, washing their clothes in the copper in the communal scullery once a week.

The long, empty afternoons were filled with visits to her mother and Bertha, window shopping in King Street, or walking by the river or in the park. Her entire day revolved around Claude's arrival home in the evening.

May came in in a blaze of glory. Blue skies and sunshine bathed the capital from dawn to dusk. Front gardens exploded into colour with tangles of pansies and pinks, irises and lupins. In the parks the neat flower beds were ablaze with early marigolds and geraniums.

These were gentle, happy times. For a while Kate was even able to stifle her frustration at having several hours each day which she was forced to idle away when they could be put to good use. Since her aimless Kensington life had ended, she had got out of the habit of time-wasting and a feeling of boredom grew. Even more so as most of the other wives in the area laboured at home, making matchboxes or putting button-holes in blouses, and some with small children under their feet too.

It wasn't as though she and Claude were on the breadline. As long as she watched every single ha'penny, they managed on his wages, providing he worked any overtime that he could get. But were she allowed to make a contribution, life could be pleasanter for them both, and he wouldn't have to work so hard. Unfortunately, his over-developed provider's instinct blinded him to reason. It was infuriating!

When she realised that their budget simply wouldn't run to any sort of a celebration to mark his twenty-first birthday in June, she decided it was time to take action . . .

Gertie had serious doubts about Kate's cunning plan to make some extra money for Claude's birthday.

'You want me to take on extra work for you to do, and I'll pay you when Maple's pay me?'

'That's right,' confirmed Kate brightly. 'And I'll come round to your place every afternoon to do the sewing, if you'll have me.'

'I'll be glad of the company, you know that,' her mother assured her. 'But I really don't think you should embark on such a scheme, since Claude is so opposed to your working.'

'What the eye doesn't see . . .'

'That's all very well, but is it fair to deceive him, dear?'

'If it's for his own good, yes,' Kate said firmly.

'I'm not so sure . . .'

'He's left me with no alternative, Mother,' said Kate. 'The man is totally unreasonable on the subject. I'm quite prepared to scrimp and scrape to make ends meet in the normal run of things. But I'm blowed if I'll sit back and let my husband's coming of age pass without some sort of a do! Not when I have the time and the skills to earn some cash to make it nice for him.'

'It does seem awfully devious, though,' persisted Gertie.

'Yes, I know,' agreed Kate, 'but it's in a good cause, and it will only be for a few weeks until I've earned enough to get him a decent present and pay for a surprise party for him.'

'I'm not questioning your reasons,' said Gertie worriedly, 'it's your methods that bother me.'

'How else can I do it?' asked Kate. 'I can't approach Maple's myself about work, not with Claude working there. He'd be sure to find out what I was up to.'

'Mmm, I suppose so.'

'Even if I was to take work direct from another milliner's, I couldn't do it at home because there's nowhere to hide it from Claude. So, you and me working together is the only way. And it *is* only for a very short time.'

'But should you do it at all?'

'Yes.'

Her mother was still very doubtful. 'It's dangerous to go against Claude's wishes in such a deceitful way,' she said. 'And anyway, even if you were to get away with it, he's bound to wonder where you got the money for the gift and the party. What will you tell him?'

'Oh, I'll worry about that when the time comes,' Kate said lightly. 'For the moment I want to earn enough money to make it a special day for him. Once it's a fait accompli and he's enjoying himself, he'll be too happy to care how it all came about.'

'I wouldn't bet on it,' warned Gertie.

'Will you ask for the extra work though?'

'Mr Maple might wonder why I want more work all of a sudden.'

'This is the height of the trade's busy season. He'll be too glad to get the work done to care,' Kate pointed out.

'That's true enough.'

'And since Maple's keep a steady flow of work all year round, producing samples, stock and soft toys in the slack season, they'll probably be able to keep us supplied into next month.'

Her mother heaved a sigh of resignation. 'Oh, all right then,' she agreed reluctantly. 'But don't blame me if it all ends in tears.'

Kate enjoyed being gainfully employed again, and found her clandestine afternoon activity exhilarating. The work was more repetitive than she had been used to, though, because it was meant for Gertie who didn't have her daughter's skills. Imbued with a new sense of purpose, Kate would fly lightheartedly through the morning chores and rush round to Dane Street, eager to get through as much work as possible to build up Claude's birthday fund.

Bertha usually joined them at some point for a cup of tea and a chat. She thought Kate's plan admirable.

'That's what I call working for love,' she said. 'Your Claude is a lucky feller to 'ave a cracking little wife like you who'll work her socks off to give 'im a knees up on 'is birthday.'

By the end of the first week in June, Kate had achieved her aim in time for Claude's birthday the next week. Excitedly, she and her mother visited a jeweller's in King Street where they purchased a silver pocket watch in a silver case for the princely sum of two pounds, ten shillings. Together they gazed in delight at an item they wouldn't have given a second glance a few years ago. In financial terms it was only a fraction of the cost of the elegant artifacts they had once taken for granted, but in terms of personal satisfaction, it was priceless.

'So you can give up work now that you've achieved what you set out to do,' said Gertie with relief.

Kate was thoughtfully silent. If she were to continue with her

106

afternoon sewing, she could gradually replace the terrible old furniture with shiny new pieces. She could make the shabby flat into a place Claude would be proud of, a home he could really look forward to coming back to in the evening. Realistically, though, she knew that to extend her scheme for such reasons would be joyless without his blessing. 'Yes, I shall revert back to being a lady of leisure,' she said regretfully.

The party was in full swing, the Brooks' small living room resounding with noise and laughter. The guests had made short work of Kate's buffet and were all beginning to get a little mellow on a selection of spoils from the off licence. A neighbour was squeezing out 'Lily of Laguna' on the mouth organ, and loud tuneless singing rose above the conversational hum. It was a warm night and the sash windows were open.

Kate made an announcement. 'Can I have your attention please, everyone?' she called, looking flushed and pretty in a flame-coloured taffeta dress. It was one she had made herself in an easy-fitting line with a lace collar, a sash tied under the bust, and a skirt which fell softly to just above her ankles.

Her words made little impact against the convivial hubbub.

'Quiet, you lot,' shouted Claude, rosy-cheeked and grinning. 'Give the little lady a bit of 'ush, for Gawd's sake.'

The volume lowered attentively.

'Thank you very much, ladies and gents,' announced Kate in the manner of a compère. 'Now I think it's about time Claude did something for his supper, don't you?'

Agreement was loud and unanimous.

'So I am going to light the candles on his cake – which he'll blow out in one go or he won't have the right to call himself a man!'

There were cheers and whistles as she put a match to the candles. Claude extinguished the flames in one breath to riotous applause, and Kate led the company in an enthusiatic version of 'Happy Birthday to You'.

Standing back from the proceedings, she allowed herself a moment of satisfaction. The event for which she had worked so hard was an unqualified success.

Claude was undoubtedly having a wonderful time. He had been thrilled, if a little bemused, by Kate's gift which she had presented to him just before the guests had arrived, leaving no time for awkward questions. If he saw fit to quiz her about it later on, she would explain to him gently and he would be too full of wellbeing to be annoyed. Especially when he heard her other piece of news . . .

She reflected with amusement on the devious tactics she had employed to ensure the party was a surprise. Fortunately Claude had been due in at the factory to paint the sale-room this particular Saturday, so she had had the place to herself while making preparations.

The birthday cake had been made in advance and put out of sight in a neighbour's flat. Kate had spent the afternoon working on the spread and when Claude got home from work the table groaned with a varied assortment of meat pies, sandwiches, pickles, jellied eels, trifle and fancy cakes.

Gertie was here with Bertha and the children, all done up to the nines. Claude's mates had been invited, and all of the other tenants in the house. Then there was Esme, looking attractive in a pale blue dress with a satin sash around her slim waist and artificial flowers under the bust.

But now the birthday song had ended and Claude was about to make a speech.

'I'd like to thank my lovely wife for organisin' all this for me,' he began, his speech slurred by a considerable intake of liquor. 'I'm a very lucky man. Thank you all for coming. Now carry on enjoying yourselves . . .'

He swept Kate into his arms and kissed her, to a loud chorus of approval.

Her happiness was complete.

Observing the proceedings from across the room, Gertie's emotions were somewhat mixed. She couldn't help being disappointed at the standards her family had come to accept as normal. One could hardly call this bun-fight the Potters' kind of thing. Frankly, Gertie thought it disgustingly rowdy, more suitable for some backstreet bar-room. But since Kate had put so much effort into it, Gertie felt obliged to put on a cheerful front. This last few years had taught her that one could get used to anything in time, but she knew she would never feel at ease in the company of these loud people who bawled out songs with no regard whatsoever for the beauties of harmony. It was all a far cry from the refined musical evenings she had once enjoyed.

Her daughters obviously had no such problems and seemed to be having the time of their lives. In fact, a stranger could be forgiven for thinking they had been born to rough and ready tenement life. Thankfully they had retained their good manners, but they seemed to be thoroughly at home in this sort of company now, such was the adaptability of youth.

Seeing Kate so happy with Claude pleased Gertie but also imbued her with a deep sense of loneliness. She still felt the loss of Cyril even now, though they had never been close. It was being a part of a couple she missed, the state of belonging to someone.

Setting aside her own personal regrets, she had to admit that it was a heartless person indeed who could watch Kate and Claude together and not feel a sense of rightness. No one except the finest gentleman was really good enough for either of Gertie's daughters. But as lesser mortals went, Claude was one of the best.

Turning her attention to her younger daughter, Gertie frowned. That young lady was a bit too giggly for her liking, and a bit too flushed. If Gertie was not mistaken, she'd been experimenting rather too liberally with the port and lemonade . . .

Esme was having a wonderful time. In fact, she felt positively ecstatic. Everything seemed so bright and funny; everyone so warm and friendly. Even old fogeys like Mother and Bertha weren't quite so boring this evening, for some reason. The port and lemonade didn't taste nearly so bitter now that she was used to it either. And on the subject of port wine, her glass was empty which was no state of affairs for the sister-in law of the birthday boy.

She was looking round the room for her sister, to ask for a refill, when her mother appeared at her side. In a vague sort of way, Esme perceived that her parent was not best pleased.

'Hello Mater, old thing,' the young woman said, giggling. 'Are you having a good time?'

'No,' snapped her mother.

'Oh, why's that? Has someone upset you?'

'Yes,' said Gertie icily.

'Oh dear,' said Esme woozily, too far gone to realise she was the culprit. 'I hope none of Kate's male neighbours has been trying to get off with you?'

'Esme,' hissed Gertie furiously, 'how dare you be so vulgar?'

She looked baffled, and stared innocently at her mother. 'What have I done? All I said was . . .'

'I heard what you said,' interrupted Gertie, lowering her voice so as not to attract attention. 'Now, I think you'd better say your goodnights and I'll take you home before you really show us up!'

'Go home?' said the girl, appalled at such a suggestion. 'I'm not leaving.'

'Oh, yes, you are.'

'I'm having far too much fun to go home yet awhile,' said Esme, with a drunken laugh. 'In fact, I'm just going to ask Kate for another drink.'

'You've had quite enough.'

'Just a teeny-weensy little drink . . .'

'A girl of seventeen getting tipsy!' Gertie hissed. 'It's down-right disgusting.'

'Course it isn't, Mumsy-wumsy.'

'Come along, Esme,' persisted her mother. 'We are leaving before anyone else notices the state you are in.'

She placed a hand on her daughter's arm, but Esme shrugged it off. 'Don't be such an old spoilsport, Mother,' she trilled, her voice rising above all the rest, bringing the chatter and singing to a halt. 'This is meant to be a party, not a funeral.'

'Esme!' warned Gertie.

Her icy disapproval, normally effective as a disciplinary measure, was impotent against the more powerful influence of alcohol.

'Trust you to spoil things for Claude,' said Esme with a giggle.

Fearing this contretemps might ruin the party altogether, Kate intervened. 'Now then, you two, let's have no family quarrels this evening.'

'She's trying to make me go home,' said Esme, pouting.

'Ah, what a shame,' sympathised someone, reckless with gin.

'Yer can't go 'ome yet,' said another, full of party spirit. 'The night's still young.'

'Exactly,' said Esme, encouraged by the support. 'Kate's gone to a lot of trouble to make this party a success, and I'm not going to spoil it for her and Claude by leaving early.'

'That's the stuff, ducks,' said one of the guests.

Realising that they were now the centre of attention, Gertie smarted with embarrassment. Not wishing to appear a killjoy, however, she said defensively: 'Esme is too young to be drinking alcohol.'

'A bit of what she fancies once in a while won't 'urt 'er,' said someone.

Perceiving that his mother-in-law was really upset, Claude stepped in. 'Esme ain't doin' no 'arm, Duchess. You forget all about 'er and concentrate on enjoyin' yerself,' he said. 'We'll be packing up soon anyway.'

Esme looked boozily at him. 'Don't be a party pooper, sending us home when we are all still enjoying ourselves!'

'Another hour or so, then . . .'

'My sister went to no end of trouble to organise all this for you. I hope you realise it,' continued Esme in a slurred voice.

'Yes, I do, Esme. I'm a lucky man.'

'All that work she did to get the money,' she blurted out, the port having reduced her memory span to the extent where she couldn't remember what had been said two seconds ago, let alone a few weeks ago when she'd been sworn to secrecy. 'Every afternoon, round at our place sewing hats. Dozens and dozens of them. That's devotion for you.'

She was far too inebriated to notice her sister's sudden pallor. Or the thunderous look on her brother-in-law's face.

'You're being childish, Claude,' Kate said later, when all the guests had gone and she and her husband were getting ready for bed. 'What can I do with a gentleman's pocket watch?'

'You can sell it, give it away, chuck it in the bloody Thames for all I care!' he said, climbing into bed. 'Just so long as you don't expect me to keep it. I don't want it, do you understand?'

'But why?'

'You know why.'

'And what's so terrible about my doing a little work to give my husband a nice birthday?' she asked, deeply hurt by his attitude.

'What you did was deceitful.'

'Maybe it was, but with the best of intentions.'

'It was still deceit.'

'How else could I have got the cash?'

'Out of the housekeeping money that I give you.'

Kate dipped the face flannel into the bowl at the washstand and wrung it out before washing her face with it. 'I stopped believing in fairy tales a long time ago. Isn't it about time you did the same?'

He glared at her from the pillow, eyes dark with rage. 'I bring in steady wages. You don't go short.'

'Not of basic necessities,' she agreed, drying her face with the towel. 'But your money doesn't run to treats.'

'Oh, so a simple life ain't good enough for yer now, is that it?' he said angrily. 'You want more than I can afford to give yer.'

'I wanted more for *you*, damn it!' It was a warm, airless night, and well into the early hours. It had been a tiring day for Kate, and having it end on such a sour note after all her hard work was almost too much to bear. 'A simple life is fine for me. But there's nothing wrong with someone striving for more if they're prepared to work for it.'

'Your la-de-da Kensington days are over,' he said defensively. 'If you wanted them back, yer shouldn't 'ave married me.'

'Oh, for God's sake,' she snapped. 'My doing a few hours' work is hardly going to change our lifestyle.'

'You went behind my back.'

'Only because you are so ridiculously sensitive about my doing anything outside the housework.' She ran a trembling hand over her brow. 'I wanted you to have something more than a pint of brown ale down the local for your birthday,' she said, 'and that's about all we could afford out of your wages.'

'I'd rather have just had that than have my wife deceive me.'

'Where was the harm in what I did?' she asked. 'It was your twenty-first birthday, for heaven's sake.'

'So what?'

'You'd have had nothing at all if I'd known how ungrateful you were going to be,' she said, brushing her dark hair back from her face with unnecessary vigour, her cheeks angrily suffused.

'And that would have suited me fine!'

'All this fuss because I showed a little initiative,' she said, through clenched teeth. 'You're being completely unreasonable.'

He leapt out of bed and headed for the door, his striped nightshirt flapping around his legs. 'And you are a deceitful little cow!' He turned at the door, glaring at her. 'I shall sleep on the sofa.'

The slam of the door felt like a jet of cold water in her face. Instinctively she made towards it, eager not to end his birthday in this horrible way. But she stopped, suddenly convinced that she must remain true to her beliefs on this occasion or regret it in the future.

After all, she had done nothing more sinful than earn a few honest shillings. And she was damned if she would beg forgiveness for that!

# *Chapter Seven*

Claude sat on a bench on Wandsworth Common, staring gloomily into space. The weather was hot and oppressive, making his boots pinch and his clothes feel damp and sticky after the long walk from Fulham. Removing his greasy cap, he wiped the sweat from his throbbing brow with his handkerchief, the brilliant sunshine hurting his eyes.

His headache couldn't be blamed on the weather though, he thought wryly. That was a mixture of last night's booze and the barney with Kate, mostly the latter which was also the reason he found himself on the wrong side of the river when he should be at home having his Sunday dinner.

It had been their first serious quarrel and had left him feeling physically ill. He'd barely slept all night on the sofa, alternating between fury at the way she had deceived him, and hope that she would come to him, soft and apologetic, to put things right. But she hadn't. Finding himself unable to cope with the arctic atmosphere between them this morning, he'd left the flat in a huff with no particular destination in mind. For once, he wished it was a working day so he could have escaped to the factory.

Surely Kate must realise how much she had humiliated him before those who would now question his ability as a provider? Perhaps it had been a mistake to marry someone who had known better things. After all, an ordinary labourer like himself could work twenty-four hours a day and still be unable to keep her in the manner to which she had once been accustomed. Oddly enough, it hadn't seemed to matter until now.

Casting his mind back to last summer, he recalled how

thrilled he'd been when Kate had returned his interest. A girl like her, a looker as well as a lady. In retrospect, it should have been obvious to him from the start that there would be problems. But he'd been far too much in love with her to see beyond the joy of the moment.

Claude was not given to delving too deeply into things. He lived from day to day and took life as it came. But in this unusual mood of introspection, he was able to admit to there being something about his wife that occasionally bothered him, a part of her held back that could never be his. It was only natural that someone with her background would have a different outlook on life to his own, but he sensed there was more to this 'other self' than just her upper crust beginnings.

It was almost as though there had been some other love in her life before him, yet he knew for a fact that he had been her first boyfriend. They said you could tell if a woman was a virgin the first time you made love to her, but he'd been in far too much of a nervous state to notice anything much beyond his own performance that first time.

The more he considered this partly acknowledged doubt, the less able he was to clarify it. It was nothing more tangible than a suspicion that things were happening behind those lovely dark eyes that had nothing to do with him. He found this painful, for he had grown up to believe that a man's wife should belong to him entirely, in thought and deed.

Then there were the bad dreams, the nights when she cried out in her sleep and woke up trembling. Those were the times when he held her in his arms and soothed her until she was calm. Caring for her as he did, he was curious as to the reason for these nightmares. But she'd been vague on the subject. She'd said they were probably caused by some lingering effect of the shock of her father's tragic death. Somehow the explanation didn't ring true. Yet he trusted her, and was certain that she loved him.

So why had she done the very thing she knew would upset him? It wasn't as though he hadn't made his feelings plain on the subject. All right so she had done it for him, but she must

116

have known he'd rather not have had the celebrations under those circumstances?

Selfish? How could the word apply to him when all he wanted was to protect her from financial responsibility? If he was one of those blokes who had their wives working for the old man's beer money, *then* she really would have something to complain about.

He was startled out of his reverie by the rumble of thunder and the darkening of the sky as black storm clouds blotted out the sun. A sudden cool breeze rustled through the trees, whipping across his sweaty skin and making him shiver. Huge spots of rain splashed on to the wooden bench, rapidly increasing in speed until a torrential downpour was pounding on to the grass, producing a glorious freshness.

Springing to his feet, he took refuge under a tree. All over the common, people in their Sunday best were running to find shelter under trees, in doorways, under railway bridges.

'Gor blimey, it's coming down in stair rods,' Claude remarked companionably to the group of people who had gathered nearby.

'At least it'll freshen things up a bit,' said a man with two little boys.

'It will an' all,' said a woman. 'This 'ot weather makes my feet swell up like bloomin' puddings.'

The tropical-style rain bounced on to the road around the common with such force that miniature lakes quickly formed. Claude had never seen such a deluge. It seemed almost unnatural, accompanied as it was by ear-splitting thunderclaps and vivid lightning that streaked across the sky and lit the whole area with blinding white flashes. It was only a storm but it seemed threatening in its freak intensity, and made him feel uneasy about having left Kate alone at home.

A policeman who was sheltering nearby answered Claude's question by telling him it was just after one o'clock. It meant he'd been out for hours. Kate might be frightened if the storm was as bad across the river. Desperate now to get home, he decided to take the tram back to Fulham. He was about to make a dash for the tram-stop when a flash of lightning lit up the common, followed almost immediately by thunder that shook the ground beneath his feet.

'It's right overhead,' said the constable.

A crack of thunder directly above them confirmed his theory.

'Phew! Blimey,' said Claude. 'It's a snorter of a storm, ain't it?'

'It'll pass over in a minute,' said the constable reassuringly to the crowd in general.

But even as his words faded, lightning lashed across the sky and Claude found himself knocked to the ground, with a peculiar ringing sensation in his ears. Hovering on the edge of consciousness, he was vaguely aware of shouts and screams around him. Dazed, he managed to scramble to his feet – and witnessed a scene of chaos.

The screams were from the children he had sheltered next to. Their father was trying to calm them. They were unhurt but shrieking with fright at the sight of a man, woman and child lying motionless on the ground under a nearby tree which was split from top to bottom. Their clothes were burned and smoking.

Still somewhat befuddled and weak from his fall, Claude's legs buckled as he suspected that they were dead and that he himself had been struck by the same flash of lightning that had killed them.

People appeared from all around. The policeman ushered the crowd back to allow a doctor, who was passing by, to do what he could to help.

'Are you all right, mate?' said the man with the children, to Claude.

'Yeah, I'm fine,' fibbed Claude, for he was trembling with shock and his legs felt like lead.

'I thought you'd 'ad your chips when you went down like that.'

'Couldn't 'ave been my turn to go,' he said shakily.

The atmosphere became even grimmer as a shocked whisper rippled through the crowd, confirming the deaths of the three people on the ground.

'They weren't so lucky, though,' said Claude, experiencing a moment of guilt that he had been spared while a child had died.

'I ain't never seen nothing like this in all me born days,' said the man, as the storm continued to rage around them and the rain fell in torrents. 'It's the last time I shelter under a tree, mate, I can tell yer!'

'Me an' all,' said Claude. 'Better to be wet than dead, ain't it?'

'Too true.' The man gathered his children to him and prepared to leave. 'I'd better be gettin' on 'ome, storm or no storm. My missis'll be worried.'

'Mine too,' said Claude.

Satisfied that he could be of no assistance here at this tragic scene, he splashed through the puddles to the tram-stop, only to be told by a passerby that the trams had stopped running because of floods. Now in a positive frenzy of concern for Kate, he began the long tramp home, drenched to the skin and knee-deep in water in places. Every step of the way, his mind was filled with the sight of those three corpses and the fact that it could so easily have been him. Supposing the flat had been struck and he got home to find Kate dead on the floor?

In fact, the storms south of the river were much more severe than on the other side of the Thames. But news travels fast and rumours of deaths in Wandsworth reached Jarman Street from someone who had been in that area.

Inevitably, exaggeration was rife as the stories spread. 'Worst storms in livin' memory, they reckon,' said one of Kate's neighbours.

'Lots o' people killed on Wandsowrth Common,' said another.

By the time the tale reached her, the few deaths had swelled to dozens in the telling. She was frantic with worry. Claude had been gone for hours. What if he was one of the victims? She couldn't imagine why he would have crossed the river, but in the mood he'd been in when he left home, he could have gone anywhere. If he was safe, why hadn't he returned? Even his bad temper wouldn't have kept him away for this length of

119

time, missing his Sunday dinner too. Weary of pacing the flat and poking her head through the window, she went out into the rainsoaked streets to look for him.

So it was that a couple of drowned rats met on the corner of Jarman Street and fell into each other's arms, their quarrel forgotten in the relief of being together.

'Thank Gawd you're safe!' he said.

'I thought you'd been struck by lightning!' she gasped.

'I nearly was,' he said, pouring out the whole frightening story. 'Made me think, I tell yer, when I saw those people laying there. I couldn't get 'ome quick enough. Sorry you've bin worried, love. The trams weren't running.'

'No need to explain,' she interrupted. 'As long as you're home safe, that's all that matters. We'll have a proper talk later when you've recovered from your ordeal.'

And Claude was far too pleased to be home with his wife to wonder what she wanted to talk about.

She waited until their reconciliation had been properly endorsed in bed that night and he had agreed to accept his birthday present in the spirit in which it had been given. Then she told him.

'I'm going to have a baby, Claude.'

'A baby? Us? Oh, gor blimey,' he said, beaming and leaving her in no doubt as to the nature of his reaction.

'You're pleased then?'

'Not 'alf.' His joy turned to concern. 'Are you feelin' all right?'

'Fit as a fiddle.'

'When?'

'At the end of the year,' she said. 'I'm three months already. I wanted to make certain before I told you.'

'Blimey! It could 'ave happened on our first night then?'

'Couldn't have been long after.'

'I wasn't as 'opeless as I thought, then.'

'Apparently not.'

They giggled and hugged and lay together contentedly while

he digested the news. 'Me a dad? Well, ain't that just the weirdest thing? I can't imagine myself lording it over some poor kid.'

'It gave me a queer feeling too,' she said. 'It makes you feel older somehow.'

'The thought of all that responsibility is enough to turn your 'air white,' he said, adding quickly, 'It's all right, I'm only teasin'.'

'It is a big responsibility, though.'

'I'll say.' He paused. 'You must take things easy.'

'Pregnancy isn't an illness,' she reminded him.

'Maybe not, but I shall see to it that you don't do too much,' he said. 'No more sewing hats behind my back.'

'You're not going to play the heavy husband, I hope?'

'I shall do me duty.'

'As long as you don't overdo it,' she said, frowning.

'This settles this question of you working, once and for all.'

'Not necessarily.'

'Of course it does,' he insisted. 'Now that we're gonna be a proper family, you'll 'ave more important things to do with your time than sewin' 'ats.'

'But there will be even more need for extra cash with another mouth to feed.'

Claude's brow furrowed. 'Don't start all that again, Kate,' he said crossly. 'I can provide for my family without any 'elp from you, so let that be an end to it.'

Something happened inside her then, causing feelings so powerful even she was surprised. In an attempt to calm herself, she sat up and perched on the edge of the bed with her back to him.

'I mean it, Kate,' he warned.

She didn't reply. It was still raining and the storms had cooled the air. But her skin burned with rage. Banks of heavy cloud obliterated the moonlight, but the gaslight outside in the street shone through the window, providing enough of a glow for her to see the outline of the hideous furniture that filled their bedroom.

121

'Don't sit there sulking all night,' he said. 'Get back into bed.'

Now she felt calm enough to speak. 'It isn't in my nature to take orders as though I was two years old and had no sensible opinions of my own.'

'But you're my wife,' he said, as though that answered everything.

'I am also a human being with a reasonable degree of intelligence.' She went over to the gas mantle and turned on the light. She felt she needed to see her husband properly for what she was about to say.

'You've been listening to too much suffragette propaganda, that's your trouble,' he said.

'I could do a lot worse.'

'Oh Gawd! I thought I'd married a woman, not a bloomin' campaigner.'

Kate stood looking down at him as he struggled into a sitting position. 'I'm not going to argue with you, Claude,' she said in an even tone, 'but I think you should listen to what I have to say.'

'All right, but get on with it, do,' he said impatiently. 'I need to get some sleep if I'm to get up for work in the morning.'

'If I think it necessary for the well-being of our child for me to earn extra money,' she announced, 'I *will* do it.'

'Against my wishes?'

'If necessary, yes,' she said firmly. 'If you refuse to allow me to work in our home I shall find somewhere else to do it, but I'll not have our child go short while I've breath in my body to do something about it.'

Claude recognised his wife's other self in this outburst, and knew he could not compete with her in this mood. The realisation frightened him. 'For Gawd's sake, Kate,' he blustered, feeling feeble against her strength. 'You're only three months pregnant. Why not wait till the baby arrives before you start issuing ultimatums?'

'Because I want to be honest with you and make my position clear from the start,' she said. 'I know it means a lot to you for me not to work, but the right to improve our circumstances is

122

important to me. And *no one* is going to stop me doing what is right for my baby.'

He heard her voice break with emotion and saw colour flood her cheeks. He was comforted only by the thought that women sometimes became irrational in pregnancy. Maybe this fierce assertiveness was only temporary? 'All right, all right, love,' he said gently, getting out of bed and opening his arms to her. 'Don't take on so.'

She moved back. 'Don't patronise me, Claude.'

'I don't even know what the word means,' he said, 'let alone 'ow to do it.'

She believed him. He was behaving in the way he genuinely thought a husband should. But she felt compelled to make her point. 'I'm not being hysterical, I really mean it.'

His eyes swept her face. Her skin seemed translucent, the bluish lights in her dark hair picked up by the gaslamp. 'Yes, I can see that you do,' he said, calmed by the thought that the baby was still six months away.

'So . . .'

'All right, let's make a deal,' he said wearily. 'I'll promise to listen to what you have to say if you think you need to earn extra money at some time in the future – so long as you promise not to go behind my back before we've talked it over.'

'That sounds fair enough to me.'

Off went the light and they climbed back into bed, cuddling close until Claude fell asleep. Kate lay awake for a long time, listening to the gentle patter of the rain on the window and wondering about these new and violent emotions she had found in herself in pregnancy. Memories of her own privileged childhood came to mind: piano lessons; pretty clothes and occasions to wear them; a comfortable home; a garden with a swing in it.

Almost irrationally protective towards her unborn child, she found herself regretting the fact that it would be deprived of these things. Compunction for setting such store by material acquisitions quickly followed. Claude was a good man. Their baby would not lack for paternal love. And that was what really mattered.

But still a nagging feeling of discontent lingered; a sense of inadequacy. Was it only because of her own grand beginnings, she wondered, or was it something more complex? Could it be that having failed her firstborn so completely, she wanted to redress the balance with the second? Poignant memories of that other little mite came to mind, as they so often did. He'd be three years old now. No longer a baby but a little boy with his own personality. Was he happy? Tears filled her eyes in the knowledge that she didn't even know what the Dexters had called him.

Admonishing herself for lapsing into sentimentality, she decided that her overly emotional state was probably just a passing phase caused by pregnancy. But the way she felt at the moment, she would move heaven and earth to give her second child the best she possibly could. In fact, the ferocity of her resolve was such that she felt ready to take on the world on her child's behalf. The world would probably be a lot easier to handle than Claude, though, she thought wryly.

War talk had been rife for months. Rumours had abounded after the assassination of the heir to the Austro-Hungarian throne in the Balkans. But nobody in Kate's circle seemed unduly worried about it. In fact, Claude found the prospect of a war quite exciting. Everyone felt that if it did come, it wouldn't amount to much.

'It won't take long for our boys to put the Hun in their place,' Claude was keen to point out.

Kate was too immersed in her own life to think much about it, though she was disturbed by the newspaper reports of the murder in Sarajevo. 'A clap of thunder over Europe' was the way the *Daily Chronicle* described it.

But it all seemed too far away to make much of an impact on someone whose energies were fully extended in trying to achieve the impossible: to make Claude's money stretch to pay for all the things they needed for the baby, as well as feed them and pay the rent.

She decided it was time to have a chat with him about the possibility of her taking on some millinery work at home for a few months. Just until she got too cumbersome and weary. With great reluctance, he agreed.

Putting in every hour she could while Claude was out at work, she sewed till her fingers were sore. And although the pay was not huge for the amount of hours she worked, at least now she was able to save something for the baby's needs. Claude was adamant about her taking August Bank Holiday Monday off, though, and suggested a day out at the seaside.

'As we're both earning, we can afford a day at Southend,' he proclaimed. 'It'll do us both the world of good, and it won't cost much on the excursion train.'

'Good idea,' she enthused.

'Let's ask your mum and Esme if they'd like to join us and make a family party of it?' he suggested. 'The more the merrier.'

Gertie wasn't at all keen. A bank holiday jaunt to Southend conjured up horrendous images of tribes of trippers pouring on to the beaches and dipping their grubby feet in the muddy waters. Esme wanted to go, though. So did Bertha, who decided to join them with the kiddies. Together they got to work on Gertie. And all of them rose at the crack of dawn on Monday morning and headed for Fenchurch Street Station.

Southend-on-Sea quivered with activity beneath a blue sky bustling with wispy white clouds and beaming with sunshine. The trippers were here in their thousands, pouring off the trains and steamers. Mum, dad and the kids; grandma and grandad; auntie, uncle, cousins – the whole jolly caboodle jostled along the seafront. They swarmed over the beach and crowded around the bandstand which was blasting out a hearty version of 'Rule Britannia' in view of the imminent outbreak of war announced on all the newspaper hoardings.

The holidaymakers queued at the cockle-stall, the doughnut maker, the seller of Southend rock; summer boaters clutched against the sea breezes, skirts billowing. They ate whelks, winkles and jellied eels from little saucers, and devoured fish and chips out of newspaper. Bunting and union jacks flapped in the sunshine from the shops and pubs; flag sellers were doing a roaring trade in the current patriotic climate.

The beach was a human carpet. Kiddies skipped barefoot over the sands; donkeys lumbered to and fro carrying excited city scamps; bathing machines rolled back and forth on their big spoked wheels, creaking and grinding; lines of people snaked from the water's edge, waiting to get on to the pleasure boats or to be rowed out to the floating baths.

'More like a bear garden than a beach,' declared Gertie disdainfully as they stood on the prom watching people pile on to the sands, the men with trousers rolled up to show paper-white shins, shoes and socks clutched in their hands.

'It's just people enjoying themselves,' said Kate defensively, since the outing had been Claude's idea.

Admittedly, it was vastly different to the seaside of Kate's childhood – the refined reaches of Eastbourne or Bognor where they had rented a cottage every summer and made sandcastles and paddled on an uncrowded beach. But the air here had a salty tang, albeit mixed with the smell of fried fish, the sun was shining, and there was an infectious friendliness among these Londoners who were far more concerned with facilities for fun than the state of the scenery.

There was a clash of interests in Kate's party. Ruby and Georgie wanted to go down on the sands, Bertha wanted to go into one of the pubs for a glass of stout, Esme wanted to parade along the front showing off her new hat to the hordes of young men, Kate and Claude weren't fussy, and Gertie wanted to go home.

In the event, they yielded to youth and all trooped on to the beach and found a place to sit down. The children removed their stockings and shoes and tore to the water's edge, squealing as the cold water caught their toes. They were soon followed by their mother who lifted her skirts to paddle, red hair flying in the breeze under her straw hat.

Kate and Claude went to the water's edge, Kate having daringly removed her stockings. She lifted her skirts, shrieking with delight as the water numbed her feet, and squeaking even more as her hat, which she'd carefully trimmed with red ribbon and wax cherries, was taken by the wind and blown into the sea where it bobbed on the waves like a raft.

'You'll have to put an extra hat-pin in it,' laughed Claude as he retrieved it for her.

There was so much to do, too much to cram into one day. Claude pushed his way into the bar of a seafront pub and got drinks all round before they all piled into a seafront café for dinner of pie and mash.

The party decided to split up for a while in the afternoon and meet up again later for a fish and chip supper before catching the train back to London. Kate and Claude took the children to the Kursal Amusement Park, Bertha and Gertie decided to take a ride on the electric train to the end of the pier before having a mooch round the town, and Esme took a walk along the front.

'My sister is getting to be the most terrible flirt,' Kate confided to her husband as they stood at the bottom of the helter-skelter, waiting for the children to slide down on mats, 'She's certainly changed since we left Kensington. She used to be so delicate when she was younger.'

'You're as different as chalk and cheese, you two,' he remarked casually.

'Meaning that I'm not a flirt, or that I'm not at all delicate?'

'Meaning neither of those two things,' he said. 'I just mean that Esme doesn't have your depth.'

'Oh? You make me sound awfully dull.'

'Gor blimey, Kate, you could never be that,' he exclaimed. 'What I mean is that Esme is all out front – what you see is what there is.'

'And you don't think I'm like that?'

'No, I don't,' he said frankly. 'Sometimes I think someone else lives inside you, a woman I don't know at all.'

Kate was glad he wasn't looking at her for she felt the colour drain from her face. Either Claude had more perception than she had given him credit for or she hadn't hidden her past as well as she might. 'You're imagining things.'

'Good. I'm pleased about that,' he said lightheartedly, indicating that he had been making conversation rather than trying to bring home a serious point.

127

The children skipped gaily through the amusement park towards the switchback railway.

'You comin' on, Claude?' they begged.

He looked at his wife.

'Go on, be a devil,' she said, and teasingly added, 'Perhaps I can come too?'

'Not likely,' he said. 'I might have given in to you about the sewin', but I draw the line at letting you on the switchback in your condition.'

'All right, keep your hair on, I was only teasing,' she told him playfully.

The children couldn't get enough of the ride that swooped and hurtled at high speed on a creaky wooden and metal structure which didn't look any too safe to Kate. Then there were the boat swings, the carousel and the dodgem cars. Then a few goes on the penny machines on the pier, and a train ride to the pierhead where the steamships were waiting to take their passengers back to London by sea.

'Time to meet the others,' said Claude eventually.

'Goodie, goodie,' said Ruby, now a thin twelve year old. 'Fish and chips – yippee!'

As they made their way back through the crowds for the final treat of the day, patriotic songs were being sung all around them.


Esme was thoroughly enjoying herself. There was nothing she liked better than to be at the centre of things. Today this little seaside town, ignored by Londoners in winter, felt like the hub of the universe. There was such a vibrancy about the place, such a wealth of entertainment – and it was positively crawling with chaps. Delicious dark ones; good-looking fair ones; even the pimply ginger ones seemed less odious in this buoyant atmosphere. There were more cloth caps and Sunday best suits about than blazers and boaters, she noticed, for this was a common crowd. But what did that matter to someone merely looking for a spot of Bank Holiday sport?

Anyway, now that she was fully adjusted to her reduced circumstances, Esme rarely thought about the past. She wouldn't say no to middle-class comforts, of course, but the extra freedom she now enjoyed compensated for the loss of those. In fact, she found life in the lower orders fun. She liked the lack of formality and the humour of the people. She valued being able to make friends with whom she liked, rather than those persons her parents thought suitable. And she enjoyed her work, especially now she was in the dress department.

This outing would have been much more of a lark in the company of her girlfriends from the store. The family were all right but they could be rather boring and restrictive to a devotee of fun like Esme. Mother kept too much of a sharp eye on her for comfort, and although Kate was only two years older, it seemed like twenty, especially now that she was married. Her 'trouble' seemed to have made her even more sensible than she'd been before, and matured her beyond her years. Not a bit like her fun-loving sister!

She strutted along the front, admiring her reflection in the shop windows. The blue dress with the white sash suited her, she thought proudly. It brightened the blue in her eyes and made her hair look blonder than ever.

'Blue is your colour, darlin',' she heard someone say, and turning round, found herself staring at a young man a little older than herself, with brown hair and smiling brown eyes.

She lowered her lids haughtily, a trick she practised when men threw admiring glances her way on public transport. 'And who asked your opinion?'

'If I wait to be asked, I might never get to know you.'

'You've got a nerve!'

'I ain't backward in coming forward, and that's a fact,' he confirmed with a saucy grin, 'which is lucky for you or you might never have got the chance of a walk along the front with me.'

'Fond of yourself, aren't you?' she said, flashing her eyes at him.

'Only because I've got good taste.'

'What makes you think I'd want to walk anywhere with you?'

'You've got "pick me up" written all over you.'

'I wasn't trying to . . .'

'Course you were! And why not? It's Bank 'oliday Monday, a day for fun.'

'Maybe it is but . . .'

'Do yer fancy a stroll or not?'

'I don't know you,' she said with feigned coyness.

'If I don't mind bein' seen with you, I don't see why you should mind bein' seen with me.'

She should have been outraged, but she burst out laughing instead. 'Come on, let's walk.'

'Take my arm then, let's do the job properly.'

Gertie was sitting in a deck-chair near the bandstand listening to a rousing rendition of 'Land of Hope and Glory'. The band were loudly accompanied by the crowds, including Bertha whose raucous tones were almost shattering Gertie's ear-drums. She was far too reserved to sing out loud in public, and was mouthing the words so as not to seem stand-offish in this mood of fervent patriotism.

The sun was warm on her face and the sea-breeze deliciously refreshing. Her hair felt windswept and sandy, her skin itched with grime and tingled from the fresh air, and her feet ached from all the tramping about. She would never get used to plebeian 'enjoyment' if she lived to be a hundred. But some-how, sitting here in the sunshine with her friend beside her, she felt unexpectedly content. Must be too tired to be anything else, she thought ruefully.

'I reckon your Esme has clicked,' said Bertha, shouting above a booming chorus.

'Why? Where is she?'

'Over there.' Bertha pointed to the bandstand enclosure railings where Esme was laughing right into the face of a young man in a checked cap.

'Oh, yes, I can see her,' said Gertie disapprovingly. 'Good-ness only knows what she thinks she's playing at, carrying on like that in public.'

'She 'aving a bit of 'oliday fun by the look of it,' said Bertha.

'That young woman really is the giddy limit,' complained

Gertie. 'What does she think she's doing, taking up with any Tom, Dick or Harry she meets on the street?'

'Don't be too 'ard on 'er,' said Bertha. 'She's young, and it *is* Bank Holiday Monday.'

'That's no excuse.'

'Why not go over there and introduce yourself if yer wanna give him the once-over?' suggested Bertha with her usual practical wisdom.

'No, I'll leave her be for the moment,' said Gertie, because she really didn't have the energy for a scene. 'I'll talk to her later about the dangers of teaming up with any old riff-raff she happens to take a fancy to.'

Esme's companion's name was Syd and he came from Stepney, she explained to her mother later when she met up with the family again and they all piled into the cafe. And, yes, she had just met him on the street, and what's more they had exchanged addresses and might meet again sometime.

'But you don't know anything about him,' reproached her mother.

'I do. I know his name and address and that he works in a butcher's shop.'

'A useful chap to know,' teased Kate, 'he's bound to get cheap meat as perks of the job. You won't go hungry if you marry him!'

'You'll be all right an' all, Duchess,' laughed Claude, entering into the spirit of the joke. 'He'll supply his mother-in-law with all the prime cuts to keep 'er sweet.'

'Don't forget me when there's any spare chops goin',' chuckled Bertha.

'I was more interested in his chunky shoulders than his potential as a Sunday joint supplier,' laughed Esme, taking it all in good part. 'He's got the most devastating brown eyes too.' She paused, surveying her tormentors with a grin. 'I've not even been out with him once yet, but I can tell you this much – if he tries to woo me with pork chops, there won't be a second time!'

'What does he do in the butcher's shop?' asked Gertie, who

had not taken part in the jesting.

'I've no idea,' said Esme with a nonchalant shrug. 'Cuts up the meat and serves at the counter, I suppose. Isn't that what butchers usually do?'

'He could be in charge,' suggested Gertie hopefully. 'If it was his father's shop, for instance.'

'More likely to be the delivery boy,' said Claude. 'If he's out on the loose at Southend.'

'I'll ask him if I see him again,' said Esme breezily

The good-humoured ribbing continued as they tucked into rock salmon and chips, bread and butter and tea.

A butcher's boy, thought Gertie dismally. And to think of the sort of man who would have courted Esme if things hadn't gone so horribly wrong. A stockbroker perhaps, or a banker. The son of the owner of a chain of butcher's shops, perhaps. But a butcher's counter hand wouldn't have got a foot in the door at Sycamore Square!

But it hurt less than she expected. She supposed she must be getting used to such disappointments.

'Do we have to go home, Mum?' said Georgie mournfully.

'After tea, yes,' said Bertha.

'Can't we stay a bit longer?'

'Afraid not, son. By the time we've finished our tea, it'll be time to get the train.'

'Not fair,' said Georgie sulkily.

'Shut up, shrimp,' said his sister.'

'Shut up yerself,' he retorted. 'I wanna stay.'

'We can't stay 'ere forever, can we? So stop your whinin',' warned his mother.

'Wish we could,' he said. 'It's better 'an 'ammersmith.'

'I bet it ain't in winter time,' said his mother.

'I bet it is too!'

'All good things come to an end, son.'

'I don't wanna go 'ome,' he complained.

Gertie took the unprecedented step of intervening between Bertha and her children. 'Now don't keep on, son. We've all had a lovely day out so don't you spoil it for your mother by making a fuss about going home.'

132

And, as she uttered the words, she realised that they were true. It *had* been a lovely day out, cockles and all.

Outside the cafe, noisy throngs were heading towards the station, waving flags and singing.

'When is the war gonna start?' asked Georgie.

'Any time now, they reckon,' said Bertha.

'Wars must be good fun if they make people so 'appy.'

'They're just being patriotic,' explained Kate.

Georgie was still trying to work that one out as they trudged to the station with the home-going masses.

# Chapter Eight

The next day Britain declared war against Germany after the latter's invasion of Belgium. The news sent crowds on to the streets of London, cheering and singing the National Anthem.

'We'll soon show those buggers that they can't march into someone's else's country and get away with it,' said Claude. 'Ain't that right, Kate?'

'I'll say,' she said, in tune with general opinion, though secretly she found the idea of war somewhat alarming. It seemed incredible to her that a murder in some distant country could set off a chain of events that would have such a dramatic effect here at home. From what she could gather from the newspapers, Britain had promised to help defend Belgium against attack many years ago in the treaty of 1839. Now, even though the Kaiser dismissed the treaty as a mere 'scrap of paper', the British were left with no honourable alternative but to declare war.

Claude heartily agreed with the government's decision and behaved as though victory was already won, insisting that they all go up West to celebrate. 'There's bound to be plenty goin' on up there,' he declared with enthusiasm.

So they joined the fervent crowds outside Buckingham Palace, waving flags and singing. When they arrived home in the middle of the evening, exhausted from such exuberant rejoicing, Claude decided to organise an impromptu party. All the neighbours were invited, and everyone pooled their resources for some bottles and a few fancy nibbles.

The shindig was a great success. In fact, they were still warbling with patriotic zeal into the small hours. Bertha's children were beside themselves with glee at having another treat so soon after their day out at Southend, a phenomenon which only served to confirm Georgie's rather distorted view of the situation.

'I wish wars would start every day,' he said. 'It's better 'an Christmas.'

Bertha introduced a serious note to the festivities. 'I bet those with a few bob in their pockets'll start fillin' their larders tomorrer,' she predicted grimly. ''Cos food is bound to be short.'

'People ought not to be allowed to hoard,' pronounced Gertie hotly, conveniently forgetting that had her own circumstances not altered, she would have been among the first to fill her cupboards with vast supplies of dried and tinned food.

'Just try stoppin' 'em, mate,' said her friend.

'But if people overbuy, it'll cause shortages for the rest of us who can't afford to buy more than we need each day,' Gertie pointed out.

'Course it will.' Bertha nodded sagely. 'But that won't worry them that's got the money to stock up.'

Bertha's prediction proved to be correct, and the newspapers condemned the panic buyers who overstocked at the expense of everyone else.

There was also a great deal of anti-German propaganda in the papers which sparked off a ferocious wave of public hatred for anyone of German origin. The vast Olympia complex in Kensington became a detention centre. The police rounded up many Germans and detained them there, some suspected of being spies.

'Cor, German spies, just down the road,' said Georgie, breathless with awe. 'Ain't that excitin'? I wish I was old enough to go away and be a soldier.'

It wasn't surprising that the nation's children were infected by the war fever prevailing among their elders, for the streets positively buzzed with patriotism. Recruiting offices were swamped each day with eager recruits queueing to join Lord Kitchener's army. There were street parades and concerts to raise money for the war effort; factories were commandeered for war work.

But for all that, the war seemed very far away for Kate and her family and life went on much as before. Until one day in early September . . .

'You've done what?' exclaimed Kate, with a mixture of shock and anger.

'I've joined up,' repeated Claude proudly, his smile fading slightly at this unexpected reaction from his wife.

'You mean, you'll be going to France?'

'I 'ope so,' he said. 'That's the general idea.'

'And not so much as a word about it to me!' she fumed. 'The least you could have done was discuss such an important step with your wife beforehand.'

'I did it on the spur of the moment when I was out on an errand from work,' he explained cheerfully. 'I saw all the blokes queuein' up at the recruitin' office when I passed, and got sort of carried away.'

'You mean you did a thing like that without even thinking about it properly?'

'I've thought of nothin' else since war broke out,' he told her firmly. 'What red-blooded man hasn't 'ad it on 'is mind? Most of my mates 'ave enlisted already.'

'And so you have to follow them, just so as not to lose face,' she ranted, fear evinced in anger. 'I've never heard anything so irresponsible!'

'How can you say that when it's me duty as an Englishman to join up?'

'Nonsense.'

'I thought you'd be proud of me,' he said disappointedly. 'Most women want their men to join up.'

'Well, I'm not one of them,' she snapped. 'You should leave heroism to single men.'

'But they need men urgently, Kate,' he said, trying to reason with her. 'There are posters all over the place.'

'I know that,' she retorted. 'You'd have to be blind not to see Lord Kitchener pointing the finger from every hoarding in London. But your duty lies here with me. Have you forgotten that we have a baby on the way?'

'Course I ain't,' he said. 'But there's a war on. We all have to do our bit.'

'You can do your bit closer to home,' she pointed out. 'Get a job in a munitions factory or something. But I suppose that's not exciting enough for you?'

She had, of course, hit the nail on the head, but he wasn't prepared to admit it. 'I'm young and 'ealthy. It's only right that I should go and fight and leave war work at 'ome for older men,' he insisted. 'Surely you can't disagree with that?'

'It isn't a game like you played as a kid, you know,' she said. 'This is for real.'

'I never said it wasn't, but the Hun won't stand a chance against us,' he said confidently. 'It'll all be over by Christmas, everyone knows that. It might even be over by the time I get to the front.'

'And that would be terrible, wouldn't it?' she said sarcastically. 'If you missed out on the fighting?'

'That isn't fair.'

'It's true though.'

'I've done what I think is right,' he persisted sharply. 'And as I've signed on the dotted line and I can't change my mind, you'll just 'ave to get used to it.'

She sighed heavily. 'So when will you be going?'

'Dunno. They're gonna send for me.'

'I see.' The fight was driven from her by the heavy weight of inevitability. She felt guilty for her selfish outburst but too miserable to give him the praise to which she knew in her heart he was entitled. 'In that case, there's nothing more to be said about it, is there?'

Kate's feeling of compunction was exacerbated by the way Claude's enlistment was greeted by the rest of the family. Gertie said Kate ought to be ashamed for having such a long face when her husband was being very brave and doing his duty to his country. Bertha said she was honoured to know such a plucky fellow who had not been slow in answering the call. Even Esme joined in the chorus of admiration, fussing around him and wittering on about how exciting it was to have a soldier in the family. There was also a great deal of hugging and back-slapping from the neighbours.

'I'm sorry I was so mean to you earlier,' Kate said in bed that night. 'Of course you did what was right, and I'm proud of you.'

'That's all right, love . . .'

'It was because I couldn't bear the thought of you going away.'

'I know.'

'It's easy for the others to be enthusiastic. Your going off to fight won't affect them in the same way.'

'That's true,' he agreed. 'But I'll be back 'ome before you've 'ad a chance to notice I've gone, you just wait and see.'

The next few weeks were rather anti-climactic as they waited for Claude's papers to arrive, both doggedly pretending nothing untoward was imminent. Every morning Kate looked for the post with her heart in her mouth, heaving a sigh of relief when they were reprieved for another day. Whilst the sensible part of her wanted to get on with what must be done, the other less rational part couldn't stop hoping that by some miracle he wouldn't have to go after all. She was glad of her millinery work to keep her occupied. At least it stopped her from brooding.

The much-dreaded envelope arrived at the beginning of October, containing a travel warrant to Aldershot. Claude turned pale at the sight of it, but soon recovered, and Kate could tell he was pleased to be on his way at last. She waved him off at the front door that misty autumn morning.

'Now you take care of yourself,' he said, as they hugged each other frantically. 'Don't you go overdoin' things with that bloomin' sewin'.'

'And don't you forget to write.'

'I won't. And don't worry, I'll be home before Christmas.'

And he was. He came home at the beginning of December for four days' embarkation leave.

'You'd think they'd give you more leave than that,' she

complained, 'when you're going off to fight for King and country.'

'They need us over there urgently,' he explained.

Kate didn't even suggest the possibility of compassionate leave when the baby was born because she could see his mind was on the job ahead. It was as though a part of him had left her already and he belonged to the army now.

'Well, since that's all they've given you, let's make the most of it.'

Which they did. They went to the Empire on the Saturday night and let their worries be swept away by the lively entertainment. They held hands in the stalls, laughing at the comedians and joining in with all the rest in 'It's a Long Way to Tipperary' and all the other patriotic songs that were on everyone's lips at the moment. They bought saveloys and pease pudding on the way home and ate by the fire before climbing into bed and shutting out the world.

It was a peculiar leave though, riddled with emotional undertones which produced a strained atmosphere. With the ominous shadow hanging over them, the much desired time alone together was often so fraught with tension they sought relief in the company of others, visiting relatives and friends.

But soon it was time to say goodbye, and neither of them knew how to do it. Claude stood at the door of their flat.

'Chin up,' he said.

'Take care,' she said, which seemed ludicrously inadequate considering the nature of the task ahead. 'And hurry home. Me and the baby will be waiting for you.'

'Don't forget to call him Sam after me grandad.'

'What if it's a girl?'

'Then you can choose.'

These were all empty words, uttered merely to help them through the trauma of the moment.

'Well, I suppose this is it then?' Kate felt her eyes smart, but maintained a brave front.

They clung together in a deep, lingering kiss. 'Don't come downstairs,' said Claude, his eyes moist. 'It's cold out.'

But she went down with him into the street anyway, and

watched him march away, his boots clicking in the sharp winter air. Determined not to upset him by breaking down, she managed to control her feelings. But at the corner he turned to give her a final wave which proved to be her undoing. She dashed back into the house, choking on her tears.

The next day Kate went into labour, almost a month early. It was a difficult confinement, and the midwife was doubtful of the outcome since the pregnancy had not gone full-term. But despite everything, little Sam Brooks arrived in fine fettle with everything in working order, albeit he was a scrap of a thing weighing only five pounds.

Realising that he would need special care if he was to survive the icy draughts that blew through the flat in winter, Kate kept him wrapped in cotton wool in a cardboard box near the fire. Minute by minute, hour by hour, she watched over him.

During this worrying time, she was very touched by the kindness she received from relatives and friends. Gertie surprised everyone by becoming something of a ministering angel, on hand with everything from nourishing food for the nursing mother to endless patience with the little one. The neighbours came to the door with broth or junket for Kate, and gifts for the baby. Everyone was eager to do what they could for the wife and baby of a soldier.

The Potters had a quiet Christmas. Gertie and Esme spent Christmas Day at Kate's. They bought a bottle of port wine and a chicken to roast for dinner. After their Christmas pudding, they drank a toast to Claude. Nobody mentioned the rumours of mass British casualties in France.

In the evening Bertha and the children came visiting. Gifts were exchanged and they played a game of charades and ate supper of cold chicken and pickles, followed by hot mince pies. They sang carols around the fire and talked about the victory they all expected which was certain to come in the new year.

Esme provided lively entertainment with amusing anecdotes of events at the store, and of various young men who had taken her fancy since she'd tired of Syd the butcher's boy from Stepney.

When they had all gone home and Kate lay in the big empty bed, with her baby feeding at the breast, she experienced a surge of love for Sam so violent her eyes felt hot with tears. She held him closer, as though he might be snatched from her in the same way as his brother.

Oddly enough Sam's arrival, which should have erased the past, had revived it more vividly than ever. This second birth had triggered off memories of the first, causing her to relive every painful moment of that parting. How she longed to see that child again!

'No one will ever take you from me,' she whispered, kissing the top of Sam's downy head. He stopped feeding and she held him against her shoulder, gently patting his back, feeling the throb of his life force, and smelling his milky-sweet baby scent. 'You're going to have the best life your parents can possibly give you.' She paused wistfully. 'But, oh, how I wish your daddy was here.'

On the other side of the Channel, in a damp and draughty tent on the site of a battle training camp, Claude was thinking exactly the same thing whilst engaged in a game of pontoon with his mates.

Not that he would admit to feeling hard done by, for the army discouraged any sort of self-pity. And to be fair, they had relaxed the rigid training programme slightly for Christmas Day. But his dream of glory on the battlefield was somewhat different to reality, and he was impatient to get into combat. After weeks of arduous training back in Blighty, it was annoying to find himself subject to even more of it here in France, without so much as a sniff of the action.

What a way to spend Christmas Day, he thought. Stuck out here in some Godforsaken French field where bitter winds howled relentlessly and the ground was always either wet or icy. Here, thousands of soldiers were being prepared for battle, mostly by means of bullying in the name of army discipline. Bayonet practice, rifle drill, — drilling again and again until their muscles were like elastic and their bones grinding with fatigue.

Claude preferred not to think of himself as 'battle hungry' because that would mean he was callous, and he wasn't. But the sooner the fight was fought, the sooner he could go home. Anyway, since their purpose in being here was to give the Hun a good trouncing they might as well get on with it. Besides, the more time you had to brood about the job in hand, the less appealing it seemed. Especially if you allowed yourself to dwell on their landing in France when they had seen crowds of wounded men on their way back to Blighty.

That had been enough to make any sane man wish he'd never joined up. Claude was no coward, but the newspapers and recruitment posters had said nothing about human carnage of the sort he had seen at that quayside. Queues of ambulances had been unloading the wounded on to a hospital ship, hundreds of stretchers carrying mud-splattered, blood-stained soldiers, fresh from the battlefield with limbs missing and bandaged heads saturated with blood.

Then there had been the walking wounded, limping, and stumbling towards the ship in orderly lines, dazed expressions on faces as pale as mushrooms. The memory of what he'd seen made him sweat. He forced himself into a positive frame of mind. Those poor devils had been unlucky whereas Claude Brooks always came up smelling of roses. No German bomb or bullet was going to get him!

Anyway, action would be a bloomin' sight better than the endless discomfort and monotony they were experiencing now. At least if he was in combat he'd feel as though he was doing something worth missing Christmas for. Playing cards with a bunch of fart-happy blokes on a Christmas night could hardly be called heroic.

Thoughts of Kate filled his mind in a tide of longing. Momentarily he wondered if she'd had the baby yet. But speculation on the maternal front was quickly superseded by images of Kate as a lover. He was hungry for her, the warmth of her body, her soft, silky skin.

'Come on, Brooksy, you playin' this game or not?' said Private Buxton, the shortest man in the battalion and hence

143

perversely known to the lads as Lofty. 'It's your turn, so what are yer gonna do?'

'Er, I dunno,' he muttered, having lost track of the game.

'Gor blimey, his mind ain't on the cards, is it?' said one of the other men.

'Thinkin' about his missus, I bet.'

'Yer know what 'appens to blokes who think about their wives too much,' said someone with lewd innuendo.

'Harder than a bobby's truncheon,' said another, causing a burst of raucous laughter.

'You lot 'ave got one-track minds,' said Claude, without taking offence since he was used to the male vulgarity of army life.

'Come on, let's get on with the game,' said Lofty.

'All right, I'll buy one.' The dealer handed Claude a card which he considered for a moment. 'Bust,' he said, relieved to be out of the game for he suddenly felt the need to write to Kate.

Leaving the others to continue, he went to his bed and began writing as best he could under the dim light of the oil lamp.

'Darling Kate,' he wrote, 'I love you so much and miss you something awful on this Christmas Day. You might have already written to tell me I'm a dad by now. I hope the nipper isn't running around before I get home.' He paused, meditatively chewing the end of his pencil and glancing around at the rows of men lying on their beds, smoking, playing cards, writing letters. Someone was playing 'Keep the Home Fires Burning' on the mouth organ. What could he tell her to make his letter interesting that would get past the censor? Nothing, he decided, so just concentrated on making sure she knew how much he loved her.

Claude's letters helped to sustain Kate. He never told her anything about what he was doing in France, but at least she knew he was safe. The winter seemed endless. Long bitter days, and freezing nights in her big empty bed. She seemed to catch one feverish cold after another which she passed on to Sam who became tetchy and fretful. What with Kate coughing

144

and Sam screaming, life was no picnic. But the strong sense of purpose bestowed on her by Sam's existence never faltered.

During the daytime, while the baby slept, she sewed hats. Despite the resistance put up by employers and unions towards women taking jobs traditionally done by men, as 1915 got underway to an extreme shortage of male labour, vacancies in office and transport work were being filled by women. This meant that there was plenty of millinery work about with so many regular women leaving the trade to do these new jobs which were better paid, even if the wages weren't the same as those given to men for exactly the same function.

As the hardship of winter yielded to spring, life became easier for Kate. While Sam thrived and was more content, her long spell of colds seemed to abate at last. Eager to take advantage of the milder weather, she hurried through her work and proudly walked Sam in his smart black perambulator to his doting grandmother in the afternoons. Sometimes they took him to the park or sat by the river in the sunshine, often in the company of Bertha who made a great fuss of Sam.

Letters continued to flow between Kate and Claude. His were always cheerful and even though the reports of casualties continued to come in, and wounded soldiers filled the streets in increasing numbers, he never mentioned anything about any fighting.

Then one spring day she received a rather cryptic note which said he was being moved and his letters might not be quite so regular for a while.

'I'll write when I can, but don't worry if you don't hear,' he said. 'I love you. Give Sam a hug for me and tell him I'll be home soon.'

Kate discussed her fears with her mother and Bertha. 'Do you think it means he's been sent to the front?'

'I shouldn't think so, dear,' said Gertie, who continued to be a tower of strength to her daughter in Claude's absence. 'He's probably just been moved to another camp.'

'Yeah, that'll be what it is, love,' agreed Bertha reassuringly. 'Claude'll be all right, don't you fret.'

And as though to confirm their theory, Sam gave one of his

gummy smiles which made them all laugh.

'Yes, I expect you're right,' said Kate.

As it happened, all three of them were wrong. Claude had scribbled that letter just before his battalion had left for the long march to the front. They were due to reinforce the weary troops who had been holding the salient around Ypres throughout the winter. Even if he had been allowed to tell Kate the truth, he would have spared her the worry.

Fresh and ready for battle, Claude's battalion were a smart, cheery bunch, singing as they marched, despite the heavy packs they carried on their backs. Trudging through mile upon mile of muddy countryside, they began to hear the distant rumble of artillery indicating that the front wasn't far away.

Despite hearty choruses of 'Pack Up Your Troubles', the signs of war became increasingly obvious. Huge stock piles of shells and tins of food; heavy artillery under camouflage or concealed among trees. More unnerving were the graveyards, and country houses and schools marked with large red crosses to indicate that they had been converted into hospitals.

At last they reached the communication trench and began to walk in single file up to the front. The gunfire grew louder, and they could see shells exploding in the direction of Ypres in the distance. Dead horses lay ominously by the track, and the landscape was torn and ravaged.

For all his eagerness to get into battle, Claude was nervous. His stomach had been griping throughout the journey, and now he wanted to vomit at the foul stench that permeated everything in the trenches which had names like 'Sniper's Alley' or 'Dead Man's Corner' painted on signs. It was a nauseating mixture of sweat, disinfectant, open latrines and rotting corpses which indicated that he had arrived at the front line on this April evening.

A young officer appeared to take charge of the new arrivals. In a brisk manner they were reminded that they were on a war footing and severe military penalties would be imposed for any dereliction of duty, such as desertion, cowardice or sleeping on sentry duty. To emphasise the gravity of this warning, he read out the names of some Tommies who had recently received the death penalty after court martial for such offences, along with the hour and date of each execution.

Claude's heart pounded and he felt the bile rise in his throat. His mates were unusually subdued too. But before anyone had time to say anything they were being shown to their dug-outs. Claude had often wondered how he would feel when it actually came to combat. Now he knew. He was shit-scared, and obviously wasn't the only one.

But the lads didn't stay downhearted for long. At least, not on the surface.

'Well, it ain't exactly the Ritz, is it?' said Lofty, managing to stir up a half-hearted ripple of nervous laughter.

'No, it bloody well ain't!' came a reply.

'What do yer think of the decor, lads?' said one man, looking round at the trench wall which was full of holes.

'Mud is all the rage,' laughed Claude, feeling better for finding the wit to crack a joke. 'I 'ear they're using it all over the front.'

'It'll never catch on in Shepherd's Bush,' said Lofty.

Camaraderie remained strong among the men despite their bowel-turning terror. Claude had never felt the same sort of bond with any of his friends at home. Must come from being part of a team, he supposed, and all in the same bloomin' boat.

The men began to settle in, unstrapping their backpacks. Some lit cigarettes, others just sat down and took the weight off their aching feet.

'Roll on tomorrow,' said Claude, for they had been told they were 'going over the top' sometime during the next day. 'The sooner we get on with the job, the sooner we'll be able to go 'ome.'

But something evil, that no soldier had ever experienced before, was already on its way towards them. A weapon so horrific it had caused guns to be abandoned and left an undefended gap in the line four miles long . . .

The sights and sound of battle were so different to those one might encounter in ordinary life, or even in training, that it wasn't easy to distinguish between the normal and the abnormal for those men who were new to the front.

So when Claude and his mates first heard the distant screams and howls, and the anguished cries in between breaks in the thunder of explosions and gunfire, it was a few minutes before they realised that something extraordinary was happening.

Then they saw it. A thick, yellow-grey cloud drifting towards them on the breeze. It was moving on the heels of crowds of terrified soldiers, desperately trying to escape, some staggering, some crawling, others vomiting as they stumbled. Men lay blind and choking on the ground, many writhing in agony.

Chaos broke out all around Claude. People were saying it was a gas attack but no one knew what to do. The young officer reappeared and hurriedly ordered the men to urinate into a sock and hold it over their nose as a protection.

Through the fog, Claude could see ambulances moving in among the banks of troops streaming back across the fields. But his eyes were smarting so badly his vision was severely impaired. A shell exploded nearby and Lofty began screaming as his arm was blown off at the elbow, a most terrible sight. The poor man was begging someone to help him as blood gushed from the wound.

Claude tried to reach him but his throat and chest were burning and he began to cough and retch, emptying his stomach, his whole body soaked with sweat and shivering uncontrollably. Everywhere men were falling to the ground, their screams of agony blasting his ear drums. He tried to run from the vapour as it closed around him, but his legs wouldn't move.

Then, with his little remaining vision, he saw an enemy infantryman looming towards him in the smoke, helmeted and masked, fixed bayonet at the ready.

Within seconds, Private Claude Brooks became a fatal statistic of war. Killed by a German bayonet without ever knowing the much-vaunted 'glory' of the battlefield.

It was autumn before Kate received official notification, confirming what she had feared ever since Claude's letters had stopped coming. All through those long months without news she had never lost faith that somehow he might still be alive. Now it was over, all hope wiped out by a few words on a slip of paper. A young man in the prime of life, rubbed out like a pencil mark. It just didn't make sense!

She was too shocked to feel anything much. There were no tears, just an awful numbness. She looked at Sam, sitting on the floor waving a teething ring, blissfully unaware of the drama unfolding around him. The fact that Claude would live on in his son was of little comfort to her at this moment.

'Well, I'm all you've got now, boy,' she said, lifting him up and hugging him. Then, with aching weariness, she got ready to go and break the sad news to her mother.

Managing alone was no problem to Kate from a practical point of view because she had got used to it while Claude had been away. It was the grief she found unbearable. When her wits fully returned, his loss registered like a body blow. It was the first thing she thought of when she woke in the morning and the last thing on her mind when she went to sleep.

When the ache didn't seem to lessen, she decided it might be easier to build a new life for herself and Sam away from the flat in Jarman Street where memories of Claude impregnated every square inch. The place had always felt more like his grandmother's home than hers anyway. Now there was no reason to stay here. She didn't need to live in a shrine to keep her husband's memory alive. That would go with her wherever she went.

With the money she earned for her millinery work added to her army pension, she was able to afford a two-roomed flat in a house a few doors from her mother to whom she had become very close since Sam's birth. Claude's grandmother's furniture was sold and replaced with some pieces more to her own taste that she managed to get second hand. A light wood table and chairs, a small sideboard, a cheerful cretonne-covered sofa and armchairs. All very basic, but at least she had chosen them herself.

A little improvisation and a great deal of elbow grease soon had the place looking more like a home than the flat in Jarman Street ever had.

She was well settled in by Christmas, the second of the war. They made a real effort for Sam's sake, even though he wasn't old enough to understand. At a year old, he was an adorable little chap who had begun to take his first tottering steps, to loud approval from his adoring elders.

He laughed and played and cheered them all up, deriving far more pleasure from the paper the gifts were wrapped in than the presents themselves. Although this Christmas was very sad for Kate, it was less fraught than last year when Sam had been so tiny and frail.

It didn't seem right to feel happy with poor Claude buried in a foreign field somewhere. But when Sam let out one of his fat chuckles, it was simply impossible not to smile.

Whilst the war brought misery and heartache, it also offered women opportunities they had never had before. Chances to work outside the home became more widespread after conscription for men was introduced in the new year. Women were needed in greater numbers and for more varied work, as the shortage of men worsened.

'I'd get a job meself if it wasn't for my Georgie,' said Bertha one day in the spring. 'Ruby's left school and is workin' in a baker's shop now, but Georgie's still only eight and I wouldn't like 'im to come 'ome to an empty place after school.'

'You've already got a job,' Gertie reminded her.

'I know that, but I'd like to do somethin' a bit more interestin' now that there's more chances around for us gels,' she explained. 'Anyway, goin' out to work is a bloomin' sight more fun that bein' stuck indoors all day sewin', I can tell yer.'

'What sort of thing did you have in mind?'

'I wouldn't mind goin' on the buses,' she explained, her eyes bright with enthusiasm. 'They're looking for women, and I've 'eard the pay's good. Better than we get makin' 'ats anyway.'

'A conductress, you mean?'

'That's right,' said Bertha. 'I really fancy the idea o' that.'

'It could be quite rough, I should think, with all the riff-raff they get on buses.'

'Wouldn't worry me, mate. I'd soon sort any trouble-makers out,' said Bertha. 'And if you're takin' home decent pay, yer don't mind goin' to a bit o' trouble for it, do yer? I was talkin' to a woman in the market the other day. She reckons 'er family ain't never eaten so well as since she's been out at work.'

'Really?'

'Yeah, it's true.'

'Get away . . .'

'What about you, Gert? You ain't tied down with kids nor nothin'. Wouldn't you like to go out to work?'

'I certainly wouldn't want to work on the buses,' she said, appalled.

'There's lots of other things yer can do,' Bertha told her eagerly. 'They need women in the munitions factories, and as railway porters. Why, they even have female undertakers these days.' She paused thoughtfully. 'They're looking for post-women, so I've 'eard. Why don't yer go down the sorting office and find out about it?'

'I'm quite happy sewing at home, thanks,' said Gertie dismissively.

'You 'ave to be up early in the morning for the post, though,' Bertha went on, far too keen on the subject to be deterred by Gertie's apparent lack of interest, 'but you're finished by dinner time, with the rest of the day to yerself. That would suit me a treat if I didn't 'ave to be at 'ome first thing to get young Georgie off to school.'

'Mmm,' murmured Gertie thoughtfully, an idea gaining momentum in her mind despite her attempts to stifle it.

Gertie tried to put it out of her mind. She really didn't want to leave the house at some unearthly hour to deliver the mail in all weathers, probably catching her death of cold. No, the whole idea was ridiculous. It wouldn't be right for a woman of her breeding to be out on the streets at the crack of dawn.

But it could be quite dull working at home, and even middle-class women had jobs these days. After all, putting linings into hats could hardly be called a top-drawer occupation.

But no, the idea simply wasn't on. She was too old for one thing, she'd be forty next year, and a grandmother at that. It was good pay, though. Just think what she could do if she had a bit more money! She might even be able to afford to brighten up the flat with a few nick-nacks. And imagine being able to treat young Sam . . .

It could solve Bertha's problem, too, she thought, growing more excited by the moment. If she herself was free in the afternoons to look after Georgie when he got home from school, Bertha could go and work on the buses. *And* she'd be able to go to the park with Kate and Sam without worrying about all the hats she should be doing. Thinking of hats made her look at the pile of them waiting for attention. Hours and hours of stitching till her fingers were sore and her shoulders ached.

There was no harm in making a few enquiries at the post office. That wouldn't commit her to anything. But even as she made plans, her courage was already ebbing away. Sewing linings into hats in the unchallenging environment of her own four walls was one thing. Actually 'going out to work' was a much more frightening prospect altogether.

# Chapter Nine

One day in May Kate answered the door to a woman dressed neatly in a navy blue uniform, her hair tucked into a matching straw hat.

'Mother,' she said uncertainly, 'why are you dressed as a postwoman?'

'Because that's what I am,' explained Gertie, who seemed to have shed about ten years. 'I've just finished my first deliveries.'

'Well, you are a dark horse,' said Kate, standing aside looking bemused as her mother swept in, having apparently found a new lease of life.

'It was rather devious of me not to say anything,' Gertie confessed, 'but I wanted to wait until I'd actually worked my first session, just in case I lost my nerve and didn't turn up at the sorting office.'

'Congratulations,' said an astonished Kate.

Her mother grinned and gave a girlish twirl. 'How do I look in uniform?'

'Fantastic.' And Kate wasn't only referring to the blue serge skirt and cape.

'And what does my best boy think of his grannie?' Gertie said, scooping Sam up from the floor where he was playing with his toy water-waggon.

'If he was old enough, he'd think that there's more to his grannie than meets the eye,' Kate said in reply.

As the months passed Kate witnessed a transformation in her mother whose interest in life expanded along with her confidence. She became healthier too. The extra walking and fresh air improved her appetite and complexion, rounding her gauntness into a softer appearance.

Kate began to feel quite envious of her and Bertha when they came home from work, bursting with stories from the outside world and clutching fatter paypackets than Kate could ever hope to earn as an outworker for a millinery firm.

But since she wasn't prepared to leave Sam in the care of a stranger while she went out to work, she accepted her lot cheerfully. Her mother's change of lifestyle proved to be practically beneficial to her too, because Gertie was free in the afternoons to take Sam off her hands for an hour or so while Kate got on with her work unhampered.

Almost without her being aware it was happening, Kate was becoming obsessive in her maternal expectations for Sam, driving herself to do more work than she could comfortably cope with so that he should have things she wouldn't otherwise be able to afford. The quality of his clothes by far outclassed those worn by the other neighbourhood children, and she was fanatical about providing him with a nourishing diet.

'You spoil that boy,' her mother often warned her. 'There's no point in giving him things you have to kill yourself to afford.'

'There's nothing wrong with my doing my best for him.'

'Of course not, dear,' agreed Gertie, 'but you're a millinery worker, not a marchioness.'

'You've certainly changed your tune,' Kate pointed out frankly. 'The time was when I had to remind you of that!'

'Yes . . . well . . . a lot of water has flowed under the bridge since war broke out,' said Gertie. 'I suppose I've finally learned to accept things as they really are, and keep my head out of the clouds.'

'That's the difference between us,' said Kate lightly, but taking the opportunity to make a valid point. 'You were being unrealistic in trying to cling on to how life was in the past. I'm just making the most of every opportunity in the present to make a better life for Sam, within my limitations.'

'Be careful you don't become a martyr to your cause,' warned Gertie.

'I don't care what I become as long as Sam gets the benefit,' said Kate forcefully. 'I'd work night and day for that boy.'

'Yes, I know you would,' said Gertie, her brows drawing together in a frown.

Time passed and still the war dragged on. Sympathy for bereaved families began to wear thin after the Battle of the Somme when those in mourning by far outweighed those who were not. Food became short as reserves ran out and German submarines continued to bomb the supply ships coming in from abroad, causing most of the food to end up at the bottom of the sea.

Steps were taken to produce more food at home. Hillsides and public parks were used to grow vegetables; waste ground in urban areas was rented out in small sections as allotments to tenement dwellers on condition that they grew food; city girls joined the specially formed Land Army in droves to work on the land to replace the farm-hands who were away fighting.

Whilst all these measures helped, they were still not enough, and rationing was finally introduced for some items. Food that was not put on ration was often in short supply, and queues trailed from many shops and market stalls. When tea was added to the list of rationed goods, the British public really cursed the Germans.

Air raids increased in the autumn of 1917. Gertie would usually appear at Kate's place at the onset of a raid and they would hurry downstairs to take shelter with a neighbour on the ground floor until the danger had passed.

Esme was rarely around. It would take more than an army of Zeppelins to interfere with her social life. Making the most of women's new freedom, most evenings she was out dancing with some soldier on leave in one of the many nightspots that were flourishing in London.

Gertie was often heard to complain of her wild, hedonistic daughter who smoked cigarettes in public, rode through the streets on a bicycle, and seemed to change boyfriends as often as her underwear. When they heard of the death at the front of the first of these, Syd from Stepney, they were all sad.

'Poor old Syd,' said Esme. 'He was a sweet boy, even if he was a bit of a twerp.'

'It's high time you settled down, my girl,' her mother would say. 'Or you'll end up as a spinster, left on the shelf.'

'No thanks,' was the standard reply. 'I'm not going to sit at home every night pining for someone who might never come back from the war. No point in getting too fond of anyone, in my opinion.'

Reports of casualties in France continued and still there seemed to be no sign of an end to the fighting. The collapse of Russia was a blow to the Allies, but would have been a great deal worse had America not already joined the war.

In August 1918, British troops joined forces with the Canadians, Australians, Americans, Belgians and French in a combined effort to burst through German defences. Despite the success of this exercise, it was still November before the Armistice came.

As the clocks struck eleven in London on that memorable day, the metropolis erupted into celebration. Almost the entire population poured on to the streets to celebrate against a deafening clatter of trumpets, church bells, police whistles, dustbin lids, and anything else that could be blown, banged or rattled.

Kate and the family went up West with Bertha and her children where every square inch was vibrant with jubilant crowds. There were fireworks and flags; bunting and balloons. People danced and sang and cheered from the roofs of department stores.

Back in Hammersmith that evening, impromptu parties were underway all over town. It was a wonderful day, but tinged with sadness for Kate as she remembered another party organised by Claude when war was declared. How many widows of servicemen of all nationalties, with children to raise alone, would be sharing a moment of regret with her now, and wondering if it had all been worth the price they had had to pay?

The government's plan to release men gradually from the

services when there were jobs available for them failed miserably because soldiers wanted to come home straight away. Many of them got back to find that in return for their service to their country, they were out of work with nowhere to live.

In February the Potters, excluding Esme, and the Brents all became victims of the influenza epidemic, more or less simultaneously. Being the only fit person among them, it fell to Esme to take time off from work to look after them all.

To make it easier for her, Gertie moved in with Kate but Esme still had to run back and forth to Bertha's place with sustenance for the invalids. They didn't go to the expense of calling in the doctor because everyone knew that you had to go to bed and take aspirin. Horrific rumours were circulating about thousands dying from the disease.

'I'll be glad to get back to work. It'll be a damned sight easier than looking after you lot,' Esme complained jovially as she administered aspirin, emptied bowls, made broth and endlessly kept them all supplied with drinks. 'But I can't very well leave you to die of neglect, can I? Now come on, Sam, try to manage some of this nice broth that your Auntie Esme has made for you . . . And how are you feeling now, Mother? Your head's still aching, is it? All right, I'll get a cool flannel for you to put on it . . . Well, Sam, let's make a deal. I'll read you a story if you eat your broth . . .'

That was Esme. Beneath that frivolous, selfish front beat a heart that cared.

March was underway before the invalids were up and about again, whereupon Esme herself went down with the dreaded bug. But as she so shrewdly put it, 'I've got the best of the deal because there's all of you to look after just one of little ole me. I shall make the most of it by languishing in bed, demanding your attention . . .'

Being laid up with 'flu proved to be very expensive for Kate and Gertie as neither was paid if she didn't work. Gertie's job at the post office had ended with the war and she was stitching hats for a living again. To help recoup their losses, she drew on the savings she had accumulated during her time on the post, insisting on helping Kate too. The latter gratefully accepted, but drove herself even harder as soon as she was well enough to thread a needle again.

The episode caused Kate to voice an opinion that had been at the back of her mind for some time.

'I ought to be working for myself, you know,' she said wistfully, 'instead of making hats for someone else all day.'

'You still wouldn't get sick pay,' Gertie pointed out.

'No, but at least I'd be able to make enough money when I was working to put something by for such eventualities.'

'What exactly do you have in mind?'

'I'd like to run my own business,' she explained dreamily. 'You know, have my own hat-shop and workroom, and design and make my own hats.'

'It's a nice idea.'

'Once I got established, you could work for me for a decent wage instead of boosting Maple's profits,' said Kate, tapping her chin meditatively with her thimbled finger

'Such is the stuff of dreams,' said Gertie, deliberately trying to stem the tide of her daughter's rising enthusiasm.

'I'm sure I could make a success of it,' Kate continued, warming to her theme. 'I've got the practical experience, and a good head for design. I've proved that by re-modelling our hats.'

'You're not serious about this though, are you?' said Gertie, sensing disappointment ahead for her daughter.

'I certainly think it's worth considering.'

'The idea is good but without capital you won't even get started.'

'I wouldn't need a huge amount.'

'Maybe not, but you'd need something behind you,' opined Gertie. 'If you want to do model millinery you'd have to have premises in the West End or you'd never get established. Then there's equipment and materials and so on. And you'd have to have something to live on until you start to make money. These things take time, and with Sam to support you can't afford to be reckless.'

'Perhaps I could apply for a bank loan?' Kate suggested impulsively.

'You don't have a bank account.'

'I would have if they loaned me the money!'

'That isn't the way banks operate and you know it,' admonished Gertie. 'And even if it was, they'd be very unlikely to take a chance on a woman setting up in business.'

'The war has changed things, Mother,' Kate reminded her. 'Women over thirty even have the vote now.'

'But where are the women who did men's jobs during the war?' Gertie asked rhetorically. 'Back home, or doing menial work again.'

'True enough,' Kate admitted, 'but we do have a little more freedom.'

'That won't change a banker's attitude towards a female trying to set up in business,' said her mother, shaking her head gravely.

'But if I could find some rundown premises to rent and do up, that would cut costs,' Kate continued eagerly. 'And I'd work without staff at first.'

Gertie chewed her lip worriedly, convinced the idea was doomed to failure. 'You'd do well to forget all about it and carry on as you are,' she said. 'At least you have an income, which is vital when you've a child to support. It would be different if you had no dependants, you could be more adventurous then.'

'It's for Sam I'd be doing it,' Kate explained determinedly. 'I mean, how can I give him a decent life the way things are now? About all I can afford to do is feed and clothe him, and that will always be a struggle, working the way I do at the moment. I'll never be able to get us into better accommodation unless drastic changes are made.'

Her mother's heart sank at the resolute look in her daughter's eye.

'I didn't realise you'd been seriously harbouring such ideas.'

'I haven't. It was being off sick that really opened my eyes to the insecurity of living from hand to mouth.' Kate paused to draw breath. 'When you think of all the profit we've made for the Maples, so that they can live in a big house near the park while we rot away in cold draughty rooms!'

'No point in dwelling on that.'

'I tell you this much, Mother,' Kate said firmly, 'somehow I'll get Sam out of these damp rooms. One day I'll do what I promised years ago and get us all back into the square.'

'But if the bank won't . . .'

'If the bank won't help, then I'll be forced to sit on the idea for a while,' she admitted. 'But I'll do it eventually. It might not be tomorrow but I can assure you, it *will* happen.'

She made an appointment with the manager of their nearest bank who treated her request with a kind of arrogant bewilderment.

'So you have no bank account and no property?' he said, as though she'd just admitted to being resident in an asylum. 'And you want me to lend you the money to set up in business?'

'That's right,' she said without any real hope. 'I have a talent for millinery and a great deal of practical experience. I know I could be a successful milliner if only I had the capital to get started.'

He treated her to a heartfelt sneer. 'No doubt you have, my dear,' he said witheringly. 'Unfortunately, we would need something a little more concrete before we could consider backing you in this venture.'

She took his point even if she didn't see the necessity for him to be quite so supercilious in making it. One day he'll be courting my custom, she thought. One day . . .

The first palais-de-dance opened in Hammersmith and started a national trend. Known as the Hammersmith Palais, it was a recreational wonder where people from all walks of life could meet informally and participate in the dance mania that was sweeping the country.

Packed to the doors every night, it had softly lit alcoves surrounding a sprung dance floor. Wide stairs curved up to a balcony where spectators could enjoy a drink in comfort whilst

160

tapping their feet to the syncopated rhythm and watching the steps of the new dances being neatly executed on the crowded dance-floor below.

As respectable widows, Kate and Gertie did not feel able to sample its pleasures, but Esme couldn't get enough of the place. It was here she met a dashing ex-pilot from the Royal Flying Corps called Johnny Betts. With his thick copper-coloured hair and laughing brown eyes, he captivated Esme from the moment she set eyes on him. From the second he swept her on to the dance-floor, she never so much as looked at another man.

He was a public school type who earned his living buying and selling property. With Johnny as gregarious as Esme, they were perfectly suited, both considering an evening spent at home as tantamount to social failure. He seemed to be as smitten with her as she was with him, wooing her determinedly with no expense spared. She was treated to dinner at all the best places, good seats at the theatre, lavish bouquets of flowers.

Kate and her mother observed all this anxiously, hoping this romance would go the same way as all the others. For, as charming as Johnny was, he had one vice which in their eyes ruled him out as a suitable husband for Esme.

He was a gambler and made no secret of it. 'I had a good hand the other night,' he'd say proudly, presenting Esme with some extravagant present. It was obvious from his manner that he played cards for high stakes.

'You can't marry a man with those sort of habits,' Kate warned her, for her sister's intentions were obvious.

'Oh. Why not?' she wanted to know.

'I should have thought that was obvious,' said Kate. 'You of all people taking up with a gambler, after what Daddy did.'

'So what if Johnny does enjoy a little flutter now and then?' she said defensively. 'It doesn't mean he's going to end up like Daddy.'

'He has more than a little flutter,' said Kate. 'And you know it!'

'So according to you,' snapped Esme, 'I shouldn't love him?'

'I wouldn't go so far as to say that, but I certainly think you should be very careful about involving yourself further with him.'

'At least Johnny isn't sly about it like Daddy was,' Esme defended hotly. 'Anyway, I can't let what happened to Daddy rule my life.'

'And I can't approve of your marriage to him,' said Kate.

'Who's asking you to? You're my sister, not my keeper. I'm over twenty-one and can marry who I like.'

Kate smarted at the truth of her statement. Being protective towards her younger sister had become a habit born of Esme's delicate childhood. 'I can't argue with that,' she admitted, 'but because I care about what happens to you, I feel duty bound to remind you of the risk you take if you marry a compulsive gambler.'

'Oh, for God's sake!' said Esme, eyes glistening with angry tears. 'You're carrying on like some maiden aunt. Anyone would think he was a convicted murderer to hear you talk.'

'No, I'm not . . .'

'Yes, you are, and I want no more of it,' she ranted furiously. 'All right, so Johnny likes to play cards for money, but that doesn't mean he isn't a good man. He's very sweet-natured, as a matter of fact, and if he asks me, I'll marry him. I shall jump at the chance. There's nothing you or Mother can do about it. Do you understand?'

'Perfectly,' said Kate.

Unable to quell her fears for Esme, Kate arranged to meet Johnny, unbeknown to her sister. They met in the West End one day while Sam was at school. Johnny insisted on taking her to an hotel for lunch.

'So what's all this about?' he asked, after a waiter had served them with beef consommé.

'My sister seems to be completely besotted by you,' Kate said frankly.

'Yes, isn't it wonderful?' he said, smiling so warmly it was easy to see why Esme had fallen for him.

'Well, I suppose it's something that her feelings seem to be reciprocated.'

He frowned. 'Was there ever any doubt in your mind about that, then?'

'I wasn't sure,' she said. 'You don't seem the marrying type.'

He sipped a glass of wine, observing her with interest. 'I don't suppose I was until I met Esme.'

'And suddenly you feel the nesting instinct?'

'Not necessarily,' he said firmly. 'I want to marry Esme because I love her and want to be with her, not because I have a sudden longing to become a pipe and slippers man.'

Kate found herself somewhat deflated by his honesty. 'Surely marriage demands a certain change of lifestyle?'

'Well, obviously.' He paused. 'But what are you getting at, exactly? I feel as though I'm being vetted by some Victorian father.'

'Gambling,' she announced. 'Would you be willing to give it up for Esme?'

'I don't know. That's the honest answer,' he said, meeting her gaze challengingly. 'Esme has never indicated that she wants me to, so I've not thought about it.'

'Would you if . . .'

'I certainly wouldn't do so because her sister suggests that I ought to,' he interrupted sharply.

Kate was surprised by his refusal to seek favour with her. She'd imagined him making promises just to smooth his path into the family, even if he had no intention of keeping them. 'So you wouldn't be prepared to give it up for her sake?'

'I don't see why I should commit myself to anything when I'm asked to do so by someone with no right to ask.'

'She *is* my sister.'

'Yes, and I can understand your caring about her,' he said, 'but I love Esme and have no intention of harming her.'

'You will if you continue to gamble,' said Kate, her cheeks burning. 'Apart from anything else, it's illegal.'

'There are worse vices,' he said mildly. 'I could be a womaniser or a drunk.'

'True. You could also be an ordinary respectable member of

the community,' she said cuttingly.

His face tightened as her remark hit home. 'You just can't bear it that your sister has found happiness, can you?' he rasped. 'When you don't have a man of your own . . .'

'That has nothing to do with it. My father . . .'

'Esme has told me all about your father,' he said, a touch scornfully. 'And I can see how all Potter problems are automatically blamed on him.'

'How dare you?'

'What's the matter, Kate,' he interjected, 'are you jealous because your sister has fallen in love and you're still struggling on alone?'

'I'm not alone. I have Sam and my mother.'

'That's hardly what I'm talking about.'

'I manage very well, thank you.'

'Managing and being happy are two different things,' he said. 'Frankly, I think you're using my gambling as an excuse to come between us.'

'Why should I want to do that?'

'I don't know,' he said with that unnerving frankness of his. 'It must be envy, I suppose. You've had a rough time, losing your husband and being left to bring up a child alone. The fact that Esme has found someone to love her and move her back up in the world must be hard for you to take.'

'That isn't fair . . .'

'It may not be fair, but I bet I'm right,' he said. 'I haven't known you long, but it's been long enough to realise that you are obsessively keen to get back to the sort of lifestyle you were robbed of by your father. Esme has told me you'd start up in business if you had the money.'

'So I'd like to better myself. That doesn't mean I'm obsessed,' she denied. 'I have a son. Are you suggesting I shouldn't strive to improve his circumstances?'

'Not at all, as long as you don't get so screwed up about what your father deprived you of, you feel you have the right to interfere in other people's lives.'

'If my father hadn't done what he did, a lot of people's lives would be different.'

Her tone was so vehement, he narrowed his eyes thought-fully. 'Why do you think so little of yourself, Kate?'

'I don't know what you mean.'

'Oh, yes, you do,' he said, observing her closely. 'You're full of self-hatred even though you keep it well hidden beneath a show of confidence. It's almost as though you're trying to make up to Sam for something that wasn't your fault.'

He was, of course, referring to her father's misdeeds, but what he said was true, albeit in another way. When she'd been married to Claude, memories of the rape and its consequences had been easier to bear. Without his love to support and strengthen her, she was constantly plagued by self-doubt.

Johnny was right about her motives, if wrong about her reasons. In wanting the best for Sam she was trying to atone for the past and the way she had failed her firstborn son. 'You're letting your imagination run away with you,' she said sharply. 'I only want what any caring mother would want for her child.'

'Perhaps, but you shouldn't live your life only for him.'

'And why not?' she rasped.

'Because children grow up and go away, and you are still a young woman.'

'How I live my life is none of your business,' she snapped.

'You're quite right, it isn't,' he agreed. 'But I think you should get your own life sorted out before you consider yourself qualified to interfere in other people's.'

She put down her spoon and reached to the floor for her handbag, preparing to leave.

'Running away from the truth won't change anything.'

'There's no point in my staying as you're clearly not pre-pared to discuss any sort of sense as regards my sister,' she said.

'Like what?' he asked, his eyes dark with anger now. 'Either I stop gambling or you try to stop Esme from marrying me?'

'I shall remind her of the insecurity of life with an inveterate gambler, certainly,' said Kate. 'Whether or not she'll listen is another matter.'

'I don't like being threatened,' he said.

She folded her linen napkin and placed it on the table. 'And

I don't enjoy having my private life poked into by a stranger.'

'Just one thing before you go . . .'

'Yes?'

'I'll lend you the money you need to start up in business, if you like.'

She gave him a cynical smile. 'Well, well. So you won't be threatened and I won't be bought.'

He looked genuinely surprised, she had to give him that. 'That wasn't why I offered,' he said. 'I happen to believe that Esme will marry me whatever you say to her, so you can go ahead and do your worst.'

'Why did you offer then?'

'I'm not short of money and you are,' he said. 'It's as simple as that.'

'Thanks, but I'd sooner stay poor than use money that had been won in a card game.'

'I do actually earn money legitimately too, you know,' he reminded her.

'No thanks,' she said, and marched away with the distinct impression that she would live to regret this meeting.

A month later Johnny and Esme were married. It was a small wedding to which Kate was not invited after Johnny told Esme about their meeting.

'Stay out of my life, you interfering bitch!' Esme had snarled at her sister. 'I don't want you to come anywhere near Johnny and me – meddling and trying to spoil things!'

Kate deeply regretted having allowed her concern for her sister to cause her to interfere. A parting of the ways was the last thing she'd wanted. But all her apologies proved to be ineffective. Esme remained adamant, despite their mother's very best endeavours to put things right between her daughters. Esme said she didn't want to see her busybody of a sister again, *ever*.

The couple moved into a pleasant house in Lilac Gardens, Kensington. It wasn't in quite the same league as Sycamore Square but it was a sight more salubrious than Dane Street according to Gertie who kept Kate informed.

Doggedly refusing to give up hope, she sent cards and presents on the birth of the couple's children: Ronnie who was born at the end of the year, and Rita a year later. She deeply regretted the fact that Sam could not see his cousins for as an only child he was often lonely. He was growing into a bright boy, though, and had a consuming interest in aeroplanes, something which could be directly attributed to Johnny. The lad pored over picture books about aircraft for hours and talked a lot about being a pilot when he grew up.

Since most little boys had dreams of driving trains or flying planes, Kate wasn't unduly worried. Fortunately the sensible ones grew out of such fanciful notions and became accountants or solicitors. That was the sort of respectable profession she wanted for Sam. If she worked very hard to pay for his training, maybe such a career would be possible for him.

For all that Gertie had changed for the better, she was still not naturally altruistic. But whereas once she had been able to turn away from some poor unfortunate needing help in the street, without the slightest compunction, nowadays it was more difficult. In her days as a Kensington lady, she had blinded herself to life's no-hopers out of sheer arrogance. Now it was inhibition that held her back, a fear of getting involved in something unsavoury with which she was not equipped to deal.

To ease her conscience, she would sometimes drop a coin into the hat of some begging ex-serviceman but anything more than that made her cringe. Some people were born do-gooders, she told herself. She wasn't one of them.

But one day in the autumn of 1922, she was drawn into an embarrassing incident in Hammersmith Broadway that turned her theory on its head.

She'd popped out for some shopping and to take a pair of Sam's shoes to the bootmender's for Kate who was snowed under with work. Passing a sweetshop and seeing the glass jars in the window, gleaming invitingly with aniseed balls and sugary pear drops, she couldn't resist going in for a ha'porth of mint bull's eyes for Sam.

The subject under discussion in the shop was the death of

Marie Lloyd which had been announced in the papers that morning.

'Only fifty-two,' said someone in the queue.

'No great age.'

'We won't 'alf miss 'er.'

'There ain't no one else like 'er, and that's a fact.'

Gertie took her turn at the counter, enjoying the tantalising aroma of liquorice and aniseed while the aproned shopkeeper weighed out the black and white boiled sweets on brass scales. The man emptied the confectionery from the scale into a small paper cone, folded the top over and handed it to Gertie, who paid the money and left. Outside she guiltily popped one of Sam's favourites into her own mouth before continuing on her way along the crowded shopping street.

Passing the Electric Palace Cinema, she noticed there was a Mary Pickford film currently showing. She made a mental note to mention it to Bertha for there was nothing the two of them liked better than a night out at the pictures if they could afford it.

'Can yer spare us the price of a cuppa tea, missus?' asked a rough female voice from behind her.

Swinging round, Gertie found herself confronted by a toothless, emaciated old woman dressed in a dirty torn coat and woolly hat, her face matching her filthy clothes.

Almost retching on the potent mixture of gin, unwashed clothes and sweat that reached her, Gertie stepped back quickly, irritated to have been approached in this way. She wanted to walk on without saying a word, but conscience manifested itself in an angry retort. 'Why should I give you money?'

'Because I'm cold and 'ungry,' came the simple reply.

Oh, really, these down-and-outs were the limit, Gertie fumed silently. How dare they intimidate decent people in this apalling way? They should learn to look after themselves and earn money for their food like decent people. 'And I'm supposed to give you my hardearned cash, am I?' she said furiously.

'Just enough for a cuppa tea,' said the woman.

'I'm not made of money, you know.'

'Compared to me yer are,' the woman croaked, shivering and pointing a bony hand towards Gertie's shopping basket.

'London is full of people down on their luck,' she said. 'And if I give to all of you, how am I supposed to pay my rent, you tell me that.'

'All right, keep yer 'air on, missus,' the woman said dully, her terrible pallor seeming to turn a greyish-green as she spoke. 'You keep yer rotten dough. I wouldn't want anythin' from a stuck-up cow like you. I've got me pride, yer know.'

Gertie walked away, glad to be rid of the smelly old hag. Damn' woman! She should spend the money she did have on food instead of gin. How on earth could people allow themselves to sink to such depths? Somewhere at the back of her mind, though, a reproachful voice nagged. She saw her own face superimposed on that of the woman. Was that what she would have come to after Cyril's death if it hadn't been for her daughters, Kate in particular? For how long would she have managed to keep a roof over her head in her feeble-minded state, if someone else hadn't looked out for her?

Annoyed with herself for entertaining such bothersome thoughts, she marched on. But her feet were leaden and wouldn't move. Heaving an exasperated sigh, she turned to see the woman slumped on the pavement outside the butcher's shop with her head leaning back against the wall and her eyes closed. People were passing by, uncaring of her plight.

Hurriedly, Gertie retraced her steps. 'Are you not feeling well?' she asked.

The woman's bloodshot eyes flickered open. 'Not feelin' well?' she said in a mocking tone. 'That's a good 'un, mate. I ain't felt well for years.'

'Here, have one of these,' said Gertie, offering her a boiled sweet. 'The sugar might make you feel better.'

The woman held out a shaky hand, but the sweet fell to the ground simultaneously with her face becoming even paler. As Gertie reached down to offer her a hand, the woman began to bring up a vile-smelling bile.

'Disgusting,' said a passer-by.

'Drunk and disorderly,' said another. 'She wants locking away.'

All Gertie wanted at that moment was to be as far away from this dreadful old woman as possible. But for some reason she heard herself saying defensively, 'She's ill. She needs help.'

'Don't let her fool yer, ducks,' said the butcher, appearing in the doorway of his shop wearing a striped apron and straw hat. 'She's always 'anging round 'ere, as drunk as a lord.' He looked down at the woman. 'Clear orf out of it, yer baggage. I don't want the likes of you cluttering up the pavement outside my shop, putting decent folks off their food. You're bad for business, you are, makin' a mess in a public place and leavin' hardworkin' people to clear up after yer.'

Feeling a trap close tightly around her, Gertie took the woman's trembling hand and helped her to her feet. 'You leave her to me,' she said to the butcher.

'You want yer 'ead examined, missus,' he said.

Moving away from the cruel tongue of the man, Gertie said, 'You can't stay here.'

''e can't keep me orf a public 'ighway,' said the woman.

'Maybe not, but you need to be inside in the warm somewhere,' Gertie told her. 'Is there nowhere at all you can go for shelter?'

'The people at the Institute'll take me in,' she said, holding tightly to Gertie's hand for support. 'They're good to me round there.'

'Where is it?'

'In Town Street.'

'We'd better go there then,' said Gertie.


'We do what we can for old Jessie,' said Marjorie Prescott, a softly spoken woman who was in charge at the Clarke Institute. She had greeted the destitute female kindly and handed her over to a middle-aged woman in a pinafore who was serving tea from an urn to a bunch of dubious-looking characters in a spartan hall down the corridor from the office, 'but whatever money she does manage to steal or beg just goes on gin. About all we can do is to give her shelter during her last days.'

'Is she very old?'

'I don't know her age but she's probably not as old as she looks,' the woman explained. 'She's drinking herself into the grave. I suppose the gin is a comfort to her in her miserable existence.'

Gertie felt shaken. 'Has she no family?'

'If she has they wouldn't want to know her in this state.'

'How has she come to such deprivation?'

'Difficult to say.' Marjorie Prescott brushed back a strand of ginger hair that had escaped from her bun. 'I think she was married once – she rambles on about it sometimes when she's drunk. Her husband either died or deserted her, and she was probably thrown out of her home when she couldn't pay the rent. I gather she's been living rough for years.' She sighed. 'Oh, well, one does what one can within the limited resources we have available.'

'Do you run the Institute?' asked Gertie.

'Much of the time, though it's officially the responsibility of a Catholic priest. He's always being called out on some errand of mercy or other, so I fill in for him. I'm here most days.'

'How did this place come into being?'

'It was started early in the century by a businessman of a philanthropic nature.'

'The work must be very depressing for you,' observed Gertie.

'The lack of donations and helpers is depressing,' said Marjorie, a pale, serene woman, 'but the actual work is very satisfying.' She sighed again. 'And funnily enough, it can be quite enjoyable.'

'Really?' said Gertie in surprise. 'That hardly seems possible.'

'Oh, yes, there's a lot of humour in these people,' she explained. 'Unfortunately, not enough of the better off are interested in doing something without financial reward, so we're terribly short of volunteers.'

'I suppose most people can't afford to work for nothing,' Gertie pointed out. 'We all have to pay the rent, after all.'

'Yes, I realise that, and I know it's easy for me to do unpaid

171

work since I have a rich husband to support me. But there are many women in similar circumstances to me who wouldn't be seen dead anywhere near this place.'

'Perhaps they have other commitments,' suggested Gertie, still struggling not to become involved.

'I expect they have,' said Marjorie. 'But most people have a few hours a week to spare.'

'Is that all the time you would expect of a helper?' asked Gertie.

'If that's all the time someone has to offer, I welcome them with open arms.'

'Well, I do have a living to earn,' Gertie heard herself say, 'but I'm sure I can find some time during the course of a week to help you out.'

# PART TWO

# Chapter Ten

Young Laurence Dexter's stomach lurched as he opened the back garden gate, returning from an errand, to see a ball whizzing towards the living-room window. His poor heart almost stopped beating altogether at the ensuing crash and splintering of glass. Oh dear, this would send Mother into one of her rages, and it wouldn't be the perpetrator of the accident, his brother Giles, who would be in the firing line.

The boy shuddered at the thought of the recriminations ahead, for he lived in constant fear of his parents, especially his mother who terrified him more than Father despite all the lashings he administered with his belt.

His mother's obvious dislike of him caused Laurence intense suffering. He felt it like a body blow every day of his life. Scorn, irritation, and even downright hatred flowed from her in a steady stream, even if she wasn't cross with him about anything in particular. For some unknown reason, he seemed to annoy her just by being around, and always had as far as he could remember. Yet his brother, who was a year younger, could do no wrong in their parents' eyes.

Earlier on that day, Laurence had reminded Giles of Mother's rule prohibiting the use of the ball in the garden. He'd told him to take it to the park or the common if he wanted to play with it. But Giles had ignored the warning, as usual. Recklessness came easy to him because he knew he would not be blamed if anything went wrong.

'Now see what you've done,' rebuked Laurence. He had been sent by his mother to the pillar box to post some letters. Odd jobs and messages were tasks that always fell to him rather than Giles. 'I told you not to play with the ball in the garden.'

'Oh, shut up, you beastly prig,' said Giles, a pale, thin-lipped boy with fair hair and button grey eyes. 'I bet you play ball in the garden when no one is looking.'

'No, I don't,' said Laurence truthfully. He was far too frightened of his parents to disobey them.

Cissy Dexter appeared at the back door. 'Come here this instant, both of you,' she summoned sternly.

'It wasn't me, Mother,' Giles called across the garden.

She considered this declaration of innocence for only a moment before responding. 'Laurence!' she yelled shrilly. 'Come here at once.'

He stared meaningfully at his brother, willing him to own up to his misdemeanour, and receiving only a complacent smile in reply. With a heavy heart, he walked fearfully up the garden path. A sudden surge of rebellion, however, made him decide not to allow his liar of a brother to get away with it yet again.

'Do you realise the cost of the damage you've caused?' his mother asked, her cold eyes making him shiver as he stood before her on the terrace in the sharp February air.

Such was his terror, he was unable to reply, thus enraging her further.

'Well, answer me, you hateful boy!' she rasped, her mouth set cruelly, bosom heaving beneath her woollen afternoon dress.

'I . . .'

'Don't just stand there looking even more stupid than you actually are.'

'I . . .'

'Answer me!'

'I . . .'

'Out with it,' she shrieked. 'Before my nerves are completely torn to shreds.

'I didn't do it,' he stammered at last.

Angry red blotches crept over her plump neck and face. Her lips twisted into a sneer. 'Oh, and who did then, may I ask?'

'It was . . .'

'I hope you're not going to make things worse for yourself by trying to pass the blame on to your brother?'

'I wasn't here when he kicked it. I'd only just got back from the letter box . . .'

'Don't tell lies,' screamed Cissy. 'I looked out of the window immediately after I heard the crash and I saw you in the garden with Giles.'

'Yes, but I'd only just . . .'

'Don't make excuses for your wicked behaviour,' she interposed, shaking her silvery-brown head wildly. 'I've had quite enough of your lies, you horrible child. Now go to your bedroom and stay there until your father gets home from work.'

Laurence turned to his brother who was now standing beside him. Giles met his accusing stare coolly, apparently without the slightest compunction. Suddenly the injustice was too much for Laurence.

'Tell her it was you, you rotten coward!' he demanded, grabbing Giles by the arms and shaking him. 'Go on, tell the truth for once.'

Cissy was at Giles's side instantly, dragging Laurence away with a rough hand. 'You're the coward, Laurence, hitting someone younger than yourself,' she shouted, dealing him a sharp blow across the cheek. 'Now get to your bedroom and out of my sight before I really lose my temper.'

He went inside without a word, holding his smarting face and choking back the tears. If his mother saw so much as a hint of his distress, she would accuse him of being a weakling since it simply wasn't done for a boy of almost twelve to cry. But once the door of his bedroom was firmly closed behind him, tears poured down his cheeks. The beating his father would give him later on wouldn't hurt nearly as much as the pain of being so blatantly unloved. Bruises only lasted a few days. The misery of rejection was permanent.

Cissy Dexter was still trembling from the after effects of her rage when she went back into the house, having sent Giles to wash his hands before joining her for tea in the drawing room.

Laurence was a real problem, she thought as she sank on to a soft leather sofa. The wretched boy seemed to get more difficult with each passing day. He was downright rude, always answering her back and trying to push the blame for his own misdeeds on to poor Giles, when anyone with a brain in their head could see that Giles didn't have a mean bone in his body.

She sighed wearily. Laurence's disobedient nature was no more than to be expected, she supposed, considering the fact that his mother had been nothing more than a common factory hand with delusions of grandeur because her parents had once been rich. Taking on that woman's brat had been a ghastly mistake, but how could Cissy have known that the incredible would happen and she would have a child of her own a year later?

Looking back over the years, she could see that she had never felt any love for Laurence. In fact, she'd begun to resent having him around immediately she'd realised she was pregnant. She'd not wanted the bother of someone else's baby once she had her own to look forward to and the discomforts of pregnancy to contend with. She'd left him in the care of a nanny almost completely during that time.

After the birth of her dear Giles, her resentment towards Laurence had increased. That nasty nuisance of a child had never fitted in with her and Reggie and Giles in their Clapham home. It wasn't as though there was anything of Reggie in him to make him seem more like one of the family. He looked like his mother, from what Cissy could remember of the girl. He had the same near-black hair and those deep brown, saucer eyes.

He had none of Reggie's boldness either. In fact, the child was far too sensitive for a boy. He won praise at school for his essays, instead of shining at something useful like mathematics which would stand him in good stead in business later on. He was squeamish too. Why, he'd almost had hysterics when Reggie had run next door's cat over in his motor car. Now what sort of behaviour was that for a boy? Reggie had had to beat him really hard that day to teach him to behave more in keeping with his gender.

Frankly, Cissy couldn't wait to get him off her hands. He'd be twelve in April, so it wouldn't be long before he was old enough to leave the nest. He certainly wouldn't be encouraged to stay on at home for any longer than necessary. A career in the army would probably be the best thing for him, she thought. That would make a man of him whilst getting him neatly out of her hair.

She smiled as Giles entered the room. Now he was a *real* boy. It would take more than a dead cat to upset her beloved Giles. He wasn't afraid to kick the stray dogs that roamed the streets either, or spit in the faces of beggars. That was how it should be for a boy who was eventually going to have to go out into the world and behave like a man.

Whereas she couldn't wait to see the back of Laurence, she dreaded Giles growing up and going away. And when he did get older, she certainly wouldn't speed him on his way. He'd be offered a place in the business, as was his birthright, something she never considered with regard to Laurence. It was *her* business and therefore *her* son and not some bastard child of Reggie's who would get the benefit. Some sort of explanation would have to be offered to Laurence when the time came, of course, but she wouldn't lose any sleep over it.

Reggie never argued with her about her preference for Giles. But then it wasn't in his interest to quarrel with the person who paid his wages, but to do as she asked. If she said Laurence needed a beating, he got on and did it. He didn't seem to share her strong dislike of Laurence, and was merely indifferent to him.

'Come and sit next to your mother, Giles dear,' she said cloyingly, patting the sofa beside her.

'How about my making some honeycomb ribbon trimming to brighten it up?' suggested Kate, standing behind her mother at the dressing-table mirror in Kate's bedroom. Gertie was wearing an old hat that her daughter was about to remodel. 'A splash of strong colour will give it just the finish it needs to make it look like new, when I've altered the shape.'

'Nothing too fussy, though, dear,' said Gertie. 'Or I won't be able to wear it to the Institute.'

'Course you will,' said Kate lightly, tilting the brim at various angles. 'Just because you work with down-and-outs doesn't mean you have to look like one.'

'I suppose not,' agreed Gertie. 'But it doesn't seem right to look too posh when I go there.'

Kate gave a dry laugh. 'If those people only knew the truth, that I'm making your new Easter hat out of one of your old ones and it will cost you nothing more than a few bits of ribbon.' She met her mother's eyes in the mirror. 'I mean, you're not exactly well-off, are you?'

'Compared to them I am,' remarked Gertie wisely, turning her head to study the hat from different angles.

It was a shabby black felt with a long front which Kate planned to make into a stylish side sweep. 'Some yellow or pink honeycomb trimming will give it a special look without being too dressy,' she said thoughtfully. 'You'll need something bright or you'll look as though you're in mourning.'

'All right then,' agreed Gertie. 'I'll get some ribbon from the market.'

'I think I'll make myself one of those cloche hats that are becoming so popular,' remarked Kate casually.

'Why not?' said her mother. 'You're still young enough to look good in one.'

'I'll be too old to start up in business if I don't soon get on with it, though,' she said gloomily.

'You're not still harbouring those ideas, surely?'

'Yes, I am,' replied Kate wistfully. 'You must admit, I do have flair.'

'You certainly have,' agreed Gertie, whose reservations about Kate's ambitions had always been purely financial. 'Bertha was thrilled with that old hat of hers you did up.'

'Good, I'm glad she was pleased with it,' said Kate. 'How is Bertha? Still enjoying her job at the factory.'

'Yes, she much prefers it to sewing at home,' Gertie replied. 'And of course things are so much easier for her now that the children are grown up.'

Bertha had never really settled back to millinery after her

job on the buses during the war. So a couple of years ago she had joined the hordes of women doing shift work in the packing room at a fruit sauce factory. The low rates of pay meant her conscience was clear about taking a 'male breadwinner's' job. With Ruby paying her way from her job in the baker's and Georgie delivering for a local greengrocer, the quality of life had improved for the Brents who now lived in a basement flat in Dane Street. It wasn't a palace but at least they had more space and only a few steps to bother Bertha who was still very bronchial.

'I'm glad she's happy,' said Kate. 'She's a good friend.'

'Mmm.'

'It's funny how things have turned out,' remarked Kate. 'It was through Bertha that we went into the millinery trade. Now she's given it up, and we're still making hats.'

'It was just a means to an end for her,' said Gertie.

'For you too, I suspect?'

'I've no ambitions to become a model milliner, if that's what you mean. But I quite like working with hats.' Their eyes locked in the mirror. 'It's more than that for you, though, isn't it?'

'Much more,' said Kate.


'I can juggle with oranges,' boasted Giles Dexter, taking two jaffas from the fruit bowl in the living room and throwing them into the air.

'Don't do that,' said Laurence, looking up from the book he was reading, and frowning. 'You'll break something.'

The two boys had been left in the care of the servants because it was their mother's day to go into the office at the factory. They had finished school for the Easter holidays and as it was raining outside, were confined to the house. The weather didn't worry Laurence who could always lose himself in a book, but Giles had a very short concentration span and needed constant amusement.

Unfortunately, his brother's current entertainment spelled disaster for Laurence. It was only a few weeks since Giles had broken the window, and Laurence could still feel the hiding he himself had taken for it. He didn't fancy the idea of another which would definitely be on the agenda if Giles damaged any of the fine china ornaments that were on display around the room.

'Don't do that,' repeated Laurence as his brother began to pound the oranges against the wall in a game of two balls.

'Who's gonna stop me?' taunted Giles, dropping the fruit which rolled across the floor and landed underneath a highly polished occasional table.

Laurence heaved a sigh, trying not to be goaded for any loss of control always got him into trouble somehow. 'You'll mark the wallpaper,' he said with forced calmness.

Giles ignored him and continued his game. 'One, two, three, O'leary, my ball's down the airy,' he chanted, in time with the rhythm of the fruit thumping against the wall. 'Don't forget to give it to Mary, early in the morning . . .'

The steady thud beat through Laurence's mind, boding calamity. Struggling to ignore it, he turned his attention back to his book, with the idea that if he didn't intervene, he couldn't possibly be implicated.

But he was drawn back despite himself just in time to see his brother miss one of the oranges so that it hurtled across the room, narrowly missing a fine crystal vase filled with spring flowers.

'Please stop it,' begged Laurence, his stomach tightening at the probable consequences.

'You can't tell me what to do,' jeered Giles, recovering the oranges from the floor and tossing them wildly into the air with the deliberate intention of provoking his brother, 'I'm the favourite. I can do what I like. Mother and Father can't stand the sight of you.'

Smarting at this confirmation of what he knew to be true but tried not to believe, Laurence ignored the jibe. Standing up, he said, 'Stop doing that and give those oranges to me.'

'Shan't!' smirked Giles.

'Give them to me,' Laurence said again.

Giles turned to his brother, gave an evil grin and threw one of the jaffas into Laurence's face so forcefully it smacked against his forehead, making his ears ring and his head pound.

When the initial shock of the blow turned to pain, the anger Laurence was trying so hard to control would be restrained no longer. 'Why, you spiteful little monster!' he said, lunging forward.

The younger boy pre-empted his brother's attack by throwing the other orange into his face with such a force it threw him off balance and sent him staggering across the room. Feeling dizzy and disorientated, Laurence instinctively reached out for something with which to steady himself. Blindly grabbing the stem of a standard lamp, it slipped from his grasp and fell against the sideboard, dislodging a delicate porcelain bowl which was perched near the edge.

'Now you've torn it,' said Giles victoriously as they stared at the remains of the bowl, which had been one of their mother's favourites, strewn across the floor in smithereens. 'They'll really have your guts for garters this time.'

'Do you have some sort of perverse ambition to drive me to an early grave, Laurence?' asked Cissy.

'No, Mother, of course not,' the boy said in a thin nervous voice.

He and his mother were alone in the living room, Giles having been sent out and Father not yet home from the factory. Laurence's knees were shaking as he stood before her, stomach griping, mouth dry. He had deemed it wise to present her with the remains of the bowl as soon as she had got back from the office, with the idea of getting his punishment over with as soon as possible.

'Why do you constantly upset me then?' she asked, through clenched teeth.

'I didn't mean to.'

'You never mean to!'

'It was an accident, honestly.'

'I've never know anyone as clumsy as you.'

'Sorry.'

'How did you come to knock the bowl off the sideboard?' she demanded grimly.

'We were . . .'

'We?' she interrupted. 'I hope you're not going to drag your brother into this.'

'No, it's just that . . .'

'Just what?'

She was beside herself with rage now and Laurence was terrified.

'What!' she screamed, a vein in her neck visibly throbbing. 'What were you doing?'

'Fighting,' he muttered, wincing as her face screwed up in temper.

'So you were hitting your little brother again?'

'No, I was trying to stop him . . . he was . . . we were . . .'

Cissy drew a deep breath, her eyes narrowing and becoming oddly vacant. 'You're a bad lot, Laurence,' she hissed, the volume of her tone lowering but becoming more venomous. 'Just like that slut of a mother of yours!'

'But you're my mother,' he croaked shakily.

Cissy gave him an evil smile, as though relishing what she was about to say. 'Oh, no, I'm not,' she explained, her voice guttural with venom. 'Do you think I would give birth to a disgusting little yob like you?'

He stared at her, his mouth dropping open, his skin chalk-white against his dark hair.

'You're not mine,' she went on viciously. 'You're the result of one of my husband's filthy flirtations. You are a bastard born to a common sewing hand who used to work in our factory.'

Speechless, he continued to stare at her.

'I took you off her hands at birth to save her from the workhouse,' she said, delighting in his pain. 'And it was the biggest mistake I've ever made. I certainly wouldn't have done it if I'd known what a miserable baby you were going to be, always snivelling and making a fuss. Not like sweet, contented Giles.'

Laurence stood frozen to the spot. It was as though the very life had been sucked from him. To have been so disliked by the woman he had believed to be his mother for all these years had been painful; to learn he had not been wanted by his real mother either was torture.

'Threw herself at my Reggie, she did, your mother, the little tart,' Cissy went on, her words flowing uncontrollably. 'But she was only too pleased to get shot of you when I offered to take you on.'

The boy closed his eyes tightly, clamping his hands over his ears to shut out the words which penetrated to his very soul. 'Stop it, stop it, stop it!' he cried.

But she went on and on, punishing him. 'Your mother didn't want you and neither do I . . .'

At last he could take no more and lunged at her with clenched fists, hitting out wildly to stop the terrible flow of words.

Vaguely, he was aware of being pulled away from her and dragged upstairs to his bedroom by his father who pushed him roughly inside and locked the door behind them.

'Just as well I came in when I did, you little heathen,' growled Reggie, 'I'll teach you to get rough with your mother. We'll soon see who's boss in this house.'

The customary lashing with the belt was replaced by violent fist blows, jabbing bruises into Laurence's face and body until he was too weak to put up any defence.

Leaving the boy in a semi-conscious heap on the floor, Reggie Dexter went downstairs to tell his wife that the job had been completed according to her instructions.

Waiting until everyone had settled down for the night, Laurence, fully dressed beneath the bedcovers, slipped cautiously from his bed, trying not to groan too loudly from the pain of the injuries he had received earlier. With heart bumping, and wincing with every movement, he limped across the room and opened the door, nerves stretched to breaking point as he listened to make sure the house was sleeping. Carefully, he made his way down the stairs and through the kitchen to the back door, his fingers trembling as he fumbled with the bolts.

Managing to unfasten them at last, he left the house, fled silently across the moonlit garden and out on to the London streets.

# *Chapter Eleven*

Leo Nash strolled along the Hammersmith waterfront in the early evening sunshine, enjoying the spring breeze and the fact that it was still daylight when he finished his day's work in a stuffy drawing office.

Having an artistic eye, every season of the river interested him. Winter was a constant fascination with its sharply defined, barren landscape. There was a curious mood then, too, which seemed to hover somewhere between tranquillity and gloom. But now, in the glorious thrust of May, with new life sprouting from every leaf and flower, Leo felt revitalised, for living afloat could be harsh indeed in cold weather.

Neatly dressed in a dark business suit and bowler hat, he paused, glancing idly at the river, delighting in the fresh vernal scents, especially the hint of May blossom in the air. Sunlight glinted on the surface of the water and was broken by the breeze into a million golden fragments. Grimy barges glided by loaded with coal or grain or sugar from the refinery. Oarsmen were out in force too, taking advantage of the daylight to practise, their skiffs skimming the surface with a gentle splashing sound.

Making his way upstream beyond some cottages and large houses, he reached a quiet stretch of the bank where willow trees overhung in leafy abandon and dog roses proliferated among burdock and thistle. Here, resting on a permanent mooring under the trees, was Leo's home.

Built towards the end of the last century for a rich business-man to use for cruising and weekend river parties, *London Lady* was a roomy boat with a spacious deck, a large saloon and sleeping accommodation for eight people. Leo had inherited her from an army pal called Billy who had acquired her at a low price in a state of neglect, renovated her and made her his permanent home. Billy had died at Leo's side on the battlefield of Passchendaele. Leo had been deeply moved to learn from his commanding officer that Billy had left *London Lady* to him in his will, for the boat had been his pride and joy.

Knowing nothing at all about houseboats, Leo had moved in only as a temporary solution to his homelessness on returning from France after the war. But from the very first morning he'd awoken to the gentle lap of water and the sun shining through the willow leaves, he had become a devotee of river life. It suited his bohemian nature so well he doubted if he could settle to a more conventional lifestyle now.

Going aboard and crossing the deck, its guardrail lined with potted geraniums and pansies, he went down a small flight of steps into the saloon. The room was cluttered with evidence of his hobby. An easel with an unfinished picture of a street scene; oil paints in tubes; a palette; a jam jar containing his brushes; the faint smell of turps permeating everything. Going through a small passageway to his cabin, he changed out of his office clothes into a pair of grey flannels and a navy blue jersey.

He wandered back into the wood-panelled saloon, a room dominated by a cast iron pot-belly stove in the centre, and the original solid wood table and chairs fixed to the floor. Pouring himself a whisky and soda, he flopped into a brown leather armchair to savour his favourite moment of the day, the time when he could divest himself of all thoughts of earning a living and let his mind run free.

His work as a draughtsman was merely a means to an end. Producing drawings of tools and equipment for an engineering firm paid him a good steady wage, for which he was grateful when so many ex-servicemen were still unemployed.

Leo's talent for drawing had been recognised at an early age. But his mother, deserted by her husband and struggling to raise him alone in an East End tenement, hadn't been able to afford any sort of artistic training for him. It had been his schoolteacher who had suggested that he apply for a job in a drawing office where at least he would be taught to put his talent to good use.

And so he could be only a part-time artist, painting when inspired and with a ruthlessly perceptive eye. He had received a limited amount of recognition over the years, mostly from winning competitions. He had even had work on display in an art gallery once. But his subject matter lacked commercial appeal, for Leo painted scenes of a kind people didn't wish to have in their homes.

His mother, who had died in the 'flu epidemic of 1919, had taught him to be true to himself, a lesson he'd never forgotten. So, not being prepared to make money at the expense of his principles, there was not much likelihood of him ever fulfilling his dream of becoming a full-time artist.

He had nothing against painting portraits as a means of financial support. Indeed, beauty and affluence were every bit as relevant as ugliness and deprivation. But his problem lay in the fact that he couldn't bring himself to indulge the vanity of the rich by painting beauty where there was none. The way nature had seen fit to arrange a person's features was a joy in itself to him, and he strove for accuracy rather than flattery.

Unfortunately those people who could afford to commission an artist usually wanted a cosmetic image of themselves rather than a true likeness. These were also the very same people with enough money to hang their walls with original paintings. Usually they preferred pretty pastoral scenes to the realistic images of everyday life that Leo preferred. So he drew tools and equipment for a living. At least that was productive.

Being only human, he had sometimes yearned for fame and fortune. But that had been in his younger days. A large slice of active service in France had clarified his priorities. Now, at thirty-two, he wanted to reach people's hearts and minds with his pictures, rather than just their eye for an ornament. Since he was most often inspired by starving, barefoot children in the slums of London, the latter was unlikely anyway.

Finishing his drink, he went to the galley in search of food, frowning at the meagre pickings in the larder. There were a few basic essentials like tea, cocoa and sugar, some digestive bisuits, a chunk of stale bread and some cheese rind with mould on it. Nothing with which to make a meal, which wasn't really surprising for he tended to be somewhat casual about domestic matters.

Disposing of the cheese rind in the rubbish bin, he went up on deck to feed the bread to the colonies of feathered hopefuls who lived in abundance on water and land around here. His own supper would probably come from the fish and chip shop later on, as usual.

Swans and ducks crowded on to the scene, squabbling noisily over the bread Leo dropped into the water, while sparrows and pigeons fought over the scraps he aimed towards the bank. There were not many people about at this time of the evening in this secluded spot. Set back from the towpath at some distance to the side of the boat stood a row of houses alongside a patch of scrub land which separated them from a group of factories further upriver. The rush of home-going workers had finished and it was too soon for entertainment seekers to appear.

Into this tranquillity came a rustling sound in a nearby clump of bushes. Too early in the evening for a courting couple, he thought, and it wasn't the unmistakable flutter of birds. Curious, he left the boat and went to investigate.

As he drew near to the bushes, the foliage became unnaturally still.

'Who's there?' he asked.

Silence.

Moving even closer, he poked the greenery with a stick.

He could just make out a pair of dark frightened eyes in the dirt-encrusted countenance of a young boy. As Leo moved closer, the urchin cowered back fearfully.

'It's all right, son,' said Leo kindly. 'I mean you no harm.'

The boy stepped back, staring at him with mistrust. His thin body was trembling beneath the grey woollen jumper which he wore with short grey trousers, the colour barely distinguishable beneath the grime which suffused every inch of him.

Leo gave him a reassuring smile. 'Don't look so scared,' he said. 'I won't hurt you.'

Making a sudden dash away from Leo, the boy tore along the dusty towpath. But confronted by an elderly couple approaching from the other direction, he stopped in his tracks as though they were a threat to him too. He moved closer to the river and hurried past them. Turning to look at Leo, as though suspecting he might be following, he tripped on uneven ground and tottered on the edge of the bank before losing his balance altogether and hitting the water with a splash.

The old couple rushed to his assistance, uttering loud exclamations of distress. The man was about to jump in after him when Leo arrived on the scene.

'I don't think he can swim,' said the old man, pale with anxiety and waving his arms dramatically. 'He's going under . . . Oh God, he's drowning.'

Off came Leo's jersey and he was in the river up to his chest. Fortunately he managed to grip the boy in a lifesaving hold. 'Trust me, son,' he said as the panicking child struggled. 'Try to keep calm and I'll have you on the bank in no time.'

'What's your name?' asked Leo a while later when the boy was sitting at the saloon table, wrapped in a towel, drinking a mug of cocoa. He had had a hot bath, thanks to the hot water system Leo had had installed a year or so ago. His clothes had been rinsed and were now hanging on the deck rail to dry, along with the ones Leo had had to change out of.

The boy lowered his eyes and didn't reply.

It didn't take a genius to see that this child was relatively new to living rough on the streets. As filthy as they were, his clothes were of good quality, and although he hadn't said much beyond please and thank you, his deportment was not that of a true street urchin.

'We won't get far if you're not going to say anything,' said Leo patiently.

Silence continued to reign.

'Put it this way then, son,' he persisted, his light brown eyes peering at the boy over the rim of his cocoa mug. 'I can't keep saying "Oi, you", now can I? So help me out by telling me what to call you.'

Huge dark eyes darted around the room as though seeing danger in every corner. 'Ozzy,' the boy said at last. 'Ozzy Perks.'

Ignoring the fact that it was obviously not his real name, Leo thrust out his hand. 'Glad to meet you, Ozzy. I'm Leo Nash. Welcome aboard.'

Clearly surprised to have his ficticious name accepted without question, the boy offered a bony hand, suspicion lingering in his eyes as though he expected Leo to attack him at any moment. Nothing could be less likely. The scars and fading bruises Leo had seen on the boy's thin body when he had been bathing indicated that he had had more than his fair share of punishment.

'I'm going to have some fish and chips for my supper,' Leo said, square face lighting up in a warm smile. 'Do you fancy joining me?'

Ozzy's expression brightened but he still looked doubtful. 'I don't want to be any trouble, sir.'

Leo laughed. 'You cause me to half drown myself to fish you out of the water, yet say you don't want to be any trouble.'

'I'm sorry, sir,' the boy said, chewing his lip anxiously. 'I slipped and fell.'

'Only because you were in such a hurry to get away from me.'

'I'm very sorry, sir.'

'Let's drop the sir, shall we, Ozzy?' he suggested. 'It makes me feel like some old walrus of a schoolmaster. My name is Leo.'

Ozzy nodded. 'I'm sorry, sir . . . er, Leo.'

Going to his cabin, Leo returned with a red woollen dressing gown. 'You'd better put this on until we can get your clothes dry. It'll be much too big, of course, but I don't have any children's clothes.'

'I'm sorry to be such a nuisance.'

'Stop apologising.'

'Sorry.'

Leo ran a worried hand across his brow, combing his thick brown hair back with his fingers. Whoever was responsible for those bruises had done much more than just physical damage. The poor lad was a nervous wreck. He walked across to the deck steps. 'I'll go and get some food then,' he said. 'What would you like, rock salmon or cod?'

Ozzy gave an uncertain smile which lit up his pathetic little countenance. 'Anything will do, thank you, sir. Er, I mean Leo.'

That same evening, sitting at her dressing-table mirror, Cissy Dexter applied rouge liberally to her cheeks. Delighted with the effect, she got to work with her lipstick. This new trend among women of using cosmetics for everyday wear was an absolute Godsend for the more mature, she thought, admiring the way her face glowed with colour. She slipped her pearl necklace on over her blue silk dress and added matching earrings.

Reggie was taking her up West to the Hippodrome to see Lupino Lane in a new revue. A night out would do her good, she'd told him. She needed a treat to help soothe her nerves after that ungrateful whelp Laurence had upset the family routine in his usual selfish manner by running away from home.

It was three weeks since he'd left and once her initial fury at his audacity had faded, she'd felt better than she had in years. It was such a relief not to have him in the house, looking at her with those forlorn, frightened eyes as though she ill treated him or something, and being spiteful to Giles and a nuisance to them all.

Had it been Giles who had gone missing, naturally she would have reported the matter to the police and urged them to find him. But Laurence could stay away forever as far as she was concerned. Let him beg on the streets for his food. A bit of hardship might make him appreciate just how much she and Reggie had done for him, providing him with a comfortable home with plenty on the table.

She cast her mind back to the afternoon of the quarrel preceding Laurence's disappearance and was annoyed to find herself assailed by a pang of conscience. Well, it was probably best that he knew who he really was, even though she hadn't meant to blurt it out and had only done so in a fit of pique. Maybe she could have broken it to him more gently. But uncouth boys like Laurence, who spent their time fighting and damaging valuable possessions without so much as a second thought, didn't deserve consideration.

Anyway, he was twelve years old, quite big enough to fend for himself. If the school board man came snooping round, she'd tell him the same as she'd told the headmaster of the school: that Laurence had gone to stay with his aunt in the country for an indefinite period. The last thing she and Reggie wanted was any sort of scandal. But the authorities were unlikely to bother a respectable family like the Dexters. It was only the proletariat who made their offspring work when they should have been learning.

She stood up and admired herself in the full-length mirror on the wardrobe door, pleased with the fashionable, low-waisted dress that made her look ten years younger and able to pass for thirty-eight. It was such a treat to be able to go out for the evening leaving dear Giles in the care of the servants, knowing that he was safe from the spitefulness of his half-brother.


When Leo got back to the boat, the boy was incongruously swathed in the enormous dressing gown and sitting at the saloon table, having hung the towel over the deck rail to dry. There was a kettle boiling on the cooking range in the galley and the table was laid with plates and cutlery.

'My word,' said Leo, 'someone's mother has trained them well.'

Ozzy's face muscles tightened but he just said, 'I thought I might as well make myself useful. I hope you don't mind me poking about in your cupboards?'

'Why on earth should I mind?' Leo put the steaming newspaper packet on the table and ruffled the boy's hair in what was meant to be a reassuring gesture. He frowned as Ozzy cowered away in fright. 'Right, you put the food on to the plates and tuck in while I make some tea.'

Returning from the galley with a tray of tea, Leo noticed

that Ozzy was wolfing the food ravenously, reminding him of the crippling hunger he himself had suffered in the trenches.

'Well, you certainly made short work of that,' said Leo a few minutes later when the boy's plate was clean. 'You must have been starving.'

'I was.'

'Would you like some of my chips?' asked Leo, pouring them both some tea.

The boy made a puffing sound and patted his stomach. 'I'm full, thank you.'

'That's good.'

Silence fell as Leo attended to his own meal.

'I don't have any money to pay you for my supper,' said Ozzy after a while

'That doesn't matter.'

'I'll work to pay you back, though. Washing the dishes, cleaning the boat, anything you like.'

'There's no need.'

'I'd rather . . . honestly.'

'Don't be daft.'

'I don't expect anything for nothing,' said Ozzy in a brittle tone.

'That's a cynical view for someone so young,' Leo remarked.

Ozzy gave a careless shrug, his lips pressed tightly together.

'How old are you?'

'Fifteen,' lied Ozzy.

Leo threw him a shrewd look. 'Now come on, old chap,' he said persuasively. 'If we're going to be friends, we must be truthful with each other. So let's try again, shall we? How old are you?'

'Twelve,' admitted Ozzy.

Leo leaned on the table with his chin on his fists, looking at him. 'And how long have you been living rough?'

'About three weeks, I think, but I've lost track of time.'

'Been begging for food, I suppose?'

'Yes.'

'And stealing from market barrows, I shouldn't wonder?' suggested Leo.

Ozzy nodded sheepishly.

'Without much success, by the look of you.'

'I managed.'

'Run away from home, have you?'

He replied with a nod.

Had Leo not seen the evidence of cruelty, he might have assumed Ozzy had left home in a childish fit of pique, and encouraged him to go back. But he didn't feel able to do this, which left him in something of a quandary given the difficulties that could arise for him personally if he gave the boy shelter. 'No need to ask if you intend going back?' he said.

'I'm never going back.'

'Your folks might have the police out looking for you,' Leo suggested.

'I very much doubt it.'

'Surely they'll be worrying about you?'

'They'll be glad to get rid of me.'

'You don't know that.'

'I do,' Ozzy interrupted fiercely, an angry flush rising. 'Anyway, I'm not going back and that's all there is to it, and if anyone does make me go back, I shall run away again.'

'So what are you planning to do?' Leo asked. 'Begging on the streets can't be much fun.'

'I'll get a job and find somewhere to live.'

Leo drew in a sharp breath, shaking his head in a cautionary manner. 'A lad of your age won't stand a chance,' he said. 'The streets are crawling with grown men looking for work.'

'So I'll live rough till I get lucky.'

'What about the rest of your schooling?'

He looked sad, but shrugged. 'I'd be leaving in a couple of years anyway.'

'You'll regret missing those two years, later on.'

'Too bad. There's nothing I can do about it.'

Leo finished his supper and drank his tea thoughtfully, guessing what was in the boy's mind. 'Look son, as much as I'd like to help you, I could be in serious trouble if your folks report you missing and you're found with me. At best I'd be accused of encouraging you to stay away from home, and they might even say I'd abducted you.'

'Yes, I understand that,' said Ozzy. 'And I don't want to cause you any bother.'

His tone was neither self-pitying nor feeble. He was simply stating a fact. It was like listening to a world-weary old man. Leo's heart went out to him and he decided to give him a reprieve. 'You can stay here tonight, and we'll discuss your future in the morning.'

The boy's emaciated face was transformed by a grin. 'Thank you. Thank you very much.'

'There'll be no wet nursing, mind,' warned Leo. 'I'm not used to children, and I'm not going to let your being here interfere with my plans.'

'Course not.'

'I shall be going out for an hour or so later on, so you'll be here on your own.'

'I can look after myself,' the boy insisted. 'I'm not a kid.'

'In that case, you can earn your keep by washing the dishes while I get a cabin ready for you.'

'Yes, certainly,' said Ozzy eagerly.

Later on that evening, snuggled up in a bunk in a modest-sized cabin overlooking the bank, the boy felt physically comfortable for the first time since he'd left home, and happier than he could ever remember. Immediately he had closed the door behind him on the house in Clapham, a weight had lifted from his shoulders. The thought of being sent back to the Dexters had worried him far more than the constant hunger and the threat of being beaten up by the gangs of street urchins who resented newcomers begging on their patch. He'd deliberately headed across the river to distance himself from the Dexters, for areas north of the Thames were foreign to them.

For the first time in his life he was not afraid. Leo had gone out so he was alone here, but a feeling of safety embraced him in a warm, comforting tide. The permanent nervous flutter in his stomach had gone and it was a lovely feeling.

The sounds from outside were oddly reassuring too: the water lapping against the side of the boat, the chug and splash of a passing craft and the slight rock of the *London Lady* in its wash. He could hear people talking and laughing as they passed by on the towpath. There was the distant rumble of traffic, the rattle of a train, a dog barking.

Ozzy liked and trusted Leo. He was surprisingly understanding for an adult too. There had been no persistent questions; no criticism even though he knew Ozzy had done wrong and run away from home. The boy was ashamed of telling lies about his name, but it made him feel safer. He felt more confident as Ozzy, too. In fact, he preferred being Ozzy Perks in every way. 'Better than Laurence Dexter any day of the week,' he muttered sleepily.

If only he could stay here with Leo, life would be perfect. He fell asleep trying to work out a way to persuade him.

Leo usually popped down to The Swan and Sparrow for an hour or so of an evening, more for the company than the beer. He knew all the regulars and never lacked for someone to chat to or play a game of darts with.

His cronies at this riverside hostelry were a diverse bunch of fellows. There was City, who was a stockbroker in the city of London and lived in one of the grand riverside houses. Then there was Pears, a street trader who had a fruit and veg barrow in Bradmore Lane Market. Blimp was a retired army officer, and Flogger made a living by peddling a variety of dubious artifacts around the pubs and clubs of the area.

Few topics escaped the notice of this loquacious group. Politics, sport, and sex were all regularly discussed.

This particular evening they had delved into the character of Stanley Baldwin, the new Prime Minister, touched on the game of cricket, and were now deeply involved in the pros and cons of 'the wireless', of which City was an ardent fan, having just bought one of the valve and battery sets.

'You can tune in to some really interesting programmes now,' he enthused. 'The wife was saying they've got a pro- gramme specially for women during the day now. Woman's Hour, it's called. They had one of the royals giving a talk on the programme to launch it, apparently. Princess Alice, I think she said.'

'Yeah, my missus was talking about that,' said Flogger, who was hoping to make some money out of the wireless craze if he could get hold of some at a low enough price.

'Oh, yes,' continued City, in the authoritative manner of the well-informed, 'the wireless is one of the greatest inventions of our time, I reckon.'

'There's less noise interference now the BBC have opened their new studios at Savoy Hill too,' said Pears. 'They 'ad dance music on the other night. It was as good as bein' at the Palais.'

'One of the kids sneezed the other night and we lost the signal altogether,' said Flogger, who was the proud owner of a crystal set.

'The wireless kills conversation, in my opinion,' snorted Blimp who was rather eccentric and opposed to technical progress.

'Cor, not 'alf!' said Pears. 'No one dare speak in our 'ouse when it's on. A bloomin' godsend, I reckon, 'cos there's no stopping my missus once she starts jabberin'.'

The men were standing at the bar counter in a room dominated by the male of the species. The few females who were present were sitting at beer-stained wooden tables with their husbands. The decor was dark with gaslight glowing from the panelled walls. A game of darts was in progress and several men were playing dominoes and shove-ha'penny. A pall of smoke hung in the air and from the other bar came the sound of 'Who's Sorry Now' being thumped out on a piano.

'You're very quiet tonight, Leo,' observed Flogger. 'You got woman trouble or somethin'?'

'No, nothing like that,' he said, finishing his drink. 'I'm off now.'

'Blimey. Well, it's either a woman or a paintin' yer want to finish to make yer go this early,' said Pears. 'You ain't been in here much more than 'alf an 'our.'

'It's neither a woman nor a painting,' he said cryptically, and left them to speculate.

Walking back to the boat along the lamplit towpath with his pals' jesting lingering in his mind, it occurred to Leo that it was a very long time since he'd had any 'woman trouble' as Flogger so eloquently put it. Being on the wrong side of thirty, it was true to say that he had had his moments with the opposite sex over the years.

He'd nearly got married once before the war. He'd actually been officially engaged. They had even started saving to set up home. Spent Saturday afternoons looking in furniture shops, and that sort of thing. She'd been a good-looking blonde who'd worked behind the counter in the dairy near his mother's place in Hackney. A warm-hearted type. A bit too warm-hearted as it turned out. She'd got herself pregnant by a commercial traveller while Leo was away in France and when Leo came home on leave, she was married to him.

His pride had been hurt, naturally, but he'd soon recovered. There had been other girlfriends since then but he'd never again felt the urge to marry. He wasn't really the marrying kind. He was far too fond of his freedom. As things were now he was free to do as he pleased, with no one to answer to. Anyway, he doubted if many women would want to give up the convenience of terra firma to live on a draughty old boat which kept him poor with its constant need for maintenance.

As he approached the *London Lady*, he turned his mind again to the problem of his house-guest, who hadn't been far from his thoughts all evening and was the reason for his early return. Making his way carefully across the gangplank, he moved stealthily over the deck and down into the saloon, anxious not to wake him. The lad had looked exhausted.

Creeping along the passage to his cabin beyond Ozzy's, aware of every step and creaking board, he decided that this sort of restricted behaviour wasn't suitable for a bachelor like himself. He couldn't have his life turned upside down by some runaway kid. Leaving the pub early because the lad was alone on the boat, sneaking about like a burglar in his own home for fear of waking him! No, it simply wasn't on! He'd tell him to leave first thing in the morning.

★ ★ ★

Since the next day was Saturday, Leo didn't have to get up early for work and awoke to find the sun streaming into his cabin through the chintz curtains. Luxuriating in the thought of a lie-in, he closed his eyes and let himself drift into a snooze.

The sound of movement somewhere on the boat reached him, reminding him he was not alone. Stumbling sleepily from bed and cursing the fact that he'd loaned the boy his dressing gown, he made his way in his pyjamas to Ozzy's cabin to get it.

The bed was made, the cabin empty. The sounds now registered properly in Leo's sleep-addled brain as being the clink of crockery from the region of the galley, leading off the saloon. Grabbing his dressing gown off the hook on the door, he struggled into it and hurried towards the activity, muttering, 'All this blasted noise first thing in the morning. The damned boy wants throttling.'

He found Ozzy, dressed in his own clothes, in the galley where the kettle was singing on the range.

'Hello,' he said brightly. 'I'm just making some tea.'

'Good for you,' said Leo gruffly.

'I found some biscuits in the larder,' announced Ozzy.

'Really?' Leo grunted, sounding unimpressed.

'I'll bring you tea and biscuits in bed, if you like.'

'No, I'll have my tea here, thank you,' said Leo abruptly, going into the saloon and sitting at the table, his brows knitting together in a frown.

Ozzy looked disappointed as he followed him into the room.

'It's no good trying to softsoap me with all this tea in bed nonsense because I've decided you have to go,' said Leo.

'Oh . . . oh, I see,' said Ozzy, sitting down opposite Leo at the table, dark eyes meeting his resolutely. 'But I've got this plan, you see . . .'

'Does it entail your staying on here?'

'Yes.'

'Then it isn't on, boy,' said Leo firmly.

'But . . .'

'It's nothing personal,' he explained, riddled with guilt. 'It's just that I don't want anyone staying here permanently.'

'You haven't heard my plan yet.' Ozzy's look of dejection

was immediately followed by a spark of determination. 'Just hear me out . . . please?'

'Oh, get on with it then,' sighed Leo irritably. 'But it won't make a scrap of difference to my decision.'

'If you let me stay,' said Ozzy eagerly, 'I'll not only pay for my keep with money, but I'll be very useful to you, too.'

'And what do you intend paying for your keep with?' asked Leo.

'I'll earn money by delivering papers and cleaning steps and things like that until I'm old enough to get a proper job,' he effused, 'and I'll do all your chores around the boat.'

'No.'

'I'll cook your meals and clean the boat from top to bottom every day if only you'll let me stay.'

'There are too many complications,' said Leo.

'Such as?'

'School, for one thing.'

'Oh, I won't bother about that.'

'You will if I have anything to do with it!'

'I'd be leaving in a couple of years anyway.'

'Two years is a lot of learning to miss.'

'All right, I'll go to school then if that's what you want,' agreed Ozzy, who had always found the schoolroom a blessed escape from the misery of homelife with the Dexters. 'I'll still have time to do all the other things.'

'And how am I supposed to explain your sudden appearance to the headmaster of the school?' Leo wanted to know.

'Tell him I'm your nephew from the country who's come to live with you because my mother has died or something,' he suggested hopefully.

Leo found himself on the horns of a real dilemma. When it came to the crunch, he simply couldn't bear to think of Ozzy roaming the streets. Neither could he bring himself to inform the police of his whereabouts, for they would surely force his real name out of him and take him home for more ill-treatment. But the alternative was going to mean a great deal of personal inconvenience. 'What about me in all this?' he asked, trying to be sensible and not let his heart rule his head. 'I need my privacy.'

'I won't get in the way,' the boy promised eagerly. 'It's a very big boat and when you want to be alone, or when you have company, there's plenty of room for me to make myself scarce.'

'But I can't have a kid about the place,' Leo insisted, shaking his head. 'It would completely cramp my style. If I was a married man it would be different, but as a bachelor I can do without that sort of responsibility.'

'It isn't as though I'm a little kid that you'd have to look after though, is it?' Ozzy wisely pointed out. 'I'll soon be old enough to be off on my own.'

'You've put me in a very awkward position.'

'I know.' Ozzy chewed his lip. 'Sorry.'

'Don't start all that damned apologising again,' snapped Leo, anxiety making him touchy. 'I prefer you when you're showing the spirit which gave you the courage to leave home in the first place.'

Ozzy fell silent for a moment. 'Just give it a try, Leo, please,' he urged. 'If it doesn't work out, I'll leave without a fuss, I promise.'

He heaved a sigh of resignation. 'All right, you win,' he said, much against his better judgement.

'Oh, thank you, thank you,' said Ozzy excitedly.

'Now, hang on a minute,' said Leo. 'Before we go any further, I am going to make some rules which I do not want broken.'

'I won't break them, honest.'

'Right,' said Leo, feeling surprisingly lighthearted now that the decision was made. 'First thing Monday morning we will go to the nearest school to register you.'

'Fine.'

'Secondly, you can earn your keep by helping with the chores and running errands for me.'

'Cor, that's good of you, but I'll pay you in money, like I said.'

Leo thought about this. He wouldn't be doing the boy any

favours by making things too easy for him, but he didn't want to be too hard on him either. 'You can earn your pocket money by doing a paper round or something if you want to.'

'All right,' he agreed. 'Is there anything else.'

'Yes. You will make yourself scarce if I have visitors.'

'I already said I would.'

'And you'll stay here alone if I go out, without any sort of fuss,' he said. 'In other words, you will not disrupt my lifestyle.'

'I understand.'

'Looks like we have a deal then,' said Leo, leaning across the table to shake his hand.

Sam Brooks decided to walk home from school by the riverside. It was a longer route because it meant a slight detour but it was more interesting than the streets, and he enjoyed watching the naval cadets on the Royal Navy's training ship *Stork* which was moored on the Thames at Hammersmith.

Officially the waterfront was out of bounds to Sam. Mother didn't allow him to go near the river without an adult. But he'd be nine soon, and kids younger than him went all over the place on their own. Grandma and Aunt Bertha said Mother fussed over him too much and that she shouldn't wrap him in cotton wool, whatever that was supposed to mean.

It was September and the trees along the bank were changing colour and carpeting the ground with russet leaves. There wasn't a breath of wind, just hazy sunshine seasoned with a slight mist. He wrinkled his nose at the stench from the mud, uncovered by the low tide.

Pausing for a moment by one of the wharves, he watched the men working on the foreshore, unloading cargo from the barges. Huge sacks and tea-chests were being piled on to horse-drawn carts to be to be taken up to the food processing plant. He lingered awhile further on to watch the cadets on the training ship, busy at work on the rigging, before continuing his homeward journey along a quiet stretch of the river.

The autumn was Sam's favourite season. He liked the nip in the air that heralded cosy winter evenings when Mum would light the fire and they'd make toast and sit round with mugs of hot cocoa. If Mum was busy sewing, he would lose himself in one of his weekly boys' adventure comics which he read over and over again. He was good at reading; his mother had encouraged him from an early age and sometimes got him books from the library. His favourites were stories about aeroplanes.

The sight of a seagull swooping and soaring, fired his childish imagination. One day I'll be flying higher than you in an aeroplane, he murmured to the ascending bird.

Reaching the turning where he usually left the river, he paused, attracted by something further along the bank. Through the trees he could see a dark-haired boy whom he recognised as one of the older boys from his school standing on the deck of a houseboat. Sam only knew him by sight because he was quite new and in the seniors, but it was enough of a connection for Sam to delay his journey home and make his way towards him. Boats couldn't compete with planes in terms of excitement, but they had enough adventure about them to evoke colourful images of journeys to faraway places.

'Hello,' said Sam brightly, for he was not a shy child. 'I've seen you at school.'

'What about it?' said the boy abruptly, eyeing Sam with suspicion.

'I was just mentioning it,' said Sam.

'What do you want?' asked Ozzy.

'Nothing in particular.' Sam scuffed his shoe on a tuft of grass. 'I just wondered what you are doing on that boat?'

'I live here, if it's any of your business.'

'You live on a boat? Cor!' he said, breathless with awe.

'That's right.'

'Cor,' said Sam again. 'That must be terrific fun.'

'I like it.'

Sam was not deterred by the other boy's unwelcoming manner. 'What's it like on there? You got cabins and that?'

'Of course.'

'Can I have a look?'

Ozzy looked doubtful for a moment, but pride eventually prevailed. 'Yeah, all right then. Come aboard.'

Tingling with excitement, Sam went aboard *London Lady*

and followed Ozzy down into what seemed to be a living room which looked very disorderly and smelled of turpentine and paint.

'Excuse the muddle,' said Ozzy, glancing proudly towards an easel. 'My uncle is an artist.'

'Can he draw aeroplanes?'

'He can draw anything,' boasted Ozzy.

'Cor,' gasped Sam again. This was getting better by the minute. He felt as though he'd stepped into something from the pages of an adventure story.

After being told his host's name and given a peep into the sleeping quarters and the galley, Sam was told firmly, 'Well, I have to go to the shops for my uncle before he gets home from work, so you'll have to go now.'

'Thanks for showing me round,' he said as they clambered up on deck.

'You can come again if you like,' said Ozzy, confident now that the boy was no threat.

'Cor, thanks,' said Sam exuberantly.

He couldn't wait to go to the boat again and called there the next day after school when he was given a warm welcome by Ozzy's Uncle Leo, who had the afternoon off from work. Sam was invited to stay for tea and they sat round the saloon table eating muffins toasted on the glowing red coals of the stove. Sam was having a wonderful time. Unfortunately, he was enjoying himself so much, he forgot the time and the fact that the evenings were drawing in . . .

He could see Mother, Grandma and Aunt Bertha standing at the front gate as he turned the corner into Dane Street, out of breath from running. It was almost dark but he could just make them out in the glow from the street lamp which was hazed with mist in the sharp evening air.

'Where have you been?' his mother demanded crossly, continuing before he had a chance to reply, 'We've been worried sick about you. I've been walking the streets for ages looking for you.'

'I've been . . .'

206

'Anything could have happened to you,' she cut in. 'You could have been run over or abducted.'

'Let the boy say his piece,' said Gertie.

'So, where have you been all this time, Sam?' asked Kate.

And, full of joy at his new friendship, he let the whole wonderful story pour out in an effusive tide.

'You had tea on a boat with river people?' said his mother worriedly.

'That's right,' said Sam excitedly. 'They actually live on the water, isn't that thrilling?'

'Do they live on the boat all the time, or do they have a house as well?'

'They live there all the time, I think,' he said, swelling with pride.

'Gypsies!' exclaimed Kate.

'Cor, are they?' said Sam, who had read about such people in adventure stories and thought them fascinating.

'Well, yes . . . sort of,' said Kate irritably. 'You'd better show me where this boat of theirs is. This fellow who calls himself Uncle Leo needs telling a thing or two. I mean, what sort of a man is it who keeps a young boy away from home while his mother goes out of her mind with worry?'

'But it was my fault, Mum,' defended Sam, 'and Ozzy did walk most of the way home with me because it was getting dark.'

'The wretched man should have known better than to keep you there so long,' she said as though Sam hadn't spoken.

He cringed at the fury in her eyes as they left their flat and headed for the river.

# *Chapter Twelve*

'How lovely to meet you, Mrs Brooks,' said Leo, standing next to Ozzy on the deck of *London Lady* and greeting Kate with a warm smile and an outstretched hand. 'Ozzy and I have heard all about you from Sam.'

'Oh . . . really?' Her anger was somewhat diminished by the discovery that the 'river gypsies' were, in fact, polite, civilised people. However, she was still dubious as she shook Leo's hand. 'You must be Ozzy's Uncle Leo?'

'That's right,' he said. 'Leo Nash, for my sins.'

Having her preconceptions thoroughly disproved by the friendliness in his shandy-coloured eyes, she reminded herself of the need to be wary of such a bohemian character who probably lived by a different set of rules to conventional society. 'My son tells me you're an artist,' she said, in a deliberately offhand manner.

'Yes, but I only paint in my spare time,' he replied amicably, apparently unworried by her tone. 'I earn my living as a draughtsman, actually.'

But that was crazy! How could this untidy, jersey-clad hunk be a draughtsman? They were serious, respectable types who wore neat business suits and lived in proper houses. They weren't sun-tanned and broad-shouldered with rich brown hair that blew across their brow in a sudden river breeze. And they certainly wouldn't do anything so out of the ordinary as to live on water. 'A draughtsman,' she said in astonishment.

'Don't sound so surprised.' He smiled. 'What did you expect me to be, a river pirate or something?'

'Of course not,' she denied haughtily, 'but a draughtsman is someone you normally associate with a more stable environment.'

'I've got news for you, Mrs Brooks,' he informed her lightly, his face crinkling with amusement, 'this boat has been on a permanent mooring for years. I've never even been as far as Chiswick on her.'

Before Kate could make a suitable retort, Sam intervened. 'If you were to travel on her, could I go with you?' he asked wistfully.

'Her travelling days are over, Sam.'

'Oh,' said the boy in disappointment.

'This lad of yours is full of adventure, isn't he?' said Leo, grinning at Kate. 'He wants to fly aeroplanes when he grows up, so he tells me.'

'He's at that imaginative age,' she said dismissively, 'but he'll grow out of it.'

'Being a train driver was the ultimate ambition for boys of my generation,' he said. 'Just shows how times have changed.'

They were observing each other in the light of an oil lamp whose glow spilled across the deck, illuminating the scarlet potted geraniums and sending a splintered yellow gleam on to the water. She shivered, and tried to rekindle the wrath that had driven her here. 'To get to the point of my visit . . .' she began.

'Let's not stand about here getting cold,' interrupted Leo. 'Why don't we continue our conversation in the cabin below?'

'I have to get back. I've work to do . . .'

'Surely you've time for a cup of tea?'

'Well . . .'

Somehow they were all trooping down a flight of steps into a room which immediately struck Kate with a feeling of warmth and cosiness, for all its disorder. Books, newspapers and art materials lay around. Leo cleared a space for her in an armchair and invited her to sit down, while he took a seat at the table.

'Make some tea will you, Ozzy?' he instructed pleasantly. 'And then you and Sam can find yourselves something to do in your cabin while Mrs Brooks and I have a chat.'

As soon as they were alone, Leo threw Kate a shrewd look and said, 'I'm not about to abduct your boy, you know.'

'I didn't say . . .'

'You didn't need to,' he interjected, his lighthearted manner becoming more serious. 'It's written all over you. When Sam came home and told you that he had had tea with a man who lives on a boat, you weren't sure if I was a dropout or some sort of a criminal on the run from the police.'

'Was I really that obvious?' she asked.

'You were rather,' he told her, his mood seeming to lift again, 'but you've nothing to fear from me, I can assure you.'

'Naturally I was worried when Sam didn't arrive home from school,' she explained defensively, 'and of course I was concerned to hear he'd been with strangers. What mother wouldn't be?'

'Yes, I'm sorry, I should have realised,' he said with genuine remorse. 'Sam and Ozzy were getting on so well together, we all just forgot the time.' He gave her a rueful look. 'I do hope you'll forgive me?'

'Apology accepted,' she said, for she was finding it almost impossible to be angry with this man.

'It must be quite a relief to find I'm just an ordinary, law-abiding draughtsman,' he said conversationally.

'Not really,' she said sharply, with the intention of re-establishing a more formal atmosphere. 'Your place in the community is no concern of mine. I merely came to ask you not to encourage Sam to visit you again.'

'Oh?' He frowned. 'May I ask why?'

'Because I don't like him playing near the river,' she explained. 'He can't swim.'

'Then he should be taught,' stated Leo categorically.

'And that's your considered opinion, is it?' she snapped.

'I should have thought it was only common sense,' he retorted. 'Any child who lives near a river should be able to swim. I taught Ozzy as soon as he came to stay with me.'

Since the wisdom of his argument could not be faulted, she just said, 'I've never got round to teaching him. If his father had lived . . .'

'I'll give him a few lessons, if you like?' offered Leo.

'In the river?'

'No. I'll take him to Lime Grove baths. It's easier to learn in a pool than in the river, not to mention cleaner.'

'I wouldn't want to put you to any trouble,' she said, feeling control of this meeting slipping from her grasp.

'No trouble at all,' he assured her. 'I'll be happy to do it.'

'Well, thank you very much, then.'

Ozzy made a timely appearance with a tray of tea and biscuits which he left on the table near Leo before making a diplomatic exit.

'So, having settled that, let's have that cup of tea,' said Leo, pouring them both a cup and handing one to her with some biscuits.

'I mustn't stay more than a few minutes,' she said, her mouth tightening as she considered the amount of sewing she still had to do to reach her daily target. 'I have a lot of work to do at home. This business with Sam has put me behind.'

'Half an hour or so won't make that much difference, surely?' he urged cheerfully, treating her to one of the disarming smiles that made his eyes dance and sparkle.

'Probably not,' she said, buffeted by shock-waves of attraction.

A pleasant atmosphere prevailed as they drank tea and munched biscuits, the stove in the centre of the room exuding a warm glow. Making conversation with him, Kate realised how much she was enjoying the stimulation of fresh adult company. Most of the time she was with either Sam or Mother. As much as she loved them both, it was nice to be neither mother nor daughter, but an intelligent person with a mind of her own.

'Making hats must be quite artistic,' he remarked conversationally.

'Working on a hat from start to finish is,' she explained, 'but I just do finishing and trimming at the moment.'

'At the moment?' he echoed questioningly. 'Does that mean you have plans of some sort?'

'Dreams more than actual plans, unfortunately,' she said. 'But, yes, I'd like to set up on my own as a model milliner.'

'That would be more creative.'

'Not to mention lucrative,' she said briskly, her mood becoming noticeably harsher. 'Fame and fortune are what I'm after.'

'To the exclusion of all else, by the sound of it,' he said with unveiled disapproval.

'I wouldn't say that exactly,' she said, 'but I certainly don't intend to rot away in two rented rooms forever, if I can possibly avoid it.'

'Really?' he said coolly.

'That's right,' she said, his obvious opposition to her ideas goading her to annoy him by making her point even more strongly. 'If I could somehow find the capital to get started, the sky would be the limit for me.'

He nibbled a biscuit without replying, his tacit criticism a palpable force in the room.

'Anyway, what about you?' she continued determinedly. 'You're obviously a man with artistic talent. Can you honestly say you don't want recognition for your art?'

'Recognition, yes,' he said. 'But not fame or fortune.'

'Surely they go together?'

'Often they do,' he admitted, in an infuriatingly calm manner, 'but that doesn't mean you have to want them all.'

'Oh, come on,' she said derisively. 'Surely you're not suggesting that you'd work for nothing if your art became well known?'

'Of course not,' he said. 'I'd like to earn a decent living from painting but I have no desire to be rich.'

'Easy to say that when you don't expect it to happen.'

'It's true, though.'

Much to her annoyance she believed him, and for a fleeting moment was envious. It must be very relaxing to be free from the need for the power and respect bestowed by financial gain. 'You'd probably enjoy the money if it came your way, though,' she said.

'Maybe,' he agreed. 'But apart from maintaining the boat to a decent standard, what would I spend it on? I'm a man of simple tastes.'

She glanced around the room, homely in the glow from the oil lamp, with its well-used furniture and fittings. It could hardly be called luxurious for all its snugness. 'You could buy yourself a house?' she suggested.

'What would I want one of those for?'

'To live in, of course,' she said. 'I assume you are only living here temporarily.'

'This is my permanent home,' he told her. 'I have no plans to move on to terra firma.'

'Oh, I see,' she said, an embarrassed flush suffusing her cheeks.

'*London Lady* was willed to me by a very dear friend,' he went on to explain. 'Originally I moved in as a temporary measure but living afloat has grown on me. I'd feel hemmed in if I moved on to land now.'

'I suppose it's cheaper to live on the river,' she remarked.

'Not when you take into account the high cost of maintaining the boat,' he said. 'I'd probably be a damned sight better off if I bought a house. I could probably get a mortgage on one of the little boxes that have been springing up in rows around London since the war.'

'Surely it makes sense for you to do that, then?'

'As I have just told you, I'm happy here,' Leo said emphatically. 'Living on a houseboat is more than just somewhere to eat and sleep. It's a way of life with a charm all of its own. I enjoy the freedom and the fresh air, the feel of the water beneath me. I'm in central London, but pleasantly detached from it, if you know what I mean.'

She knew exactly what he meant. There was a tranquillity about the rocking of the boat, the echo of a ship's hooter, the urban rumble muted but still reassuringly audible. Nice enough for a visit, but not as a permanent residence, she thought, and said, 'Oh, well, to each his own. It wouldn't suit me. I'm after grander things.'

'You seem very determined.'

'I am. I haven't always roughed it in the backstreets of Hammersmith, you know,' she explained. 'I was brought up in a fashionable Kensington square until my people fell on hard times.'

'And to move back to a fashionable address has become your life's ambition, has it?' he enquired wryly.

'Something like that,' she admitted, without a hint of apology. 'I've been rich and I've been poor and I know which I prefer.'

'You're too young to be so hard,' he said.

'Not really so young,' she said. 'I'm twenty-eight.'

'That's still too young to be so cynical.'

'And too young to settle for two rooms in a backstreet when I have a talent that hasn't yet begun to be used,' she informed him brusquely.

'Why are you so desperate to prove yourself?' he asked, observing her with interest.

'I just want the best I can get for Sam and myself,' she said without really answering his question. 'I want to be able to afford to keep him on at school so that he can make something of himself.'

'An understandable ambition for a mother to have for her son,' he remarked. 'As long as you make sure what you want for him is what he wants for himself.'

'What he might want to do when the time comes for him to leave school, isn't necessarily what's best for his future,' she said, 'I mean, what do any of us know at fourteen?'

'Enough to get by, that's about all.'

'Mmm, and not enough to make the right decisions,' she said. 'That's why I intend to guide Sam in the right direction.'

'Towards a job offering security, I'll bet?'

'Correct,' she said assertively. 'I make no bones about it. Anyway, that's all a long time into the future.' She grinned. 'I have my fortune to make before then.' She stood up. 'And more immediately, I have a pile of hats to finish if I'm going to be able to pay next week's rent.'

Kate walked to the steps and was about to call Sam, when Leo said, 'When I've taught Sam to swim, will you allow him to come to the boat to visit Ozzy? Only they've become such good pals, despite the age difference.'

'I don't think my life will be worth living if I try to stop him,' laughed Kate.

'What did you think of Sam's mother?' asked Ozzy when the visitors had gone and he and Leo sat chatting across the saloon table.

'She seemed all right.'

'Only all right?' said Ozzy, who hadn't realised mothers came in such charming packages. 'I thought she was beautiful.'

'Oh, she's beautiful all right,' agreed Leo. 'I thought you were asking what kind of person I thought she was.'

'What was the matter with her, then?'

'I thought she seemed a bit hard,' Leo declared impulsively, for Ozzy had become more of a pal than a lodger, with a maturity way beyond his years.

'That was only because she was cross about Sam being late home from school,' said Ozzy wisely. Compared to his own mother Sam's had seemed as warm as the saloon stove on a chilly morning.

'It was more than that,' said Leo, thinking aloud. 'She's very ambitious, seemed almost obsessed by the idea of making lots of money.'

'What's wrong with that?'

'Nothing actually wrong with it,' said Leo. 'I just don't happen to think it's healthy to want it as much as she does.'

'At least she's prepared to work hard for it, from what I've heard.' When Ozzy had first learned that Sam's mother worked in the millinery trade, he'd been uneasy, fearing some connection with the Dexters even though the large numbers of hat-making firms employing outworkers made it very unlikely that Mrs Brooks would be working for them. However, an ostensibly casual enquiry had finally eased his mind. 'Sam said she's always sewing so that they can live decently. It isn't as though he has a father to support them.'

'I'm sure she's a very industrious lady,' said Leo, indicating that the subject was at an end, mainly because he was confused about his feelings towards Sam's mother and feared he had already been too presumptuous in his judgement. He certainly wasn't displeased to hear Ozzy stating an opinion. In fact he encouraged it as a general rule for the boy was still far too afraid of causing offence.

'Will you be going down the pub later on?' asked Ozzy companionably.

'No, I won't bother tonight,' said Leo. 'I've got a painting I want to get on with.'

'Shall I go and get us some pie and mash or saveloys and pease pudding for supper?'

'Whichever you like.'

'It isn't for me to say what we have.'

'Now what have I told you about your right to an opinion,' said Leo, frowning.

'It's your boat.'

'But it's your home too now,' he said firmly. 'You earn your right to a say by pulling your weight around here.'

'All right then, I'd like pie and mash,' said Ozzy, adding quickly, 'if that suits you.'

Leo laughed and shook his head. 'You're a hopeless case, do you know that, Ozzy? You must learn to stand up for what you want. I appreciate your consideration, of course. But consideration is one thing, unreasoning acquiescence quite another.'

'Being too humble, you mean?'

'Yes.'

'Sorry.'

'There you go, apologising again!' said Leo. 'You really must learn not to do so much of it before you go out into the world, or you'll get trampled on by all and sundry.'

But despite this gentle reproof, Leo had grown very fond of the boy. For all his youth, Ozzy made a pleasant companion. Over the last few months, he had become less nervous even if he was still too eager to please. Leo was determined not to let him grow up into a spineless 'yes man' just because some thoughtless people had beaten him into submission in his formative years.

Leo's earlier reservations about having a lodger had proved to be groundless. Ozzy never intruded on Leo's privacy. Surprisingly sensitive for someone so young, he seemed to know when Leo wanted company and when he wanted to be left alone. Frequently they set the world to rights over supper. Ozzy was hungry for knowledge, and drew Leo into discussion of everything from geography to politics.

Leo had noticed a keen social awareness in him too, probably because of his own harrowing experiences. He had still told Leo nothing about his background. If a tentative probe was made, Ozzy retreated into himself, so Leo had decided to leave the past alone.

'Anyway, whatever you think about Mrs Brooks,' Ozzy said, bravely standing his ground, 'I think she's very nice and Sam is lucky to have her as his mother.'

'Good, you're learning,' said Leo with a grin. 'You've stuck to your own opinion, regardless of what I think.'

Leo found his own thoughts returning to Kate Brooks. He didn't quite know what to make of her. She certainly seemed to know what she wanted, and made no secret of it. And since she was originally from a rich background, was it not only natural she would wish to regain her former social standing? For all that though, he sensed a deep sense of inferiority beneath that brittle self-assurance. Could a change in circumstances alone produce such soulless aspirations, or was there something else that generated her driving need for success? Somehow, he found it hard to believe that she was as hard and materialistic as she seemed.

One thing he did know for certain – he was intrigued by her. There could be few women in London more unsuited to him, but he wanted to see her again, with a kind of desperation.

Later that night, long after Sam had gone to bed, Kate finally finished sewing for the day. Her eyes were gritty with tiredness, her body ached. She yawned and stretched, feeling barely able to raise the energy to make it to the bedroom.

She had only herself to blame. If she hadn't stayed so long at that damned boat, she would have been finished ages ago. The whole episode had cost her more time than just the length of the visit because thoughts of Leo Nash had slowed her pace.

What a peculiar fellow he was, with his fine ideals. As for all that nonsense he talked about not wanting to be rich, well, he sounded like one of those left-wing idealists one heard so much about these days. It was all very well now, but he would undoubtedly dance to a different tune if he was suddenly rocketed to riches through his art.

He was very attractive for all that, even if he wasn't her type. She grinned to herself. Surely there could be no two people so different in outlook in the whole of the metropolis than herself and Leo Nash? Yet, still, she felt drawn to him.

As she slipped into her empty bed, next to Sam's, the sheets striking cold in the chilly night, she imagined the warmth of Leo's body next to hers.

The next day, however, something happened which pushed all lustful imaginings from her mind completely.

# *Chapter Thirteen*

An anxious Gertie arrived at Kate's door the next morning.
'I've had a telegram from Esme, telling me to not to pay my
usual Friday visit because young Ronnie has gone down with
scarlet fever.'

'Oh, no.' Kate's legs turned to jelly at the mention of this
dreaded illness that claimed so many young lives.

'It's a worry and no mistake,' said her mother.

'I feel so helpless,' said Kate later as she made tea for her
distraught parent. 'I feel I should be there with Esme, doing
something to help.'

'Me too, but we mustn't go near the place in case we bring it
home to Sam,' said Gertie. 'I expect Esme is having to keep
young Rita away from the sickroom, and disinfect all Ronnie's
bedlinen and destroy all the toys that have been anywhere near
him.'

'The poor little mite,' said Kate.

'Not quite three years old,' said Gertie, 'dear little chap,
too.'

'What can we do?'

'Just wait and pray.'

As it happened they didn't do either for very long, because
the next day Gertie received a telegram to say the child had
died.


'Hello, Esme.'

'Hello, Kate. Thanks for coming.'

'Wild horses wouldn't have kept me away.'

'The doctor said we're clear of infection now,' her sister said
dully.

'So Rita will be all right?'

'Hopefully, yes.'

It was the day of the funeral and Kate and Gertie had just arrived at Esme's house in Lilac Gardens. Kate had not thought it wise to subject Sam to such a sad occasion, so had let him go to school in the normal way, having made provision with Leo for him to go to the boat after school with Ozzy just in case she was delayed.

They were standing in the hall, an imposing tiled area reflecting colour from the stained glass window in the porch door. There was a barometer on the wall and a vase of flowers on a semi-circular table beneath a gilt-edged mirror.

Gertie disappeared into one of the rooms where people were gathered. Johnny stood by his wife's side with a steadying hand on her arm, as though afraid she might collapse. Indeed, she looked almost frail enough to be knocked over by the draught from the opening of the front door.

It was three years since the sisters had last met, and Kate barely recognised Esme. Her black calf-length dress hung loose on a skinny frame, red-rimmed eyes staring vacantly at Kate from an ashen face so thin the bones protruded. The silky fair hair that Kate remembered was dragged back from her sister's face in an untidy bun.

'He was so ill, Kate,' she said tearfully, 'so very ill. There were convulsions, delirium . . . he wasn't like our little boy any more.' She moved closer to her husband whose arm instinctively went round her. Esme looked up at him. 'Was he, Johnny?'

'No, love, he wasn't,' he said tenderly 'but he's at peace now. No more sickness, no more pain.'

A lump gathered in Kate's throat at the unity of these two people. She realised she had been wrong to doubt Johnny's rightness for her sister. Whatever his faults, he really was the only man for Esme. Being in the presence of such deep affection made it difficult for Kate to suppress her own emotion. 'I'm sorry I never met your little boy,' she said in a quivering voice.

'Oh, Kate.' Esme fell towards her sister and flung her arms

around her. 'Johnny is very brave, but I can't be. It hurts too much.'

'There, there,' said Kate, holding her close.

'This is the worst thing that ever happened in the whole of my life.'

'I know.'

'I've never been strong at the best of times, you know that,' sobbed Esme, 'but *this*, Kate. It's knocked me for six.'

The sisters clung to each other, reunited, while Johnny stood nearby in case his wife needed him.

Gertie had agreed to sleep at Esme's for a few days after the funeral for moral support, which meant that Kate travelled back to Hammersmith alone. Calling at the boat to collect Sam, she stayed much longer than she'd intended. Being a relative stranger, Leo was just the person she needed to soothe her after that heartbreaking burial during which her sister had become hysterical.

*London Lady*, with her soothing sense of other worldliness, supplied Kate with a much-needed respite, especially as Leo produced a glass of brandy from his cupboard, saying she looked as though she needed it. Having greeted her, the two boys had disappeared into Ozzy's cabin to look at comics. With the curtains drawn, the atmosphere in the saloon was so relaxing it loosened Kate's tongue.

'I don't know how my sister will ever get over it,' she said, her cheeks rosy from the brandy and the heat from the stove.

'Time is the only thing that will do it, I suppose,' said Leo.

'I don't think I would ever recover if I lost Sam,' she confessed, reminded of the fact that she had never forgotten the son she had lost, albeit not through death. 'I doubt if a mother ever gets over losing a child. A parent or partner, in time, yes. But a child, never!'

'What makes you so sure?' he asked. 'You've never lost one, have you?'

She gave him a sharp look, and answered rather too quickly, he thought, 'You don't have to burn in oil to guess what it feels like.'

'She'll probably never get over it,' Leo said gravely, 'but she'll learn to live with it in time. Nature provides us all with an immense capacity for endurance, you know.'

'Is that the wisdom of personal experience?'

'I was at the front for three years, on and off,' he reminded her.

'Enough said. I'm sorry . . .'

'There's no need.'

She sighed wearily. 'I feel such empathy for her, and Johnny of course. But he's a tower of strength.'

The brandy relaxed her into telling him about her split with Esme. One thing led to another and he was given the complete story of the Potters' downturn in fortune.

'At least the tragedy has brought Esme and me together again,' she said. 'Not that it's any real consolation for her, but at least I can be there for her now.'

Leo knew then that Kate was a woman of immense heart beneath her tough exterior. Anyone who cared so deeply for the members of her family could never be totally ruthless, however much they might wish to be.

'They say it's an ill wind that blows nobody any good, don't they?' he reminded her.

All day and every day Esme sat brooding and smoking cigarettes. She neither ate nor slept properly and was prone to frequent bouts of uncontrollable weeping. Her attitude towards her little daughter alternated between impatience and over-protectiveness. The doctor prescribed a nerve tonic and said grief had to take its course, but she wasn't to be left alone too much in the meantime.

Kate and Gertie took it in turns to be with her during the day while Johnny was out at business. Between them they were unsparing in their efforts to help her to pull herself together, all without success. Since they both had a living to earn they were worried about falling behind with the rent as the amount of work they could get through in a day was drastically reduced. To solve that problem, Johnny made up the deficit in their earnings from his own pocket.

'I'm so grateful to you both for spending so much time with her,' he confided to Kate one day when she was about to leave. 'I'd do anything to help her, anything at all.'

'Even give up gambling, if that was what she wanted.'

'You're talking to a reformed character,' he informed her proudly. 'I put all that behind me some time ago.'

'You've never!'

'I have, you know,' he told her. 'It won't bring Ronnie back or pull Esme out of the doldrums, but it might help her to know I'm at home at night and not out playing poker.'

'It must make her feel more secure knowing that you're not putting everything you have at risk at the card table.'

'I hope it will do when she comes out of this trough, though nothing much seems to register with her at the moment.'

'She'll come out of it in time,' said Kate. 'And your turning over a new leaf is good news indeed. What brought it on exactly?'

'Ronnie's death put my priorities sharply into focus, even though it had nothing to do with my gambling,' Johnny explained. 'It made me realise that Esme and Rita are far more important to me than anything, even the thrill of a card game. Esme accepted my gambling when she married me and has never tried to stop me. But it must have been a worry for her. I don't want to add to the burden she has to carry now.'

'Well, good for you,' said Kate. 'I hope you keep to it.'

'I will, don't you fret.'

So Leo was right about that ill wind, she thought, as she made her way home.

Life continued to be harrowing for Kate over the next few months when there was no improvement in Esme's condition. Kate and Gertie carried on with their rota system so that she was not alone too much with just her maid-of-all-work and little Rita.

But although solitude only sent her deeper into depression, all she really wanted was to be left alone to wallow in her grief and self-pity. This was both frustrating and exhausting for those who were trying to help her.

'Oh no, are *you* here again?' she'd say ungratefully when Kate arrived. 'Why don't you go home? Can't you see all I want is to be left alone to think about my Ronnie.'

'You've a daughter too, you know,' Kate reminded her.

'I haven't forgotten, but she's here so I can't forget her, can I?' Esme reasoned with her sick logic 'But I might forget my little boy if I don't keep thinking about him.'

'You won't forget him, love,' Kate assured her patiently.

But Esme was deeply immersed in a world of her own which blinded her to other people's feelings, particularly those of her loved ones.

One day early in 1924, Esme was at a very low ebb and brought pain upon her sister which shocked them both.

'How can you possibly know how I feel?' she raged when Kate tried to persuade her to take Rita for a walk in the park. 'You've never lost a child, have you?' Her eyes glinted with memory. 'You've given one away though, haven't you? Oh, yes, just like that, you gave your son away.'

'Esme, that is uncalled for,' rasped Kate, flinching with the agony the words recalled.

'You did it though, didn't you?' Esme cried hysterically.

'Yes, I did, but . . .'

'Anyone who can give a child away as though it's of no more importance than a pound of potatoes cannot possible know how I feel!' shouted Esme, a feverish flush suffusing her cheeks.

Although Kate knew her sister's words came from a temporary imbalance of mind and she was not really responsible, they increased the sorrow Kate had never lost, causing her to retaliate vehemently. 'You know nothing about the way I felt about that, and still feel. So just shut up about it.'

A tense silence rocked the room as the sisters were locked in confrontation. Esme looked puzzled, as though her own appalling behaviour had taken her by surprise.

'I'm sorry, Kate,' she said at last, her whole body seeming to crumple as the tears began to fall. 'I didn't mean it.'

'Don't you dare assume you know how I feel,' said Kate, still smarting from the accusation and not prepared to let her off scot free.

'I'm so sorry, Kate,' she sobbed, hanging her head in shame. 'Please forgive me.'

Kate hugged her sister and they wept copious tears together. 'I'll forgive you,' she said eventually, 'but you mustn't hurt other people just because you're feeling so bad.'

'I'll try not to.'

'You must do more than just try,' Kate said firmly. 'You must make damned sure you don't do it.'

Leo Nash had become Kate's salvation during the gruelling time following Ronnie's death. As well as supplying Sam with food and shelter whenever his mother was detained in Lilac Gardens with Esme, his boat provided a welcome retreat for her when she got back from Kensington. It was very relaxing to have company to talk to outside the family who sooner or later ended up discussing the tragedy.

She fell into the habit of staying to have something to eat with Leo and the boys when she collected Sam, before going home to stitch hats until the small hours. She looked forward to those times when the four of them would sit round the saloon table chatting companionably, either over something cooked from the shop or a simple feast from Leo's galley like sausage and mash, or ham and eggs with chunks of fresh crusty bread.

Sometimes it seemed as though the foursome was all part of one little family. Every Saturday morning Leo took the boys swimming at the baths, and in the afternoon the male trio usually went to watch a football match. This meant that Kate didn't see much of Sam on a Saturday, even though she didn't have to spend so much time with Esme because Johnny was at home. But knowing he was in good hands and enjoying himself, she didn't mind.

On the day of the quarrel with Esme, she was feeling particularly exhausted when she arrived at the boat in the early evening.

'You look worn out,' remarked Leo, having sent the boys to the chip shop to buy supper.

'I feel it,' she admitted, going on to tell him that she'd had an altercation with Esme, carefully omitting the subject matter.

'From what I've heard, it's a wonder you haven't lost your temper with her before,' he said, for he was kept fairly well up to date with events in Lilac Gardens. 'You're only human, after all.'

'She went too far this time.'

'Do you want to talk about it?'

Since she didn't feel able to tell him the reason for the eruption, she just said, 'Oh, it was something and nothing, you know how these things start. She seems to have forgotten that the rest of us have feelings. Today I just couldn't take it.'

'A few home truths will probably be the best thing for her.'

She made a face. 'That's a bit brutal, isn't it? She *has* lost her little boy.'

'And it's very sad, but life goes on. She'll have to come to terms with it sooner or later.'

'Sometimes you have to be cruel to be kind, you mean?'

'Exactly.'

A need to forget the whole painful episode for a while prompted her to say, 'Can we change the subject? I need a break from family problems.'

'Certainly,' he said. 'And on the subject of a break, how about us having a night out next Saturday? You know what they say about all work and no play . . .'

'Why not?' she agreed, cheered by the idea. 'The boys will love it.'

'I wasn't including the boys.'

'Oh.' She gave him an uncertain smile. 'Just you and me?'

He nodded.

'On a date?'

'That's right,' he said, with one of his warmest smiles. 'Ozzy is quite old enough to take charge for a few hours. Or you could leave Sam with your mother if you'd feel happier about it.'

'I'm not sure . . .'

'Don't look so astounded.' He grinned. 'I'm a man as well as a child minder.'

'Yes, I know that. It's me. I'm out of the habit of that sort of thing.'

'High time you got back into it then, isn't it?' he said with a roguish grin.

'If you say so,' she said, laughing and feeling almost youthfully exuberant. 'And I'd love to come out on a date with you.'

Being the scrupulous mother that she was, Kate decided to leave Sam in her mother's care while she went out for the evening. Gertie suggested that her grandson stay overnight to save Kate having to rush back. She also invited Ozzy to join him, as long as he didn't mind sleeping on the sofa.

So, having finished her work for the day, Kate was free to enjoy herself when Leo called for her on Saturday evening, looking unusually smart in a lounge suit worn with a sparkling white shirt, his hair neatly combed to the side. He wasn't handsome exactly; in fact he had rather an untidy face with a square prominent jaw, a snub nose with a bump on the bridge, and a mouth that became lop-sided when he smiled. But he certainly wasn't lacking in sex appeal, his weathered countenance seeming even more deeply tanned in contrast to the white shirt.

For the first time in ages Kate had taken real trouble with her appearance. Obviously, with a growing child to support, most of her income was swallowed up in basic essentials which severely limited her wardrobe. Her skill with a needle and thread, however, enabled her to make a few things and bring others up to date. This evening, she wore a red winter suit with a long jacket and calf-length skirt, and black shoes with a strap. Her dark hair was worn in a medium-length bob which swung loosely beneath her cloche hat.

'Wow!' said Leo, tucking her arm into his as they walked down the street. 'You look lovely.'

'You don't look so bad yourself.'

They went to the Silver Cinema to see the latest Rudolph Valentino. All the trauma of the last few months melted away as Kate let herself be swept into another world by the idol of the silver screen. With great panache, he wooed his lady-love through heart-stopping adventures, accompanied by cheers and boos from the audience and the pianist energetically emphasising the drama.

Since they were in no hurry to get home, they called at Brown's Oyster Bar afterwards for supper.

'You look like a young girl this evening,' said Leo, studying her across the table as they tucked into oysters served with masses of bread and butter.

'I feel completely revitalised,' Kate's eyes were shining. 'It's years since I've been out to have fun. Not since my husband and I were courting, and it's nearly ten years since he died.'

'We must do it again sometime soon.'

'Yes, please,' she agreed merrily.

They walked back to her place, arm in arm. And since she was rather beyond the age of being kissed goodnight at the front door, she asked him in.

'My reputation will be in ruins by tomorrow morning, of course,' she laughed. 'It'll be all round the houses that I've had a man in my flat after ten o'clock at night, and me a respectable widow with a growing boy to raise too.'

'If you'd rather I didn't . . .'

'I'd rather you did,' she assured him recklessly.

They drank cocoa by the fire, chatting about the film. After saying goodnight rather passionately, Leo crept quietly down the stairs, leaving her feeling as though she had been reborn.

It soon became obvious to Kate that the quarrel she had had with Esme was taking effect. Although her moods were still unpredictable, Esme did begin to improve. Some days were better than others, but she became less aggressive and gradually began to take an interest in life again.

This meant Kate's visits became less fraught. But although she no longer needed Leo's company as a means of therapy, she continued to spend a lot of time with him for the sheer pleasure of it. Saturday night became their regular, child-free night out together when they usually went to a cinema or theatre.

Other times they took the boys on outings: to shows and exhibitions at Olympia, to see the waxworks at Madame Tussaud's, to London Zoo, and many other places. Their trips were made all the more exciting when Leo bought a little motor car. This meant they could go further afield to places like Richmond and Hampton Court. The whole period was a time of acute happiness for Kate, which she wanted to last forever.

The boys groaned good-humouredly when their elders let their joy in each other get out of hand.

'Oh, no, not kissing again!' they could be heard to mutter. 'They're always at it.'

The relationship between Kate and Leo was not the only one to blossom. Sam and Ozzy's friendship deepened too. So much so that Ozzy became almost like one of Kate's family. The fact that he was older meant that Sam tended to regard him as something of a hero. But Kate was impressed by the fact that Ozzy didn't seem to be irritated by Sam's childish affection. In fact, they were more like brothers than friends, ribbing each other and uniting against their elders on occasions.

Kate was amazed when Leo told her that he was not really Ozzy's uncle at all, and went on to explain how the boy had come into his care. It just didn't seem possible to her that anyone would want to mistreat such a sweet-natured boy.

'Don't let Sam hold you back if you want to go off with your older friends,' Kate said to Ozzy one spring afternoon at her flat when Sam was out of the room.

'He doesn't hold me back,' said Ozzy. 'He's a good pal.'

One Saturday afternoon in the spring, Kate took some time off from her millinery work to enjoy the sunshine with Leo on the deck of *London Lady*. This particular Saturday, the boys had deserted Leo and gone off with some pals, so he and Kate were quite alone. It was wonderfully peaceful sitting there with the sun on her face, and Leo close by busily planting seedlings in

231

pots. They were so comfortable together, words weren't necessary.

This atmosphere of contentment was shattered when Leo said lightly, 'You realise you've ruined my comfortable bachelor existence.'

'Oh, and why is that?'

Looking across at her, a streak of mud smudged across his cheek, he said, 'You know the answer.'

He was right, of course. During the last few months she had grown to love Leo with a passionate intensity that far exceeded the youthful first love she had felt for Claude. She and Leo had been so happy together, lighthearted and uncommitted but bound by mutual affection and trust, she didn't want the magic to end. And she was certain that would happen if they tried to alter what was between them. So she had refused to think about the future of their relationship, even though it was obvious they couldn't continue as they had been indefinitely.

'I thought you liked having Sam and me around?' she said evasively, because she didn't want to face up to what she knew was on his mind.

He put the plant pot down, wiped his muddy hands on the old gardening trousers he was wearing, and sat down in a deck chair facing her. 'You know very well what I'm getting at,' he said gruffly. 'You know that I'm in love with you.'

'Yes, I had gathered that,' she said. 'And I feel the same way about you.'

'Oh, Kate.' He was on his feet, sweeping her into his arms. 'Let's go inside.'

She pulled away. 'Not here. Not now,' she said. 'The boys might come back.'

'Let's get married as soon as possible,' he suggested eagerly.

'Married?' she gasped.

'Of course,' he said. 'What else did you think I had in mind?'

'I don't think marriage would be right for us,' she said solemnly.

'What have the last few months been about then?' he asked, his expression darkening.

'About falling in love,' she said. 'But we'd pretty soon fall out of love if we got married.'

'Of course we wouldn't.'

'Oh yes we would,' she insisted. 'Because we want such different things from life, we'd become incompatible after a very short time.'

'What you're trying to say is that you don't want to live on a boat.'

'That's only part of it,' she said. 'I've never made any secret of what I want from life.'

'And marriage to me isn't in your plans?'

'I have a son to consider,' she said, without answering his question. 'Even if I wanted to, I couldn't just up sticks to live on a boat without so much as a second thought.'

'The boat is a damned sight more comfortable than those rooms you live in now.'

'I agree, but whereas I consider my accommodation to be only temporary, you intend to stay here indefinitely.'

Some people walking along the towpath led them to go below to continue the discussion in more private surroundings. The saloon was awash with sunlight, gleaming on the polished table and splashing a pale light across the wood panelling. The freshness of spring poured through the open windows, the curtains gently flapping in the breeze. Leo was right to rate his accommodation above hers, she thought. This bright, attractive room was a palace compared to her flat which was usually filled with soot from the street and other people's stale cooking smells.

As always, the matter was thrashed out across the saloon table.

'It isn't as though I wouldn't improve your quality of life, Kate,' he declared ardently.

'Yes, I know . . .'

'All right, so I might not be able to keep you in luxury,' he interrupted, eager to persuade her, 'but I can afford to keep you and Sam in reasonable comfort. You certainly wouldn't have to sew hats day and night in order to live. And I'd be really proud to have Sam as a stepson.'

'I know that, Leo,' she said with feeling. 'You're a good man, and I love you very much.'

'Marry me then,' he urged her.

'It isn't as simple as that,' she sighed. 'Apart from all the practical complications, I'm not sure if I want to get married again.'

'I can't give you that fashionable Kensington address you want so badly, is that it?'

'It isn't that you can't give it to me,' she said. 'But that you wouldn't want it if it was given to you as a gift.'

'Too right I wouldn't!' he exclaimed. 'I don't want to live among people who will judge me by my possessions.'

'And I wouldn't want to ask that of you,' she said. 'So you can see how impossible it would be.'

'All couples have problems,' he said, 'and if you really do object to living on the boat, I'd be willing to move into a little house – little being the operative word. Posh houses in Kensington are out of my league, I'm afraid.'

'So you're prepared to give up the lifestyle you enjoy so much, for me?'

'Yes, I am.'

'Oh, Leo, you're wonderful.' She was up from her seat and in his arms. 'But we're so happy as we are, why don't we just carry on?'

It was his turn to draw back. 'Because it isn't enough for me, Kate.'

She felt emotionally torn and very confused. There was nothing she wanted more at this moment than to be Leo's wife. And when she really thought about it, she had no serious objections to living afloat. In fact she had become almost as fond of the *London Lady* as he was. But there was a stubborn part of her that just wouldn't allow her to take the most desirable option at the expense of her ambitions.

'Can we let things stay as they are for a while longer, please, Leo? Just until I've had time to think about it properly?'

He gave a resigned sigh. 'Oh, all right then, if you insist.'

# Chapter Fourteen

Such were the advances in modern technology, millions of wireless owners were able to join the enthusiastic multitudes in Wembley Stadium to hear the King open the largest British exhibition ever planned.

Kate was one of the thousands on the terraces at the opening of the British Empire Exhibition. Leo had suggested that they be there in person, deeming the occasion to be of educational value to the boys as well as a blooming good day out for them all. Kate's nearest and dearest had soon latched on to the idea and were here en masse, Gertie and Bertha having squeezed into Leo's Ford with Kate and the boys, Esme and her family meeting them here.

Despite the chilly mist on this cool spring morning, the atmosphere in the stadium was warm and exuberant as the crowds waited for the royal party to arrive. From their places in the upper balconies, Kate and company witnessed a most colourful and moving preliminary spectacle.

The massed bands of the Brigade of Guards marched into the amphitheatre and swung smartly into position, followed by the massed pipers of the Scots and Irish Guards. The exultant crowds were then entertained by rousing band music and the glorious singing of the joint choirs of three thousand voices. The Guards of Honour were played into the arena by the bands, and after some more military pageantry the King appeared, with the Queen and his three younger sons, to tumultuous applause.

His Majesty spoke from the grand dais which had been temporarily erected and fitted with all the latest miracles of science which would make his voice audible to his subjects in all parts of his Empire. He delivered his message of confidence for the future with clarity and sincerity, touching on the 'co-operation between brothers for the development of the family state'.

After the ceremony, Kate and her party found plenty to interest them at the exhibition. With throngs of other visitors, they were given an insight into life on such distant shores as Canada, Australia, New Zealand and India, views of which delighted them from a good vantage point on one of the bridges over the lake.

There were Palaces of Industry and Engineering, and buildings full of enthralling exhibits from faraway places like Ceylon and South Africa. There was the magnificent Burma Pavilion, and a fortress of dark red stone containing the native West Africa exhibitions. Ubiquitous in the gardens were banks of budding tulips planted in profusion. There was even a cobbled Old English street with quaint rows of shops.

Interrupting their sightseeing only to eat lunch in one of the many restaurants, they trooped from one building to the next, lingering along the way to enjoy such pleasures as a brightly coloured bandstand, a gorgeous Indian courtyard, and Hong Kong represented in a whole street. There was something to please everyone in this diverse landscape: tall towers, small native huts, sparkling waterfalls.

Eventually sated with culture, they moved on to the thrills and spills of the amusement park where Sam and Ozzy paid sixpence for four minutes of breathless excitement on the only one of the three scenic railways that was ready for use.

By the end of the afternoon, they were all exhausted so decided to take a break for a late tea at a cafe. Hundreds of weary visitors filled the place in noisy abundance. Deciding not to wait for a table to become vacant where they could all sit together, Kate and company parked their tired bones wherever the waitress could find space for them. In the chaotic scramble for seats, Kate found herself sharing a table for two with her brother-in-law.

'Actually I'm glad of this opportunity to have a chat with you, Kate,' said Johnny intriguingly, helping himself to one of the iced fancies from a silver-plated cake-stand. 'I've been thinking of coming to see you, as a matter of fact.'

'Oh? What's on your mind?'

'I was wondering if you're still keen to start up in business on your own?'

'As much as ever,' she said, puzzled by the question. 'But why the sudden interest?'

'It isn't all that sudden,' he reminded her. 'I offered to help you once, remember?'

'Yes, I remember.'

'Well, just lately it's been on my mind again,' he explained. 'I got to thinking that you might feel more inclined to accept a helping hand from me now that my habits have changed. I'm not rich by any means but I could let you have enough to get started.'

'It's very tempting,' she confessed, 'but you've Esme and Rita to support. I'd feel as though I was depriving them.'

'Naturally, I wouldn't make the offer if I couldn't afford to help you without it affecting my family commitments,' he explained. 'Anyway, I've spoken to Esme about it and she's all in favour.'

'I see, but why should either of you want to help me?'

'Because we're grateful to you,' he told her.

'What on earth do you have to be grateful to me for?' she asked, genuinely baffled.

'You've been very good to Esme since Ronnie's death.'

'No more than any sister would have been,' she interrupted.

'I disagree,' he said. 'You didn't have to spend so much time with her when she was low, coming over to the house every day no matter how busy you were and putting up with her difficult moods. It isn't as though life is easy for you, with a child to raise alone.'

'So I spent time with her. What's so special about that?'

'You helped her come through it, believe me.'

'Esme would have battled her way through it anyway,' argued Kate. 'She may not be the toughest person in the world but neither is she a quitter.'

'I have no way of proving it but I think your contribution

237

made a lot of difference. At least she's learning to live with her grief as best she can now.'

'Yes, she does seem much better.'

'It eased my mind too in those early days, knowing that you were with her while I was out at work.'

'I'm not sure Esme was too pleased about it, when all she wanted was to be left alone to feel sorry for herself!'

'All the more credit to you for sticking it out then.'

'It wasn't all down to me,' Kate reminded him. 'Mother did her share too.'

'Yes, I must find a way to repay her, too.'

'There's no need for you to repay either of us,' she said emphatically. 'Families stick together. At least, that's what I've always believed.'

'But it would please me to do something for you in return,' he said earnestly. 'And it would be very foolish of you to miss the chance of being able to turn your dream into reality.'

She stirred her tea thoughtfully. 'You really are keen to help me, aren't you?'

'That's right.'

'And as you say, I'd be a fool to turn my back on such an opportunity.'

'Sure.'

'I would only accept the money as a loan, not a gift.'

'Oh? Why?'

'As keen as I am to set up on my own, I want to do it without handouts, and standing firmly on my own two feet.'

'How about a compromise, then?' he suggested 'Let's make it an interest-free loan.'

'You'd still be giving me something.'

'Only the interest.' He gave her a wicked grin. 'And, anyway, families stick together.'

'Touché.' She smiled happily, conceding defeat, 'But I would want to repay the loan as soon as possible.'

'That's entirely up to you.'

'What sort of sum do you have in mind?'

'I couldn't go higher than about two hundred pounds,' he explained, 'but I've taken the liberty of making some enquiries

238

about the cost of setting up a millinery business, and I think that should cover everything you'd need and give you enough to live on until you start to draw an income.'

'That would be ample, I'm sure.' Now that the idea stood a chance of reaching fruition, she was assailed by doubts. 'Supposing the project fails?'

'It won't fail with you in charge,' he said. 'I might have given up gambling but I haven't lost my feel for a winner.'

'You're very kind.'

'I'm not just being kind, I'm saying what I believe to be true.' He looked seriously into her face. 'So, do we have a deal then?'

She nodded. 'Oh, Johnny, I've wanted to do this for so long, but now I can actually go ahead, I'm scared stiff!'

'The best way of dealing with cold feet is to plunge them straight into the water.'

'I expect you're right.' She leaned across the table and squeezed his hand with gratitude and affection. 'You'll get your money back, if I have to kill myself to do it.'

'I'm sure such lengths won't be necessary.'

'Can we work out the details later?' she said, anxious to share the good news. 'I can't wait to tell Leo and the boys.'

Leo thought Kate looked years younger as she excitedly broke the news, her cheeks flushed, eyes shining. With a sinking heart he suspected that his plans for marriage must be abandoned, for the time being anyway.

'Oh, Leo, isn't it wonderful? Isn't Johnny a sweetheart to give me this chance? I must start looking for suitable premises right away . . . will you help me? Oh, boys, isn't it going to be fun? I'm going to make us rich, Sam, rich! What do you think about that?'

'Er . . . it's good,' he said doubtfully. 'But we won't have to move away, will we?'

'No. I'll have to find a shop to let in the West End, if I'm to stand any chance of making a name for myself,' she explained, 'but I won't be able to afford anything in that area with living accommodation, so we'll stay where we are for the moment.'

'Thank goodness for that,' he said, grinning with relief, 'Only I wouldn't want to be too far away from Ozzy and Leo.'

'Don't worry, Sam,' she said, looking meaningfully at Leo, 'I wouldn't want that either.'

Meeting her eyes, his fears were confirmed. He knew he must not exert pressure if their relationship was to stand a chance of surviving into the future. Whatever it was that drove her to crave success so badly, she must be allowed her head or it would haunt her forever. He consoled himself with the thought that at least she seemed to want to share the excitement of this new project with him.

Kate found herself plunged into a period of hectic activity. There were premises to find; materials and equipment to buy; a stock of hats to be made; marketing to be studied. Locating a shop was the major priority though, and that was not an easy task for someone on a strict budget who needed to trade in the West End. Rents were high in this desirable region and she daren't be reckless with the loan, not with a child to support and the possibility of its taking a while to build a steady income.

Leo was a great help, putting his advice, his spare time and his motor car at her disposal whenever she needed it. Indeed, the setting up of this enterprise was a family affair with everyone taking an interest, including Ozzy. In fact, it was that young man who spotted the dilapidated shop premises for rent in one of the backstreets near Oxford Street one Sunday afternoon when Leo was driving them around in search of anything the estate agents didn't have on their books.

Situated in Litchman Street, the shop had been standing empty for some time on account of its small window space. A dusty 'To Let' board led them to the owner who gave them a tour of inspection. At first glance the property seemed to be completely without potential, being in a bad state of repair with rotting floorboards and peeling wallpaper. But the instant Kate walked through the door she knew that, with some redecoration, the place would be perfect.

The premises comprised a shop area and two other rooms.

The one at the back with nice big windows she saw as a workroom; the other would make an ideal office. A couple of other high-class hat shops were already established in the street but Kate did not see this as fearful competition but a confirmation that she had chosen the right area in which to set up in business as a model milliner.

'I hope you boys don't have anything planned for your spare time over the next few weeks,' said Leo, seeing the gleam in Kate's eye, 'because the three of us are going to be busy painting and decorating.'

'It'll be something to do,' said Ozzy.

'Cor, what a lark!' said Sam.

'My heroes,' she said, hugging all three of them in turn.

Even before the lease was signed, Kate had worked out the decor for her shop. Aiming for a modern look with an air of spaciousness, she chose white walls liberally covered with mirrors, royal blue carpet and chairs with dove-grey upholstery.

While the three men in her life became spare-time decorators, she visited a milliner's closing down sale where she managed to obtain a sewing machine, papier mâché dollies, wax heads for window display, chrome millinery stands, various shopfittings and a batch of hoods and other materials. At a furniture sale she acquired a second-hand desk and some workroom tables.

With the practical tasks well underway, the opening was set for August with winter headwear in mind. This meant she needed to get to work on a collection of hats. Dreaming up the designs was easy compared to finding a suitable helper. She had decided to employ one assistant apart from her mother, whose hours were to be part-time and flexible to enable her to be at home when Sam got in from school if Kate was not.

Kate's advertisement in the *Evening News* produced a string of applicants, but none who met her criteria, for she was looking for someone who could do more than just sew. She needed a good all-rounder who would be willing to be a general dogsbody, as well as look after the place if it was necessary for Kate to go out on business.

The solution was unexpectedly solved by the most unlikely contender, a cockney school-leaver called Poppy Brown, who breezed into the chaos of the embryo milliner's for an interview one late summer afternoon without making an appointment. Kate was busy at the time, battling to get the workroom into some sort of order, surrounded by paper bags and cardboard boxes full of materials. Ozzy was perched on a ladder in the shop putting the finishing touches to the paintwork. Sam had gone on an errand, both boys being on their summer holidays from school.

Feeling rather harassed by this intrusion, Kate took her into the room which would eventually be the office and found her a seat by the desk, currently shrouded in a dust sheet. A pile of hat-boxes prevented the door from being closed but the interview went ahead anyway.

Kate was not initially impressed by the girl's demeanour, especially the way she dominated the interview.

'I've been workin' in millinery since I was about ten years old,' she informed Kate brightly. 'Mum sews 'ats at 'ome, yer see, and she's always taken on enough work for me to do an' all to bring in more money.'

'I see but . . .'

'Now that I've left school I can get a proper job,' she continued with staggering self-confidence. 'Mum and Dad need my wages 'cos there are four at 'ome younger than me, and Dad's out o' work.'

'Oh dear, what a shame . . .'

'Lost his job down the docks and can't find nothin' else,' she continued, ignoring Kate's attempts to speak, 'and 'e ain't been well since he came back from the war neither. Gone a bit funny in the 'ead, 'e 'as. Talks to 'imself an' gets terrible shakin' fits. Mum says it's a bloomin' shame after what he did for 'is country.'

'So, as you've only worked on hats at home, you don't actually have any workroom experience?' interrupted Kate, determined to get to the point of the interview.

'Not as such, no,' said the girl without a hint of regret. 'But I can sew as good as anyone, better 'an most. I'll give yer an example if yer give me something to work on.'

Since the girl's sewing ability was not the issue in question, Kate said, 'No, that won't be necessary, thank you.' She ran a judicial eye over this spindle of a thing who looked as though she hadn't had a decent meal or any new clothes in ages. Two earnest brown eyes shone from a tiny face surrounded by a mop of curly, chestnut-coloured hair. Her skin looked freshly scrubbed but her frayed dress was too small and pulling across an expanding bust, her shoes scuffed at the toes and worn down at the heels. 'I'm looking for someone who has workshop as well as sewing experience.'

'Wouldn't take me long to pick it up,' she said, 'I can promise yer that.'

'I'm sure it wouldn't, my dear, but I'm only in business in a small way, so I need someone older who can work on their own initiative,' Kate said. 'There will be occasions when I have to leave the shop, you see.'

'Everyone says I'm a quick learner,' Poppy persisted. 'An' we all 'ave to start somewhere, don't we?'

Kate steeled herself against the persuasive eyes that were meeting her own determinedly. She really must be strong about this, she couldn't afford to carry passengers. 'I'm sorry, my dear,' she said, rising from her seat with an air of finality, 'but you won't be suitable. I'm sure you'll find a position with a larger, well-established milliner's.'

The girl looked downhearted but not defeated. 'Give us a chance, missus,' she begged. 'You won't regret it, honest.'

'I'm sorry, dear.'

'Oh well,' the young woman sighed, getting up from her seat. 'You know yer own business best, I s'pose, but yer won't get many who'll work as 'ard as me.'

'Thank you for coming,' said Kate, riddled with guilt without really knowing why.

'That's all right.'

Poppy Brown marched with spirit out of the office and across the shop, watched by Ozzy who had been listening intently to every word.

'What yer looking at?' she asked, halting in her step to throw him an icy glare. 'Don't yer know it's rude to stare at a lady?'

'Sorry,' he said, turning scarlet.

'You will be if I catch yer clockin' an eyeful again,' she said as a parting shot.

When the shop-door closed behind her, the whole place seemed dismally silent.

'I think you ought to have given her a chance,' Ozzy ventured impulsively, his voice quivering slightly at his own impertinence.

'Oh, you do, do you?' said Kate, too taken aback by his nerve to be angry. 'And why is that?'

'Lots of reasons,' he said, pausing in his work with his paintbrush poised in the air. 'She's obviously experienced at sewing, she's the sort to work her fingers to the bone and take a real interest in the firm, and because she really needs the job.'

'So do hundreds of other girls,' Kate pointed out.

'But you haven't found anyone suitable, even though you've plenty of choice.'

'That's true but . . .'

'There was something special about her,' he said as though thinking aloud. 'I don't know what it was exactly . . .'

Kate had noticed Ozzy's sensitivity before, and on this occasion he was in tune with her own thoughts. On the face of it, Poppy Brown was completely unsuitable for a West End milliner's, yet she was the only one of the applicants Kate really wanted to employ. She heard herself saying, 'You'd better get off after her then, hadn't you, and tell her to come back so that we can arrange a starting date.'

Perceiving his joy as he almost fell off the ladder in his hurry to get down and after the girl, Kate realised she was standing on the sidelines of a schoolboy crush. Poppy Brown should be honoured indeed to have Ozzy's admiration, she thought. He really was the nicest boy.

Kate, Gertie and Poppy made a good team as they worked feverishly to have a good selection of hats ready for the opening. Making her own sparterie blocks for shaping, Kate got busy with scissors, steam kettle and flat iron. She cut, shaped, pressed, pulled, twisted; Gertie and Poppy pinned and stitched until their fingers ached.

Among the growing accumulation of stock were toques, tricornes, cloches and berets, all made unique by variations of style and trimmings. There were neat head-hugging hats and large floppy extravaganzas. There was a close-fitting cap with a feather trim; a white felt pill-box with a swirl of red ribbon around it caught with diamanté clasps. Frivolous fun hats and sober shopping hats made an imaginative and varied collection in all shades and materials. One of Kate's favourites was a glorious autumn creation in rust-coloured felt, trimmed with orange petersham ribbon and clusters of crimson wax berries.

Every day the workroom table was littered with snippets of felt, velour, velvet, scraps of ribbon, thread, sewing silk. Pins, drawing pins and tape covered the floor until, at last, the collection was ready.

Now came the task of finding customers. This was where the private school that had taught Kate how to put pen to paper in an intelligent manner came in useful. She sent letters to the fashion editors of various magazines and newspapers informing them of the opening of her shop and inviting them to a small launch party. She also placed advertisements in the top fashion magazines.

The day before the official opening, every last bow and button, feather and fold was sewn into place. A couple of bottles of sherry had been purchased with which to entertain her guests. Kate Brooks, Model Milliner, was about to make her debut.

# Chapter Fifteen

Outside the shop all seemed tranquil. The window was elegantly dressed with hats in a variety of colours displayed against a dark blue backdrop. Written in black on a white fascia board above the window was the simple announcement KATE BROOKS – MILLINER.

Inside, the atmosphere was fraught with tension. The blue-carpeted shop area, divested of every last speck of dust, had several display counters with hats on view on heads and stands.

A comfortable chair was placed in front of every mirror, a few other seats dotted around for general use. Anything with the slightest potential to shine had been polished until it gleamed; vases of fresh flowers, some of which had been delivered to Kate as a personal opening day gift from Leo, were dotted about on occasional tables.

On a table in the corner stood a sherry decanter and glasses. Poppy, neatly accoutred in a crisp white apron bought for the occasion by Kate, waited to serve the drinks to ladies of the fashion press. It was almost twelve noon. The time given on the invitations had been eleven-thirty.

'They'll all turn up at the same time, I reckon,' said Poppy hopefully.

'Like trams and buses,' added Gertie.

'I shouldn't think they'd come now,' said Kate, trying to hide her disappointment for a couple of sentences by a fashion reporter was better advertising than any that could be bought. 'They've probably got more important things to do. Never mind, I expect we'll have better luck when we open to the public this afternoon.'

Despite her calm exterior, the enormous responsibility of

this project weighed heavily on Kate. Up until half an hour ago, she had been too busy with the preparations to dwell on the possibility of failure. Now, in the sobering light of an empty shop that should be filled with fashion reporters, her imagination ran wild. Supposing she didn't even sell one hat! *Not ever!* And her with a child to support and two people relying on her for their wages. She felt quite ill with worry.

She was about to suggest that they forget about the party and get on with some work when a taxi drew up outside, and a smart woman in a Chanel-style summer suit stepped out.

The visitor turned out to be Rose Matthews of *Fashion Monthly*. She offered profuse apologies for her late arrival, which had apparently been caused by a traffic hold-up at Oxford Circus. Other guests followed, all with the same explanation. Only a handful of those who had received invitations actually appeared, but there was enough to create a festive mood, and a sociable hubbub soon filled the shop.

'An interesting collection, my dear,' said Rose Matthews, smoking a cigarette in a long holder. 'I'm quite impressed.'

'Thank you.'

'You'll have to do something more outlandish to get noticed, though.'

'Really?'

'Oh, yes, fashion is a highly competitive business as I'm sure you know.'

'I just want to make beautiful hats, hats to bring out the best in people . . .'

Rose interrupted with a shrill laugh. 'It's a sweet idea, and I'm not saying you won't manage to struggle along making a living that way, but you'll never be a top milliner unless you stand out from the crowd, somehow.' She sipped her third sherry, her cheeks glowing pinkly. 'You'll have to stud your hats with drawing pins or paper clips or something.'

'I wouldn't want to do anything like that just to get noticed.'

'Designers have done worse things to put themselves on the map,' said Rose flippantly.

'I won't be using gimmicks,' Kate said, standing her ground.

'I intend to produce hats to make my customers feel good about themselves. If I please people, they'll come back.'

'Oh, well, if you're aiming to build a list of nonentities, that's up to you,' Rose said, guzzling her sherry and taking a refill from the tray Poppy was handing around.

'I'm hoping to please a wide range of women,' said Kate. 'We all know how important a woman's hat is to to her self-esteem.'

'And we all know how you designers crave commercial success,' Rose said, hiccuping.

'Doesn't anyone who starts in business?'

Adopting a chummy manner, Rose took her arm. 'I'm not being bitchy, my dear, just realistic,' she said, looking into Kate's face. 'I make a living by knowing about these things. I'm not saying you'll not earn your daily bread, just that you'll have to come up with a new angle if you want caviare.'

'Thanks for the advice,' said Kate. 'Now if you'll excuse me, I must circulate.'

Fortunately, not all of her guests were as cynical as Rose Matthews. In fact most of them were kind and supportive. But as Kate moved among them, she found herself longing for the proper business to start this afternoon when she opened her doors to the people who really mattered – the customers.

'I saw your advertisement in a magazine and thought I'd come along to see if you have anything to suit me,' said their first customer that afternoon, an expensively dressed lady with white hair but a youngish air about her. 'Since my hair turned white I have difficulty finding anything that doesn't either make me look as though I'm in my dotage or like mutton dressed as lamb.'

'I'm sure we can find something to suit you,' Kate assured her. 'What colour did you have in mind?'

'That green one is rather attractive,' said the woman, pointing towards an apple-green felt with a feather trimming. 'But I'd rather be advised by you.'

'Certainly.'

Kate settled the customer on a chair in front of a mirror and tried the hat on her. The colour was perfect, bringing out the greenish tones in her eyes and enhancing her olive skin.

'I love the colour,' the client said, 'but there's something not quite right about it.'

'Mmm, I agree.' Kate pondered on the problem for a moment before pushing the brim into a sidesweep which instantly changed the image, combining stylishness with dignity which was perfect for a woman of her years. 'There, how about something like that?'

'Oh, yes, that's much better,' the customer enthused. 'Yes, I like that a lot.'

'Leave it with me then and I'll have it altered for you,' Kate said. 'Are there any other modifications you'd like? A tuck here and a twist there can make a world of difference.'

'Don't you mind changing one of your model hats?' enquired the woman.

'On the contrary, there is headwear and there are hats. I make hats with a life of their own to suit individual owners. Since every one of us is unique, a little modification is bound to be necessary.'

'This green will be fine the way you have it,' said the woman eagerly. 'But I need a few other hats for the winter season. May I try some more on?'

'Certainly,' said Kate, her heart leaping for joy as another potential client entered and began browsing. 'I'll bring a selection over to you.'

'So, your first day was a success then,' said Leo when he called round at Kate's flat that evening to find her in good spirits.

'I think I can honestly count it as one, yes,' she said, pouring him a cup of tea. 'I didn't enjoy the press party very much, but once the real business started, I was in my element.'

'Did you sell many hats?'

'Yes, quite a few.'

'Good. Once word gets around, you'll be inundated.'

'I hope so, but I suspect it won't be quite as easy as that.'

'Maybe not, but I'm glad today went well, anyway,' he said, sitting in a chair by the open window to drink his tea. 'I was wondering how you were getting on while I was working at my drawing board.'

'Thanks for the flowers,' she said, going over to him and kissing him. 'It was a lovely thought.'

'My pleasure.'

Sam appeared looking hot and dusty from playing in the street.

'Hello, Sam,' said Leo.

'Hello. Where's Ozzy?'

'On the boat.'

'Can I go and see him, Mum?'

'All right, but make sure you're back before dark.'

'I will. Cheerio.'

'Cheerio.'

'He's growing faster than a weed,' commented Leo.

'Mmm, as soon as I can afford it, I must get us into some larger accommodation,' she said. 'He's getting too big to be sharing a bedroom with his mother.'

'Give yourself time,' said Leo. 'You've only been open one day and already you're planning to move house.'

'Nothing expensive, just something with two bedrooms,' she said, adding waggishly, 'but perhaps I had better leave it until the end of the week.'

'In the meantime, how about us going out for a meal to celebrate your first day in business?' he suggested. 'We could go up West.'

'I'd love to . . .'

'Good. Let's get organised then. Sam can stay with Ozzy . . .'

'But I can't,' she interrupted ruefully. 'I have some work to do.'

'Oh, no. Not work again, morning noon and night,' he said crossly.

'I've a few alterations to do for a customer,' she explained. 'I've brought the hats home to work on.'

'They can wait, surely?'

'I promised to have them ready for her tomorrow.'

'That's ridiculous,' he snapped.

'I need to build a reputation, Leo,' Kate reminded him, 'and if that means putting myself out, then that's what I'll do.'

'You should end your working day at a reasonable time now that you're running a business of your own,' he snapped. 'Otherwise you'll be a slave to it like you were when you were working for someone else.'

'I'm even more of a slave to it now I'm working for myself!'

'More fool you.'

'It doesn't seem like work now that I'm doing something I really enjoy. Anyway, no one ever found success by working nine till five.'

'Success, success!' he shouted. 'That's all you ever think about.'

'Maybe you're right,' she retaliated, 'and I've never pretended otherwise. You've known the sort of person I am from the start.'

'That doesn't make it any easier for me to take,' he said angrily. 'I'm in love with you, Kate. I want to be with you. All right, so I've agreed to mark time on the question of marriage, but I want to see something of you, for heaven's sake.'

'I'm sorry to have upset you.'

'Are you?'

'Yes, I am,' she said with genuine concern, 'but I don't see what I can do about it because I'm into this thing up to my neck. I *have* to make it work.'

'And that means living and breathing it, I suppose?'

'I wouldn't go so far as to say that, but it certainly means commitment,' she said. 'Don't spoil it for me, Leo. I've wanted this for a very long time.'

'I'm sorry,' he said in a tone of weary resignation. 'I suppose I'm being selfish.'

'No, you're not,' she said, sitting on his lap and slipping her arms around him. 'We'll go out together another night sometime soon, I promise.'

'Fair enough,' he agreed, but he had a strong suspicion it was going to be a very long time before they had any sort of life together.

★  ★  ★

From sheer necessity work dominated Kate's life over the next few months as the difficulties facing a new milliner with no reputation or contacts became apparent. Design and production were no problem for she was brimming over with creative energy and had good back-up staff. Marketing was the thing that gave her sleepless nights.

It wasn't that they didn't sell any hats. After a short fallow period following the opening, when the few lines written about her in the fashion press were forgotten, regular advertising and a well-kept window produced a reasonable flow of custom. Women of all shapes, ages and temperaments visited her shop. Her workshop was kept busy. She could meet her overheads and feed and clothe Sam and herself. She was even able to afford a small increase in rent and move into a modest two-bedroomed flat a few streets away from her mother near some public gardens.

But her turnover varied little from week to week. She wasn't progressing in the way she had hoped. There were a million hats in her mind and she wanted to make them all. She wanted clients who consulted her on a regular basis. But building a client list took time and for the moment she needed to sell more hats to anyone who would buy them.

Frequently the London streets burned beneath her aching feet as she trudged along them with a bag full of hats, calling at the little Baker Street shops usually called 'Madam' something or other. Occasionally they would buy a few from her. She tried to make her work known to the couture houses, but none of them would see her.

A breakthrough came one day in the spring of 1925. Having toured the department stores trying to see millinery buyers without even getting past the reception office, she decided to make one last call before giving up, and arrived at the prestigious Whitton's store, exhausted and windswept. Miraculously, the buyer agreed to see her, liked what she had on offer and ordered fifty hats.

Kate traded regularly with Whitton's after that, which meant an increased turnover and the need for another couple of workroom hands, especially as the shop trade was also increasing.

London fashion was reckless and revolutionary just now, especially for young women. Cloches were worn so low on the forehead that eyes were almost concealed in some cases, and there was a vogue for attaching a sparkling ornament to the front or side of these sort of hats.

Immersed in her frantic lifestyle, events outside work seemed to happen on the periphery of Kate's existence. Sam grew tall as his eleventh birthday approached, and Ozzy left school and started work as an office boy on the local paper with the idea of working his way up to becoming a reporter. His friendship with Poppy seemed to be continuing, judging by the amount of time he spent hanging around the shop waiting for her to finish work. Inevitably, Sam saw less of Ozzy now that he was no longer a schoolboy, but Kate was pleased he hadn't deserted Sam altogether and was still a regular visitor to the flat at weekends.

Gertie continued to work for Kate, except on Thurdays when she spent the day helping out at the Institute.

As for Leo, he seemed to have accepted her career and no longer complained about the long hours she put in or pressured her to see him. He invited her to dinner on the boat one Saturday in late summer, though, and she found herself free to accept. Sam was away camping for the weekend with the Cubs. Ozzy had gone to stay with a friend from work for the weekend, so they were to have the place to themselves.

It was a warm humid evening, with the late sun shining through the willow trees and a river breeze stirring the leaves. The boat made a welcome retreat from the airless streets which were buzzing with bluebottles, the accumulation of motor fumes, horse dung and drains rising in a nauseating miasma.

Since Kate and Leo didn't socialise very often these days, she had made a special effort with her appearance and looked lovely in a yellow silk blouse with matching pleated skirt which fell just below the knee. Her hair was fashionably bobbed beneath her summer boater which was trimmed with yellow ribbons.

At thirty she was more attractive than she'd been as a girl because her raw thinness had become gently curved, her dark eyes reflecting her increased self-confidence. The sophistication she had gained from being in business suited her. In common with many other fashion-conscious women, she had begun to use cosmetics which gave her face a new glow.

'My word, you look as though you're about to dine on a millionaire's yacht instead of a creaky old houseboat with ordinary old me,' said Leo as she came aboard.

'There's nothing ordinary about you,' she said, kissing him in greeting and noticing that he was looking smart in a blazer and flannels. 'You look more handsome than Douglas Fairbanks.'

'Flattery will get you everywhere,' he laughed.

'I mean it.'

'Would you like to eat on deck as it's such a pleasant evening?'

'I'd love to,' she said. 'But what's with all this home cooking?'

'I thought it would be more private than a restaurant.'

'You're right,' she agreed, 'and something smells delicious.'

He had excelled himself by cooking steak with mushrooms and sauté potatoes which they at a small deck table. He surprised her by producing a bottle of champagne.

'This is all very romantic,' she said. 'You're spoiling me.'

'It isn't often I get the chance.'

She looked into his eyes, so warm and tender. 'No, we don't have enough evenings like this together.'

'And whose fault is that?'

'Mine,' she admitted, raising her hands in self-defence. 'I take the blame entirely.'

'Well, here's to your first year in business,' he said, raising his glass.

'I'll drink to that,' she said as their glasses chinked.

'Are you pleased with the way things have gone for you this year?'

'Moderately,' she said.

'Only moderately?' He was frowning.

'I still don't have the sort of client list I'm after,' she said, and hurriedly sought to change the subject because she knew how Leo disapproved of her avid quest for success. 'How's Ozzy getting on at his job?'

'Quite well, I think, though he's another one who wants to run before he can walk,' he told her. 'He's impatient to get into print.'

'Oh dear, poor Ozzy.'

'I've told him he's got years of making tea and running errands in front of him before he can even begin to think of that sort of thing.'

'He's a sweet boy, I hope he makes it.'

'Oh, he'll make it all right,' said Leo adamantly. 'Not only is he determined, he's very clever with words too.'

'It's good to know that I'm not the only one with ambition in your circle,' she said lightly.

'Perhaps it flows towards people with big dark eyes,' he said.

She giggled. 'Yes, Ozzy and I both have those, now you come to mention it.'

'Than God I'm not bitten by ambition,' he said. 'I couldn't bear all the anguish.'

The steak was followed by fruit salad, then they lingered over coffee and brandy. A pleasant sense of relaxation turned to lightheadedness. Kate felt feminine and filled with desire. In this amorous mood, her pulses quickened with every look, every touch . . .

'It was a lovely meal,' she said. 'Thank you.'

'My pleasure.'

'I'll wash the dishes as you cooked the meal,' she offered in an effort to temper the sexual chemistry that was flowing between than as palpably as the river itself.

'Certainly not.' He was smiling. 'Tonight is not for domestic chores.'

'I've done them often enough in the past,' she said.

'But not tonight,' he insisted, adding jokingly, 'I should have servants to do it for me.'

'One day perhaps you will, when you are a successful artist.'

'God forbid,' he said. 'I can't imagine anything more awful than having one's privacy invaded in such a way.'

She didn't reply because she didn't want to risk a quarrel and spoil the mood. They sat for a long time, sipping coffee and watching the sun sink behind the rooftops. Even as darkness fell and dampness rose, the air was still warm and balmy. Swarms of midges gathered like dust around the deck lamp.

'How about a walk?' he suggested.

'Lovely,' she said.

They ambled along the river bank, arm in arm, with no particular destination in mind. They passed wharves, still and silent at this time. Patches of light dotted the dark industrial shapes of the sugar refinery, the brick factory and brewery. They passed boathouses and rowing clubs and clusters of cottages. Crossing the creek by the wooden High Bridge, they passed various riverside pubs, their windows glowing cosily and punters spilling out on to the towpath.

'Sunday tomorrow,' she said, 'I can have a lie in as Sam's away.' She paused. 'I miss having him around though.'

'That's something you're going to have to get more used to as he grows up.'

'Don't remind me,' she said. 'I'm dreading it.'

'You are a complete mystery to me, you know,' he said.

'Why is that?'

'Well, you set convention on its head by wanting a life outside the home when most women are happy to settle for marriage,' he said. 'Yet you're the most devoted mother anyone could ever wish to meet. It's all seems such a contradiction.'

'Not really,' she argued gently, her tongue loosened by champagne and brandy. 'It's all part of the same thing. It's because of Sam that I want the success so much.'

'All this hard work and effort just because you want to give him a good start?'

'That's right.'

'Is it *only* that, Kate?' he asked.

His words unexpectedly jogged her memory, dealing her a body blow from the past . . .

Reggie Dexter was on top of her, crushing, bruising, forcing. Cissy Dexter's nurse-maid was dragging her baby away, tearing the very heart from her. The images poured into her mind so vividly, she re-lived every sensation with utmost pain. It all came back: the self-hatred, the humiliation, the crippling powerlessness, the heartache she still felt for her firstborn son. Her skin was burning but she was covered in goose pimples.

'Are you cold?' asked Leo, feeling her shiver against him.

'Just someone walking over my grave,' she fibbed.

'You haven't answered my question,' he persisted.

She knew she could never tell him the truth about her past. In fact, she wasn't even sure she knew the answer to his question herself. The only thing she did know for certain was that her craving for success somehow dated back to that day in the packing room at Dexter's when she had been so cruelly robbed of her self-respect.

'Well?'

'Just leave it, will you, Leo?' she snapped, but her voice was shaky.

'Sure, if that's what you want.' He stopped in his tracks and turned to her, drawing her into his arms. 'What is it, Kate, what's the matter?'

'Nothing.'

'You're still shivering.'

'For God's sake stop questioning me and let's go back to the boat,' she rasped.

'All right, all right.'

They walked back, barely saying a word. 'I appear to have upset you. I'm sorry,' he said as they climbed on board.

'Don't worry about it.'

'Shall I make us some more coffee or do you have to rush off?'

'No, I don't have to rush off.'

'Good.'

'Hold me, Leo, *please*.'

He took her in his arms, stroking her hair, kissing her gently.

'Can I stay here tonight?' she asked.

'Of course,' he said in surprise, 'but what about your reputation?'

'Being with you means more to me than my reputation.'

# Chapter Sixteen

Kate opened her eyes to the glare of sunlight shining through a gap in the curtains and striking the wall of Leo's bedroom cabin. He was fast asleep beside her with his arm flung across her chest. Carefully removing it, she sat up and observed him with deep affection. He was lying on his side, his suntanned profile etched against the white pillow, the mop of straight brown hair sticking up in spiky disorder.

Although theirs was not a platonic relationship, this was the first time they had actually breached the rules of social convention and spent the night together. Even the sobering daylight didn't fill her with regret, though she was not unaware of the fact that such behaviour must certainly force a watershed in their relationship.

She frowned as she anticipated the difficult choice now facing her. Obviously things could no longer drift along as they had been between herself and Leo. With a son to whom she must set an example, she could not brush aside convention as regular practice, nor could she expect Leo to endure the frustrations of an indefinite courtship, especially with the presence of two growing boys making finding time alone together so difficult.

The boat rocked softly in the wash from a passing craft but Leo slept on, a picture of contentment. Unlike him she was restless in her dilemma, so slipped from the sheets and into his dressing gown before padding along to the galley to make some tea. Filling the kettle and setting it to boil on the range, she stared idly through the window at the dew-covered tangle of wild flowers on the bank. Unexpectedly, the sight produced a moment of pure serenity.

The feeling was short-lived, however, under the weight of her problem. Having the chance to marry Leo should make her the happiest woman alive. Oh, if only life was that simple.

'Now who's being spoiled?' he said when she woke him with tea and biscuits.

'You deserve it.'

'Are you not joining me?' he asked, frowning, when she didn't get back into bed.

'I have to go home to change into some comfortable day clothes,' she said with false levity.

'Ah, yes, of course.'

'And some nice juicy gossip I'll cause too, if I'm seen arriving home in my best togs at this time of the morning.'

'Why not leave it till later on then?'

'No, I'll risk it,' she said, for she needed time alone to think. 'Then I can relax.'

'Off you go then, you fallen woman,' he teased.

'It's no laughing matter,' she rebuked him lightheartedly. 'I *am* supposed to be a respectable widow, remember.'

'The sooner we change that unsatisfactory state of affairs, the better.'

She didn't reply but concentrated on changing out of his dressing gown into her own clothes.

'You'll come back and spend the day with me, I hope,' he said. 'We might as well make the most of the peace and quiet. There'll be precious little of it once the lads get back.'

'Yes, I'll be back later.'

'Don't be long, then,' he urged, blissfully unaware of the turmoil that was raging beneath her lighthearted mood.

'I won't.'

It was midday before she returned, dressed in a practical cotton dress with short sleeves and a dropped waistline.

'You've been ages,' he reproached mildly.

'Isn't the female of the species expected to take a long time to dress?' she said, though she had actually lingered at home agonising over her predicament.

'Not by me,' he chided lightly. 'But now that you are here,

how about a walk before lunch?'

'Good idea.'

They took a stroll along the riverside before returning to a feast of bread and cheese and pickles, eaten on deck in the sunshine.

'What a thoroughly degenerate weekend this is turning out to be,' she laughed with forced brightness. 'Not only do we spend the night together, we spurn the traditional Sunday roast in favour of bread and cheese.'

'That's the good thing about my kind of lifestyle,' he remarked casually, 'you don't have to adhere to such conventional rituals if you don't feel like it.'

'I must admit I'm usually quite a stickler about Sunday lunch, however busy I am,' she confessed. 'I think it gives Sam a sense of stability. We generally go to Mother's place.'

'You're enjoying the break from routine, I hope?'

'You bet.'

'Good.'

It was after they had finished washing the dishes and were relaxing in the saloon that Kate knew she could avoid the issue no longer.

'No, Leo,' she said, as she found herself being led from the room in the direction of his sleeping cabin.

'Is sex on a Sunday afternoon a little *too* degenerate for you?' he said lightly.

'It isn't that,' she said gravely.

'We have the place to ourselves for a few more hours,' he pointed out, 'we'd be silly not to take advantage.'

'I have something to tell you, Leo.'

'Oh dear, that sounds ominous. Don't say you're going home to work on hats?'

'No, it isn't that, but it very well could be,' she told him solemnly. 'And because of that sort of thing, I feel compelled to end our affair.'

His face tightened. 'Just like that?'

'Not just like that,' she said. 'I've given the matter a lot of thought and I'm sure it's the best thing for both of us.'

'Well . . .' He was breathless with shock. 'I've heard of men losing their woman to another man, but never to millinery!'

'There's no call for sarcasm,' she snapped, because this was equally as painful for her as it was for him. 'It isn't like that at all.'

'Why else am I being given the brush-off, then?'

'Because I have decided that I don't want to get married, and don't think it's fair to expect you to continue as we have been when I know it isn't what you want.'

'Too true it isn't,' he said briskly, 'but what's so terrible about marrying me?'

'Nothing at all,' she assured him. 'I just don't want to marry anyone. I want to be free to concentrate on my business.'

'Do I seem like the sort of man who would stop you doing what you want to do?'

'Of course not.'

'Well then . . .'

'If I married again I would want my husband to be number one priority in my life, which would mean having my business as a sideline,' she explained. 'And that isn't what I want.'

'So it was a straight choice between me and your ruddy ambitions?'

She flinched at his choice of words which made her seem so callous. In fact, quite apart from the fact that she loved him, it would be the easiest thing in the world for her to settle for what society taught women to believe was their sole purpose in life. But there was too much restlessness within her, still this aching need to prove herself.

'It isn't a crime for a woman to want to stay single, you know,' she pointed out curtly. 'Plenty of men spend their lives trying to avoid marriage, and no one condemns them for it.'

'True, but even the most confirmed bachelors usually get married in the end.'

'Maybe, but it isn't what I want to do and I don't see why I should be made to feel guilty about it,' she told him determinedly.

'I'm not trying to make you feel guilty,' he said sadly, 'but you can hardly expect me to jump for joy.'

'Of course not. I'm sorry.' Her tone was full of remorse

because she despised herself for hurting him. 'But I've made up my mind.'

'There's something else bothering you, isn't there, Kate?' he said, his tone softening as he sensed her anguish. 'Something that I don't know about.'

She smarted at the truth of his assumption but just said, 'Of course not.'

'Why don't we try to work this thing out together?' he persisted. 'A problem shared . . .'

'There's nothing to work out,' she interrupted brusquely. 'You're imagining things.'

'Be that as it may,' he said, remaining unconvinced, 'you're a fool if you think you'll find happiness from a healthy bank balance and an address in some posh Kensington square.'

'Why is everyone so obsessed with the idea of finding happiness?' she said, bewildered by the complexity of her emotions. 'There are other things in life to strive for.'

'Such as?'

'Peace of mind, self-respect . . .'

'I could give you both.'

'Those things can't be given,' she said, 'they have to be earned.'

'I just don't understand you, Kate,' he said, looking completely baffled. 'You admit to being in love with me, yet you're determined to cut me out of your life when you know I won't interfere with your work. It doesn't make sense.'

'It does to me.'

'You're one hell of a complicated woman.'

'It's just as well we're splitting up then, isn't it?' she said. 'You'll be better off with some easygoing female who wants nothing more from life than to marry and look after you.'

'If that was all I wanted, I'd have got married years ago,' he said, adding bitterly, 'But, yes, maybe it *is* time I looked around.'

'I hope you find someone.'

'So do I,' he lied.

She picked up her handbag and marched across the room,

turning at the steps. 'No doubt we shall meet from time to time because of the boys.'

'Don't worry, I won't embarrass you by trying to persuade you to change your mind,' he growled. 'I shan't bother you again in that respect, *ever*, I can promise you that.'

An icy silence filled the room as they stood locked in conflict. At that moment she wanted nothing more than to abandon her plans and run into his arms. But good sense prevailed and she left the boat in a dignified manner, the finality of his words throbbing in her brain.

Having changed so much over the years, Gertie was embarrassed to remember the feeble creature she had been when they had first arrived at Beaver Terrace, fifteen years ago. How terrified she'd been of life and her new neighbours, with their vulgar jollity and unnerving capacity to cope with the most dire discomfort.

She supposed it was inevitable that she would eventually begin to see life from a new perspective. But she hadn't become saintly – far from it. On the contrary, she had been forced to accept the fact that she was never going to be the sort of person to whom kindness came easy. Unlike Marjorie Prescott, Gertie had to work hard to find tolerance and compassion within herself. Sometimes she even felt moments of superiority towards the poor unfortunates with whom she was involved at the Institute. Fortunately, she was able to conceal and control these lapses, and most of the time gave of her services with a genuine desire to help. It had been a long time coming, but at last she had matured sufficiently to realise that giving was its own reward.

Now, seated at her Sunday lunch table, perceiving her daughter's obvious despair as she picked at her food, Gertie knew that it was Kate who needed to get her life into proper focus. She'd been at a very low ebb indeed since she'd ended her affair with Leo a month ago, despite her pretence to the contrary.

The woman Gertie had once been would undoubtedly have applauded her daughter for ending her association with an unconventional type like Leo with nothing to offer in the way of prospects. But the more enlightened Gertie liked him, and thought the couple were made for each other.

She couldn't fail to see the irony of the situation where she herself had settled for a lower status in life only to find that her daughter had become obsessed with the idea of bettering herself. It worried Gertie to see Kate working so ridiculously hard, following even the most tenuous leads to improve her sales, constantly pursuing fashion editors to try to get her hats into the public eye. She even wrote to celebrities through the magazines and newspapers in which they were featured, telling them about her millinery services. And when she wasn't frantically seeking to promote her hats, she was busy on the production side.

Gertie feared that this ruthless dedication would only get worse as Sam grew older and needed his mother less. At least now her strong sense of maternal duty forced her to take some time off to be with him. God only knew where it would all end. It wasn't natural for a woman to be so preoccupied with a career, in Gertie's opinion.

She blamed herself for setting such store by their Kensington lifestyle all those years ago. Kate had been at an impressionable age when it had all been taken from them, and Gertie had been far too full of her own problems to notice just how much it was affecting her daughters. Then there had been Kate's 'trouble'. Who was to say that that hadn't had some lasting psychological effect that had helped to make her the complex woman she now was? Since no one ever discussed such things, Gertie could only guess at that.

'Can I leave the table please, Gran?' asked Sam. 'I'm going over to the boat to see Ozzy.'

'Certainly, dear,' said Gertie.

'Don't be late back for tea,' said Kate rather absently.

'I won't.'

The boy hurried from the flat and clattered down the stairs, whistling cheerfully.

'Why don't you go with him?' suggested Gertie. 'You can easily catch him up.'

'Why would I do that?'

'You know very well why,' said Gertie in exasperation. 'You've been going about with a face like a yard of elastic ever since you gave Leo his marching orders.'

'I'll get over it,' said Kate.

'But why put yourself through it at all when there's no need?'

'There's every need.'

'Why, for heaven's sake?'

'Because it wouldn't be fair to him to carry on when I'm not going to marry him.'

'You're mad to turn him down.'

'I must be the judge of that.'

'I don't understand you, Kate, I really don't,' her mother sighed.

'That makes two of you then,' retorted Kate, gulping back the tears. 'Because he doesn't either.'

'Understandably.'

'For goodness' sake, let's drop the subject.'

'All right, all right.'

Kate finally gave up on her meal and rose from her seat and began stacking the dishes. 'I'll do the washing up while you put your feet up.'

'Thank you, dear,' said Gertie.


Kate put away the last plate in the kitchen cabinet and joined her mother on the sofa in the living room where she was looking at the Sunday paper. As much as Kate wanted to leave, she knew that an early departure would give rise to well-meant advice about solitude being bad for her while she was in her present mood.

Her mother was right though, she had been feeling utterly miserable this last month. Rather than improve her concentration at work, the break-up with Leo had left her so lacking in spirit she'd barely had the heart to do more than keep the firm ticking over. What she needed to cure the doldrums was some really exciting project to work on, something more challenging than the type of hats that would bring safe sales from the middle-class matrons who were the backbone of her clientèle.

'Anything interesting in the paper?' she asked, pretending an interest.

'I'm just reading about this new scheme they're introducing to try to reduce accidents on the roads. There are so many motor cars nowadays they're going to paint white lines down the middle of the road to separate the traffic streams.'

'Sounds like a good idea.'

'What will they think of next?'

'Heaven knows,' said Kate.

Gertie studied the newspaper in silence. 'Eve Lorimar is in the news again,' she said after a while.

'What's she done this time?' asked Kate, though the woman in question didn't really need a reason to get into the papers. She was a well-known actress who was almost as famous for her bad temper and glamorous persona as her acting ability.

'She's been threatening to leave the cast of the farce she's in because of a row with the producer, but they've talked her into staying.'

'So what's new?' said Kate without any real interest. 'I think her publicity manager invents these dramas just to get her into the papers.'

'There's a terrible photograph of her,' said Gertie.

'I haven't thought she looked as stunning as usual in the last few pictures I've seen of her,' remarked Kate casually. 'She seems to wear such unsuitable hats lately.'

'She looks positively dowdy in this one.' Her mother handed the newspaper to Kate. 'Don't you agree?'

She peered at the picture which was of the actress about to get into a taxi outside the theatre. She was wearing a fashionable blazer-style jacket over a striped dress, and a cloche hat pulled so far down you could barely see her eyes. 'It's the hat she's wearing,' said Kate. 'It's far too austere for her sharp features.'

'That style of hat is all the rage and she's known to be a devotee of fashion.'

'Mmm. She could be still with something less extreme.'

Gertie looked at the picture again. 'You're right, Kate. That

hat doesn't do anything for her at all.'

Taking the newspaper from her mother, Kate read the article accompanying the picture and stroked her chin meditatively. 'She's appearing at the Royalty Theatre,' she said thoughtfully. 'I think I ought to write a letter to her there, don't you, Mother?'

'I doubt if you'll get a reply, dear.'

'Don't you be so sure about that,' said Kate with a wicked grin.'

'How *dare* you send me such an insulting letter?' said Eve Lorimar, clutching it as she swept into the drawing room of her Chelsea house where Kate had been shown by the maid.

'It's good of you to see me,' said Kate, whose communication had been deliberately hard-hitting with the idea of shocking the actress into seeing her.

'I only asked you here so that I can tell you what I think of you to your face,' said Eve, sinking on to a pale green sofa, the folds of a cream satin housecoat draped luxuriously around her. 'And what I think is, you have a damned cheek!'

'I didn't intend to insult *you*,' explained Kate. 'It was the hat you were wearing in the picture on which I was expressing an opinion.'

'And you're arrogant enough to think I'd be interested in your opinion?'

'I'm arrogant enough to want to give it,' said Kate.

'Not a hint of apology?'

'It would be pointless to apologise for speaking out in your best interests.'

'Honestly, you really have the most appalling manners!'

'You've built up a reputation for looking special,' continued Kate, ignoring the other woman's protests, 'and whoever is making your hats at the moment is failing to do that for you, if the latest few creations are anything to go by.'

'How dare you?' blustered the actress, blue eyes flashing, pointed face angrily suffused.

'I'm sorry if you're upset by what I have to say, but it's only what I believe to be true,' said Kate boldly. 'Other people must have noticed it even if they've been too polite to mention it to you.'

'My dear Mrs Brooks,' Eve said haughtily, but there was more than a hint of concern in her eyes now. 'I patronise only the most respected milliners in London. Talented people with specialist skills. Why, I'm a client of those who serve the aristocracy.'

'I don't doubt it, and the hats are obviously well made,' said Kate. 'But the styles are not right for someone as smart as you. They won't turn heads in admiration, and *certainly* won't make you stand out as a leader of fashion. You have been known to start crazes – well, you won't start many with your recent headwear.'

'The public would emulate me if I was to go out wearing a duster on my head!'

'Only if you looked good in it,' said Kate with brutal frankness.

Eve Lorimar looked about to explode, but turned her attention to Kate's letter-heading instead. 'Kate Brooks – model milliner,' she read in a derisive manner. 'I'd never heard of you before receiving this and I don't suppose anyone of any importance on the London fashion scene has either.'

'I make no claim to fame.'

'And I'm not a fool,' Eve ranted. 'I know what all of this is about. You want to make hats for me to get them into the public eye and put yourself on the map. You want to use *me* to promote *your* name.'

'What's wrong with that?' asked Kate. 'I expect you used every avenue you could find to get publicity in the early days of your career.'

'My talent got me where I am today.'

'Yes, but you had to get that talent noticed initially,' said Kate. 'It's the same for me.'

'You can hardly equate acting talent with the work of a milliner,' said Eve dismissively.

'Maybe not, but making model hats requires something beyond just a working ability,' Kate explained. 'I have that something. But although I do a good trade in middle of the

269

road millinery, I need the chance to do something more imaginative, something deliciously bold. I admit that I wrote to you with my own career in mind, but had I genuinely thought the hats you have been photographed in lately were right for you, I would never have taken such a liberty.'

'Really?'

'Yes, I truly believe that I could do more for you than your present milliners,' Kate continued. 'My satisfaction comes from doing a really good job for my clients. Any boost my business gets as a result is purely incidental.'

'You've certainly got a nerve.'

'Essential in business as in acting, don't you think?'

Eve Lorimar stood up dramatically, her housecoat flowing around her ankles. She was a peroxide blonde of about thirty with a slim, willowy figure. Her face was not pretty, for she had rather prominent features, but she was extremely attractive with high cheekbones and huge eyes.

In a theatrical gesture, she tore Kate's letter to pieces and let it flutter to the floor. 'That's how far your outrageous cheek has got you with me!' she said. 'Now get out!'

Before Kate had time to comply, they were interrupted by the maid announcing the arrival of a male guest whom Eve said was to be shown in immediately. A man wearing a blazer and silk cravat marched in carrying a bouquet of flowers which he handed to the actress.

Seeming to forget Kate's presence, Eve embarked on an effusive greeting. 'Darling, how sweet of you to bring flowers for your little Evie. Come here and let me kiss you . . .'

Kate slipped unnoticed from the room while they were embracing, leaving one of her business cards in a prominent place on an occasional table.

One afternoon about two weeks later, the actress appeared at Kate's shop in a charming mood, behaving as though a cross word had never passed between them.

'I thought I'd come along to see some examples of your work as I don't have a matinee today,' she explained.

'You won't have a wasted trip, I can assure you,' said Kate, feeling almost childishly triumphant.

She showed Eve her range, suggesting that the less severe lines of the toque, with its looser crown, were more suitable for her than the cloche. In an extravagant frame of mind, Eve purchased several hats, then got around to the real purpose of her visit.

'Actually, I want a very special hat for a showbusiness charity luncheon at which I am to be the guest of honour,' she explained. 'I need something really stunning to outshine the fierce competition. Anyone who's anyone in the theatre will be there, and all dressed to kill. You said you wanted to do something out of the ordinary. Now's your chance to show what you can do.'

'Do you have any particular colour or style in mind?'

Eve handed Kate a snippet of red silk. 'This is the material of the dress I shall be wearing. It's going to be very plain and sleek with a matching jacket.'

'You need something dramatic,' suggested Kate. 'As the outfit is plain.'

'You can be as dramatic as you like,' Eve said, adding in her famous acid manner, 'but it will have to be good or I shall see to it that your life isn't worth living.'

'Leave it with me. I'll telephone you when I have something ready for fitting.'

Although Kate discussed this project with her staff, she did the labour herself, from the first cut to the very last stitch. In a few days she had a choice of three hats at the fitting stage: a halo hat worn off the face, a tiny plain cap made startling by an enormous feather, and an exotic thing with a great waving brim with red silk trimmings.

Having been asked to take the hats to Eve's house, she arrived laden with boxes.

'Absolutely divine,' said the actress, trying on the halo. 'My dear, I love it.'

'If we take a tuck here,' said Kate, standing behind her client at her dressing-table mirror, 'and a little pleat here . . .'

'Whatever you say,' Eve agreed.

Such was the woman's good humour, she purchased all three

hats and insisted Kate join her for a sherry. She then supplied her with a detailed account of the men in her life, all of whom became 'impossibly possessive' when they should understand she was an artiste 'married to the theatre'.

Finding her pretentiousness somewhat tedious Kate was glad to leave, but did so confident that a definite breakthrough had been made in her career.

During the next couple of months, however, she began to think she must have been mistaken when there were no further orders from Miss Lorimar, nor recommendations. Naturally Kate was disapointed, but counted the incident as valuable experience and put it out of her mind.

Then, one winter's day, a well-known lady of the theatre appeared at Kate's shop having seen a photograph of Eve Lorimar in *Vogue*, wearing a Kate Brooks hat.

This was the real turning point. Other showbusiness people became clients and were photographed in Kate's hats. She became a name on the London fashion scene. Trade increased dramatically. By the end of 1927 her turnover had trebled and she had the security of a healthy bank balance. Now, at last, she could afford to do something about Sam's future.

# Chapter Seventeen

Why is it that acting in the best interests of one's child always hurts so much? Kate asked herself. It was Sunday afternoon, the first day of 1928, and she was standing on the station platform with Ozzy to see Sam off on the train to his new school in Hampshire. She'd managed to get him into a highly reputable boarding school, which she was assured would provide him with the necessary grounding to train for one of the professions later on, albeit that he was late to private education.

She'd thought it only natural for a boy of thirteen to eschew the idea of having his mother travel down with him for his first term. But she could see from the ashen tinge of his skin that he was terrfied of this new venture, for all his brave front as he chatted to them through the open carriage window.

'Don't forget to write to me, Sam,' she said, her voice quivering with emotion.

'Don't fuss, Mum,' he said with boyish nonchalance, though his mouth was dry with nerves.

Kate felt a powerful urge to drag him off the train and clutch him in her protective arms forever. It reminded her of the way she had felt about another child one April afternoon in 1911 in a certain seaside boarding house.

'If there's anything you need during the term, just let me know,' she said, hoping she wasn't going to disgrace herself by bursting into tears.

'I will, Mum.'

'Let me know if you're not warm enough in bed and I'll bring some blankets down.'

'Give over, Mum,' he warned, making a face and looking at Ozzy in embarrassment.

'Sorry.' He seemed such a baby even though he was almost as tall as her. The mere thought of him sleeping in a spartan dormitory, at the mercy of some hateful bully, almost crucified her. Banishing such negative thoughts, she concentrated on the positive aspect. At least this way there was a possibility of his securing a decent future. What chance would he stand if he stayed at home with her and left school in a year's time? If he was lucky he might be apprenticed to some manual trade. But if he wanted any sort of white collar job, he'd have to do the same as Ozzy and try his luck at working his way up, with no guarantee of rising much beyond office boy in twenty years' time.

The whistle blew and Sam's face grew even paler. She hugged him. 'Bye, bye, darling. I'll see you at half term.'

'Cheerio, Mum,' he said stiffly.

'Ta ta, mate,' said Ozzy, shaking his hand. 'See you soon.'

'Bye, Oz. See you in the hols.'

'Sure.'

The train steamed out of the station, taking Sam and a chunk of Kate's heart with it.

'He'll be all right, Mrs Brooks,' said Ozzy kindly as tears slid down her cheeks. 'He'll be home for half term before you know it.'

'I'm being stupid,' she said, sniffing into her handkerchief. 'What it is to be a mother, eh? Thanks for coming to see him off, Ozzy, you're a good friend to him.'

'I'll miss having him around,' he said chattily as they walked towards the Underground station to catch the train back to Hammersmith.

'I feel like the villain of the piece, sending him away,' she confessed, 'but it wouldn't be right not to give him the benefit of certain privileges now that I can afford it.'

Ozzy wasn't sorry he'd missed out on that particular 'privilege' because he'd heard horrendous tales of cruelty and bullying at boarding schools from some of the sons of friends of the Dexters who'd been pupils. But he deemed it wise not to mention this to Mrs Brooks because she obviously had Sam's long-term interests at heart. What a warm and generous person she was, so far removed from the cold-hearted woman who had brought Ozzy up.

'I'm sure you've done the best thing for him in the long run,' said Ozzy, partly to reassure her and partly because he thought it was probably true. 'He's a good mixer so he'll soon make friends.'

'I certainly hope so.'

'He'll be full of it when he comes home for the hols,' he said to cheer her up, 'and he'll make lots of useful contacts.'

'Everything you say is true,' she said, turning and smiling at him. 'You've been a real comfort to me today.'

On the train journey to Hammersmith they sat in companionable silence. She found herself thinking what a nice young man Ozzy was growing up to be. He must be going on for seventeen now, and not a bit moody like some boys at that age. In fact, he seemed very well-balanced, something for which Leo must be given credit. As her thoughts lingered on the latter, she longed to see him with a ferocious ache. It was at times like this, when she was feeling sad, that she missed him most. They met in passing occasionally, but only ever exchanged a few polite words. Lately he always seemed frantically busy and in a hurry to get away, which wasn't surprising since he was something of a celebrity these days.

'How's Leo?' she asked.

'He's fine,' he said. 'Busy getting his new exhibition ready for the spring.'

'It's amazing how his painting took off all of a sudden like that,' she said. 'He's getting to be quite famous.'

'The press have taken an interest in him, it's true.'

'Has all the attention he's been getting changed him?'

'You know Leo better than that,' Ozzy said. 'He's got a bit more money in his pocket, of course, but no pretensions. The only reason he's given up his job in the drawing office is because he thinks it will make way for someone else, not because he thinks he's too good for it.'

'He won't be buying some posh house then?

'No chance,' he laughed. 'You know how he loves that boat.'

'Don't I just?' she said, almost to herself.

The train rattled into their station, bringing with it a fresh surge of loneliness for Kate. 'Do you fancy coming home with me for a cup of tea?' she said impulsively, the thought of the empty flat without Sam almost too much to bear.

Ozzy looked into her tearful eyes. He couldn't remember ever seeing her look depressed before, which indicated the depth of her feelings for Sam. He thought about the piece of writing he had in progress about Hammersmith Creek which he had planned to finish this afternoon. He was hoping to have it on the editor's desk first thing tomorrow morning with a view to getting it into this week's edition. It was part of his plan to impress the editor into realising that Ozzy had a future as a reporter.

He remembered Mrs Brooks's kindness over the years. The way she had always welcomed him into her home even when she'd been struggling to make ends meet in the cramped rooms in Dane Street with piles of hats to sew every night. The sight of her looking so gloomy twisted his heart for he had grown fond of her.

'Don't worry if you've other things to do,' she said. 'I can always go and spend an hour or so with Mother. I just don't fancy my own company at the moment.'

'I've no plans,' he lied. 'And I'd love to join you for a cuppa.'

When he left her an hour or so later, he was glowing with well-being. She really was a charming lady. What a pity she no longer came to the boat. Leo wasn't the same man since they'd stopped seeing each other. He'd found artistic success, but he didn't laugh much these days. Oh, well, it wasn't Ozzy's place to say anything, but some people just didn't know what was good for them.

Bertha stood shivering at the front door of her basement flat, watching Gertie climb the small flight of stone steps up to the pavement.

'Mind you don't fall,' she called against the howling wind. 'It can be just as slippery when the snow starts to melt as when it's rock hard.'

'It's blowing a gale out here,' said Gertie, shouting to make herself heard.

'Good job you ain't got far to go.'

'I'll say,' said Gertie. 'See you tomorrow, Bertha, thanks for supper.'

'A pleasure, Gert.'

'My turn next week.'

'Righto. Ta ta, love.'

'Bye.'

Giving her friend a last wave, Bertha went inside to her tiny kitchen and washed the plates from which they had eaten large helpings of faggots and rice. Bertha yawned contentedly. Gertie was a good pal and she enjoyed her company. Their Friday night suppers together had become something of a tradition. You needed your friends when the kids left home, she thought, making herself a last cup of cocoa and sitting in an armchair by the fire in her cosy living room.

Bertha didn't lack for company even though Ruby had married a tram driver and now lived in the East End, and Georgie had gone away to sea. She had her workmates and the Potters, and the neighbours were a friendly bunch. She didn't see as much of the children as she would have liked, but you had to expect that when they grew up. Even Kate had had her first taste of what that felt like last Sunday when she'd sent young Sam away to school.

Finishing her cocoa, she trotted to the bedroom and got her thick winceyette pyjamas from under her pillow and hurried back to the fireside to undress. The fire was almost out for the night, but the living room was still warmer than her ice-box of a bedroom. She loved her little home though for all its freezing draughts. She was grateful to Georgie for sending her money to help with the rent, for on her wages from the factory she could only afford one room.

Ah, well, that's another day done, she thought as she slipped into the icy cold sheets, slapped her feet onto the stone hot-water bottle and curled up into a ball. Saturday tomorrow which meant she could lie in. Good job an' all, she thought, as she drifted off to sleep.

Gertie woke up with a start. Must be indigestion from too many faggots at Bertha's place, she thought, sitting up sleepily. She was about to get some of her chalky medicine from the kitchen when she realised that it was not her stomach that had woken her but her ears which were being assaulted by a persistent noise. It sounded like a motor car roaring outside. Damned nuisance, she muttered, getting out of bed and going to the window. People ought not to be allowed to make such a racket when decent folks were trying to sleep.

She drew back the curtains and looked down into the street, her heart lurching at the sight that greeted her. Water was cascading towards the house like a giant tidal wave. Even as she stood there, paralysed with shock, it poured across the tiny front garden and rose around the house. Cold with terror, she was vaguely aware of the sound of men shouting. In the light from the street lamp, she could just make out a skiff in which two men appeared to be making their way along the flooded street calling out a warning.

Her instinctive fear for Kate was short-lived in the realisation that people sleeping on upper floors were probably not in danger. It was those on the ground floor and basements who were at risk. The thought of Bertha galvanised her into action, and she rushed from the room without even stopping to slip her dressing gown over her flannelette nightdress.

Bewildered residents in their nightclothes were already gathering on the landing as she tore past them and tried to get down the stairs, hindered by a stream of people from the lower floors moving up to safety. People were screaming and shouting, children crying with fright.

'Don't go down, Mrs Potter,' they warned her. 'The water is coming in.'

'My friend lives in a basement flat near here. I have to go and warn her.'

'You can't get out, love,' said a man in a maroon dressing gown who seemed to have taken charge and was helping the refugees from below up the stairs. 'Come on now, get off the stairs. You're blocking the path.'

'My friend needs to be warned.'

'She'll be all right, someone in her own buildin' 'll tell her,' he said, counting everyone and declaring that all the lower residents were out of danger.

Sick with worry for her friend, Gertie stumbled blindly down the stairs, only to be physically restrained by maroon dressing gown.

'Let me go,' she gasped, struggling violently as he dragged her back up the stairs. 'I have to get to my friend.'

A loud crash boomed through the house, stunning them all into silence. The terrified residents were horror-stricken as the front door was broken down by the force of the water which gushed inside in a filthy torrent.

The distant sound of children shrieking awakened Bertha. One of the kids upstairs must be having a nightmare or something, she thought drowsily, pulling the blankets over her head to block out the noise. But there was something going on outside too. Men were shouting.

'Bloomin' drunks ought to be locked up, disturbing the peace at this time of night. No wonder they've woken the kids,' she muttered. An explosion rocked the room. 'What the bloody 'ell . . .?'

She jumped out of bed, startled by the fact that her feet were immersed in water. Bewildered, she paddled to the gaslight and turned it on to see the window had crashed in and bricks from the wall were hurtling towards her on an avalanche of filthy water. She tried to get to the door leading to the living room, but the flood knocked her down as it poured through the room, sweeping aside everything in its wake: the mattress, the chest of drawers, even the wardrobe was floating.

Managing to get to her feet, she made another attempt to get to the door, but the icy water was already numbing her waist, her chest, her shoulders. She couldn't move. She opened her mouth to scream, but it was filled with water . . .

★ ★ ★

Immediately the flood waters receded sufficiently for Gertie to leave the house, she went to the Institute which was being used as a refuge for flood victims whose homes were not habitable. She worked with ferocious dedication, collecting blankets from well wishers, making endless pots of broth, and tea, helping people scrub their homes with disinfectant to erase the stench of the sewage that had been left behind by the flood waters.

She daren't stop working for fear she would revert back to the pathetic heap she had once been, completely unable to cope in the face of adversity. The news of Bertha's death on Saturday morning had hurt her more deeply than anything before. More violent than her grief for Cyril or even for her little grandson, Ronnie, the void she felt at the loss of her friend was simply unbearable.

Leo worked with hammer and nails on the deck of *London Lady*. He was replacing the planking that had been torn from its housing when the railings had been wrenched away by a tree branch in the floods. It was hard to believe on this calm afternoon, with nothing more threatening than a shiver on the water's surface and the blue sky scudding with little white clouds, that this had been a scene of such chaos a week ago. The much feared combination of high winds and a very high tide, coinciding with a sudden thaw, had caused the Thames to burst its banks in the early hours of last Saturday morning, bringing death and destruction to London's riverside.

What a shocking night that had been! He and Ozzy had joined the rescue workers rowing or wading through the water to help people to safety. In some cases they had been too late. There had been several fatalities. He'd attended the funeral yesterday of poor Bertha Brent. Kate and her mother had shown such courage, he'd thought, looking after Bertha's heartbroken daughter when they must have been devastated themselves, particularly Gertie who had been Bertha's closest friend.

He was lucky. His only legacy was minor damage to the boat. Some people had lost all their furniture and belongings, ruined by the filthy water. Many of them were poor and had little chance of recouping their losses, being without jobs. Thank God he was in a position to donate a substantial sum to the relief fund.

It was amazing how his circumstances had changed so suddenly. After he and Kate had parted, he had found solace in his work, spending all his spare time sketching and painting in a bid to forget her. In that aim he had been unsuccessful, but creativity had thrived in his mood of despair. Having more finished work than space to store it, he had come to an arrangement with a stallholder in Petticoat Lane Market. The man had agreed to put some of Leo's paintings on the stall, on the understanding that he took a commission on every sale.

Neither he nor Leo had held out much hope. But not only had the paintings found buyers, they had also attracted the attention of a gallery owner who had offered to put them on show. The work had been well received there too. Art critics had written about the sensitivity of the artist. Suddenly Leo was being hailed as an exciting new talent.

He was completely baffled as to why his work had been ignored for so long, since the talent must have been there all the time. He could only put it down to a change in public taste. They say everything has its time, and apparently his time was now.

If rumour was to be believed, the same could be said for Kate. She was making hats for the highest in the land these days. She now had the sort of recognition she had craved. And the money too, enough to send young Sam to an expensive boarding school. The poor little beggar had Leo's sympathy, if boarding school stories were to be believed. Still, he'd come out of it with all the necessary social graces to enable him to make something of himself. In all due credit to Kate, she left no stone unturned to give that boy the best.

Even now Leo missed her though he had made a determined effort to find female company. He had had a few girlfriends since Kate, some of whom had lasted several months. But each relationship had petered out eventually because they had lacked the spark he had shared with Kate. She had captured his heart irrevocably even though he now accepted the fact that their values differed too greatly for them ever to have a life together. He loved her but he didn't like what she was, a ruthless businesswoman who valued material success above all else.

Quite honestly, he could lose all the trappings of success tomorrow and wouldn't give a damn. Recognition as an artist was enough for him.

'Oh, well,' he sighed, hammering a nail with unnecessary vigour, 'at the rate Kate's going she'll be moving back into her beloved Sycamore Square before very long.'

Personally, he couldn't imagine anything more hellish, but good luck to her if that was what she really wanted.

It was, in fact, more than three years before Kate was in a position to look out for a property in that sought-after square, having by then fully repaid her debt to Johnny.

Sam was nearing the age when he would leave school to train as a solicitor. Kate thought of all the advantages he would derive from a more salubrious address. The quiet ambience would be ideal for study, and it would be a much more suitable atmosphere in which to entertain his friends.

He was a dear, intelligent boy but Kate often worried about his tendency to cling to boyish fantasies. When he was home for the holidays, he still spent hours poring over books and magazines about aircraft and talked a lot about flying.

She consoled herself with the thought that it was probably just a need for some light relief, because he worked hard at his studies in term time. She was glad he was doing well at school. It meant a lot to her for him to be accepted into the school of law. His training was going to be very expensive for her though. For, as well as supporting him and paying his tuition fees, she was also going to have to pay a premium to the principal of the law firm to which he would be articled. But she didn't begrudge a penny.

Despite all the well-connected friends Sam had made at boarding school, his closest pal was still Ozzy Perks, even though Ozzy was now involved in a serious relationship with Poppy Brown. It had all worked out well enough. Kate was fond of both Poppy and Ozzy and looked on them as part of her family, so she was quite happy for them all to get together at her place during Sam's holidays.

It took some time to find a property in the square, but eventually in the summer of 1931 the estate agent telephoned to say that a house had come on to the market that would be perfect for her.

It was on the opposite side of the gardens to the former Potter home, but similar in style with a gleaming stucco front, shiny black railings and a solid oak front door.

Her mother declined the invitation to move in with Kate. She wanted to stay on in the modern flat Kate had made it possible for her to move into after the floods because it wasn't far from the Institute and because she liked it there.

Seeing her mother's point of view, as well as the irony in the situation, Kate excitedly made plans for this move that marked the fruition of all her ambitions.

# *Chapter Eighteen*

With completion of her house purchase imminent, Kate was spending her lunch break in her office, browsing through some home-making magazines. Her mother had joined her for a sandwich and they were enjoying a pleasant half-hour studying all the latest furnishing ideas. Kate had just spotted a room-setting that she particularly liked when the peace was shattered by a telephone call from a distraught Esme, begging them to go over to Lilac Gardens right away.

Leaving Poppy in charge of the shop, they hurried to Kensington to find a shamefaced Johnny trying to pacify Esme, who was almost hysterical.

'History is repeating itself,' she wailed, waving her arms dramatically. 'I should have listened to you, Kate, when you told me not to marry this . . . this weak-willed fool!'

'Calm down and tell us what's happened,' urged Kate.

Esme threw her husband an accusing glare. 'He's lost everything through his blasted gambling, just like Daddy did,' she whimpered, wringing her hands. 'We're going to be evicted.'

'Oh, Johnny, how could you?' said Gertie.

'I'd no idea you'd been playing cards again,' said Kate, pale with shock.

'Neither had I,' shrieked Esme. 'He's been doing it on the sly, just like Daddy used to. He's been telling me he was out on business, and because I trusted him and he hasn't been staying out all night, I believed him. At least in the old days he didn't lie to me about it.'

'I didn't need to then, you didn't mind.'

'I've grown up a bit since then.'

'Anyway, I was too ashamed to tell you,' confessed her ashen-faced husband. 'After I'd promised never to do it again. I haven't been gambling as a regular habit, there've only been a few games . . .'

'Enough to lose everything you've worked for,' she wept. 'You bloody idiot!'

'She's right, Johnny,' said Kate. 'Why – after kicking the habit for so long?'

'It wasn't for kicks but necessity,' he explained. 'I lost a lot of money on a couple of bad property deals. I bought too high and had to sell low. It happens in my line of work. I didn't have the resources to sustain such a loss so I've been under constant threat from the bank as my overdraft got out of hand.'

'You should have told me,' rebuked Esme.

'I didn't want to worry you,' he said. 'I thought your nerves had taken enough of a battering when we lost Ronnie. Besides, I hoped I could get out of trouble without your ever knowing anything about it.' He looked towards Kate and Gertie. 'I needed a large sum of money to pay off the bank and the only way I knew of getting it was in a card game. But I was on a losing streak.' He bit his lip anxiously. 'So now I've no choice but to sell the house to pay my debts.'

'I see,' said Kate.

'We've nowhere to go,' sobbed Esme. 'We'll be out on the streets, and us with a child to look after!'

'Do try to calm down, dear,' said her mother patiently. 'You know perfectly well that Kate and I won't see you walking the streets. We'll sort something out between us.'

It took Kate just a few seconds to make her decision.

'Just how much money do you need to pay off the bank so that you can keep the house, Johnny?' she asked, taking her cheque book from her handbag.

'There's been a change of plan. We're not moving house,' said Sam to Ozzy the following Sunday. The former was on summer holiday from school and the pair of them were on their way to a local cricket match on which Ozzy was to write a report for the paper.

286

'Oh, so I won't be able to boast about my posh Kensington friends after all?' joked Ozzy, his dark eyes smiling.

'Afraid not,' laughed Sam, who grew more like his father every day, with the same chunky build and vivid blue eyes.

'But I thought the deal was tied up, all bar the shouting?'

'It was.'

'What happened then?'

'It's all a bit hush-hush,' Sam explained in a confidential manner, 'but my Aunt Esme and Uncle Johnny are in terrible financial trouble.'

'So?'

'Mother gave them the money she was going to use for our new house so that they wouldn't lose theirs.'

'Cor, that was good of her.'

'Uncle Johnny helped her to get started in business,' explained Sam, 'so I suppose that has something to do with it.'

'It's still a really nice thing to do.'

'Oh, yes, Mum's heart's in the right place for all her dedication to business,' said Sam. 'That's why I can't bring myself to tell her that I don't want to be a solicitor. She's so keen on the idea and she's already spent a fortune on my education so that I'll be able to get into the profession. It would break her heart if I was to tell her I'd rather do something else.'

'Mmm, I can see that it's difficult for you,' agreed Ozzy, 'but you'll have a rotten life if you're miserable in your work.'

'She's set her heart on my having the security of a profession, you see,' he continued. 'And considering all the unemployment that's around, I suppose she does have a point.'

'There is that to it,' said Ozzy. 'We're lucky to have a job at all.'

'That doesn't make me dislike the idea of going into law any the less, though.'

'I suppose not.'

'I'll do it, though.'

'It's your life, Sam.'

'Don't let on about how I really feel. I don't want to hurt

Mum's feelings. No one could have done more for a son than she has.'

'I won't breathe a word,' Ozzy promised.

'Sam Brooks and his mother aren't moving house after all,' Ozzy said to Leo when he got home that night.

'Oh, really, why's that?'

'She's given the money she was going to use for the Kensington house to her sister to stop her being evicted,' Ozzy said warmly.

'Has she now?' So Kate hadn't completely lost her way after all, Leo thought, greatly cheered by this news.

'A nice gesture, don't you think?'

'Indeed,' Leo said thoughtfully, 'but no more than you'd expect from someone like her.'

'That's true,' agreed Ozzy, managing to resist the urge to break his word and tell Leo about Sam's career problem.

There were two groups of Londoners existing side by side in the capital in the early 1930s, the 'haves' and the 'have-nots'. Ironically, as unemployment figures soared, so did the amount of cheap mass-produced goods that were now available to ordinary people. While riots erupted among the unemployed, who organised demonstrations to bring attention to their plight, those people who were lucky enough to have a job were enjoying such pleasures as talking pictures, holidays and motoring.

Kate's millinery trade was not unduly affected by the depression, since she catered primarily for the middle and upper classes. She wasn't blind to the suffering of the hard-up housewives she saw every day on the streets, though, and thought their shabby, old-fashioned clothes must add to their misery. It was a recognised fact that a smart new hat could do wonders for the morale, even if a whole new outfit wasn't possible. It occurred to her that there was a real need for stylish headwear of the sort she produced, but at a price to suit the pocket of those who were struggling.

This was a gap in the market that was not easy for Kate to

fill, however. Were she to launch a range of very cheap hats under her own name, she stood to lose many of her high-class clients who would not want to patronise a milliner whose hats could be bought across the counter by the hoi-polloi. Snobbery it undoubtedly was, but it was something Kate could not afford to ignore. As well as her own livelihood to protect, she also felt responsible for her workforce who relied on her staying in business for their daily bread.

The solution came after a great deal of consideration. She took on some freelance designing for a firm who mass produced headwear for the very cheapest end of the market. This meant that low-priced hats with a real touch of chic became available to the public under the brand name of the factory, thus leaving Kate's exclusive clientèle unoffended.

For all her professional triumph, Kate was beginning to realise that the sweet smell of success was distinctly lacking when there was no one with whom to share it. Immersed in her work, she had virtually no social life. An occasional trip to the pictures with her mother and Esme was about the limit. But since this had been the path she had chosen, she knew she had no cause for complaint. And as reports of hunger marches continued to fill the papers, she counted her blessings.

'Oh, well, it's time for me to toddle off to bed,' said Esme, yawning as she rose from her armchair where she had spent a pleasant evening listening to the wireless. 'Are you coming up, dear?'

'No, I need to unwind a bit first,' said Johnny, pouring himself a glass of whisky from a decanter on the sideboard. 'You go on up, I won't be long.'

'All right, darling,' she said, understanding her husband's need to relax for he had not long returned home from seeing someone about a property deal.

She went over and pecked him on the cheek. 'Goodnight, dear, just in case I'm asleep when you come up.'

He surprised her by taking her in his arms and kissing her with a kind of urgency. 'I love you,' he said.

'Goodness me, what's brought all this on?' she asked lightly.

'Nothing. I love you, that's all.'

'After all these years of marriage, I thought you'd be tired of me?'

'Never.'

'How sweet, Johnny,' she said, smiling. 'And I feel the same way about you.'

When the door had closed behind her, he sank gloomily into the armchair. Draining his whisky glass, he poured another drink which he swallowed swiftly, then went over to the bureau. Taking out some writing paper, a pen and a bottle of ink, he sat with nib poised, despising himself for deceiving Esme yet again, for he had no more been out on business this evening than she had. He chewed the end of the pen, searching for the words which must be said.

Full of self-disgust, he dwelled on the fact that fortune had been kind to him. He had the love of a good woman, and together they shared the joys of a fine healthy daughter. He'd been spared in the war and blessed with a keen brain with which to earn a good living when many other ex-servicemen were unemployed. Yet, despite all these advantages, he'd still managed to make a complete mess of his life.

Kate's generosity a year ago had meant he'd been able to keep his house and support his family. But there had not been enough money to buy property to improve and resell at a profit, which was how he made his living. Too ashamed to admit the truth to anyone, he had turned in desperation to gambling again and sustained heavy losses.

But tonight his luck had changed, though his winnings fell short of the amount he needed to get back into the property-dealing business. His initial reaction to this upturn in fortune had been to increase the amount by risking it in other card games.

On the way home, however, he had mulled over the possibility of losing what he already had, and had decided that *now* was the time to stop, not tomorrow or the next day. He had also come to the painful conclusion that the kindest thing he could do for Esme was to leave the money with her and disappear from her life altogether. It wasn't a huge sum but it was enough to keep her and Rita for a while. He was no use to anyone unless he could change his ways. If and when he could trust himself never to gamble again, he would return.

Everything he'd done went into the letter, along with his true feelings. Nothing was held back. He put it into a large envelope with his winnings. Then he poured himself another whisky and gulped it quickly to deaden the pain. When he was sure Esme was asleep, he crept upstairs to his dressing room and packed a small suitcase. Then, feeling as though his heart would break, he left the house.

When Esme showed Kate the letter the next day, it was as much as the latter could do to hold back the tears. She was angry with Johnny, of course, and knew she shouldn't waste her compassion on a man who had behaved in such an irresponsible manner. But it was such a sad letter, and somehow she could see the peculiar logic that had made him think he was acting in Esme's best interests by going away. Recalling the fuss her sister had made during the last crisis, when she'd been about to lose her home, it wasn't surprising he had reached that conclusion.

Now that Esme was faced with the horrible reality of not having her husband around, it was obvious to Kate that her sister would rather forfeit every material possession than lose him. In fact, the courageous way Esme seemed to be accepting her predicament was quite astonishing. Having been told what had happened on the telephone, Kate had expected to arrive at Lilac Gardens to find Esme in a state of collapse. But although a puffiness around the eyes betrayed the fact that she had been crying, she was surprisingly calm.

'He'll come back,' she said bravely. 'I know he will.'

'But will you want to have him back?' asked Kate.

'Oh, yes,' said Esme. 'He's a damned fool but I love him. Anyway, maybe none of this would have happened if I'd put my foot down about the gambling from the start. I could have taken more of an interest in his business affairs too.'

'There might be something in that,' agreed Kate, beginning to see her sister in a new light.

'Anyway, since he's deserted me, I'm going to need a part-time job.'

'You've enough to live on for a while.'

'Yes, but that won't won't last forever,' she said. 'And with Rita out at school all day, it will do me good to get out of the house.' She paused, struggling against tears. 'It will take my mind off the fact that Johnny won't be coming home in the evening.'

Kate was pleased to see her frivolous sister showing such strength. Perhaps she was growing up at last. 'I could use another assistant in the shop,' she said. 'You'd be well suited to it, having worked in a West End store. But you'll have to earn your wages, I can't afford passengers.'

'When can I start?' asked Esme, managing a smile.

The wedding of Ozzy Perks to Poppy Brown in the autumn of 1934 was a lively occasion, with the bride's guests outnumbering the groom's by a great number on account of the fact that Poppy was related to a large proportion of the population of Fulham. The Browns were loud, cheerful cockneys who were no strangers to hard times and therefore determined to squeeze every ounce of enjoyment from this special occasion. Their side of the church was awash with sentiment as the couple took their vows, and risqué humour abounded back at the reception in a Fulham hall.

Sam was Ozzy's best man. Leo, Kate and her relatives were a stand-in family to him. Kate was delighted that the couple had made it to the altar, having watched their on-off romance develop since that first adolescent meeting.

Poppy had grown into an attractive, homely woman who today was radiant in a long white dress with orange blossom in her brown hair. Ozzy looked proud and handsome, darkly good-looking in his smart new suit.

It was only natural that Kate and Leo should find themselves thrown together on this occasion. 'They make a smashing couple, don't they?' she remarked to him at the wedding meal, at which they were seated together.

'Yes, they're very well matched,' he agreed. 'I'm glad to see

Ozzy settled down with a nice girl. He's been through a lot.'

'That doesn't seem to have stopped him getting on,' she said. 'I understand he's doing well as a reporter now?'

'That's right.'

'Credit must go to you for encouraging him.'

'Nonsense, he's the one who's done it.'

'From what you've said, I gather he didn't have much going for him when you took him in.'

'True, but success has come from his own efforts.'

But Ozzy himself, in his speech, mentioned how much Leo had done for him. He also took Kate by suprise by saying that he had valued being treated like one of the best man's family over the years. It was a moving speech, Ozzy's emotions stirred, Kate suspected, by substantial amounts of best bitter, though sincere nonetheless.

Speeches and toasts over, the couple departed for their honeymoon amid clouds of confetti and the usual assortment of honeymoon jokes. Tables were moved to make way for dancing to a small band. Couples quickstepped round the floor to an out of tune rendering of 'You're the Top'. The drink flowed and everyone was having a good time. Even Gertie, who still tended to be rather inhibited at this sort of gathering, let her hair down and joined in the 'Lambeth Walk'. Esme had no shortage of partners among Poppy's ubiquitous uncles, and Rita found plenty of company among the younger Browns.

Typically diligent in his duties as best man, Sam, now working at a firm of City solicitors, presided over the party in dignified manner, causing his mother to swell with pride. No one at this jovial get-together spoiled the mood by mentioning unemployment, or what they read in the papers nearly every day about the terrible things that were happening in Germany under Adolf Hitler who had recently become Head of State as well as Chancellor.

The sedate waltzes and foxtrots changed to an unruly hokey-cokey, then the whole place erupted into a riotous knees up.

'As much as I've enjoyed myself, enough is enough,' Leo confided to Kate. 'How about us slipping away?'

293

'I thought you'd never ask.'

Leo drove them to the riverside, parked the car in his usual place in a sidestreet, and they walked to the boat along the towpath in the spicy autumn air. Kate was swamped with memories as *London Lady* came into view.

Below deck in the saloon there had been changes since she was here last. She was pleased to see that the dining table and chairs had not been replaced but there were smart new red leather armchairs, and some of the wood panelling had been renewed in keeping with the original style.

'You've been splashing out, I see,' she said, sinking into one of the armchairs holding a glass of sherry.

'At least I can afford to maintain her properly now I've more money in my pocket,' said Leo. 'I've updated the galley and installed a more reliable hot water system. A lot of the exterior wood needed replacing too.'

'Fame hasn't made you want to move to an easier way of life, then?'

'No,' he laughed. 'I've got this ruddy boat in my bones, for all its inconveniences.'

'I'm quite fond of her myself.'

'I must say I'm surprised you agreed to come back here with me,' he said, sitting opposite her with a glass of whisky.

'I think I'm a bit long in the tooth for girlish modesty. I'll be forty next year.' Kate leaned back against the soft upholstery, looking at him. 'I've missed you terribly, Leo.'

'Likewise.'

'You didn't find a nice, uncomplicated female then?' she said quietly.

'I found several, but none was right for me.'

'There's been no one else for me either.'

'I know,' he told her. 'I've kept my ear to the ground on that subject.'

'I'm glad you took the trouble to bother.'

Sipping his drink, he observed her in the light from the oil lamp. 'Are you content now you have the success you wanted so much?'

'Good lord, no,' she laughed. 'It isn't in my nature to sit

back feeling pleased with myself. Anyway, I still have that fashionable address to strive for.'

'You could have had that a few years ago though, couldn't you?'

'I suppose Sam told Ozzy, and Ozzy told you?'

He nodded. 'It must have been a blow for you, having to abandon the idea at the last minute like that.'

'Esme's need was greater than mine,' she explained. 'I'm very fond of Johnny too, you know, despite everything he's done.' She went on to tell him about the current situation. 'Anyway, I'll get my posh house eventually.'

'You still want it?'

'Of course, but I have to find new premises for my business first,' she explained. 'I need a bigger place. We're bursting out of the shop in Litchman Street.'

'I see,' said Leo quietly.

The atmosphere was tender and relaxed. Maturity had made them both more tolerant.

'Why did you come back to the boat with me, Kate?' he asked, adding with a half smile, 'We both know what will happen.'

'Just because I chose not to marry you doesn't mean I don't love you.'

'Still?'

'More than ever.'

'Come here,' he said, opening his arms to her.


'Let's get married, Kate,' he said the next morning as they lingered over toast and coffee in the sun-washed saloon.

'Don't rush me, Leo. Let's just see how things go.'

'Rush you?' he echoed with a dry laugh. 'That's rich since ours must be one of the longest running courtships in London.'

'So what?'

'We're too old for the strain of this hole and corner carry on.'

'Oh, I don't know,' she said thoughtfully. 'Getting older does have its advantages.'

'Such as?'

'It makes you realise that life is too short to spend time bothering about trivialities – such as what people might think of someone who has been out all night.'

'Some people care more about that sort of thing as they get older.'

'Not me.'

'Not even about Sam's opinion?'

'I care, of course, but I hope I've raised him to be broad-minded enough not to judge me too harshly.'

'You may have succeeded in that, but I'm still childish enough to mind about you living in one place and me in another.'

'Please don't let's complicate things for the moment,' she implored.

'All right,' he sighed 'if that's what you really want, but I don't like it.'

Neither did she, but she simply could not bring herself to make the total commitment he wanted from her. Apart from their conflicting values, she still felt fully pledged to her work. There was so much to think about and do.

'If it's any comfort,' she said, covering his hand with hers across the table and looking into his eyes, 'I'm yours completely, even if I am hesitant about tying the knot.'

'I suppose I shall have to make do with that for now, then.'


It was the Tuesday morning after August Bank Holiday, and Giles Dexter was sitting at his desk reading an article in a magazine. It was about a top West End milliner who had just moved her business into larger premises. Some people had all the luck, he thought resentfully. Everything that woman touched, turned to gold. You only had to open a fashion magazine to see her hats plastered all over the pages. Oh, yes, everyone in the millinery trade knew about Kate Brooks. Some of the fashion reporters even rated her beside star milliners like Aage Thaarup.

To Giles it didn't seem fair that she had all that while mass producers like Dexter's struggled for orders against such enemies as an economic depression and a trend by some of the more daring young women to defy convention and go hatless. Fortunately, a hat was still as essential to any decent middle-aged woman as her shoes and stockings, but the possibility of such crazes spreading were a threat to the hat trade. The papers claimed that the depression was coming to an end but it still wasn't over according to Dexter's sales figures.

Of course, it was all very well for model milliners like that Brooks woman, whose rich clients could afford to buy three hats at a time, regardless of the economic situation. Model millinery was the branch of the trade Giles would like to go into, and he'd said as much to his mother the other day. He would never make a name for himself running a factory, but he would if he made exclusive models. He could design. He'd done enough of it for Dexter's, copying bits and pieces from other people's hats to make an original. But you had to have West End premises to succeed in that field and decent places were like gold dust around there. If he did decide to pursue this idea, he had no intention of waiting until something suitable became available.

He leaned back in the office chair that had once been his father's, recalling the pearls of wisdom the old man had passed on to him. 'If someone is in your path, son, don't walk round them. Find a way to get them out of the way. If someone has something you want, take it from them by any means at your disposal. All's fair in business, boy,' he used to say. 'Look after your own and sod the rest.'

Giles had gone into the family business with his parents after leaving school and had soon been given a seat on the board. He had bright ideas and a good head for business. The refined demeanour he had acquired at boarding school and his inherent single-mindedness had given him the hard edge necessary for management of a large concern like Dexter's. When his father's health had begun to fail, Giles had removed much of the worry from Reggie's shoulders; when he had died of a heart attack six months ago, his son had been competent enough to step into his shoes.

He and his mother ran the business together, though he took most of the responsibility as she was getting on in years. Giles got on well with her which wasn't difficult since they had a similar outlook on life, and also because she let him have his own way about practically everything. It was second nature to him to exploit her devotion to the full. He'd been doing it for as long as he could remember.

After that beastly Laurence had left home, things had got even better for Giles because Mother was then able to indulge her feelings for him without Laurence's miserable presence about the place. Giles had missed the perverse pleasure of tormenting his elder brother and seeing him take the blame for his own misdemeanours. But he certainly never lost any sleep over Laurence's departure, because with him out of the picture the whole shooting match, the business, the house in Clapham and all the rest of his mother's worldly goods, would eventually come to Giles alone.

He studied the magazine again, observing the picture of Kate Brooks outside her new shop in Feather Street W1, smart double-fronted shop premises with spacious bow windows. A place like that would be just right for him to set up in as an exclusive milliner. The idea grew on him by the moment. Mother could manage the factory here with the help of the general manager, and he himself would divide his time between the two operations. This new venture would be an additional part of the Dexter firm but Giles's own baby, rather than something he had taken over from someone else.

Tingling with excitement, he went into his mother's office next door. 'You know, I've been thinking of setting up an exclusive hat shop in the West End,' he said, putting the magazine on her desk, open at the appropriate page. 'Well, I think I've found just the place.'

Cissy read the article with more interest than her son could possibly have predicted. She looked up at him, her wrinkled face creasing into an evil smile, eyes gleaming spitefully from behind her spectacles. 'I agree with you, dear. This shop would be perfect.'

'Shall I go and see this Brooks woman to find out how much she'll want to move out?'

'No, son, leave it to me.' Cissy didn't intend to confide the secrets of the past to her beloved Giles, but she knew who Kate Brooks was. She might have changed her name and her appearance but Cissy never forgot a face. Especially the face of the hussy who had seduced her husband and left her with her brat to look after. And here the trollop was, dripping with success that would never have been hers had she not had her disgrace taken care of by Cissy.

'Oh, why's that?' asked Giles, for pressurising people into doing things against their will was his speciality.

'A female approach will probably be the best thing initially, dear,' she said, excited by the idea of seeing the little whore again and reminding her that the Dexters were still a force to be reckoned with, even if Reggie was no longer around. 'You can take over if she proves to be difficult.'

'As you wish, Mother,' he said.

That particular morning, Kate was still glowing from an enjoyable Bank Holiday Monday at Brighton with Leo. The sunshine had brought the crowds out in their thousands, and there hadn't been room to breathe, but it was good to see signs of prosperity again which confirmed the reports that unemployment figures were beginning to decrease slightly at last.

Every inch of the beach and promenade had been packed; every pub and restaurant was overflowing; long queues tailed from every kiosk and street vendor. But Kate and Leo hadn't minded the pushing and shoving because it spoke of better times ahead. They'd sat in deckchairs on the pebbles, and paddled in the foamy waves; they'd eaten winkles and shrimps and toffee apples; and eventually they drove home in Leo's car, singing 'Red Sails in the Sunset'.

Since their reunion nearly a year ago, their relationship had continued on the lines she wanted. They were friends and lovers, committed to each other but still living apart. Sometimes, like yesterday, it seemed enough. Other times she wanted more. But there were plenty of arguments against, not least their contrasting views on fundamental issues. So, she lived from day to day, enjoying his love and friendship and pretending it could go on like this forever.

This last year had been a hectic time for them both. Leo had been busy with exhibitions, involving several trips to Paris; she'd been chasing her tail finding and moving her business into new spacious premises.

But now, as she sat at her desk in her light, roomy office, she was feeling too happy to dwell on the negative side of her love life. The sun was shining. She had the love of a good man; a caring son she had set up in his own flat a few minutes' walk from hers; a smart new shop. Even the newspapers didn't seem to be carrying any horror stories of cruelty to the Jews in Germany, for a change. It would take something really bad to alter her lighthearted mood.

A few moments later she knew that that 'something' had happened when she answered the telephone to Cissy Dexter.

# Chapter Nineteen

It had been twenty-four years since Kate had last seen Cissy Dexter, but she would have known that face anywhere.

'Do take a seat,' she said with tense politeness when the older woman swept into her office that afternoon.

'Thank you.' As it had been on the telephone, Cissy's manner was courteous but cool.

'Would you like some tea?'

'That would be most welcome,' said Cissy, making little sucking sounds as her lips caught against her ill-fitting dentures.

Kate went out into the shop and asked Esme to organise a tea-tray, then moved briskly back to her desk, though her legs felt weak. After all these years, this woman still had the power to frighten her.

'The tea won't be long,' she said, sinking gratefully into her chair and observing her visitor across the desk. Kate guessed she must be about sixty now but she was well-preserved and smart, albeit rather over made-up. Her iron-waved hair was white beneath her large-brimmed hat and her skin withered, but the cut of the navy and white linen suit she was wearing gave her a groomed, expensive look. Kate decided to try to ease this awkward moment with the normal social graces, however meaningless. 'So, how have you been keeping, Mrs Dexter?'

'Quite well, thank you.'

'And Mr Dexter?'

'He died six months ago.'

'Oh.'

Cissy cast a critical eye around the room, with its oak desk and Axminster carpet. 'Well, you've certainly done well for yourself. I've been reading about this new shop of yours in one of the magazines.'

'I can't complain,' Kate said, inwardly quaking as she waited for her visitor to come to the point, guessing it would not be to her advantage.

'I should think not indeed,' Cissy said icily.

Since there was only one thing that linked Kate with Cissy, she assumed this visit must be connected in some way with her son. Fear made her blood run cold. Why would she come here unless something was wrong with him? Anxious to move things on, she said, 'I'm sure you haven't come here just to compliment me on my new premises.'

'I certainly haven't.'

'Has something happened to my son?'

'No,' Cissy said dismissively.

'Thank God,' Kate sighed involuntarily.

On perceiving her concern, Cissy's first impulse was to hurt Kate by telling her that her wretched baby had grown into a wicked, ungrateful brat who had brought nothing but misery and trouble on his adoptive parents. But it didn't suit her to mention this. In fact, the least said about Kate Brooks's bastard child the better.

On hearing of Giles's scheme, the possibility of using Kate Brooks's colourful past to exert pressure should she refuse to co-operate had occurred to Cissy. But after giving the matter further consideration, she had decided it would be a mistake to rake up the past. People might dig deeper than she intended. Kate Brooks could even retaliate by naming the father. However much Cissy denied it, the matter would become one for speculation, making the Dexter name a subject of gossip among their workforce as well as their neighbours. So it was best to let the whole mucky business rest, especially as dear Giles knew nothing about it.

'I'm here on a matter of business, as a matter of fact.'

'Is the boy well and happy?' Kate asked eagerly, as though the other woman hadn't spoken.

'As far as I know,' she snapped. 'Why shouldn't he be? And

302

he isn't a boy but a grown man now and living away from home. I don't see much of him these days. What mother does see her children, once they leave the nest?'

'Didn't he go into the family business then?' Kate asked.

'No, he didn't,' Cissy said in a tone designed to discourage further enquiry. 'But I haven't come here to talk about him, I've come to offer you a proposition.'

'Oh?'

'It's my son Giles's idea actually.'

'*Your* son?'

'That's right. He was born a year after we took Laurence in.'

This information made Kate uneasy. 'So you called my baby Laurence?' she said. 'I've often wondered.'

'Yes, yes,' Cissy said impatiently.

'It's rather a nice name.'

'Anyway, Giles came into the business with us when he left school so is very experienced in the hat trade,' she said, ignoring Kate's last comment, 'and now he wants to branch out and set up a retail outlet in the West End. Dealing in exclusive models, of course.'

'Naturally, but what has that to do with me?' asked Kate. 'Does he want advice about the model millinery trade or something?'

'No, he wants your premises,' Cissy stated frankly. 'We want to buy you out of here.'

'Buy me out?' she said incredulously.

'We'd make it worth your while financially, of course.'

'I'm not interested,' said Kate, gathering her wits. 'I waited a long time for something suitable to become available, and having only just moved in, I'd be a fool to move out and have the job of finding a place all over again.'

'You'd be paid a fair price.'

'No thanks.'

Cissy gave a cynical smile, revealing the join where the orange-coloured dental plate met her gums. 'Perhaps I haven't made myself clear,' she said dogmatically. 'When I say we want to take over this place, I actually mean we *intend* to do so.'

'And if I won't budge?'

'You will.'

'Meaning that you'll use force to get me out?'

'Meaning that you would be wise to think very carefully before refusing,' she said, 'because Giles is the sort of fellow who makes an absolute point of getting what he wants, one way or another. He had an excellent teacher in his father. I'm sure you remember how much Reggie enjoyed having his own way?'

'You're threatening me!'

'Not threatening,' she said, 'just giving you some friendly advice.'

The years fell away for Kate to a time when, as a naive young girl, she had stood before this woman and allowed herself to be manipulated because there had been no other choice. Now she was neither young nor naive, and there *was* a choice. She leaned back in her chair with an authoritative air and met the challenge in the other woman's eyes. 'Well, Mrs Dexter, age has not mellowed you,' she said. 'You're still the vicious bitch you always were.' She stood up to indicate that the interview was at an end. 'Now get out, and take your proposition with you.'

Cissy didn't move. 'We'd give you a fair price to move out. You'd not be out of pocket.'

'I wouldn't sell out to you for a barrel-load of bank notes.'

'Why not?'

'Firstly because I'm not prepared to be forced into anything by thugs like you, and secondly because I want to keep these premises.'

Cissy's face worked, her neck flushing with rage. With a factory full of workers reliant on her for their employment, she was used to being in a position of power. The lack of it infuriated her. 'Fancy yourself as a lady nowadays, don't you?' she snarled, driven by anger into raising the subject she had intended to leave alone. 'But I know what a slut you really are. You wouldn't have any of this if I hadn't taken your brat off your hands.'

'You wanted him,' said Kate, reeling from all the old guilt.

304

'You left me with no choice but to give him up. I didn't want to . . .'

'Don't make me laugh,' rasped Cissy. 'You wanted shot of him so that you could be free to get on with your own life. You wanted your pleasure, but you didn't want the shame and responsibility that went with it.'

'It wasn't like that!'

'You'd have been an outcast in society if I hadn't taken care of your trouble,' Cissy ranted. 'Never mind having all this, you'd probably be skivvying to make end meets now.'

The accusations of a malicious woman didn't have the power to hurt Kate, but they brought something home to her with devastating certainty. It was obvious from the way Cissy spoke of Kate's child that she had not been kind to him. Even now, with the boy a grown man, this cut deep with Kate.

'Are you suggesting I should give in to your demands out of gratitude for the past?'

'It might save a lot of unpleasantness.'

'No.'

'Oh well, if you're determined to be stupid, you'll have to take the consequences.' Cissy rose and walked towards the door, turning when she got there. 'Are you sure you wouldn't rather settle this matter in a civilised manner?'

Kate shook her head.

'You'll regret it.'

'Esme said to tell you she's gone home,' said Poppy half an hour later when she went into Kate's office to give her a progress report on the hats they were making for a society wedding. 'She didn't want to disturb you when you had a visitor.'

'I hadn't realised it was time for her to leave,' said Kate absently. Esme only worked from ten till three.

'Is there anything wrong, Kate?' asked Poppy, noticing that her employer looked pale and worried.

'No, I'm all right,' she lied.

'That woman's upset yer, ain't she?' said the indomitable

Poppy. 'I thought she looked an 'ard-faced cow. We can do without 'er sort on our books.'

Kate was warmed by her genuine concern. Over the years, Poppy had become Kate's right arm in business as well as a close personal friend. Kate was very glad that Ozzy had not gone along with the opinions of most men and objected to her continuing with her job after marriage.

An assistant like Poppy, who knew the business inside out, was invaluable to Kate. Although both Mother and Esme were useful, neither had the same sort of commitment as Poppy, and both only worked part-time. Mother's main interest lay in her work for the Institute these days, and Esme looked on her job merely as a diversion from the emptiness of her life without Johnny.

'She wasn't a potential customer,' explained Kate.

'Good job an' all,' said Poppy. 'But whoever she was, she's taken the colour out of your cheeks good and proper.'

Deciding not to burden Poppy with problems that were not her concern, Kate forced a smile and said, 'I'm all right, honestly. Now about the wedding order, are we on schedule?'

'Yes, the hats will be ready for fitting tomorrow.'

'Good.'

'It's a nice big order an' all. Practically every female relative on the bride's side wants us to make their hat.' She paused and consulted a piece of paper she was clutching in her hand. 'I'll have to send one of the juniors over to Clerkenwell for some more trimmings, though. We won't have enough and the rep isn't due to call until next week.' She handed Kate the paper. 'I've made a list of what we need.'

'Fine,' she said, glancing at the list. 'You go ahead. Is everything else all right in the workroom?'

'No problems at all.'

'Good,' said Kate, the threatening shadow of Cissy's visit fading from her mind in Poppy's cheerful company.

Kate usually got to the shop before the staff in the morning. She found it useful to catch up on outstanding paperwork while

306

it was quiet, or have the workroom to herself with any new designs she had in progress.

What greeted her when she arrived one morning a week after Cissy's visit turned her to stone. The wax heads on her interior displays were bare, the hats that had been adorning them lying slashed to ribbons on the floor. The contents of the stock cupboards had met a similar fate. Numb with shock, she made her way into the workroom to find the window broken and swinging open, the perpetrators of the crime having obviously made their escape through it.

Going back into the shop, her eyes filled with tears at the sight of the ruined hats on the floor. Months of creative thought and craftsmanship completely destroyed. All that beautiful silk, velvet and velour as limp as rag on the floor. Someone must have been at work with a razor. It had obviously been done under contract to Cissy Dexter and her son, but she doubted if they would actually have taken the risk of being involved in the physical work themselves.

She was about to call the police when the telephone rang. 'This is Giles Dexter.'

'You bastard!'

'Just to let you know that there's plenty more where that came from unless we can come to an arrangement.'

'I won't give in.'

'You will, eventually.'

'I'm going to report it to the police, and I shall tell them it was you.'

He chuckled down the line. 'They can't do a thing without proof,' he said. 'And they won't find anything to incriminate us.'

'They'll get you,' she hissed. 'Don't you worry about that.'

'You'll be the one in trouble for wasting police time, not to mention facing a slander action if we feel like bringing one against you,' he said. 'Now why don't you be sensible and we can get together and discuss terms?'

'No.'

'All right, if it's war you want, we'll be happy to oblige.'

★  ★  ★

'There's no question of my being forced out of this shop, Poppy.' It was later that same day. Everyone else had gone home and Kate and Poppy were in Kate's office discussing the attack. 'So you and the rest of the staff needn't worry about being thrown out of work while I find new premises.'

Deciding that she owed Poppy some sort of explanation, in the light of this new development, Kate had told her about the Dexters' scheme, omitting any reference to her previous connection with them. She had been hesitant about calling the police though. As much as she wanted to bring the Dexters to justice, they were the family of the boy to whom she had given life, and she feared he might be implicated somehow. But thinking back on what Cissy had said about Laurence not being involved in the business, or in her life for that matter, Kate had finally gone ahead and done her public duty. Whilst seeming to believe her story about the threat, there was not much the police could do without evidence.

Now the clearing up had been done and work was already in progress to replace the damaged stock. Fortunately it was Gertie's day for the Institute. She would be given a watered down version of what had happened from Kate later on so as not to alarm her too much.

'I'm glad you're standing up to 'em,' said Poppy.

'Wouldn't you?'

'Not 'alf! Bloomin' crooks, they want locking up,' she said. 'The police'll soon nail 'em.'

'I doubt if it will be as simple as that,' said Kate. 'Without proof the police are powerless, and you can be sure the Dexters will have seen to it that the attacks can't be linked to them.'

'*Attacks?*' Poppy said emphatically. 'You mean there might be more of 'em?'

'I should think this is just the beginning.'

'Oh Gawd,' gasped Poppy. 'And there's nothing we can do?'

'Not really. Short of sleeping here to guard the place, and I'll do that if necessary.'

'You mustn't,' said Poppy anxiously. 'You could get 'urt.'

'I'll risk it rather than be dictated to by a couple of thugs.

But I doubt if anything will happen for a few nights. They won't risk acting again so soon. It's when the police lose interest in the place that we'll need to worry.'

'It makes my blood boil,' Poppy fumed. 'How dare these criminals terrorise a decent hardworking woman like yourself? If they want to set up in business around 'ere, they should look for their own place, like we had to.'

'I agree.'

'Ooh, it makes me so mad,' she said, cheeks flaming with anger.


Poppy was still furious when she related the story to Ozzy that evening as they sat down to supper in their Fulham flat.

'I'll kill the buggers if I ever meet them,' she said.

'Me too.'

'Kate's thinking of staying at the shop all night, though I doubt if she's told any of her relatives about it,' she said. 'They'd soon talk her out of it. I mean, she could get hurt, couldn't she, Ozzy?'

'Course she could,' he agreed. 'We mustn't let her stay there on her own.'

'But I think she's right not to give in to these people, don't you?'

'Too true, and it's up to all her friends to give her their support,' he said heatedly. 'I'll have a word with Sam and see if we can't get together and do something ourselves about stopping this scum as the police can't do anything. You said she knows who's doing it?'

'Mm, that's right.'

'Did she tell you who they are?'

'Yeah, they're a firm of hat-makers across the river at Wandsworth,' she said, trying to remember the name. 'Er . . . Dexwood, Dexly or something.'

'Not Dexter's?' he breathed.

'That's it,' she said, starting on her toad-in-the hole.

'My God!'

'Whatever's the matter, love? You look as though you've seen a ghost,' she said. 'Do you know them, or something?'

'Oh, I know them all right,' he said, leaping from his seat.

'Ozzy, what's going on?'

'I have to go out, love,' he said, planting an absent kiss on the top of her head.

'But your supper!' she said. But Ozzy was already on his way out of the flat.


Ozzy caught the bus to Clapham and walked to the Dexters' house, seething with rage, completely forgetting that he had changed in appearance since he had last been there. The door was opened by a maid he couldn't remember having seen before.

'Yes?'

'Is Giles at home.'

'Is he expecting you?'

'No.'

'Oh, well then, I'm not sure . . .'

'I'm his brother.'

'Sorry, sir,' she said, flushing and standing aside for him to enter. 'I didn't realise you were a relative.'

'Don't worry,' he said, making his way into the front sitting room, feeling faint just to be here. The room had been modernised, he noticed, and thought Giles's youthful influence had probably been at work in the choice of white and orange walls and cube-like furniture that was all the rage.

Just being again in this house brought back all the pain he had experienced here. He was a young boy again, lonely and despised. Every moment of that miserable childhood was imprinted on his memory. He would never forgive the Dexters for robbing him of those few carefree years that should be every child's right.

Voices whispering outside the door brought him back to the present. 'The man said he was Mr Giles's brother, madam,' the maid was saying apologetically. 'I thought I'd better let him in.'

The sitting-room door burst open and in marched Giles, followed by his mother. Ozzy stared at them in silence, trying to match the tall, moustached man dressed in blazer and cravat with the skinny young boy in short pants he remembered. Cissy was more easily recognisable for she had not changed from child to adult as Giles had.

He was obviously having similar problems identifying his half brother. 'Laurence?' he said.

'That's me, though I haven't used that name for years.'

Giles nodded thoughtfully. 'Yes, I can see it's you now. I'd know those shifty dark eyes anywhere.'

'You've not lost your charm then?' came the sarcastic retort.

'My God, you've got a nerve coming back here!' said Giles. 'After what you did to Mother, going off like that.'

'All I did was to relieve her of the misery of having me around,' he said. 'I'm sure you were all delighted.'

'After all I'd done for you,' said Cissy, 'you show your gratitude by clearing off and leaving me worried half to death.'

'Don't tell lies,' he snapped. 'You were glad to see the back of me. I bet you didn't lift a finger to try to find me.'

Ignoring his accusation, she said, 'I suppose you've heard about your father's death and that's what's brought you sniffing around? Well, you needn't have bothered because he didn't leave you anything in his will.'

He laughed with the sheer joy of knowing he was free from the tyranny of these people. 'I wouldn't have accepted it if he had. I want nothing from this family, nothing at all.'

'Why have you come back, then?' asked Giles.

'I'm here on business.'

'Business?'

'Yes, I'm a reporter.'

'What has that to do with us?' asked Giles.

'Nothing in itself,' said Ozzy. 'But added to the fact that Kate Brooks is a very good friend of mine, it has plenty to do with you.'

Cissy and Giles exchanged glances. 'I don't see why,' said Giles, observing him warily.

'I think you do. I know that you were behind the break-in at her shop last night.'

'You could find yourself in trouble, making accusations like that without a shred of evidence,' said Giles.

'And you'll find the story of your treachery splashed all over

311

the pages of my paper unless you give me your word that you'll leave her alone.'

'Print what you like,' said Giles haughtily, but he had turned very pale. 'And we'll sue the paper for libel.'

'A libel suit won't give you back your good name,' said Ozzy. 'Print is a powerful thing. And the truth will be obvious to anyone who reads the paper, I'll make damned sure of that.'

Stepping forward, Cissy glared into his face. 'So this is the way you repay the hand that fed you for the first twelve years of your life, is it?' she squawked. 'Taking sides with that slut against me who put food in your belly and clothes on your back.'

'Kate is a very dear friend, and what you're doing to her is criminal . . .'

'She couldn't wait to get rid of you,' interrupted Cissy, her spiteful words flowing almost of their own volition. 'She could hardly wait for the umbilical cord to be cut . . .'

'What cord? What are you rambling on about, woman?'

'How you found out is a mystery to me,' Cissy continued, too absorbed in her own feelings to notice his puzzlement.

'Found out about what?'

'No one knew except us and her family,' she went on. 'You were registered in our name, mine and Reggie's, not hers.'

'I don't understand . . .'

'Must be a journalist's nose for a story, I suppose,' she continued, oblivious to everything except the sound of her own voice.

'Are you saying that Kate Brooks is my mother?' he gasped, hardly able to say the words they were so astonishing.

'Of course she's your mother!' snapped Cissy. 'If you can call someone who gives a baby away hours after it's born a mother.'

'Good God!' said Giles.

'She was Kate Potter then, of course, a shameless baggage who worked for us in the factory.' Cissy slipped into a fantasy world of her own where the truth was shaped to suit herself. The lies flowed with ease because she had grown to believe them over the years.

'Poor Reggie didn't stand a chance against her, with her posh ways and come-to-bed eyes. She didn't like the consequences though. Oh, no. It was left to me to help out when she got pregnant with you. Now she's a big name in the millinery business she carries on like Lady Muck, but I know different. I know what a tart she really is!'

'I don't believe any of it,' said Ozzy. 'You're making it up just to hurt me.'

'Ask her if you don't believe me,' said Cissy.

'It's all lies . . .'

'I tell you this much,' she said, ignoring his anguish, 'she wouldn't be where she is today if I hadn't taken you off her hands. With a bastard child around her neck she'd have been an outcast with no chance of getting a husband, let alone a decent job. She'd be scrubbing floors to keep herself now, and that's a fact.'

'Shut up!' yelled Ozzy, clamping his hands over his ears.

Looking at him as though his comments finally registered, she said, 'But surely you know she's your mother? Isn't that why you've taken her side against us?'

He shook his head. 'Her son's a pal of mine,' he said stiffly, 'I've been a friend of the family for years. I never dreamed she was . . .'

'Well, she is, and now you know the truth about her perhaps you'll not be so quick to defend her,' she said. 'Your loyalty lies with us.'

Ozzy was dazed, numb with shock but conscious of a debilitating ache in the pit of his stomach. The woman he had admired and respected, even loved in a filial kind of way, was the woman who had carelessly handed him over to the Dexters. Somehow he managed to remain standing, though he felt as though his legs were about to give way. 'My loyalty lies on the side of right,' he said dully. 'So, stop harassing her or I'll go to my editor with the story.'

'You wouldn't dare!'

'Try me.'

'Go on then, do your worst,' shrieked Cissy hysterically, 'but get out of this house.'

313

'With the greatest of pleasure.' Stiffly, he walked to the door, his head spinning.

Giles was an astute and artful businessman. He knew how damaging adverse publicity would be to the company, and it certainly wouldn't help his chances with the upper echelons from whom he would draw clients as a model milliner. Maybe it would be simpler just to find premises through the normal channels. Or stick to mass production.

'Look, let's not be too hasty about this, old boy,' he said. 'Why don't we all calm down and talk about it sensibly?'

'Hello, Ozzy,' said Kate, opening the door of her flat to see him standing there. 'What a nice surprise.'

'Hello, Kate.'

'Is Poppy not with you?'

'No, she's at home.'

'Come on in, I'll make some coffee.'

She left him in an armchair in her homely living room, with its red furnishings and soft orange curtains, while she went to the kitchen to make some coffee.

'I expect Poppy will have told you about the break-in last night?' she said as she offered him coffee and biscuits from a tray.

'Yes, she did,' he said, taking a cup and setting it down on the table beside him.

'It's good of you to call in to see me,' she said. 'I've had no end of people dropping by to give me their support. It's very reassuring.'

'I'm sure it must be.'

'The lengths some people will go to to get their own way, eh, Ozzy?' she said, sitting down opposite him. 'But I'll not give in to those villains, however much they try to scare me.'

'Good for you.'

'You're very subdued this evening,' she said, looking at him thoughtfully, 'is anything the matter?'

'I'm all right,' he lied. He couldn't take his eyes off her. People had often remarked on their having the same dark eyes. Now it seemed as though he was looking at a mirror image of

314

himself. It was the most peculiar feeling to know that he had once been a part of this woman's body.

'That's good. I thought perhaps you weren't feeling well.' She stirred her coffee. 'This business last night has made me scared to leave the shop for fear of what will happen while I'm away.'

'I imagine it would,' he said dully.

'The police won't be able to keep a special eye on the place for long, they simply don't have the men.'

'You'll have no more trouble,' he said coolly. 'I can promise you that.'

'Oh.' She held her cup in mid air, eying him quizzically.

'I've fixed the Dexters,' he said in a monotonous voice, 'they'll not bother you again.'

'Fixed them? Ozzy, I don't understand.'

He told her how he'd reached an agreement with the Dexters. 'I've just come from their place, actually.'

'How clever of you,' she said, smiling at him. 'And how kind of you to go to such trouble on my behalf.'

'It was no trouble.' He could hear the words but could not feel himself uttering them.

Noticing from the walnut clock on the mantelpiece that the time was nine-thirty, she said, 'You were lucky to catch them at the factory this late at night.'

'I went to their house.'

'Found their address in the phone book, I suppose?' she said, 'My word, Ozzy, you *have* been working hard on my account.'

'I didn't need to look them up,' he explained. 'I knew where they lived.'

'Really?' she said in surprise.

'I used to live with them.'

'Good heavens!' she exclaimed. 'They're not at all the sort of people you would expect to take in lodgers.'

'I wasn't a lodger.' He gave a stiff smile. 'Well, not officially anyway.'

'What then?' She sipped her coffee, looking at him questioningly over the rim of the cup and waiting for him to continue.

He stared at her so hard his dark eyes seemed to mesmerise her.

'Ozzy,' she said, becoming uneasy, 'what's the matter with you?'

He didn't reply but continued to stare.

'You're in a very strange mood this evening,' she said nervously. 'In fact, you don't seem yourself at all.'

Still his eyes didn't leave her face.

'What is it?' she persisted, her mouth drying with nerves. 'Tell me, for goodness' sake!'

'I wasn't christened Ozzy Perks,' he said at last in a cracked dry voice.

'Oh, really?'

'No. I was registered as Laurence Dexter. I am the eldest son of Reggie and Cissy Dexter,' he said, his words thundering in Kate's ears, 'Only it wasn't Cissy Dexter who gave birth to me, was it, Kate? It was you!'

# Chapter Twenty

When the room stopped spinning, Kate focused her eyes on Ozzy, speechless with emotion.

'You . . . you . . . are my son?' she managed at last, tears streaming down her cheeks as she stumbled towards him with her arms outstretched. 'Oh, Ozzy, if you only knew how much I've longed for this moment!'

He leapt up and out of her way, staring at her coldly. 'Don't add insult to injury by coming out with a load of sentimental drivel.'

'It's true,' she wept. 'I've thought about you so much. On your birthday every year I said a special prayer for you.'

'Oh, yes, I've noticed you pining for me,' he said with biting sarcasm.

'That sort of suffering is done on the inside.'

'Suffering, my eye!' he said cynically.

'I realise how it must seem to you,' she said, 'but having given my word to the Dexters that I would never try to contact you, I had to put the past behind me, on the surface anyway, and make a life for Sam.'

Staring at her in silent reproach, he found that all the qualities he had so admired in the mother of his best friend seemed like failings in his own mother, a woman capable of discarding her child. The hard work and determination to succeed which he'd seen as the efforts of someone struggling to give her child a good start in life, now became distorted in his troubled mind to represent the ruthless ambition of a woman out for self-gratification.

'Sam was all right to have around, I suppose, as long as he

'didn't interfere with your precious career,' he said, driven to calumny by his wretchedness.

'Now that isn't fair, Ozzy,' she reproached. 'Sam has never suffered because of my work. He certainly wouldn't be enjoying the sort of life he has now if I hadn't dedicated myself to it.'

'Yes, I know. I'm sorry,' he said stiffly.

'That's all right.'

His face twisted with pain. 'Sam was the lucky one. He didn't get thrown out like garbage.'

Kate winced but remained silent. He was entitled to be upset, especially as Cissy Dexter's version of the story had probably been a million miles from the truth.

'I did what I thought was best for you at the time.'

'How can giving your own child away possibly be the best thing for it?'

'In some circumstances it can,' she said. 'I was sixteen years old and living in one damp room with my mother and sister when you were born. Cissy Dexter wanted you so badly she made sure I would never find a job if I didn't agree to let them have you. I would have been destitute, we'd have been sent to the workhouse. The Dexters had plenty of money, a comfortable home. I had nothing.'

'You had yourself. That would have been enough for me.'

'Fine words,' she said. 'And easy enough to say when you've never known poverty.'

'Poverty isn't the only instrument of torture, you know.'

'With the Dexters you had the chance of a good life . . .'

'Living in a snake pit would have been easier,' he interrupted coldly.

'Surely it wasn't that bad?'

'Oh yes it was! Cissy always hated me. It wasn't until I was twelve, and she told me in a fit of temper that I wasn't hers, that I realised why. That was when I left.'

'Oh, Ozzy, I'm so sorry,' she said, making another unsuccessful attempt to embrace him.

'So am I.' He threw her an icy glare. 'Cissy Dexter thought I had gone there this evening to stop them harassing you because I had found out that you were my mother and that's why I was taking up the cudgels on your behalf. That's how it came out. I almost wish it hadn't.'

'It must have been a shock.'

'All the years that I've been Sam's friend, I've admired your spirit, the way you worked to give him a good life. I even loved you in a way because you made me feel at home, a part of your family. I valued that because it was something that I never had from the Dexters who always made sure I felt like an outsider in their home.' He paused and moistened his dry lips. 'Can you imagine what it feels like to discover that the woman I respected and loved is actually someone who slept with a married man and left the consequences to someone else to deal with?'

The crack of her hand against his face echoed from the walls in the quiet room. He seemed dazed, rubbing his cheek in bewilderment, cowering away from her with his mouth open.

Kate was ashen-faced with shock at her action, but she knew it was justified. Just because he had been hurt, that didn't give him the right to play God over something he knew nothing about.

'All right, Ozzy, you've made your opinion on the subject very clear. Now perhaps you'll pay me the courtesy of listening to my side of the story?' she said assertively. 'It isn't a pretty tale but you're quite old enough to know the truth about what happened. So sit down, and be quiet.'

Without a word he did as she said, barely moving as the true story unfolded, filling Kate with painful memories.

'So now can you understand how impossible it would have been for me to keep you?' she said in conclusion.

'I can see that it would have been difficult,' he said in a dull, weary tone.

'Do you believe me about the rape?'

He shrugged with mock nonchalance. 'Why shouldn't I believe you? I'm sure my father was capable of such a thing. He was a very cruel man. I've still got the scars to prove it.'

'I'm sorry.'

'Too late to be sorry,' he said sharply. 'You must have known what wicked people they were. If they could treat you so badly, it was obvious they weren't going to be kind to your child.'

'It wasn't obvious at all,' she defended hotly. 'Cissy wanted a baby so badly, I thought she would dote on you. Had they not had a child of their own, I think things would have been different.'

'That's something we shall never know, isn't it?' he said coolly. 'It's all immaterial anyway. I've put the past behind me and found a life of my own with Poppy.'

'I can understand your feeling bitter.'

'Can you really?' he said icily.

'Yes, I can.'

'Well, you understand more than I do then because I just feel empty,' he said, rising as though to leave. 'Perhaps I should feel as though my life has been enriched because I've found my real mother, but I feel as though I've lost everything.'

'How can you say that?'

'You were a valued friend.'

'I still am.'

'Oh no, not now,' he said. 'Things have changed too much for that.'

'Nothing's changed in that respect,' she pointed out. 'We're still the same people as we were yesterday.'

'Maybe nothing is different for you, but it certainly is for me.'

'In what way?'

'I feel like I did before I met Leo,' he told her. 'Like an unwanted bastard. Inferior, unclean.'

She clasped her hands to her head in horror. 'Oh, don't be so silly, Ozzy! There's absolutely no call for you to feel like that.'

'Maybe not, but it's there inside me,' he told her gravely.

'We can work this thing out together,' she said persuasively. 'It might take a little time, but we'll come through it. Perhaps it's too late for us to be like mother and son, but there's no reason at all why we can't still be friends.'

'I don't want to work through it with you,' he said. 'I want you out of my life.'

'Oh no, Ozzy. Please don't be rash . . . you're angry and upset . . .'

His eyes were dark pools of despair as they looked into hers. 'I'm not angry with you now, Kate. I just don't want to see you again. I don't want Sam or any other members of your family in my life either, to remind me of who I really am.'

'Don't be a fool.' She forced her arms around his rigid, quivering body. 'We've been friends for a long time. Both Sam and I love you. Please don't shut us out.'

He clung to her in a sudden embrace, his body shaking with stifled emotion. But almost immediately, he let go of her and moved away. 'Goodbye, Kate,' he said calmly, though his face was working against tears. 'At least this time I'm leaving of my own free will.'

Choking back the lump in her throat, she watched him walk across the room, knowing from his determined manner that any further attempts at persuasion would be useless. The careful way he closed the door behind him emphasised the fact that he was in control. She was filled with despair at the finality of his departure.

Sinking disconsolately into an armchair, she tried to clear her muddled brain, still reeling from the shock of actually finding her son. Amid the confusion, one fact prevailed. She was proud that Ozzy was her son, and didn't want their friendship to end.

For a long time she sat still, immersed in thought. Then she slipped on a jacket and headed for the one person in the world she needed to see right now.

Ozzy felt duty-bound to tell Poppy the whole story when he got home. 'So now you know who you're really married to,' he said bitterly in conclusion. 'A bastard who wasn't even wanted by his adopted parents, let alone his own mother. Someone who has been using a false name since he was twelve years old.'

Until now he had never said much about his past, just that he'd run away from home as a boy and been taken in by Leo Nash. But Poppy's only interest in the matter was the effect this newfound truth was having on him.

'So if you want to leave me, I'll understand why,' he continued.

'Don't be so bloomin' daft! It's you I married, not who yer were before we met. I don't give a toss whether you came from rape or true love, as long as you got born some'ow.'

'She gave me away.'

'So, you had a rotten childhood,' she said, being deliberately harsh in the hope of dispelling his mood of self-pity. 'It was a long time ago. Now is what matters. Forget the past and enjoy the present. You've people around you who really care about you, including Kate Brooks.'

'I don't want to see her again,' he said emphatically.

Poppy tutted, looking at her husband anxiously. 'I expect she thought she was doin' the right thing for yer. She was very young . . .'

'I know all that,' he snapped. 'And as long as I don't have to see her, everything will be fine. As far as I'm concerned, she no longer exists.'

'Being a bit dramatic, ain't yer?' she said, hoping to bring him to his senses.

'What if I am?'

'Don't you think you're bein' a bit 'ard on yourself as well as on 'er?' she persisted. 'I mean, Kate and Sam have been a part of your life for a long time. It was through 'er that you and me got together.'

'I don't want that woman in my life,' he insisted. 'Surely I'm entitled to that much?'

'All right, all right, keep yer 'air on, yer stubborn man,' said Poppy crossly. 'If yer wanna cut off yer nose to spite yer face, I can't stop yer, but you can't stop me 'aving my say.'

For all her apparent lack of sympathy, she was full of compassion for him, knowing he was going through hell. It was her firm belief, however, that any hint of pity from her would only push him deeper into the abyss.

Listening to Kate's bizarre tale, a lot of things became clear to Leo. Now he could understand why she craved self-respect and power. She was obviously still deeply scarred by what had

322

happened. Also the mystery of Ozzy's past was revealed. Caring for them both as he did, Leo was very moved by the story.

'So now you know who I really am,' she said, 'a woman who didn't have the courage to face up to her responsibilities and look after her own child.'

'Now, you know it wasn't like that.'

'That's how Ozzy sees it,' she said. 'He hates me for what I did to him.'

'Give him time,' he said kindly. 'He'll realise you acted in his best interests when he's had time to think about it properly.'

As well as feeling concerned for Kate and Ozzy, Leo was also suffering some personal turmoil. It was a very traumatic experience to discover that the woman you loved had been a victim of rape. As well as feeling blistering anger towards the perpetrator of the crime, he was also having difficulty closing his mind to the disturbing mental images the knowledge evoked.

They were sitting in the saloon of *London Lady*. The chintz curtains were drawn and the stove was taking the chill off the autumn night. Beside Kate on a small table was a half finished glass of brandy which Leo had given her to calm her when she had arrived, trembling and close to tears.

'Ozzy has a perfect right to shut Sam and me out of his life.' She made a face. 'And that's another problem. I shall have to tell Sam the truth. He'll be upset. You know how much he thinks of Ozzy. He'll probably blame me for ruining their friendship, so I shall be seen as a villain by both my sons.'

'If Sam turns against you over this, he'll be well out of order after all you've done for him.'

'Maybe he won't.'

'He'd better not,' Leo said protectively. 'For heaven's sake, Kate, for how much longer are you going to punish yourself? Ozzy has had a hard time, no one can deny that. I saw the state he was in after he left the Dexters, and I can vouch for it. But that isn't your fault. You did what you thought was best for him at the time. And at least he was given a name and a place in a family, and not branded a bastard and made an outcast as he would have been if you'd kept him.'

'Oh, Leo,' she said, brightening considerably, 'I knew I could rely on you to make me feel better. What would I do without you?'

'Come here.'

She went and sat on his lap, feeling his strong arms around her. 'You must regret the day you ever got involved with someone as complicated as me?'

'Things would be simpler if we could choose who we fall in love with,' he said, 'but that isn't the way life works.'

'I can understand your being upset, but is it really necessary for you to end your friendship with Kate and her family altogether?' Leo said to Ozzy the next day when the latter called at the boat in his lunch-hour with his version of the story.

'Yes, it is.'

'You'll only hurt yourself more, you know,' Leo warned, shaking his head in admonishment. 'Kate is very sorry for the way things turned out for you with the Dexters. She came to see me last night, after you'd left her, in quite a state.'

'You're bound to take her side,' said Ozzy, facing Leo across the saloon table having been invited to join him for cheese on toast.

'I'm trying not to take sides,' he said, 'but I can't just stand by and see two people I care about being made miserable when there's no need. You've been friends a long time, and there's no reason for that not to continue. Kate knows you can't become mother and son overnight.'

'We can't *ever* do that.'

'All right, so you think she's done wrong by you, but you can't punish someone forever for one mistake.'

'I'm not trying to punish her,' said Ozzy irritably, his eyes shadowed from a sleepless night. 'She had every right to do what she did. But so have I the right not to see her again.'

'But what about poor Sam in all this?' Leo asked worriedly. 'He's your best mate. He doesn't deserve to be dumped because of something that happened before he was even born. He's your brother. Enjoy it.'

Ozzy pushed his uneaten food aside. 'Perhaps if I explain to you how I feel, you might understand why I need to get them out of my life.'

'Go ahead, I'm listening.'

'When you took me in twelve years ago I didn't have much in the way of self-esteem, did I?'

'None at all.'

'Well, I'd always felt like that until then,' Ozzy explained, 'I'd been used to being on the receiving end of irritation and dislike. I knew I was a nuisance. I was frightened of everyone.'

'You were very jumpy, I agree.'

'Living with you made me feel as though I might be worth something after all,' he continued. 'I enjoyed a new sense of belonging, a feeling of being wanted which I also got from Sam and his mother. Now, just the thought of who I really am to Kate and Sam, the unwanted illegitimate son and half-brother, just crushes me, brings back all the pain and destroys my self-confidence so that I feel like a clumsy kid again who can't do a thing right. I just don't need that sort of punishment, Leo. I'm a married man with a duty to Poppy. I've a good job and . . .' He paused. 'I haven't told anyone about this yet in case it doesn't come off but I've applied for a position on one of the national papers.'

'Good for you.'

'But this thing with Kate has knocked me sideways, made me feel stupid and incompetent just like the Dexters always said I was.' His mouth twitched slightly and his drawn face was suffused with a fine layer of sweat. 'It could ruin Poppy's life as well as mine, and I'm not prepared to let that happen. It's very important to me that I make something of myself. Can you understand that?'

Like mother like son, Leo thought, but said, 'Yes, I can.'

'I need Kate and Sam out of my life altogether so that I can forget the past and make a decent life for Poppy and myself.'

'How do you actually feel about Kate now that you've calmed down?' asked Leo, wondering if there was any hope of reversing his decision.

Ozzy pondered on this for a few moments. 'I honestly don't

know. I just screw up inside every time I think of her and what she did, even though I know I'm probably being unreasonable.'

'It will hurt less as time goes on.'

'Yes, I think so too, as long as she's not around me to bring it all back.' He paused. 'I've been awake most of the night thinking about it, Leo, and I've made up my mind.'

'I see,' he said sadly, realising this was not an impulsive decision.

'I don't want her or Sam to approach me to try to talk me out of it, either.'

'And you want me to make sure she understands this and leaves you alone?'

'I would appreciate it,' said Ozzy. 'You're closer to her than anyone.'

'All right. I'll make sure she's left in no doubt.'

'Thanks, Leo, you're a pal.'

'I hope this doesn't mean that you'll stop coming to see me?' he said. 'Knowing that Kate and I are such close friends.'

'Don't worry, I'll come to see you when she's not here.'


Leo hated being the messenger of such sad tidings that evening. His heart turned over as he watched Kate put a brave face on it.

'I can see his point,' she said.

'He isn't doing it just to hurt you,' he said, hoping to soften the blow. 'I think he genuinely believes that life will be easier for him without you and Sam around.'

'The damage I did to him is irreparable, isn't it?'

'Nonsense. He might feel a whole lot different later on.'

'But for now I have to let him go, don't I?'

'I think so,' he advised her. 'Any attempt at reconciliation must come from him.'

'If only we had some way of knowing how far-reaching the consequences are going to be when we make decisions.' She cleared her throat and gave him an overly-bright smile. 'Oh, well, we can't re-write history, as they say. I did what I did, and that's all there is to it.'

They were in the living room of her flat. She was standing with her back to the window across which the curtains were drawn. He was standing by the sideboard on which the wireless-set was playing very low. She looked so pale against the orange curtains, and so achingly vulnerable, he would willingly have gone through this for her if he could. He went to her and slipped his arms around her.

She stiffened and moved back. 'Thanks for telling me, Leo,' she said in a small, polite voice. 'I'm so sorry you've got mixed up in this wretched business.'

'Don't be silly,' he said. 'Your problems are mine too.'

'Thank you,' she said in a distant tone.

'Don't shut me out, Kate, please?' he entreated emotionally. 'I can bear anything but that.'

'Sorry. I didn't realise I was.'

He tried to embrace her again and this time she didn't move away, but was unable to respond. She merely stood stiffly in his arms. Realising how much she must be hurting him, she said, 'I'm sorry, Leo.' She shook her head. 'Oh God, I feel so bloody guilty about everything. About Ozzy, about you . . .'

'There's no need.'

'Give me time,' she said wearily. 'I think I need to be alone for a while.'

'I understand,' he said, letting her go and walking to the door.

Poppy was a very sincere and fair-minded person, which meant she agonised over the decision she felt compelled to take.

'I don't wanna leave the firm, Kate,' she said one morning a week after the truth about Ozzy's origins had come to light. 'I enjoy my job and you've been good to me over the years. Don't think I'm not grateful, 'cos I am, but I don't think it's fair to Ozzy for me to stay on 'ere, not with things being as they are between the two of yer.'

'Oh!' Kate felt the words like a hammer blow. She'd have to search long and hard to find anyone as loyal as Poppy, both as an employee and a friend. 'Oh, I see . . . well, if you really think that's the best thing, far be it for me to come between husband and wife.'

'Ozzy 'asn't told me to leave, nothin' like that,' Poppy said. 'But I feel awkward about it. Disloyal to 'im, if yer know what I mean?'

'I quite understand.'

'Ozzy is me 'usband when all is said and done,' said Poppy, chewing her lip.

'Don't worry about it,' Kate forced herself to say. 'I'll miss you terribly, of course, but I can see your point of view.'

'Thanks for being so nice about it.'

'It's the very least I can do,' said Kate, forcing a smile to cover the ache in her heart.


The unsatisfactory state of Kate's personal life was not reflected in her business performance. Quite the reverse, in fact. Seeking escape from personal worries, she channelled all her efforts into her work, finding endless creative energy.

She made little beret hats with metallic trimmings and large hats decorated with swirls of plaited wool. She made saucy hats with enormous feathers for music-hall stars and tasteful creations for matrons of the middle classes. She even had an order from an American film star who was staying in London.

Most evenings she busied herself in the workroom until quite late, shaping, moulding, sewing, snipping. Now more than ever before her work became her life. Within this business environment she could forget that she had ever been Kate Potter and be Kate Brooks, respected and sought after as a professional woman who was one of the best in her field.

Now firmly established as a milliner of imagination and flair, her client list swelled almost daily. As well as ladies of the peerage, she catered for the wives of prominent businessmen and members of parliament.

Even the terrible news from abroad was easier to bear when she was caught up in the hustle and bustle of the shop. Such shocking things were happening in this year of 1936. Alarming reports filled the papers almost every day. Hitler's troops marched into the Rhineland; the Italian use of poison gas on the Abyssinians caused widespread horror; civil war erupted in Spain.

'Nothing but trouble everywhere,' said Gertie in disgust. 'Every time you open the paper there's people killing each other for power, while there's poor souls on the streets of London who'd be grateful for a crust of bread to keep them alive till tomorrow. It just doesn't make sense.'

In the autumn, a year after Kate's split from Ozzy, two things happened much closer to home to shock her out of the protective shell she had built around herself.

# Chapter Twenty-One

'I'm leaving the legal profession, Mum,' said Sam, avoiding his mother's eyes by staring at the pattern on her living-room carpet.

'Giving up law?' she said, a puzzled smile hovering on her lips. 'You're having me on.'

'No, I'm not,' he said, raising his eyes sheepishly to hers. 'I do hope you're not too upset.'

'*Upset?*' she echoed crossly. 'You calmly announce that you're about to throw away everything you've studied so hard for, and expect me *not* to be upset?'

'Sorry.'

'What on earth has got into you?' she interjected angrily. 'Have you lost your mind or something?'

'I'm going into the RAF.'

'The RAF!' she exclaimed in astonishment.

'That's right,' he said, unable to stop his voice lifting with excitement as he added, 'I've been accepted.'

'But what's brought this on, all of a sudden?' she asked, her anger turning to stunned resignation with the realisation that he was serious.

He bit his lip guiltily. He knew how much his legal career meant to his mother and hated having to disappoint her, especially as Ozzy had wounded her so deeply last year. Frankly, Sam thought it was callous of Ozzy to banish them both from his life altogether. It was understandable that he would feel sore at Mother, having suffered such a miserable childhood, but did it really warrant such drastic action that must be hurting him as well as them?

Sam himself had been shocked to learn of what had happened

to his mother as a girl, and even now, couldn't bear to dwell on the sickening details. But, instinctively protective towards someone who had been a good and loving mother to him, all his acrimony flowed towards the Dexters.

Now, as he braced himself to tell her what lay behind his decision, he trusted her not to want him to continue along a path that was wasn't right for him.

'The decision to leave law isn't sudden,' he said ruefully. 'I've been thinking about it for some time.'

'Oh, really?'

'I've never wanted to be a solicitor,' he explained anxiously.

'Why start along that path then?'

'I only went along with the idea because you wanted it so much. I thought I'd get to like it eventually, but that hasn't happened.'

It was as though he'd thrown cold water in her face. So she'd failed Sam as well as Ozzy? What was the matter with her? Was she completely lacking in judgement as to what was right for her children? 'Why didn't you tell me, Sam? I'd have understood.'

'You were working so hard to pay for my training,' he said, despising himself for causing that hurt look in her eyes, 'I just didn't have the heart to tell you it wasn't for me.'

She shook her head slowly from side to side, despairing. 'You mean, for all those years you've gone through the whole gruelling procedure, hating every minute?' She was full of compunction for subjecting him to such a grim fate.

'No, Mum, it hasn't been as bad as that,' he said kindly, 'I don't hate it. I just find it very boring, that's all. Now I've the chance to do something I *really* want to do, and I feel I must be true to myself and pursue it. I've always been very interested in anything to do with aeroplanes, as you know.'

'I thought that was just a boyish hobby,' she said. 'I never took it seriously.'

'It probably would have stayed just a hobby if the RAF hadn't launched their recruitment campaign,' he told her, 'They're trebling the strength of the air force and need well-educated men to train as pilots.'

'A pilot,' she said numbly.

He went over to where she was sitting and knelt in front of her. 'Flying isn't as dangerous as it used to be in the early days,' he said, looking reassuringly into her worried face.

'I know, Sam,' she said. 'Just give me time to get used to the idea.'

'I want to do this so much, Mum.'

Shaking her head quickly as though to clear her muddled mind, she said, 'Well, you certainly don't do things by halves, do you? There can't be two occupations much more different than solicitor and pilot.' She sighed. 'I'm only sorry I encouraged you to go into something that wasn't right for you. I do feel bad about it.'

'There's no need, honestly.'

'I wanted you to have respect and security,' she continued. 'I wanted people to look up to you.' She couldn't help but grin. 'I didn't mean literally!'

'I know you've always done your best for me,' he said, relieved to see her smile. 'And I'll always be grateful, but we only get one life and it's time now for me to make my own decisions about mine.'

'Of course it is.'

'Please be happy for me.'

She studied his face, so clean-cut and fresh, his fair hair falling on to his brow youthfully. He was handsome in the same mould as his father, square-jawed and solid, with Claude's twinkling eyes and a smile that lit his whole face. Her heart stirred with a mixture of pride and sadness. This moment marked the end of an era. Sam had finally severed the umbilical bond and become his own person.

'If it's what you really want, son, then I want it too,' she said. 'And I'm so very proud of you.'

She hugged him tight and said nothing about the way her heart leapt with fear at the thought of her dear boy flying the skies, especially with all this talk of war.

In December the British people had something to take their minds off the gloom from abroad that had been filling the papers when news broke of a secret love affair between the King and Wallis Simpson, an American divorcee.

When King Edward VIII told his subjects on the wireless of his decision to abdicate, the whole country reeled from the shock.

'I have found it impossible to carry the heavy burden of responsibility and to discharge my duties as King as I would wish to do without the help and support of the woman I love . . .'

'It's a damned disgrace,' fumed Gertie, the day after the broadcast when she and her daughters met at Kate's shop for work. 'How would it be if we all gave up our responsibilities just because we happen to feel like it?'

'Now be fair, Mum, there's more to it than that.'

'He's deserted his people, that's what he's done,' Gertie ranted.

'I think it's quite touching,' said Kate, who had actually been moved to tears by the speech. 'Being royal doesn't make them immune to falling in love.'

'Love be buggered!' said Gertie, borrowing a phrase from her late friend Bertha. 'Lust would be nearer the mark.'

'Poor fellow,' said Esme. 'It's only natural he would want to be with the woman he loves.'

'Being King isn't like being the gas man, you know, Esme,' her mother reminded her hotly. 'He can't just do as he likes in his spare time. I don't know what he was thinking of, getting involved with a married woman in the first place. He must have known they wouldn't let him marry her.'

'You must admit it takes courage to do what he's done though, Mother,' said Kate.

'Where's the courage in going off and leaving your brother to do your job?' she said. 'Now he's the one I'm sorry for, what with being so shy and stuttering when he speaks.'

As the subject continued to be heatedly debated in pubs, clubs and living rooms all over the country well into the new year of 1937, Leo wrestled with a dilemma of his own.

One spring evening as he and Kate strolled along the

towpath for a sociable hour in the historical ambience of the Doves, with its low ceilings and dark woodwork, he finally decided what to do about it.

'You're very quiet this evening,' she said as they settled at a table in a secluded corner of the terrace, shielded from the cool river breeze by a vine-covered roof.

'Am I?'

'Is there something on your mind?'

'There is, a matter of fact.'

'Anything I can help with?'

He sipped his beer ponderously. 'Yes, you can, actually.'

'Oh?'

'Will you marry me?' he asked simply.

In as much as the companionable relationship they had been enjoying for the last few years had seemed to suit them both, she was surprised at the question. She'd assumed he had become happy with the way things were and no longer wanted marriage, since the subject hadn't been mentioned for a long time.

'What's brought this up again all of a sudden?'

'I've been offered a job in America.'

'Really? How exciting,' she said, feeling winded by this news.

'Yes, it's a teaching post in a college of art in New York,' he informed her. 'I'd like to feel I was putting something back by helping students develop their talent.'

'It sounds like the chance of a lifetime.'

'It's certainly an interesting opportunity,' he said. 'And as I've been invited to do a particular job, I doubt if there'll be a problem with their immigration laws.'

'I see.'

'I'd like you to come with me . . . as my wife.'

'Oh, Leo,' she said. 'I'm so honoured to have been asked.'

'But the answer is no, I suppose?' he interrupted brusquely.

'I'm not sure. I have commitments here . . .' she began, anxiously fiddling with a lock of hair.

'Sam is off your hands now,' he pointed out, 'and your

mother and Esme will have each other. We wouldn't be away forever.'

'What about the shop?' she said, trying to marshal her confused thoughts into some sort of order. 'There would be no point in putting it under management since my designs are the business.'

'You could set up in New York.'

'This is a bad time to have something like this thrown at me,' she said. 'I've orders in hand for the summer season. There's Ascot and Henley and so on . . .'

'Is there ever a good time for you?' he asked coldly. 'If it wasn't your spring collection you were fretting about, it would be your autumn hats, or Christmas orders, or some other damned thing!'

'Yes, I know it seems like that.'

'It *is* like that.'

'You really want to take this job, don't you?'

'It seems silly not to make the most of the opportunity since I've no ties here,' he explained. 'My parents are dead. Ozzy is married and no longer needs me. That just leaves you.'

'This feels very much like a turning point,' she said.

'It is,' he told her frankly. 'I'm forty-six years old, Kate. It's time to take stock, time to stop drifting along in the hope that you might decide to make a proper commitment to me one day.'

'Oh, Leo!'

'This American job is just the jolt I needed to bring me to my senses,' he cut in. 'I've been in love with you for years, and still am. But I've decided that if you turn me down again this time, I shall make a life for myself without you. In other words, I'm not prepared to continue with this ridiculous arrangement any longer.'

'So you're offering me an ultimatum?' she said through gritted teeth, angry at being forced to make such an impossible decision. 'Either I leave everything I've worked for and go to America with you, or we're finished.'

'America isn't the issue. Marriage is,' he said. 'If you really don't want to go abroad because you can't bear the thought of

336

leaving England, well then, we'll have to talk about it some more. But if your objection is simply this aversion you have to marriage, then I shall accept the job and end this ludicrous relationship.'

The alarming prospect of losing him evinced itself in anger. 'Oh, really, Leo,' she snapped. 'We're both mature people. This sort of dramatic behaviour is for youngsters in the first flush of romance.'

'If you think the need to make a commitment to someone ends when you're forty, you're more out of touch than I thought.'

'Just because I haven't wanted to conform and get married again makes me a freak, I suppose?'

'Don't be stupid,' he said, his voice rough with emotion. 'You're quite at liberty to stay single for the rest of your life. But don't expect me to be on hand when you need comfort or friendship.' He paused. 'Or anything else, for that matter.'

'Really, Leo,' she admonished, flushing.

'I'm only saying what's true,' he said. 'My God, anyone would think I was offering you a life of misery tied to my shirt-tails. You know very well that I'm not the sort of man to stop you working or doing what you want to do. I just want us to have a proper life together.'

'And you're supposed to be so bohemian,' she said sarcastically.

'Don't try to make me feel guilty because I want to get married.'

'And don't try to make me feel guilty because I don't!' she retorted.

Their words clashed, leaving a shuddering silence in their wake.

'There's nothing more to say then, is there?' he said at last.

'No, there isn't,' she said. And leaving her drink unfinished on the table, got up and marched away along the towpath.


'I shall be telling an American friend of mine all about you when she comes to England for a visit later this year, my dear,' said one of Kate's clients one afternoon two weeks later. 'So

337

you can expect to get a call from her.'

'That's kind of you, Lady Rimley, thank you,' said Kate, standing behind the woman and talking to her in the mirror at which she was seated.

'It always strikes me as odd how one is hesitant to disclose the name of one's dressmaker but postively boasts about one's milliner,' the client remarked conversationally.

Lady Rimley was a woman of middle years who was no stranger to Kate's shop. She was large and loquacious with a penchant for big, brightly coloured hats. Kate was trying a variety of trimmings against the creation she was in the process of fitting.

'Curious it may be, but I'm not complaining.' Kate smiled. 'Recommendations are valuable to me.' She turned her head to various angles to judge the effect of the white tulle and artificial daisies she had pinned on to the royal blue picture-hat sitting on her customer's head. 'I think the combination of white and blue really does something special for you. It brings out the blue in your eyes, don't you agree?'

'I think it's perfect.'

'Good. I'll get it into the workroom and have it ready for you within a day or two.'

'How do you manage to be so prompt?' Lady Rimley asked. 'When you must be one of the busiest milliners in London.'

'I have a very good staff.'

'And an understanding husband who doesn't complain when you work late, I expect?'

'No, my husband was killed in the war and I've never remarried.'

'A career woman, eh?'

'I suppose you could say that.'

'I always admire you gels who break away from the traditional female role by setting up in business,' she said. 'Still, I expect you've some nice man in the background, giving you moral support.'

'No,' Kate admitted, smarting at the reality of it.

'You obviously have your reasons, my dear,' said the customer lightly. 'But I don't know what I'd do without my dear Cuthbert. He can be an irritating sort of a cove at times but he's there when I need him, someone to share things with, even if I could cheerfully murder him sometimes!' She stood up. 'Well, I must be on my way.'

'I'll be in touch in a day or two.'

'Very well.'

Kate watched through the window while the aristocratic lady was helped into her car by a uniformed chauffeur. As the vehicle rolled away, Kate went into the workroom and passed the hat over to the head work-girl with instructions for finishing. Then she scuttled into her office and closed the door behind her, something she had done all too often this past two weeks since that final parting with Leo.

Before very long, however, she was forced into the hurly-burly of business routine dealing with customers, taking telephone calls, organising deliveries, and a million and one other jobs that fell to her as proprietor of the firm. When all the staff had gone home, she stayed at her desk moodily staring into space. There was nothing to hurry home for and she was too listless to search for millinery inspiration.

Her mother telephoned. 'Esme and I are going to the pictures this evening. Do you fancy joining us?'

'Not tonight thanks, Mother,' she said.

'You'll get morbid if you stay at the shop on your own.'

'I've plenty to keep me occupied.'

Her mother sounded exasperated. 'Working every evening won't do you any good.'

'I'll be all right.'

'Of course you won't be all right!' Gertie argued. 'You can't hide behind your work forever, my girl. Sooner or later you'll have to face up to the fact that there *is* more to life, and then it will be too late. How many more chances do you think you'll get at your age?'

'We'll talk about it another time,' said Kate, and hung up.

Finding herself devoid of concentration, she stared absently out of the window. Then she thumbed through her impressive client list. All these names are here because they like what I produce, she thought, seeking some sort of consolation. None came. She wandered into the shop with its polished wooden floor and gleaming mahogany counters.

There were hats displayed on chrome stands all around the shop; small plain ones, large extravagant ones; some trimmed with feathers, others with ribbons; some adorned with shimmering costume jewellery. Millinery creations in every colour and style, and every single one designed by her. So where was the feeling of triumph?

She ambled into the workroom and wandered idly among the rows of tables. On some there were sewing machines, others housed dollies. There were wooden blocks, all lit by the evening sunshine streaming through the window and making undulating patterns on the wall.

Hardly aware of her actions, she found herself in the place where inspiration most often came, the stockroom, in which all the materials of her trade were kept. Letting the silence wash over her, she stood among the hoods, wire, ribbon, tulle and feathers, hoping to lift her spirits somehow.

Her brain refused to serve her with positive thoughts. She tried to find solace in the fact that she had a full order book. But one question refused to go away. What was all this worth if her private life was empty?

As she stood there among the essentials of her craft, it occurred to her that she had used her work as a crutch for so long it had become a habit. The driving ambition had become such second nature, she hadn't been able to stop even when success was hers. Her job as provider to Sam was over but still she clung to her precious ambitions, seeking even more self-satisfaction at the expense of the happiness of the man she loved. Just because Leo was strong and self-sufficient didn't mean he didn't need her equally as much as she needed him.

The truth shamed her. She had used success as a drug and become dependent on it. As she accepted this fact, she knew she no longer needed it. Leo thought she was wonderful, for all her faults and weaknesses. He didn't hold past mistakes against her, and would love her if she was the biggest failure on earth.

She thought of all the empty time ahead after he had sailed to America. Days without his telephone calls; evenings after work without his company to look forward to. In a sudden frenzy, she tore back to her office and grabbed her bag. Without even stopping to tidy her hair, she made the shop secure for the night and ran from the premises as though a gang of villains was after her.

He was sitting on deck sketching, dressed in an old brown jersey and paint-splattered beige slacks. The sun on his face showed up the lines and emphasised the fact that his hair was turning grey.

'Hello,' he said amicably, as though they had never quarrelled.

'Hello.' Kate stood behind him, looking over his shoulder at his sketch pad. 'The view from here? It looks good.'

'I'm doing it to take with me to the States,' he explained. 'It will probably make me homesick, but still . . .' He added some shading with a few deft pencil strokes. 'The light is fascinating at this time of day. I want to try to capture it so that I can actually feel this place when I'm in my New York apartment.'

'You're not still cross me with me then?'

'No. You're entitled to live your life in whichever way you choose,' he said. 'Life's too short for grudges.'

'I couldn't agree more.'

'Would you like a cup of tea?'

'Stop being so damned polite,' she said, grinning. 'And ask me why I'm here.'

'All right,' he said, narrowing his eyes quizzically. 'Tell me.'

'Well . . . I got to thinking that you might find life in America awfully dull without my complex nature to keep you on your toes,' she said, smiling and slipping her arms around him. 'So I've come to ask if I can come with you as your wife?'

Later, they got around to discussing more practical matters.

'I shall complete the orders I have in hand,' she said, languishing happily beside him in the big double bed, the creaking and chugging of river traffic drifting through the window. 'There's no point in my trying to sell the business as a going concern since my designs are what brings customers in.

341

I'll find another milliner to take over the lease on condition they keep the staff on. I couldn't bear to go away leaving them out of work.'

He stared at the ceiling thoughtfully. 'It will be very hard for you to turn your back on it all, won't it?'

'It certainly will,' she confessed, 'and I'm dreading that part.'

'But you're willing to give it all up for me?'

'You bet.'

'It will be a wrench.'

'You've changed your tune! You were brushing aside my objections when you were trying to talk me into it a couple of weeks ago,' she said with an uncertain smile. 'Now all you seem to want to do is talk me out of it. You haven't changed your mind about my coming, have you?'

'Don't be daft,' he assured her. 'It's just that now you've actually agreed to come, I've realised just how much you have to give up.'

'You're worth it.'

'I'll try to make sure you don't regret it.'

'I won't regret it, don't you worry,' she assured him confidently. 'I shall miss the shop enormously, of course, but it would be worthless without you in my life, even if it has taken me a long time to wake up to the fact. I've been a selfish bitch and I don't deserve you.'

'I won't argue with that,' he teased, ducking as she aimed a pillow at him.

'So when are you planning to leave?'

'The end of May,'

'That soon?' she said, frowning. 'I might not be able to get things tied up here by then as regards the shop, and there's all the red tape of going abroad to sort out.'

'A week or two either way won't matter.'

'I'd like to get married before we go, so that the family can be there.' She made a face. 'I shall miss them terribly.'

'You'll get used to it.'

'I know.'

'We can get a special licence.'

'Oh, yes,' she enthused. 'Isn't it exciting?'
'You're happy then?'
'Ecstatic.'

# Chapter Twenty-Two

The Scholar was one of the regulars at the Institute who came in search of food and shelter. Shuffling through the streets, twitching and muttering to himself in a battered old trilby hat and raincoat tied at the waist with a pyjama cord, he was a sad figure, though every inch a gentleman. It was an accepted fact that he was as 'nutty as a fruitcake', and he was generally thought to be one of the war's shell-shock victims.

His nickname originated from his refined accent and wide vocabulary, indicating that he was a man of learning, albeit what he said was often incomprehensible. His nervous affliction was greatly exacerbated by the fact that he used gin as his staple diet. Sometimes his emaciated body shook so violently he could hardly get his words out at all.

'It's a crying shame,' Marjorie was often heard to remark. 'He was obviously a useful and respected member of society once, probably a schoolteacher or something. Now the poor devil can't even remember his own name half the time. My God, the war has left its mark, and here we are drifting towards another one.'

One wet afternoon a few days after news of Kate's forthcoming wedding to Leo, Gertie was in Marjorie's office telling her that her daughter had seen sense at last.

'Naturally I wish she wasn't going away to live,' confessed Gertie, 'but at least she's had the sense not to let him go.'

'What will happen about your job at her shop?' asked Marjorie.

'Kate said that I can stay on with whoever takes over the lease if I wish, but she's going to see me all right financially so that I can retire if I'd rather.'

'If everyone had relatives like your daughter, there would be no need for places like this,' said Marjorie.

'I know,' agreed Gertie, 'I'm very lucky.'

'You are indeed.'

'I'll be able to put in more time here, if I do retire from paid work,' said Gertie. 'I wouldn't want to just sit at home . . .'

An urgent knocking at the door interrupted their conversation, and a volunteer helper called Joan appeared, looking flushed and harassed.

'Sorry to interrupt,' she said breathlessly, 'but it's the Scholar.'

'What's the matter with him this time?' Marjorie asked, bracing herself for trouble. 'Don't say he's wet himself again?'

'Nothing like that. In fact, it isn't him I'm bothered about,' Joan said, chewing her lip worriedly. 'He's brought another man in with him and I think his friend is ill.'

'Drunk more like,' said Marjorie, being realistic rather than malicious.

'No, I'm sure this one is genuinely sick,' Joan insisted. 'He seems to have a fever.'

'All right,' sighed Marjorie, rising. 'Let's go and have a look at him.'

'I managed to get him up to the dormitory and into bed,' Joan explained. 'But can I leave him with you now? There's a crowd in the canteen wanting tea. The rain brings them in in hordes. Typical British spring weather.'

'Yes, you carry on, dear. Gertie and I will see to him,' said Marjorie, marching purposefully towards the door.

The two women hurried through the dreary building, along a stone-floored corridor and up a flight of stairs to the men's dormitory. They could hear the rattle of his breathing even before they entered the spartan room, dank and chilly from the rain that leaked in places through the crumbling window frames. Shivering beneath a rough grey blanket on one of the beds was a man with matted hair surrounding a haggard countenance. Two unhealthy patches of colour were visible on his sunken cheeks, despite a thick coating of grime.

'Well, you've got yourself into a proper state, haven't you?'

said Marjorie, managing as ever to tread the fine line between compassion and condescension. 'I think we'd better get a doctor in to have a look at you.'

His eyelids flickered open. 'Sorry to be a bother,' he croaked in a parched whisper, 'but please could I have a drink of water?'

'My God,' gasped Gertie, grabbing Marjorie's arm for support as her legs almost gave way.

'Whatever's the matter?' she asked, turning to see her companion's ashen face.

'This man. I can hardly recognise him but . . .'

'But what?'

'It's Johnny, my son-in-law!'

Kate was surprised to see Leo at her shop one afternoon a week later, especially as he was looking decidedly out of character in a grey suit and trilby hat.

'Don't tell me you've given up art and taken a job as a tailor's dummy,' she teased.

'Cheeky bitch,' he laughed, and there was no mistaking the gleam in his eye.

'What's it all in aid of?' She ran her eye over his smart apparel. 'Are you going to a cocktail party or something?'

He shook his head, eyes shining with mischief.

'Not a funeral either because you'd be all in black.'

His reply to that was an infuriating grin.

'It has to be something really special for you to be done up like a dog's dinner in the middle of the day.'

'You'll soon find out,' he informed her. 'Get your coat and hat, we're going out.'

'I can't go out,' she said. 'I still have a business to run for a few weeks yet.'

'Is there anything urgent you need to deal with in the next hour or so?'

'Well, no, but . . .'

'So, leave someone in charge and let's be on our way.'

'On our way where?' she asked in exasperation, but she couldn't help but be infected by the levity of his mood.

'You just wait and see,' he said, his eyes twinkling.

Donning a straw boater and a blazer over her cream pleated dress, she allowed herself to be escorted into the street where his car was waiting. 'Your carriage awaits, madam,' he said, bowing and opening the door for her.

'I don't know what's got into you today,' she said lightly as he drove them through the back streets of the West End. 'You're behaving like a schoolboy.'

'Today I feel seventeen again.'

'Mmm, well, that's as may be,' she muttered good-humouredly, 'but I'm a bit long in the tooth for all this suspense.' She paused, staring out of the window. 'Kensington . . . what are we doing in Kensington? Esme won't be at home. She'll be at the hospital visiting Johnny.'

'We're not going to Esme's.'

'What the blazes? This is Sycamore Square . . . why are we stopping? We're not on visiting terms with any of the residents here now.'

'I know that.'

Kate stared in amazement as he drew up outside a house on the opposite side of the square to her former home. The central gardens were bright with spring colour, the trees bursting with tender young leaves, daffodils and tulips swaying in the breeze. Leo got out of the car and went round to open her door. 'Out you get then, madam.'

Dumbfounded, she followed him up the steps to the front door of a house in a gleaming stucco terrace, and watched him turn a key in the lock. Gingerly following him into the marble-tiled hall, she felt uneasy, half expecting someone to appear and accuse them of trespassing.

But the house was unoccupied. Sunlight streamed through the windows into silent, empty rooms, spacious interiors graced with wood panelling and moulded ceilings. They went up a polished staircase to airy bedrooms with wide windows.

'Whose house is it?' she whispered, feeling like an intruder.

'Ours if you want it to be,' he explained, his face wreathed in smiles.

'Ours?' she echoed feebly.

'That's right,' he told her exuberantly. 'Hence the suit. I thought the occasion of visiting our first home together was special enough to warrant my best bib and tucker.'

'Leo, I . . .'

'I've paid a deposit to the agent to hold it for us,' he went on effusively. 'But it's returnable if you're not happy with the place.'

'But Leo!'

'I was lucky to find one for sale round here,' he continued, unable to stem the excited words. 'This one has only become available because the owners have moved to the country in case war breaks out. If you don't like it, though . . .'

She was completely confused. 'Like it?' she exclaimed. 'I love it! But what's the point of buying a house when we are going abroad?'

'Ah, well,' he said, 'I've had second thoughts about that.'

Since there were no chairs to sit on, they perched on the window seat.

'I've been giving some serious thought to the matter of our going to America,' he explained in more serious mood. 'And when it comes to the crunch, I think it would just be too heartbreaking for you to leave your family and your business, however much you might pretend otherwise.'

'I'll survive,' she assured him, 'and you mustn't throw this chance away.'

'It's not really that important,' he told her. 'In fact, I think I'd rather we stayed here. I mean, London is where we both belong.'

'Now you're being parochial,' she chided.

'Very probably.'

'I'll never forgive myself if you miss this opportunity because of me,' she said earnestly, 'so let's forget this house and revert to the original plan.'

'What I'm trying to say, Kate, is that it's enough for me to know that you would give up everything you care about to go with me,' he said. 'And it is *my* decision not to hold you to it. So you mustn't feel that you are letting me down in any way.'

'But I'll be happy to go with you, I've told you.'

He shook his head. 'I know you'd *go* with me, but I don't think your heart would be in it, not really.'

In all honesty she couldn't deny it so she just said. 'Are you sure this is what you want?'

'Positive,' he told her. 'I'll start a class here in London. I'm already quite excited about it. So there must be no guilt on your part, no regrets.'

'I just don't know what to say.'

'Tell me that we can go ahead with the house?' he said. 'That'll do for now.'

'Oh, yes,' she said, kissing him. 'And thank you so much.'

'I've enjoyed myself enormously, planning it as a surprise.'

Her brows met as something else came to mind. 'But you've always hated the idea of living on terra firma,' she reminded him. 'Especially somewhere as conventional as this.'

'I suppose I must be getting soft in my old age.' He gave a wry smile. 'Perhaps I just fancy the idea of having my home comforts without all the hard work and inconvenience of river life.'

Kate wasn't totally naive, she knew there was more to it than that. But, somehow, to probe further seemed wrong. And anyway she did genuinely believe that life on shore would be easier for him as the years passed.

'Will you sell the boat?'

'No. I don't need the money to buy this place,' he explained. 'My work has made me a rich man this last few years. I've decided to make Ozzy a present of it. It'll make a nice home for him and Poppy, and they'll have something they can sell later on if they wish.'

'What a lovely idea.'

'I hope they'll be pleased,' he said. 'It will be better for them than the rented flat they're in at the moment.'

Kate cast an eye around the spacious empty room upon which she and Leo would stamp their own personalities. Already her thoughts were turning to warm-coloured curtains and soft sofas upholstered in pastel shades. 'I feel at home here already,' she said. 'Thank you for making a dream come true.'

'It's my pleasure.'

Realising that his words came from the heart and had not been uttered merely as a formality, she knew that she would give him far more pleasure by receiving this loving gesture with grace and enthusiasm than reiterating her concern about his losing his chance to go to America because of it.

Although Kate and her mother shared Esme's relief that Johnny was recovering from a severe bout of pneuomonia, they were both concerned about what was going to happen when he came out of hospital.

'It would be a mistake to take him back out of pity,' Kate warned her sister.

'Yes, I know that,' Esme said, 'but even after everything he's done, I still love him.'

'It's easy to mistake pity for love.'

'I think I'm old enough to know the difference,' replied Esme.

'Well,' sighed Kate, 'you know what you could be letting yourself in for if you get together with him again.'

'Once a gambler, always a gambler, eh, Kate?'

'That's what they say.'

'He says he hasn't played cards for years and I believe him,' she said. 'He hasn't had anything to gamble with, for one thing.'

'What about when he gets back on his feet and does have money again?'

'Someone has to have faith in him,' declared Esme calmly, 'or he'll never learn to trust himself again.'

And Kate certainly wasn't going to argue with that.

'Hello, my dear old fruit,' Kate said to Johnny, smacking a kiss on his cheek and putting a paper-bag full of grapes on his bedside table.

'Hello, Kate,' he said, relieved that she had adopted the same old friendly attitude towards him since he'd been back. 'Thanks for the grapes.'

'You're welcome,' she said, giving him a glance. 'You're

looking better, thank goodness. You've had us all chewing our nails.'

'I'm surprised you bothered,' he said gloomily, 'after what I've done.'

'Us Potters are gluttons for punishment,' she said lightly, sitting down by his bed in the men's ward at Hammersmith Hospital.

'I'm a complete dead loss,' he said mournfully.

'My, my, you are feeling sorry for yourself today,' she chided gently.

'Not sorry for myself. Sorry for the people I've hurt,' he corrected.

'It'll do you no good to brood about it at this stage of your recovery.'

'How can I do otherwise?' he said. 'I mean, first I lose everything, then desert my wife and daughter, and cap it all by becoming a tramp.'

'Not a very inspiring track record, I agree,' said Kate, deciding that a little mild admonishment wouldn't do him any harm. 'You didn't even write to Esme and that was cruel. You could have been dead for all she knew.'

'I was too ashamed to write because I didn't have any money to send to her,' he explained. 'Things are tough on the streets.'

'You should have stayed at home and faced the music,' she said. 'Running away never solved anything.'

'At the time it seemed right that I should go away,' he said. 'I'd made such a mess of everything, I thought Esme would be better off without me. I wanted to kick the habit in a new area where there were none of my gambling cronies around.'

'What went wrong?'

He licked his dry lips. 'I didn't have the money to stay in the property business so I went to the Midlands because I'd heard there was work there in the light industries. But because I only took a little cash with me I couldn't get accommodation. They all wanted rent in advance. I soon got caught in a vicious circle. Without a place to live I couldn't get a job, and without an income I couldn't get a place to live. I managed to get odd jobs from time to time, gardening and labouring, but I could only earn enough to eat, not pay rent too.' He sighed. 'I just sank lower and lower.'

'So what brought you back to London?'

'I suppose I was feeling homesick,' he explained thoughtfully. 'I hadn't been feeling well for some time, rundown I expect, and it's natural to want to be close to home when you're sick. I didn't plan to see Esme, but I thought being in London would make me feel closer to her. With jobs being easier down here now, I hoped to find work. But by the time I got back to London, I was too ill to do anything. I just drifted in and out of consciousness.'

'How awful.'

'Anyway, I met the chap they call Scholar who looked after me as best as he could. Somehow he got me to the Institute. I was too ill to realise it was the place where Gertie worked or I'd never have gone there.' His eyes filled with tears. 'The last thing I wanted was for Esme, or any of you, to see what I'd become.'

'Oh, Johnny, you have made things hard for yourself, haven't you?'

'I've been a fool.'

'There's no point in dwelling on past mistakes,' she said. 'The important thing is to get back on your feet again.'

'Easier said than done.'

'What will you do when you leave here?' she asked.

'I've no idea.' He threw her a shrewd look. 'But don't worry, I'm not going to dump myself on Esme, even though she says she wants me back.'

'Esme has changed a lot,' Kate told him thoughtfully. 'Your going away seems to have strengthened her. She's learned to stand on her own two feet at last.'

'At least some good has come out of it then,' he said, 'but I'll not burden her when they discharge me from here.'

Kate lapsed into a ponderous silence. She had given his predicament a lot of thought since her discussion with Esme. 'Well, that's something for you to work out between you,' she said. 'But if you do decide to stay in London, there will be a job at my place for you when you've fully recovered, if you want it.'

His cracked lips formed into an uncertain smile. 'You wouldn't want me . . .'

'Yes, I would,' she assured him. 'I need someone to look after the promotional side of my business. Organising hat shows, looking after publicity and so on. A chap like you with the gift of the gab would be ideal.'

'Just because I'm down and out doesn't mean I'll accept charity,' he said, his thin fingers trembling slightly as they fiddled with the starched white sheet.

'And you won't get it from me,' she said. 'I *really* do need someone. I am about to reorganise my working life so that I have more free time to spend with Leo after we're married. I've never had much of a life outside of work before, and I want to be able to enjoy it, which means delegation.'

Her heart lurched as two giant tears rolled down his cheeks. He bent his head in embarrassment and fumbled in his pyjama pocket for a handkerchief.

'How can you bear to put your faith in me after everything that's happened?' he asked, managing to compose himself.

'Where would I be today, Johnny, if you hadn't given me a start?'

'You'd have got there somehow, with or without my help.'

'And so will you, without mine,' she said. 'I firmly believe that.'

'You don't owe me anything, Kate,' he said. 'You paid back the money you borrowed and bailed me out when I was in trouble.'

'I'm not paying you back for anything,' she said firmly. 'I'm merely offering you a job. It isn't an act of pity, it's simply a practical solution for us both. I need a promotions manager and you need a job. You won't make anything like the sort of money you made in property, but you'll find the work a darned sight more interesting than doing odd jobs.'

'Kate, I just don't know what to say.'

'No need to give me an answer now,' she said. 'Get yourself properly well first. Then, if you fancy the idea of working for me, let me know and we'll talk terms.'

'Aren't you going to ask me to swear that I'll never gamble again?'

'What's the point of getting you to make promises you can't be sure of keeping?' she asked. 'You know what's at stake if you blow this chance. You're a grown man, I can't tell you how to live your life. I'm just hoping that you've learned your lesson this time.'

'You're a good sort, Kate,' he said, reaching out his bony hand to grasp hers.

'You're not so bad yourself,' she replied, giving it an affectionate squeeze.

Kate stayed with him until Esme arrived, then made a diplomatic exit. She was thoughtful all the way home because, despite her show of confidence in Johnny, she knew she was taking a terrible risk in offering a position of responsibility to a man with a compulsion like his. But there was a lot of good in him, and it was worth sticking her neck out for someone who had given her the opportunity to make something of herself. And, anyway, who else was going to give him a chance?

The marriage of Kate to Leo took place the weekend after the Coronation of George VI. After all the patriotic celebrations, when the capital heaved with visitors, London had returned to normal. Memories of the festivities lived on, though, in the flags and bunting that still adorned many of the streets.

It was a small but stylish family wedding. A register office ceremony with a celebration lunch afterwards at a Kensington hotel. Kate wore a cream-coloured suit with lime green trimming that matched her picture hat, beneath which her hair fell in a sleek pageboy. Leo looked smart in a dark suit.

Sam managed to get a forty-eight-hour pass and came up from camp in Kent to join Gertie, Esme and Rita, who were there with a much recovered Johnny. Poppy and Ozzy put in an appearance, the latter under protest, Kate guessed, and only for the sake of Leo.

It was a very happy occasion filled with all the usual sentimental speeches, toasts and jokes about newlyweds.

Immediately the formalities were over, Poppy announced that she and Ozzy had to leave because he was covering an important story.

'Is it the big political story?' asked Leo, referring to the fact than an announcement was expected from Downing Street at any moment. It was thought that Stanley Baldwin would resign and Neville Chamberlain would take over as Prime Minister.

'All a bit hush-hush, I'm afraid,' bluffed Ozzy.

'Ah, well, we wouldn't dream of asking you to break your professional code of conduct,' said Leo lightly.

When Poppy made a last minute visit to the ladies' powder-room, and Leo was engaged in conversation with Johnny, Kate managed a quiet word alone with Ozzy.

'Thanks for coming,' she said. 'Leo would have been very upset if you hadn't.'

'I wouldn't have missed seeing him getting spliced for anything,' said Ozzy politely.

'Don't stop visiting him just because he's going to be living with me, will you?' she said. 'You know you'll be welcome at our house any time.'

'Well, I . . .'

'It's a big house, Ozzy,' she said pointedly. 'You'll be able to come and visit without even seeing me.'

Put like that, the situation between them seemed noticeably odd. Kate was embarrassed. For a moment she thought he looked uneasy too, but he soon recovered.

'Don't worry, I won't ditch him. Leo's been a good mate to me.'

There was an awkward silence. 'You're doing very well in your job, I understand?' she said in an effort to ease the tension.

'Yes, I'm quite happy with the way things are going.'

'I expect Poppy is proud of you,' she said. 'I know I am.'

'Oh, are you really?'

He was obviously taken aback and she thought she saw a hint of pleasure in his eyes. Looking at him now, it seemed incredible that the likeness between them had not seemed significant during their long association. It wasn't just a similarity around the eyes they shared, but also the same high forehead and deeply bowed mouth.

'I suppose you were bound to be ambitious,' she said meaningfully, trying to force him to speak of the subject that was so often on her mind. 'You take after me.'

Poppy arrived back on the scene before he had a chance to reply, and the couple said their goodbyes and left.

He has to leave because of a story like I've been invited to Buckingham Palace for tea, thought Kate.

Determined not to allow the sadness of their continuing estrangement to cast a shadow on this happy occasion, however, she banished it from her mind and went to mingle with the wedding guests.

Outside the hotel, Poppy was annoyed with her husband. 'I really don't enjoy tellin' lies, Ozzy,' she said. 'Even for you.'

'I know, love, but it was necessary so as not to hurt Leo's feelings.'

'If he 'as any sense he'll 'ave guessed it was just an excuse to get away so you wouldn't have to spend any more time in Kate's company than was absolutely necessary. I didn't know where to put meself when you came out with the bit about it bein' hush-hush.'

'I thought it sounded quite convincing.'

'The story of Cinderella is more believable! Honestly, Ozzy as if you'd 'ave to rush off in the middle of a weddin' reception because of some news story, even if you do work for a national paper!'

'It happens . . .'

'Well, it didn't 'appen today, and anyone with 'alf a brain in their 'ead must have known we were makin' it up,' she said. 'I'd be amazed if Kate believed it.'

'I couldn't care less what that woman believes,' he said. But he wasn't speaking the truth. Not having Kate and Sam in his life left a void that could not be filled by anyone else, not even his wife. And despite himself, he had been unable to stifle a feeling of pleasure when Kate had admitted to being proud of him just now.

But he wasn't going to let these feelings get the better of him. She wasn't going to worm her way back into his life just because she was married to Leo. He'd meet Leo for a drink in a pub rather than go to his house and risk seeing her. He didn't want them to include him in any of their family events either. Poppy was all his family now. And that was the way he intended it to stay.

After a short honeymoon in Paris, Kate and Leo settled to married life in Sycamore Square. The days were hectic but fun as each balanced a busy career with new domestic bliss.

Kate was glad, if more than a little apprehensive, that Esme and Johnny had decided to give their marriage another try. A very much quieter and more mature Johnny took charge of her promotions. By the end of the year he seemed to be in control of the job, organising hat shows for the following year's spring collection and finding new publicity leads.

An exciting commission came Kate's way early in 1938 when she was asked to make the hats the film star Diana Dix was to wear in her new film. It was to be set in the Edwardian era, and was one of Kate's most challenging tasks to date. Hours were spent poring over historical costume books and browsing in the archives of fashion magazines.

For all that she was enjoying the project, it was enormously stressful because there were many more aspects to be considered than in normal millinery work. The star didn't want the hat to be too pretty and detract from her good looks; the dress designer was concerned as to whether or not the hat expressed the 'emotion' of the dress; the producer was trying to capture the overall effect of the scene and the character of the heroine; the cameraman complained if a brim shadowed her face; and even the electrician had a say because he had problems getting her face properly lit if the hat was shading it.

It was a period of frantic telephone calls and frequent trips to Ealing Studios. But it was an interesting experience and life seemed quite dull when the job was finally finished and business returned to a more steady bustle.

★ ★ ★

For all that life was good for Kate, it was becoming impossible to ignore the threat of war which seemed to become more likely with every passing day as frightening stories from Germany continued to fill the papers.

In March, reports appeared about Adolf Hitler's latest tyranny, a pogrom called 'the great spring cleaning' that was happening in Austria. Jews were being excluded from their professions. Jewish judges were dismissed, Jewish artistes were removed from theatres and music halls.

'Can't someone do something about that bloody man?' said Kate to Leo one morning at breakfast as they looked at the papers. 'It's scandalous that he can be allowed to get away with it.'

'He's brainwashing the people into supporting him,' he said gravely, 'drumming Nationalism into them, threatening German parents with the loss of their children if they don't teach them Nazism.'

'Surely the world governments won't let it escalate into war?' she said. 'They must have learned the lesson from the last one.'

'Let's hope it doesn't come to that.'

But towards the end of the year, after Hitler marched into Czechoslovakia, worrying signs of war preparations began to appear at home. Gasmasks were distributed as a protection against poison gas; posters appeared on hoardings and trees appealing for people to enrol as air raid wardens.

After Christmas, Hyde Park joined most other public parks and became honeycombed with trenches to be used as shelter in the event of an air raid. And soon after that, the Home Office announced plans to provide shelters to homes in the districts most likely to be bombed, with priority being given to the London area. It was all very frightening.

Kate had sleepless nights worrying about it, and nightmares about Sam fighting battles in the air. Ozzy, too, would be eligible for call up if the worst happened. She thanked God for Leo's advanced years. He'd done his bit last time.

She was somewhat alarmed when he came home one day with the news that he had joined the ARP.

'Are things really getting that serious?' she asked.

'It's still just precautions,' he told her reassuringly, 'but I want to do my bit.'

Johnny followed him into the service soon after. Gertie answered Lady Reading's call for volunteers and joined the WVS. She was in her element, assisting with gasmask distribution and rushing all over London helping to organise recruitment meetings.

Even the cinema could no longer be relied upon as an escape from the gloom because the newsreels were full of horror from abroad.

# Chapter Twenty-Three

'Poppy! What a lovely surprise,' she smiled, answering the door to Ozzy's wife one showery spring evening. 'Come on in.'

'Ozzy's workin' late tonight so I thought I'd take the chance to nip over for a chat,' Poppy explained as Kate ushered her into the porch. 'I hope you don't mind my turnin' up out of the blue like this?'

'Course not, I'm delighted to see you,' Kate assured her, taking her dripping umbrella and putting it in the stand. 'Leo's out at an ARP meeting so we can have a good old chinwag in peace.'

'Bloomin' rain,' complained Poppy chattily as Kate helped her out of her wet mackintosh and hung it on a peg. 'It came down in stair rods when I was in the bus queue, and stopped like a tap once I was on the bus soaked right through. Ain't that just typical?'

The weather certainly was in a changeable mood. The wet pavements were already steaming and sunlight was pouring through the sitting-room windows and forming squares of light on the rose-patterned carpet. Kate settled her visitor on the sofa and went to the kitchen to make some coffee, far too polite to mention the young woman's increase in weight.

Poppy had no such inhibitions, however. 'End of October it's due,' she announced brightly when Kate returned with a tray. 'That's why I've come over really, to let yer know.' She grinned. 'I could see you'd noticed my disappearin' waistline.'

'Was I that obvious?' Kate laughed, setting the tray down on a small table and giving Poppy a hug. 'Congratulations! It's wonderful news and I'm thrilled for you.'

'Thrilled for yerself an' all, I 'ope,' came her chirpy retort.

'You realise this is gonna make you a grannie?'

'So it is,' Kate said, smiling then making a face. 'I'm not sure I'm ready for sensible shoes and a shawl, though.'

'I couldn't imagine you in either,' laughed Poppy.

They drank coffee and munched biscuits in companionable silence for a short time.

'I bet Ozzy's tickled pink, isn't he?' said Kate after a while.

'You bet.'

'How is he?'

'Fine. Still chasing after a good story,' she told her, 'though all the papers seem to have in 'em these days is bloomin' war talk.'

Kate nodded in agreement. 'Today they're full of the government's plan to call up men of twenty for military service.'

'I 'eard that on the wireless,' said Poppy, shaking her head gravely. 'It's enough to give yer the screamin' willies, ain't it? They'll 'ave fit men of all ages in the army if war does break out, I reckon.'

'Let's hope it doesn't come to that.'

'There's nothin' the likes of us can do about it anyway, except get on with it if the worst 'appens,' declared Poppy.

'You're right.'

'This is no time to be 'anging on to old grudges, I know that much,' said Poppy pointedly. 'Especially with the baby coming, an' all.'

'It certainly isn't,' agreed Kate. 'And I can't tell you how much I wish things could be different between Ozzy and myself, but I can't force myself on to him if he doesn't want to see me.'

'He does want to see yer, though,' Poppy told her. 'But he's too bloomin' stubborn to admit it.'

'You really think so?'

'Not 'alf,' she said. 'Maybe he'll never be able to accept you as 'is mum, but he misses havin' you and Sam as friends.'

'How can you be so sure?'

'Oh, little things slip out when he's off 'is guard,' Poppy

explained thoughtfully. 'Now and again 'e forgets 'imself and rambles on about the days when you were all so close. He gets quite emotional sometimes an' all.'

'I'd give a lot for us to be friends again,' confessed Kate.

'Why not go and see him?' suggested Poppy.

'Do you think that's a good idea?'

'It's worth a try,' said Poppy with a wise nod. ''Cos if *you* don't try to put things right, this daft feud is likely to last forever. He'll never approach you, he's too bloomin' proud!'

'Well . . . I'm willing to have a go.'

'Good,' said Poppy. 'It will probably be best if I'm not at 'ome when you come, then he'll be forced to talk to you – even if 'e does just tell yer to go to hell. So let me know when you'll be comin' over to the boat and I'll go and visit me mum.'

Ozzy was smiling when he poked his head out of the cabin door to see who'd come on board. But his expression soon darkened when he saw who it was.

'Oh, it's you,' he said coldly. 'I thought it was Poppy come back for something. She's gone to visit her mum.'

'May I come down?' asked Kate.

He hesitated. 'I suppose so,' he said grudgingly at last.

Kate was struck by Poppy's feminine influence as she climbed down into the saloon. The fresh scent of lavender polish filled the room which gleamed from floor to ceiling. There were daffodils in vases; flowering pot plants; embroidered cushion covers; bright contemporary curtains gently fluttering at the window in the evening breeze.

'As I said, Poppy's not here.'

'It's you I came to see.'

'Oh?' he said.

'Poppy told me about the baby. Congratulations.'

'Thank you.' He gave her an inquiring look. 'Surely you didn't come here just to say that?'

'No, I came because I think it's time you and me had a chat,' she said, her confident manner belying the fact that her heart was fluttering nervously. It meant so much to her for things to be right between them.

363

'What could you and I possibly have to say to each other?' he asked rhetorically.

'Plenty.' She stared at him, forcing him to meet her eyes. 'Isn't it time to let bygones be bygones? Especially with all this talk of war about, and you with a baby on the way.'

'Surely you're not going to stake any sort of claim as grandmother to the baby?'

She hadn't expected that and it cut deep. 'Not if you'd rather I didn't. I realise I have no rights in that direction,' she said, 'I'd like very much for us all to be friends again, though.'

'Too much has changed for that.'

'We like each other as people,' she said. 'Surely that's worth something?'

'I can't pretend not to know the truth.'

'Of course you can't,' she agreed. 'But you can try to see it from another angle. That by giving you away I could have been putting your happiness before my own.'

'There's no need for you to justify your actions to me,' he snapped. 'I've already told you that I don't blame you.'

'Even so . . .'

'Look,' he interrupted crossly, 'I've never tried to stop Poppy from seeing you, and I've no intention of doing so after the baby is born as long as you don't start playing grannie, so you've nothing to complain about.'

'I wasn't complaining, I just . . .'

'All I ask is that you leave me alone,' he shouted, his voice cracked with emotion.

Sighing, she said, 'Oh, well, if that's the way you *really* want it, there's nothing more to be said.' She walked to the steps and turned. 'You know where I am if you need me.'

'You're twenty-eight years too late,' he said cuttingly.

Watching her through the window as she walked sadly along the towpath, he sank into an armchair smarting with a perverse kind of empathy for the suffering he had inflicted upon her. Guilty? Why should he feel guilty? He owed that woman nothing. Well, perhaps that wasn't quite true . . . maybe she had helped to build his confidence after he'd left the Dexters.

He remembered how wholeheartedly she had welcomed him into her home, a runaway with no family background that she knew of. Still, she'd probably only been kind because he was a friend of Sam's, he told his troubled conscience.

In moments of real honesty, Ozzy felt bad about the way he had treated Sam who could hardly be blamed for being the favoured son. But what other way forward had there been for him but a clean break? Anyway, he doubted if Sam lost any sleep over it. He was far too busy making a success of his air force career.

Things were best left as they were, Ozzy told himself. He couldn't live with the feeling of rejection and self-hatred the Brooks engendered in him. He had inherited enough of that from the Dexters. The further he was from Kate and Sam Brooks, the better he would like it.

Despite her regrets over Ozzy, and signs of war preparations appearing everywhere, life went on more or less as normal for Kate.

Disused buildings might well be turning into ARP Control and First Aid Centres, walls of sandbags might have become an established part of the landscape, but business carried on regardless. In fact, there was an increase in demand for hats among those clients who feared a shortage if war did break out. Kate guessed that would be the case even though she still lived in hope that a solution could be found and war would be averted.

Her faith was severely tried one day in June, however. She was on her way to see a client in Chelsea when she was held up in Sloane Square by throngs of people lining the pavements. The traffic was at a standstill and the area was swarming with policeman and air raid wardens, the latter distinctive in their brown overalls and steel helmets.

'What's going on?' Kate asked a woman standing next to her in the crowd.

'Some sort of ARP experiment, apparently,' the woman explained. 'They're going to stage an air raid so that they can test their precautions.'

The information was confirmed by the high-pitched wavering wail of the air raid sirens. Wardens immediately sprang into action, blowing their whistles vigorously. Moving with the crowd, who had been given instructions before she arrived, Kate walked in an orderly manner towards the roped-off enclosures which represented the shelters.

There was a hushed silence as the sirens died away, broken by a voice through the loudspeaker warning the public that bombers would be here in seven or eight minutes. Soon there were bells clanging and fire engines rushing off to deal with imaginary fires. Mobile first aid units, ambulances and stretcher bearers hurried about their duties, showing off their expertise and creating an authentic atmosphere. Even the schoolchildren had been included in the exercise and were being transported from schools to various railway stations, partly to keep the streets clear while the experiment was in progress and partly to test the evacuation arrangements.

Eventually the 'all clear' was sounded on the sirens and Chelsea began to grind back to normal. Kate was still feeling weak-kneed as the crowds started to disperse.

'It might have been just a trial run,' said her companion in the crowd, 'but it's set my nerves jangling all right.'

'Mine too,' said Kate.

'The situation must be really serious,' said the woman, shaking her head sagely. 'They wouldn't go to the trouble of setting up something on that scale if it wasn't.'

'No, they wouldn't,' agreed Kate gloomily.


Poppy Perks switched off the wireless with tears in her eyes on the morning of Friday, September 1st, having just heard that Germany had invaded Poland. Throughout the summer months she had joined her fellow Londoners in putting a brave face on events as the country drifted towards the inevitable. Even when reports had come through of a non-aggression pact between Russia and Germany, she had not allowed herself to get too ruffled. Because of her condition, she had tried to stay calm. But this latest news, coming on top of reports that the mass evacuation of city schoolchildren to the country was well underway, finally snapped her self-control.

'Bleedin' Hitler,' she fumed to the walls of *London Lady*, angry tears gushing down her cheeks. 'All these terrible things are 'appening because of that evil sod. Those poor little beggars bein' dragged away from their families. It's nothin' short of criminal.'

She'd been sitting in an armchair in the boat's saloon listening to the news. Now she staggered over to the sofa and lay down, mopping her brow with a handkerchief for the hot sticky weather was uncomfortable for someone as heavily pregnant as she was. In fact, she hadn't felt right since she woke up this morning after a restless night. What with the humid weather and the bloomin' war, it was a wonder anyone was managing to sleep.

As well as having a sick headache, there was also a dragging ache in her back which probably accounted for the fact that she was so tearful, for she wasn't the type to cry easily. She dried her eyes, ashamed of her feebleness. It's no use you blubbing, she admonished herself, it ain't any worse for you than anyone else. At least by the time the baby arrives it'll be all over bar the shouting. They say it won't last beyond Christmas.

The gnawing in her back nagged relentlessly like a very bad period pain. Unable to lie still, she got up and paced the room. Staring absently through the open window, she found herself unexpectedly reassured by the ordinary sight of an old man walking a dog along the river bank.

Half an hour or so later, she came out of the bathroom, trembling with fear. There was a large bloodstain on her pants, and the baby wasn't due for two months . . .

Armed with reporter's notepad and pencil, Ozzy stood outside Paddington Station with a lump in his throat. An unending stream of small persons, labelled like luggage and clutching a few personal belongings, gasmasks in cardboard boxes strung across their shoulders, were being bundled off buses and herded into the station by schoolteachers who were to escort them to havens in the country.

Ozzy had been reliably informed that the number of children

367

to be evacuated in the government scheme was officially estimated at 1.5 million, and a large proportion of them seemed to be passing before his eyes at this very minute. There were the ragged and the neat, the shy and the ebullient, children of all shapes and sizes were here this morning.

Out of sight of the watchful eye of the teacher at the head of the crocodile, angel-eyed slum urchins with filthy faces and broken shoes jostled each other, uttering invective with the casual ease of navvies. Ozzy heard one little boy tell another to 'Stop bloody well shoving, yer sod, or I'll tell me dad and he'll punch yer bleedin' 'ead in!'

Many of the more reserved ones clung to the hands of elder sisters or brothers, looking pale and bewildered. One little boy made a nervous puddle on the pavement, but it went unnoticed in the feverish activity and he was marched off in a line into the station. Ozzy had been told that family farewells had been said outside the schools where the evacuation parties had assembled. He was also aware of the fact that parents had been instructed to send their children to school with nothing more cumbersome to carry than spare clothing, a toothbrush, comb, handkerchief, and a bag of food for the day.

'Why are we going away without Mummy?' Ozzy heard one little boy in owlish spectacles ask his elder sister.

''Cos she's got to stay 'ome to look after Dad,' said the girl.

'I don't wanna go,' he said tearfully.

'Well, we've gotta go and that's that,' she said, her own face working against tears. 'It'll be nice when we get there. There'll be farms and that, like in the picture books.'

He continued to cry.

'Pack it up, 'enry, or we'll cop it from miss,' she said.

'She ain't our mum,' he sobbed. 'She can't tell us what to do when we're not at school.'

'She can, 'cos she's in charge of us till we get to the country.'

'Who's gonna look after us when we get there?'

'Dunno. The people we're gonna stay with, I s'pose,' she said uncertainly.

Some of the older boys were much more sanguine and were

sparring and showing off in front of their female counterparts in this mass exodus.

Because of the congestion inside the station, most of the press were covering events from outside.

'Poor little devils,' said Ozzy to a fellow reporter from another newspaper who was standing next to him.

'You got any kids?' asked the man.

'Not yet,' Ozzy told him. 'One on the way though.'

'It's the parents I really feel sorry for.'

'I shouldn't think it's any picnic for the children,' Ozzy pointed out, 'being uprooted and sent to live with strangers.'

'They'll soon get used to it, the little ones especially,' the man said. 'Kids are quick to adapt, but their parents will go through hell every minute they're away.'

'You reckon so?'

'I know so, mate. My two nippers have gone away with their school today,' he explained, 'and making the decision to send them was one of the hardest things me and the wife have ever had to do.'

'Really?'

'Oh, yeah. Knowing your kids will be safe from the bombs doesn't help much when you're wondering if their foster parents will be kind to them, or if you'll ever see them again. We weren't going to send them since it isn't compulsory, but you've got to do what's best for them even though it breaks your heart, haven't you? My wife has been crying all night over it.'

Ozzy completed his shorthand notes and pushed his way through the crowds to catch the bus back to the office. He was so immersed in his thoughts, he hardly noticed the disruption to transport caused by the evacuation or the ubiquitous posters warning the public that black-out was officially coming into force today at sunset.

All the way back to Fleet Street, the conversation with the reporter lingered in his mind. It must be agonising having to decide whether to put the good of your child before your own feelings, he thought. How many parents would put their children's lives at risk by taking the soft option and keeping them at home? It occurred to him that it was not dissimilar to the decision Kate had had to make about him all those years ago.

Back at the office, all such cogitation was banished by the sight of a piece of paper tucked into his typewriter with a message on it. Her mother had telephoned to say that Poppy had gone into labour and been rushed into Hammersmith Hospital.

'The doctor is with your wife now, Mr Perks,' said the ward sister rather hurriedly, speaking to Ozzy in the corridor outside the ward.

'Is it serious?' he asked, somewhat unnecessarily since childbirth was a thing that usually happened at home and she wouldn't be here at all unless her condition was critical.

'She *is* two months early, Mr Perks.'

'Oh.' It was almost a whisper because he could hardly breathe. 'You mean she might lose the baby?'

Her gaze rested on him gravely.

'Not both of them?'

'We're doing everything we can,' she said kindly. 'If you sit down, I'll get one of the nurses to bring you a cup of tea.'

Grey with worry, he did as she said. The smell of disinfectant and floor polish caught in his constricted throat, making him want to retch. He couldn't stop shaking. He'd never been this terrified of anything before. Poppy was everything to him. If he lost her, what was left? She *couldn't* die. Please God, don't let her die . . .

Her mother had been here when he arrived and had filled him in on the details. Apparently Poppy had fled to her in a panic about a show of blood. The doctor had been called and he'd sent for an ambulance.

Guessing that his mother-in-law was anxious about leaving her husband alone, because he suffered so badly with nervous debility, Ozzy advised her to go home, promising to telephone the grocer on the corner of her street as soon as there was any news. As fond as he was of Mrs Brown, he'd been relieved to see her go because, for some unknown reason, he didn't want

370

her with him at this traumatic time.

People were going about their business around him. Nurses in starched uniforms hurried past; white-coated doctors marched purposefully along the corridor; porters wheeled patients in wheelchairs. The squeak of rubber-soled shoes on the polished floor heralded the arrival of a nurse with a cup of tea.

'Try not to worry too much, Mr Perks,' she said, noticing the cup rattling in the saucer as she handed it to him. 'Your wife is in good hands.'

'Thank you, nurse. You're very kind.' He looked into her sympathetic eyes and made a sudden, unexpected decision. 'Is there a telephone anywhere I could use, please?'

'Yes, you can use the one in Sister's office,' she said. 'Follow me.'

He put his tea-cup on the floor under his chair and went after her.


The weather was so oppressive that afternoon, Kate was finding it difficult to concentrate on the pile of paperwork she was dealing with at her desk. An air of expectancy hung over the shop as they all waited for the news everyone now knew had to come. The black-out was due to start this evening, the children were being sent away. Indeed, many business people in the metropolis were preparing to move their firms to the country too.

Kate was not planning to evacuate her business. In fact, she preferred not to speculate beyond the immediate crisis since no one knew exactly how things would be in wartime. She was hoping to keep the shop going somehow, if they weren't all bombed or poisoned by this time next week. Business was certainly booming at the moment. The workroom staff were busy with a batch of orders for rich clients about to take up permanent residence at their country homes for the duration of the war.

Outside, the streets were full of people in uniform; the roads jammed with cars leaving London, piled high with luggage and prams and bicycles strapped to the roofs.

Answering the telephone on her desk, she was surprised to hear Ozzy's voice, and alarmed by what he had to say.

'I wonder if you could come to the hospital, Kate?' he said, having explained the situation with Poppy. 'I know I don't deserve it, but I need you. *Please* say you'll come?'

The whole of London appeared to be on the move as Kate battled her way to Hammersmith. The queues at the bus-stops seemed to stretch for miles, and a sea of people was surging into the Tube station. She eventually managed to flag down a taxi but only after waving her arms frantically at the kerbside for ages.

When she finally arrived at the hospital, she found Ozzy sitting on a bench in the corridor outside the ward. Without a word she sat down beside him and took his hand.

'Thanks for coming,' he said, turning and meeting her eyes. 'It was really good of you, considering the way I've treated you.'

'Nonsense. It's the least I can do.'

'You must think I'm totally pathetic,' he said. 'I mean, a grown man of twenty-eight, asking his mother to come and hold his hand.'

'Don't be so daft,' she said emphatically. 'We all need someone beside us at times like this.'

'It wasn't just anyone, though, Kate,' he explained through dry lips. 'Poppy's mum was here earlier. I'm very fond of her but I didn't want her with me. I just can't explain what came over me when I telephoned you. I just wanted *you* to be here with me so much.' He shook his head. 'Is that very selfish of me?'

'Not selfish,' she said. 'Just human. And I'm very glad you called me.'

Just after six o'clock that evening a hush ran through the hospital. Medical personnel chatted in groups; shocked whispers echoed in the corridors.

'The Civil Defence has been officially mobilised,' explained a passing nurse, her stiff skirts rustling as she moved. 'It's just been announced on the six o'clock news. All volunteers have to report for duty.'

'Oh God,' said Kate, but she was in such a high state of anxiety about Poppy, the effect of this important announcement was muted.

'I reckon war will be declared over the weekend,' a porter was saying to a man he was pushing in a wheelchair.

Kate's heart lurched as a doctor hurried towards them. 'Oh God,' she said again, perceiving his strained expression.

'You have a little daughter, Mr Perks,' he said, and Kate realised that what she had mistaken for anxiety was simply exhaustion.

'What?' muttered Ozzy in a daze.

'She's very small and is going to need special care for a while,' beamed the doctor, 'but she's quite healthy.'

All Ozzy could think of was Poppy. 'My wife?' he said, hardly daring to ask the question.

'Very tired and weak,' the doctor explained calmly. 'She's lost a lot of blood. But she's going to be all right.'

'Oh . . . oh, thank you, doctor!' Ozzy leapt up and shook the man's hand, then turned to Kate and hugged her.

'You can go in and see your wife and daughter for a few minutes, Mr Perks.'

Ozzy looked at Kate, and then at the doctor. 'Can we both go in?'

The doctor frowned. 'I'm afraid not. Only fathers are allowed into the ward.'

'Not even close relatives?'

'Only under very special circumstances.'

'But this lady is the baby's grandmother,' said Ozzy persuasively.

The doctor gave a tired grin. 'Well, I suppose as we are about to be plunged into war, this could be called special circumstances,' he said. 'But only for a few minutes, mind.'

Walking proudly at her son's side, Kate went to welcome her first grandchild into the world. War was almost inevitable now, and the future uncertain, but at that moment she felt indestructible.

★ ★ ★

Later that evening Kate had a houseful at Sycamore Square. Sam arrived unexpectedly from Kent on an overnight pass. He had an emotional reunion with Ozzy who had accepted Kate's invitation to join her and Leo for the evening rather than stay at home alone. Johnny dropped Esme, Gertie and Rita off in the car at Kate's place before going to an ARP meeting with Leo.

The war dominated everything. The black-out curtains were drawn and the wireless was switched on continuously for news bulletins, a tense silence descending at every one. To further emphasise the scale of the emergency, the BBC announced that it was to merge its National and Regional services and would only be broadcasting one programme in future.

When Leo and Johnny returned from their meeting looking grim, Kate decided it was time for the small celebration she had planned, war or no war.

Producing a tray of glasses and the champagne she had purchased from the wine store on the way home from the hospital, she made an announcement.

'I'd just like to remind you that it isn't all bad news today,' she said. 'So let's all drink a toast: Ozzy and Poppy on the birth of their little daughter, Matilda.'

The cork popped and glasses were filled. 'To baby Matilda,' she said, lifting her own glass.

Glasses were raised and the air resounded with laughter and congratulations. Standing at Leo's side, Kate felt happy and complete as her two sons exchanged a congratulatory handshake, Sam slapping Ozzy's back chummily. Catching her eye, Ozzy gave her an affectionate wink.

There were some things that would never die, no matter what hardship lay ahead. Some sixth sense told Kate that the memory of the way she felt at this moment was one of them.

*More Compelling Fiction from Headline:*

# PAMELA EVANS

# LAMPLIGHT on the THAMES

The new London saga from the
author of *A Barrow in the Broadway*

*The fog swirled around the crowd at the graveside; Bob
Brown had been a popular man. But Bella's thoughts were
darker than the earth that was to cover the coffin – Frank
Bennett had killed her father as surely as if he had taken a
knife to him.*

Since the end of the war, when Bob Brown had taken
over the car workshop on Fulworth High Street in
London, Frank Bennett had been trying to get his hands
on it. An East Ender who had made good by his quick
wits and unscrupulous business methods, Frank was
determined to get the prime site – whatever the cost.

For as long as she could remember, Bella had been drawn
to the river, and to the ivy-covered house on the
promenade where she had first met Dezi Bennett. The
child and the young airman had become unlikely friends,
though both families had disapproved. Years later, their
love blossomed, and it seemed that nothing, not even the
feud between their fathers, could prevent their marriage.
Until Bob's tragic death and his dying request to Bella . . .

Also by Pamela Evans from Headline
**A BARROW IN THE BROADWAY**

**FICTION/SAGA   0 7472 3335 7**

*More Compelling Fiction from Headline:*

# —— PAMELA EVANS ——
# STAR QUALITY

The new London saga
from the author of
*Maggie of Moss Street*

Young Tess Trent works at Emerson's department store in
London's West End, its affluence a far remove from her own
ordinary, respectable home in Briar Park in Hammersmith.
Unlike her parents, Tess does not believe the fine and beautiful
things she sells each day will be beyond her reach for ever.

The son of a Sheffield miner, Max Bentley wants to earn his
living as a musician in a dance band in London. His parents are
horrified: 'You'll find nowt worth having down South, lad,' his
father warns.

Meeting at a dance one Saturday night, Tess and Max are
instantly attracted, and soon discover they share the same
dreams. But Max's ambitions drive them apart.

Betrayed by the man she loves and desperate to leave home, Tess
tries to find fulfilment in marriage, and her ambition to open a
fineware shop. Over the years her business expands, and then
Tess's nineteen-year-old daughter, Judy, meets and falls in love
with a musician. It is Max Bentley...

STAR QUALITY is a warm-hearted saga of love, conflict and
ambition set against the changing kaleidoscope of London
through the depression of the thirties, the heartbreak and
austerity of the war years to the reckless sixties.

Don't miss Pamela Evans's other London sagas from Headline
MAGGIE OF MOSS STREET
LAMPLIGHT ON THE THAMES
A BARROW IN THE BROADWAY

FICTION/SAGA   0 7472 3711 5

*More Enthralling Fiction from Headline:*

# ELIZABETH MURPHY

## THE NEW LIVERPOOL SAGA FROM THE AUTHOR OF *THERE IS A SEASON*

Nicknamed 'Happy Annie', Anne is the youngest of the eight
Fitzgerald children, loved and petted by her older brothers and
sisters and secure amid their extended family in Liverpool's Everton
district. Her childhood is blessedly free from worries: although
conditions are hard in the 1920s and '30s, Patrick Fitzgerald's
building firm provides a steady income and there is always food on
the table and the sound of music and laughter in the house.

When Sarah Redmond introduces Anne to her brother John, there is
an unspoken attraction between the two young people, but John goes
to Spain to fight with the International Brigade, and when he returns,
it is to find that he is a social outcast. He is unwilling to involve Anne
in his troubles and she is too proud to admit to feelings she believes
are not returned.

Only when war breaks out do they marry and have three children,
with whom Anne hopes to recreate her happy childhood home. But
John is busy pursuing his own ambitions and this leads to
misunderstandings and unhappiness until in the end Anne's dream is
fulfilled and she can truly describe her home as her childhood home
was once described – a nest of singing birds.

Don't miss Elizabeth Murphy's poignant sagas of life on Merseyside,
*The Land is Bright*, *To Give and To Take* and *There is a Season*, all
available from Headline.

FICTION/SAGA   0 7472 4010 8

# A selection of bestsellers
# from Headline

| | | |
|---|---|---|
| THE GIRL FROM COTTON LANE | Harry Bowling | £5.99 □ |
| MAYFIELD | Joy Chambers | £5.99 □ |
| DANGEROUS LADY | Martina Cole | £4.99 □ |
| DON'T CRY ALONE | Josephine Cox | £5.99 □ |
| DIAMONDS IN DANBY WALK | Pamela Evans | £4.99 □ |
| STARS | Kathryn Harvey | £5.99 □ |
| THIS TIME NEXT YEAR | Evelyn Hood | £4.99 □ |
| LOVE, COME NO MORE | Adam Kennedy | £5.99 □ |
| AN IMPOSSIBLE WOMAN | James Mitchell | £5.99 □ |
| FORBIDDEN FEELINGS | Una-Mary Parker | £5.99 □ |
| A WOMAN POSSESSED | Malcolm Ross | £5.99 □ |
| THE FEATHER AND THE STONE | Patricia Shaw | £4.99 □ |
| WYCHWOOD | E V Thompson | £4.99 □ |
| ADAM'S DAUGHTERS | Elizabeth Villars | £4.99 □ |

*All Headline books are available at your local bookshop or newsagent, or can be ordered direct from the publisher. Just tick the titles you want and fill in the form below. Prices and availability subject to change without notice.*

Headline Book Publishing PLC, Cash Sales Department, Bookpoint, 39 Milton Park, Abingdon, OXON, OX14 4TD, UK. If you have a credit card you may order by telephone — 0235 831700.

Please enclose a cheque or postal order made payable to Bookpoint Ltd to the value of the cover price and allow the following for postage and packing:

UK & BFPO: £1.00 for the first book, 50p for the second book and 30p for each additional book ordered up to a maximum charge of £3.00.

OVERSEAS & EIRE: £2.00 for the first book, £1.00 for the second book and 50p for each additional book.

Name ...................................................................................................

Address ................................................................................................

..............................................................................................................

..............................................................................................................

If you would prefer to pay by credit card, please complete:
Please debit my Visa/Access/Diner's Card/American Express (delete as applicable) card no:

| | | | | | | | | | | | | | | | |
|---|---|---|---|---|---|---|---|---|---|---|---|---|---|---|---|
| | | | | | | | | | | | | | | | |

Signature ...........................................................Expiry Date .......